Praise for ABSOL

Best Mystery-Suspense-Thriller -- 20

"A New Orleans killer thriller." -- Jan Herman, Arts Journal

"Relentless tempo and sharp writing." -- Kirkus Discoveries

"Creole-flavored suspense, colored with musical connections which Fleet handles with particular deftness." -- The Attleboro Sun Chronicle

"Fleet has created a crime drama that stands far above the ordinary whodunit. A wholehearted bravo!" -- K. G. Hunt, The Florida Times-Union

"First class writing! Fleet goes inside the head of the killer with a rare talent. An 'I couldn't put it down' thriller." -- C. J. Gregory

"I so enjoyed this well-written, exciting novel. I liked the characters, the plot, the way [Fleet] uses words to convey the fear and imagery associated with stalking and serial murders." -- Diana Hockley, author of *The Naked Room*.

Praise for DIVA

"Great character development [and] an absolutely fascinating ending ... a very suspenseful book!" -- Feathered Quill Book Reviews

"Fleet subtitles *Diva*, her new killer thriller, a novel of psychological suspense. That's an understatement." -- Jan Herman, *Arts Journal*

"NOPD detective Frank Renzi returns in a relentless hunt through ravaged, drug infested neighborhoods in search of murderous thugs and a psychotic stalker. Fleet weaves . . . another nail-biting page-turner!" -- K. G. Hunt

"Fleet takes us inside the head of the obsessed stalker as he lusts after his victim ... one must-buy book." -- Tom Bryson, author of *Too Smart To Die*

"Absolution was the first - Diva the second - I can not WAIT to see what's in store for us with the third! This is one writer who gives the `Big Six' in publishing a new, fresh voice to listen to, and seeing her on the bestseller list very soon will not be a surprise. Enjoy this one!" -- Amy Lignor, author of *Until Next Time*

NATALIE'S REVENGE

A FRANK RENZI NOVEL

"I shall be a champion of justice and freedom."

-- from the student oath of the

International Taekwondo Federation

Susan Fleet

Music and Mayhem Press

This book contains an excerpt from Susan Fleet's next novel, *Jackpot*. This excerpt may not be identical to the final content of the forthcoming edition.

ISBN-13 978-0-9847235-3-9

ISBN-10 0-9847235-3-6

Cover photographs used with permission:
Sexy gun woman © *Jason Stitt - Fotolia.com*
Dragon © *Dimitar Marinov - Fotolia.com*

Author photo by Pete Wolbrette

Printed in the United States of America

Crime novels by Susan Fleet

Absolution

Diva

Natalie's Revenge

Non-fiction by Susan Fleet

Women Who Dared: Trailblazing 20th Century Musicians
Volume 1: Violinist Maud Powell and Trumpeter Edna White

DEDICATION

To all victims of violence and to their relatives, who suffer the consequences of violent crimes long after their loved ones are gone.

PROLOGUE

October 1988   New Orleans

One night Mom didn't come home.

Every morning she'd come in my room, wake me with a kiss and say in a cheery voice, "Rise and shine, Natalie. Your breakfast is ready."

Not today. Today I woke with a start. Right away I got a creepy feeling. Except for the rain splattering my bedroom window, our apartment was silent and still. I looked at my clock radio. The big red numbers said 8:35.

I was late for school. Even if I stayed up late watching TV, Mom always got me up in time for school.

Last night before Mom left she said, "Do your homework and go to bed and I'll see you tomorrow."

I buried my face in the pillow and tried to pretend it was a dream.

But down deep I knew it wasn't. I don't know why. Last night Mom left for work at nine o'clock same as always, wearing a pretty emerald-green dress and her lemony perfume. Mom was beautiful, long chestnut-brown hair and big green eyes that she made look even prettier with glittery eye-shadow.

Every night before she left, she always said the same thing:

Don't answer the phone. Don't open the door to anyone. Don't leave the apartment.

One night I snuck out to the corner store to buy a snack and the clerk told Mom the next day. Mom got mad and said if I ever did that again, I wouldn't get my allowance.

I clenched my teeth, but it didn't make the sick feeling inside me go away.

I threw off the sheet, got out of bed and opened my bedroom door.

The lumpy futon in the living room where Mom slept was still upright, no sheet, no pillow. That scared me even more than the silence. After I left for school Mom usually went back to bed. She needed to sleep because she got home really late. Mom worked as a hostess at a fancy restaurant.

1

Or so she said. I'd never been there. I was only ten, but I watched TV, and I didn't think hostesses wore fancy dresses and glittery eye shadow and smelled the way I imagined the women on my favorite TV shows did when they went out on dates with important men.

A delivery truck rumbled past our door, thumping over the potholes in our street. Our first floor apartment was noisy, but Mom said hearing traffic noise beat lugging laundry and groceries up two or three flights of stairs. Mom can sleep through anything, but I'm a light sleeper. Sometimes the sounds outside my bedroom window woke me up at night.

Opposite Mom's futon was the breakfast bar where we ate our meals.

Normally, my milk and Cheerios and fruit would be there.

But nothing was normal now.

I felt sick, like I might throw up, and my hands felt weird, hot and cold at the same time and damp with sweat. Mom always said to call her cell phone if there was an emergency. And if this wasn't an emergency, what was?

Padding barefoot over the worn linoleum, I went around the breakfast bar to the alcove kitchen. The telephone was on the wall beside a boxy old refrigerator with chipped enamel. Mom had printed her cell phone number on a pink Post-It and stuck it to the fridge. Beside it was another pink Post-It with the numbers for police and fire and medical emergencies.

I couldn't decide what to do. Maybe Mom was just late.

Maybe the taxi that was bringing her home had a flat tire.

I looked at the calendar beside the fridge. Right after Christmas last year Mom bought a wall calendar with twelve paintings by Vermeer. Mom loved art. Every month we got to look at a different painting while we ate our meals. The October painting was The Girl With the Pearl Earring.

The girl was pretty and she had beautiful eyes. But she looked sad.

Looking at her made me feel worse. My stomach cramped.

Where was Mom?

I noticed she'd penciled something on the calendar for tomorrow.

Natalie. Dentist. 4 PM.

Then the doorbell rang. My heart stopped, at least it felt like it did.

Don't open the door to anyone.

A few weeks ago the doorbell rang right after I got in bed. That never happened and it scared me. When I went to the door and looked out the peephole, some guy with a scraggly gray beard was outside our door. I could see his lips moving, like he was talking to himself. After a couple of minutes, he went away. I figured he was probably a drunk from the French Quarter two blocks away. I went back to bed, but it took me a long time to fall asleep.

I never told Mom about it. I didn't want to worry her. Mom was already worried about me staying here by myself. She didn't say so, but I could tell.

The doorbell rang again. My legs felt like Jell-O, all quivery and shaky.

I crept to the door and looked through the peephole the way Mom taught me. A woman in a dark-blue police uniform was standing outside in the rain.

Police meant trouble. That's what Mom always said.

But I was already in trouble.

Late for school. And Mom wasn't here.

And a policewoman was ringing our doorbell.

I looked through the peephole again.

The expression on the woman's face scared me. Frown lines grooved her forehead the way Mom's did when she was worried about something, like when she didn't have enough money to pay the bills.

My hands were shaking, but I worked all the locks and opened the door.

"Natalie?" The policewoman didn't smile when she said my name.

I nodded. I was too scared to think, too scared to breathe.

"I'm Detective Fontenot from the New Orleans Police Department. Your mother's been hurt."

My throat closed up. Mom was hurt. Badly hurt, or she'd have called me.

I wanted to ask her if Mom was okay, but I was too scared.

The policewoman rolled her lips together. Her eyes looked sad. Sadder than the girl on the calendar. "I'm sorry to have to tell you this, Natalie, but someone attacked your mother last night."

She looked away, like she didn't want to say anything more.

Then she said in a low voice, "Natalie, your mother is dead."

CHAPTER 1

July 24, 2008   New Orleans

The stench, a pungent mix of urine, feces and rank body odor, was brutal. Twenty-plus years as a detective, he'd smelled his share of stinky corpses, but not many in ritzy hotel rooms. This one was naked, sprawled on a four-poster double bed. A large yellow urine stain soiled the sheet. His head lay on a blood-soaked pillow, a gunshot entry-wound centered in his forehead.

Sometime after midnight someone had called the Hotel Bienvenue desk to report a problem in Room 635. A big problem, big enough for the hotel security guard to call NOPD and have them roust Homicide Detective Frank Renzi out of bed at one A.M.

Whoever popped the guy shut off the A/C, maybe after the shot, maybe before. Maybe the guy was into hot sex.

He studied the corpse. No defense wounds, no visible bruises. No doubt about the cause of death. One shot to the head, over and out.

Adrenaline boosted his energy level, upping his heart rate. No matter how many murder cases he worked, each one was a fresh puzzle. Who's the victim? Who killed him? And why?

The person who'd called in the problem hadn't hung around. Now it was 1:35 A.M. An NOPD officer posted outside the room would fend off any unauthorized visitors. The crime scene techs and a coroner's investigator were on their way, and so was Kenyon Miller, his partner.

The cherry-wood desk beside the window was squeaky clean, no dust, no notes. Heavy drapes covered the window, not that anyone could see into a room on the sixth floor. The victim's clothes lay in a heap on the floor beside the bed, a pair of white jockey shorts on top.

His partner ambled into the room. "Yo, Frank, smells like we got a stinker," Miller said, his voice a deep rumble like a slow-moving freight train. He eyed the corpse. "Mm, mm, mm. This'll cause a shitstorm."

4

"Why? You know him?"

"Yeah, and I'm not talking about his Yankee Doodle."

Every black guy he'd ever worked with had an arsenal of terms for male genitalia, but Yankee Doodle? That was a new one. "Who is he?"

Built like an NFL linebacker, Miller mopped sweat off his shaven pate with a handkerchief. "Arnold Peterson. Be all kinds of pressure on this one. He's marketing director for The Babylon."

The Babylon, a recent addition to the French Quarter, was a big gambling casino similar to Harrah's.

"You positive it's Peterson?"

"No doubt in my mind. He's a high profile guy. I've seen him at Saint's games hanging with his bigwig buddies in a VIP Suite."

It had taken Frank a while to understand that pro football reigned in New Orleans. Everyone here was a Saints fan. Where he came from the Celtics ruled. Or the Red Sox.

He gestured at the corpse. "Looks like a hit. One shot to the head."

"Wouldn't surprise me. What I hear, Peterson's a real prick, screwed a few people to get the job."

"Feels like the A/C's been off for a while, might complicate the TOD."

Miller shrugged. "The COD is obvious enough."

"I'm going down to the desk and find out who rented the room. Nail down the time of the problem call, too. I want to know who called it in."

"Sure. Head on down to the *delightfully* cool lobby while I sweat it out with the smelly corpse." Miller shot him an aggrieved look. "Why not have a beverage in the nice air-conditioned lounge and ask the bartender if Peterson was there tonight?"

"Hey, partner, cut the jive. Neither of us will get much sleep for a while. I'll do the notification. After the coroner's investigator releases the body, canvas the guests on this floor to see if they heard anything. Then you can head on home to Tanya and catch a few winks."

Miller had a wife and two teenagers at home, but no one was waiting for Frank Renzi. Thanks to the real estate slump after Katrina, he'd bought a small condo a year ago. Thanks to his workaholic tendencies, he wasn't there much. He spent most of his free time at Kelly's house. She was a cop, too.

On the way to the elevator, he spotted a security camera at the end of the hall. Maybe they'd catch a break with that. They might need one. New Orleans was the murder capitol of the country, but most of the vics were drug dealers and gangbangers. A VIP corpse? The media vultures would go crazy. Summers here were brutal, hot and humid, no telling when a hurricane might churn into the Gulf and spawn a massive evacuation with horrendous traffic jams. Just what he needed to go with a murder in a ritzy French Quarter hotel.

He didn't care if the vic was a VIP or not. Peterson might be a rich and powerful, but rich pricks deserved justice too, and he intended to get it for him. Which meant he wouldn't catch up on sleep anytime soon.

It also meant he wouldn't see much of Kelly. Bummer.

He got in the elevator, recalling his last high-profile case. Two years ago a black drug dealer had killed a white woman. All kinds of black on black crime in New Orleans, but black on white crime? Fuggedaboudit! The ball-busters in the local media put on a full-court-press, badgering NOPD to solve the case on which Homicide Detective Frank Renzi was the lead investigator.

That's how he'd met Kelly. He hadn't seen her since Sunday, and if Miller was right and the corpse was Peterson, he wouldn't be seeing her anytime soon. As lead investigator, he'd be under the gun. Nothing new there.

Working for Boston PD he'd taken plenty of heat.

And he knew exactly how unpleasant that could be.

The elevator swooped to a stop and he stepped into the Hotel Bienvenue lobby. To his left, beyond glass double doors, Royal Street was shrouded in darkness. Just another sweltering night in New Orleans, except for the corpse upstairs. The lobby was deserted. Most of the guests were out partying on Bourbon Street or asleep in their rooms.

Except for Arnold Peterson, who was in permanent slumberland.

Light from recessed spotlights in the two-story ceiling dappled the marble floor and tastefully upholstered sofas grouped around low tables. Off to his right, the desk clerk was talking on the phone. He stifled a yawn.

Those cushiony sofas looked mighty inviting. Thanks to his always-iffy sleep patterns, he hadn't had a good night's sleep in a week. Two nights ago a recurring nightmare jolted him awake. A little girl's face, innocent in death, tears on her cheeks, a blood-soaked shirt. The image still haunted him. He went out for a run, dozed on his couch until it was time to go to work. Last night, weary and exhausted, he'd fallen asleep at midnight, but his ex-wife called at two-thirty, in the midst of one of her frequent panic attacks. He talked to her for a half hour until she calmed down. But could he get back to sleep? Of course not. He'd tossed and turned until sunrise.

And now he had a murder to solve. He went to the desk and flashed his ID at a frazzled-looking man in a dark suit. Got no welcoming smile. Bad for business, a guest found murdered in a luxury French Quarter hotel.

"Did you take the call about the problem in room six-thirty-five?"

"Yes, sir." A muscle bunched in the desk clerk's jaw.

"What time was that?"

"I'm not sure, exactly. Sometime after midnight."

"Was the caller male or female?"

"I couldn't tell you. I was checking in two guests at the time."

"What did the caller say, exactly?"

"Exactly?"

He wanted to smack the guy. He needed to talk to the bartender, and the dull ache in his temples did nothing to improve his mood. "Tell me what the caller said. Tell me whether the voice sounded like a man or a woman. Pretend your job depends on it."

Clearly annoyed, the clerk heaved a sigh. "The caller said there was a problem in Room 635 and hung up. I called security, told them to check the room and got back to registering our guests. I can't tell you if the caller was a man or a woman."

He could tell this was going nowhere. "Okay, who rented Room 635?"

The clerk got on the computer, hit some keys and stared at the screen. Anything to avoid the eyes of the pissed-off homicide detective before him.

Laughter floated across the lobby, high-pitched trills and low-pitched guffaws. Frank turned and watched two well-dressed couples leave the lounge and approach the elevator.

"The room was registered to Arnold Peterson," the clerk said.

Bada-bing. VIP murder case coming right up.

"Is the security camera on the sixth floor working or just for show?"

"No, sir, not for show. All our security cameras are fully functional."

"How do I get a copy of the tape?"

"You'd have to speak with Mr. Taylor about that. He's our security director."

"Is he here now?"

"No, but I'm sure he'll be along soon." The clerk didn't seem happy about it. Maybe he wasn't looking forward to answering the security director's questions either.

"When he gets here, tell him I need to watch all the security videos that were operational tonight. All of them, not just the one on the sixth floor. Tell him if anything happens to them he'll catch hell from NOPD."

———

Recessed lighting in the Bienvenue cast a discreet glow over the opulent teak-paneled room. Below a crystal chandelier with twinkly lights, high-backed barstools flanked a circular polished-wood bar. Small tables sat between the bar and the tall windows that faced Royal Street, only one occupied, a well-dressed young woman and her male companion. Two older couples and a couple of singletons sat at the bar, nursing the last of their drinks.

Frank eased onto an isolated barstool, and the bartender came over, a distinguished-looking gray-haired man. He was wearing a white shirt, a black bow tie and a red cummerbund. And a professional smile.

"Good evening, sir. May I get you something?"

"NOPD," he said quietly. "I've got some questions about a guest." He opened his jacket to flash his ID, but the bartender waved him off.

"No need for that, sir. I've seen you on TV a time or two."

He flashed the disarming smile he used to cajole witnesses. "Man, I hate when they put me on TV. Could I trouble you for a glass of ice water?" The lounge was cool but he'd worked up a thirst in the sweltering room upstairs, not to mention questioning the not-so-forthcoming desk clerk.

"Ice water coming up." The bartender scooped ice cubes into a tall glass, filled it with water and set it in front of Frank. "My name's Syd. How can I help you?"

"Thanks, Syd. I'm Frank Renzi. Does Arnold Peterson stay here a lot?"

Syd's face took on a guarded look. "Yes. Mr. Peterson rents a crash-pad on the sixth floor by the month. To be close to his office, I guess."

He guzzled some ice water. Given Syd's expression, Peterson might have had reasons other than work to stay here. "Does he use it often?"

"He's here most weeknights."

"A hard worker, huh?"

Syd's gaze shifted away. "I don't know about that."

He heard raised voices and turned to look at the young couple at the table. The woman appeared to be on the verge of tears, no telling about the man, whose back was turned.

When they quieted, he said to Syd, "Tell me about Mr. Peterson."

"He comes in here most weeknights around eight."

"Alone, or with somebody?"

"Mostly alone." Syd hesitated. "But when he leaves sometimes he isn't, if you get my drift."

"I do. And the person he leaves with is usually female?"

"Definitely."

"Working girls?"

"No, sir. We don't allow that in here." Syd tipped his hand back-and-forth. "Well, I've seen a few that were questionable, but I keep an eye on them if they come in alone and sit beside a man. No, I think Peterson sometimes picked up women who stayed in the hotel."

The sound of shattering glass interrupted their conversation.

Syd frowned. Frank left the bar and approached the table with the young couple. The woman was crying.

"You fucking bitch," said her companion. "I don't know why I bothered with you." The guy looked like a wrestler, broad shoulders inside a snug polo shirt, muscular forearms.

Frank squeezed his shoulder and Loudmouth rose to his feet. He was three inches taller than Frank, at least six-four, but when he tried to turn he stumbled, his coordination impaired by alcohol. "Who the hell—"

He twisted the guy's arm and rammed him against the wall. "You want to come down to the station and cool off in a cell or you want to play nice?"

"Let go of my arm. You're gonna break it!"

8

"I'll let go when you tell me you're gonna get in a cab and go home. Without the young lady." When he got no response he jerked the guy's arm.

"Okay, o-*kay*. I'm going."

Frank pushed him toward the exit and Loudmouth shuffled away.

"Are you okay?" he said to the woman, who was wiping her eyes with a tissue. She appeared to be in her mid-twenties, about the same age as his daughter. But he couldn't imagine Maureen putting up with the kind of crap this jerk had been dishing out.

"I guess." She took a deep breath. "Yeah, I'm okay."

"Will he be waiting for you when you get home?"

"No. But he drove me here. I'll have to take a cab home."

Through the window he saw the doorman help the drunk into a cab. "Go powder your nose. By then that jerk will be gone. The doorman will get you a cab."

"Thank you." She balled up the tissue and gave him a tremulous smile. "Are you a cop or something?"

"Or something. Take my advice and ditch this guy. You deserve better."

He watched her leave the lounge and reclaimed his seat at the bar.

"Thank you," Syd said. "If you hadn't run him off I'd have had to. I owe you one."

"No problem. I hate men that beat on women. And I get the feeling that would have been the next step, the kind of language he was using."

Syd nodded his agreement, then leaned closer and whispered, "Is something wrong with Mr. Peterson? Or am I allowed to ask?"

"Sure. You'll hear about it tomorrow anyway. Mr. Peterson is upstairs in his room. Dead."

Syd seemed genuinely shocked. "Lord-a-Mercy! He came in tonight around nine, a bit later than usual. He had a Jack Daniels on the rocks and left just before ten. Alone."

"Thanks." Syd would make a far better witness than the tight-assed twerp on the desk. Frank gave him his card. "I'll be in touch, but if you think of anything important, call my cell anytime."

"I will." Syd shook his head. "I feel bad for Mr. Peterson's wife."

Frank did too. He wasn't looking forward to telling Mrs. Peterson her husband was dead, but that was his next task.

Any kind of luck, he'd catch a few winks afterwards.

———

The notification did not go well. Not that Peterson's wife got hysterical. Far from it. When he arrived, the Peterson house was dark. He had to ring the bell four times before Mrs. Peterson opened the door. Wrapped in a white terrycloth robe, she glared at him, clearly angry.

"Why are you ringing my bell at this hour?"

He flashed his photo-ID. "I'm sorry, but I have some unpleasant news. Could I come in?"

She grudgingly allowed him into the foyer, but not a step farther.

"I'm very sorry, Mrs. Peterson, but your husband was found dead in his room at the Hotel Bienvenue tonight."

He studied her reaction. The spouse is always a prime suspect, but other than a slight widening of her eyes, she remained stone-faced.

"What happened? A heart attack?"

"No. Someone shot him in the head." That got a reaction, but not the one he was expecting.

She laughed, an ugly guttural sound. "Someone shot Arnold?"

Working homicide he'd done plenty of death notifications, had watched people react in different ways. Some got hysterical. Some just cried quietly. He'd even seen people react with nervous laughter, but Mrs. Peterson's laugh was different. Cold. Verging on vindictive.

A voice from upstairs called, "Mom? What's wrong?"

"Go back to bed, Louisa. I'll be up in a minute."

"I'm sorry, Mrs. Peterson, but I need to ask you a few questions."

An outraged expression froze her face. "Questions? Now? I can't talk to you now. I've got three children upstairs and I need to figure out how to . . ." She took a deep breath and lowered her voice. "How to tell them their father is dead."

"Have you been home all evening?"

"Yesss," she hissed. "Now please leave. If you have questions, come back tomorrow morning at nine o'clock. By then I'll have things under control." Another a curt laugh. "Well, a semblance of control anyway."

The not-so-grieving widow practically shoved him out the door.

CHAPTER 2

Thursday, July 24, 2008   8:30 A.M.

Frank slid a mug under the LavAzza Espresso Machine spout and waited for his caffeine hit. His kitchen was tiny. When he ate meals here, which he seldom did, he ate in the living room. Two dirty coffee mugs sat in the sink. On the counter, the inexpensive toaster-oven and microwave he'd bought at Wal-Mart stood against the white ceramic tile backsplash. The espresso maker, a concession to his Italian heritage, had cost a small fortune. But the strong full-bodied flavor was worth it. Hell, the aroma alone was worth it.

After mailing the monthly alimony check to his ex-wife, he could barely afford the condo, but paying a mortgage beat pissing rent down the toilet. The two bedrooms were small, but he loved the living room, spacious and airy with high ceilings and a window overlooking the street. With his espresso mug in hand, he stood at the window. Two floors below, unaware he was watching, people were scurrying off to work and whatever tasks awaited them.

He sipped the espresso, relishing the rich taste, recalling the time his mother had jived his father about the fancy Italian-made espresso machine he'd bought for her. "The Italians make beautiful cars and typewriters and appliances, but half the time they don't work."

His father said nothing. Salvatore Renzi knew when to keep quiet.

A Maureen O'Hara look-alike, Mary Sullivan had beguiled his father with her intelligence and fiery spirit. For their twentieth wedding anniversary, his father had taken her to Italy, a trip she greatly enjoyed. But she loved teasing him, and her hair-trigger temper was a thing to behold when she got going.

Franklin Sullivan Renzi hadn't inherited his mother's auburn hair and green eyes, but he liked to think he channeled her fiery passion and empathy for the downtrodden. Salvatore Renzi was seventy-five now, still an appellate court judge in Boston. Six years ago, after battling a particularly aggressive form of breast cancer, Mary Sullivan Renzi had died. For the first time in his life, he had seen his father cry.

A heartbreaking moment, one he'd never forget. But a normal reaction to grief, one he hadn't seen from Peterson's widow last night.

11

His second visit to the Peterson home was starkly different. The Petersons lived in an exclusive enclave near the Metairie Country Club. At three A.M. their street had been dark and quiet. Now, bathed in sunlight, four television vans and a pack reporters surrounded the house, an imposing English Tudor with an attached three-car garage. Dark-brown wood outlined the cream-painted exterior, and gables jutted out from the steep-slanted roof.

Waving off the reporters, he mounted the semi-circular terraced steps and rang the bell. The door opened immediately.

Corrine Peterson was only forty-five, but her matronly dress wasn't particularly flattering. Nor was it widow's black, though the aquamarine color complimented her short ash-brown hair. Her eyes were puffy and bloodshot, and deep lines grooved the corners of her mouth.

Urgently motioning him inside, the widow led him into the living room and said in a business-like voice, "Would you like some iced tea?"

"Water would be fine," he said.

Left alone, he studied the room, stunned by the décor. Unlike the English Tudor exterior, the interior was stark-modern. Off-white walls and carpeting, floor-to-ceiling glass on the wall facing the golf course. In the center of the room, a smoked glass coffee table stood between a black leather couch and a white leather settee. The room felt cold and impersonal, like the painting mounted on one wall, mono-chrome geometric shapes on a black background.

The one trace of humanity was a color photograph on the mantle of the white-brick fireplace: the Petersons with their children, two girls and a boy. No sign of them now, no pitter-pat of footsteps, no young voices. He hoped there was a playroom. They sure didn't fool around in here. The photograph appeared to have been done by a professional, for a Christmas card perhaps.

He tried to reconcile the man in the photo with the dead man in the hotel. The man with the ugly grimace on his face. In the photo Arnold sported a cocky, used-car-salesman grin. Dark hair flecked with gray slicked back from his fair-skinned brow. No tan. Indoor sports appeared to be Arnold's specialty. His hands rested on the boy in front of him. Corrine stood behind the two girls, a fake smile on her heavily made-up face. The girls were pretty, dark haired like their father, smiling into the camera. The boy looked to be about six. His smile seemed forced, as if it had taken a million shots to get a decent one. A not-so-happy family?

Stifling a yawn, he took a seat on the couch. Corrine Peterson returned, set a cut-crystal glass of ice water on the table in front of him and arranged herself on the white settee. The amber liquid in her glass looked like iced tea. But it might have been something stronger. Was Corrine a drinker?

"Do you have family around here?" he said, his usual icebreaker when interviewing a bereaved spouse.

"My mother's flying in from Iowa City today. To help with the children."

He took out his spiral notepad. "I know this isn't a good time, but I need to ask you some questions."

She sipped her drink and gazed at him with her bloodshot blue eyes.

He tried to think of a word to describe her, came up with *fleshy*. Twenty years ago she was probably a looker. Now her arms were flabby, her waist was as wide as her hips, and her face was lined and haggard, as though years of misery had worn her down.

"Any reason why someone might want to kill your husband?"

Seemingly shocked by the blunt question, she stared at him.

"Did he have any enemies?"

She barked a curt laugh similar to the one he'd heard last night. "You mean all the other ruthless men he screwed to get where he is?"

Pow! Ask a simple question, get a rip-snorting answer. Corrine was an angry woman. "Can you give me some names?"

"You can get all the names you want from Arnold's assistant. Ask Fenwick Holt. He'll tell you." A cold smile. "He's another man on his way up."

Make that angry and bitter and not afraid to show it. "How long were you and Mr. Peterson married?"

"Fourteen years. We met in Chicago. I was a real estate agent. Corporate, not residential. Arnold was there on a business trip. Back then he worked for Gillette, signing pro athletes for endorsements." Another icy smile. "A man on his way up." The phone rang and she flinched.

"Go ahead and take it if you need to. I can wait."

"No. The damn thing's been ringing off the hook for hours. The buzzards want to talk to the grieving widow. You saw them outside."

Indeed he had. As Miller had predicted, the shit was hitting the fan. The Peterson murder had led the news on the local TV stations this morning. And it was only going to get worse.

"They want juicy tidbits from the widow." Her lips formed a grim line.

Not a good lead-in for his next question, but he had no time to waste. He still had to interview Peterson's assistant. Miller was at the hotel questioning guests. After lunch they had to watch the hotel security tapes.

"How were you and Mr. Peterson getting along? Any problems?"

Her jaw tightened, deepening the lines at the corners of her mouth. She fixed him with an icy stare. "Problems? I had problems but Arnold didn't. He did whatever he wanted. The powerful man's privilege. I'm sure you'll hear all about his *girl*friends. It's common knowledge."

And that must hurt, Frank thought. "Were any of them married?"

Shock flitted across her face. Corrine was no dummy. She knew where he was headed. "Well, well. I hadn't thought of that. You think some angry *husband* shot Arnold?"

13

"That's one possibility." One of many. "Did you know any of his . . . girlfriends?"

"Detective Renzi, I stopped trying to figure out which girl Arnold was screwing a long time ago. What good would it do? He'd just find another one."

Terrific. His unknown suspect list was expanding exponentially. "Did you discuss this with him?"

"Once, years ago, after our son was born."

"How old is your son? And your girls?"

"Tim is seven. Julia's ten and Louisa is thirteen."

"This must be difficult for them. How are they doing?"

Her eyes welled with tears and her face imploded. "They're devastated," she whispered.

She might not love Arnold, but she clearly loved her kids.

"Where are they now?"

"At a friend's house. I'm picking them up for lunch."

"We didn't find your husband's wallet. Do you know if he carried any credit cards?"

"I don't know for sure, but I assume so."

"You need to cancel them. Do you have the account numbers?"

Her mouth quirked. "Arnold deposited money into my bank account every month. I took care of my bills and he took care of his. I'll have to go through his file cabinet to find his credit card statements."

"Do it soon. Someone may try to use the credit cards." He drank some ice water and segued into his next question. "How often did your husband stay at the Hotel Bienvenue?"

"He'd go there Sunday night and come home on Saturday to spend time with the children." Her eyes welled with tears. "If one of them was in a school play or a concert, he'd come home for that. We'd go together." She clenched her jaw, squeezed out a grudging, "Arnold was a good father at least."

He tried to imagine it. Peterson stayed in a hotel all week to avoid his wife. Even when he and Evelyn weren't getting along, they'd slept in the same room every night. In twin beds.

"Did you and Mr. Peterson have any arguments recently?"

"No. I lived my life and Arnold lived his."

Maybe. But Arnold's philandering must have caused her considerable embarrassment. He could picture her having a few pops and getting into a screaming match with Arnold. Maybe more than one. Maybe the fights got so bad she decided to kill him. She might love her kids, but any love between her and Arnold had died years ago. He had only her word that she'd been home last night. Had she tucked the kids in bed, driven to the Bienvenue and popped him? Possible, though it would have been hard to cover her tracks.

"Do you own a gun, Mrs. Peterson?"

Her mouth sagged open and she stared at him.

14

"A gun? What would I do with a gun?" A brittle laugh. "Oh, I get it. You think I shot Arnold. Well, I didn't. I don't own a gun."

Maybe not, but Corrine wasn't off the hook yet. If she got rid of Arnold, she wouldn't have to put up with the ugly rumors. Or other people's pity.

"Why didn't you leave him?"

Her lips twisted. "Last time I checked there isn't a big market for middle-aged women with three children. Men my age want trophy wives. I have a nice home and my country club friends and status in the community. If I divorced him, I'd lose all of that. I might have money, but money isn't everything."

And some husbands fought like tigers to stop their wives from getting their money, Frank thought. So their wives killed them.

———

"Thank you for coming, Detective Renzi. Have a seat." Fenwick Holt gestured at the visitor chair in front of a massive mahogany desk with an inlaid leather top.

Irritated, Frank said nothing. Holt was acting like he'd invited him up to discuss a business matter, not a murder, shuffling papers around to show how busy he was. The self-important little twerp was maybe thirty-five and clearly not grieving. Why should he? Now that Peterson was dead, he was in charge.

Before he could zap Holt with a question, the phone rang. Holt swiveled his high-backed leather chair, grabbed the phone and said in an officious voice, "Babylon East Marketing, Fenwick Holt." And after a pause, "We'll distribute a statement to all media outlets in an hour. Thank you for calling."

He stabbed a button on the executive phone. "Hold my calls, Marjory. Tell the reporters we'll give them a statement in plenty of time for the early news." He ran a hand over his dirty-blond military-style buzz cut. "Sorry for the interruption, Detective. It's been crazy around here as you can imagine."

He could imagine it all right, but The Babylon was still open for business. Downstairs he'd zigzagged through gaming tables, roulette wheels and dozens of slot machines with dazzling electronic displays that emitted ugly annoying sounds. On his way to the elevator he dodged gamblers of both genders clutching drinks and several uniformed guards. When he left the elevator on the second floor, he'd passed the Babylon Security Center. An armed guard stood outside the door. Inside, Frank knew, eagle-eyed watchers scrutinized banks of video monitors to make sure nobody ripped off the casino.

"I understand your CEO is on vacation. Does he know about Peterson?"

"Yes. I texted his Blackberry. Mr. Weston and his wife are vacationing on the French Riviera."

"And his reaction was?"

"Well, he was shocked, of course."

"Can you elaborate?" *You self-important prick.*

15

"Detective Renzi, this may come as a surprise to you, but Arnold was on his way out."

A surprise? It sure was. "What do you mean?"

Holt pursed his lips like a prissy old maid. "He was about to be fired."

"Fenwick, we'd save a lot of time if I didn't have to pull every detail out of you like I was pulling bubblegum out of my daughter's hair. Why was Peterson about to be fired?"

"He had a gambling problem. He asked Mr. Weston for an advance on his salary. When Mr. Weston asked why, Arnold said he had gambling debts." Holt smiled tightly. "I don't know how much he asked for, but Mr. Weston told me it was more than Arnold made in a year."

Letting him know he was tight with the CEO. "Did you know he had a gambling problem?"

"No."

"Was Peterson gambling here?" He couldn't imagine it, but things were getting weird.

"No, he wasn't stupid enough to do that. He was into sports betting."

Frank thought about Corrine's statement: When they'd met in Chicago, Peterson had been recruiting athletes to endorse Gillette products. Lots of pro teams in Chicago: the Bears, Black Hawks, Cubs and White Sox. Maybe that's when he started gambling. Big cities offered plenty of betting opportunities, legit and otherwise. He wondered if Corrine Peterson knew about the debts.

Holt ostentatiously looked at his watch. A busy man.

"Tell me about Peterson's schedule yesterday. Did he have any unusual appointments?"

"No."

"I'd like to see his appointment calendar."

Holt flipped a page in a leather-bound calendar and handed it to him.

"Thanks. I'll need to keep this for a while."

Holt frowned, "Well, I don't know . . ."

"I can get a court order, Fenwick, but why don't we play nice. I'll sign a receipt for it, let you off the hook. I'm sure your employer would want you to help us solve Mr. Peterson's murder."

Holt's mouth quirked. "Fine. Take it. I'll have to reconstruct his schedule from his computer--"

"I hear Peterson made some enemies on his way up. Can you give me some names?"

"Who told you that, his wife?" Holt sneered. "She's got no complaints, takes her fat ass to the country club every day to booze it up with her friends."

He revised his take on Fenwick Holt: self-important, snotty, and misogynistic. "Do you know anyone who wanted Arnold *dead*?" Leaning on the word to shake him up.

Holt's ferrety eyes widened. "No, I don't. I mean, I'm sure some people didn't like him, but I don't know of anyone who'd want to kill him."

"Seems like you're next in line for his job."

Holt's jaw dropped halfway to his chest. "You think I killed Arnold?"

"Where were you last night between ten and midnight?"

"Home with my wife! Ask Linda. She'll tell you."

"I'll do that." He stifled a yawn, calculating how much sleep he'd get tonight. First thing tomorrow he had a meeting with his boss. He was willing to bet the NOPD brass and the local politicians were already leaning Detective Lieutenant Morgan Vobitch. A Babylon East executive murdered in one of the French Quarter's premier hotels? Hell, that was a sure thing.

And his suspect list was growing. If Peterson borrowed money from a loan shark, maybe the shark sent his enforcer to collect the vig and the guy killed him because he wouldn't pay. Great. Add loan shark to an angry widow, disgruntled co-workers, and a self-important asswipe after the dead man's job. Throw in the jealous husband of one of Peterson's girlfriends, the possibilities were endless.

"If you think of anything helpful give me a call. I'll ask your wife to confirm your alibi."

Holt stared at him, looking much less self-important. "Hey, you want names? Talk to Ken Volpe and Ivan Ludlow. They weren't too happy when Arnold landed the Marketing Director position."

Nothing like being a murder suspect to cause an attitude adjustment.

"Do they still work here?"

"Hell no. Arnold forced them out." Holt shot him a sanctimonious smile. "They aren't grieving over Arnold's death, I can promise you that."

———

Outside The Babylon, he dug out his cell and called Miller.

"Yo, Frank, how'd it go with the widow? You think she killed him?"

"Hard to say at this point. Did you get anything from the hotel guests?"

"Got diddly. Two rooms on the sixth floor were unoccupied. The guy next door to Peterson's room went to Harrah's last night, didn't get back to his room till four A.M. The couple on the other side are on their honeymoon, went barhopping on Bourbon Street, didn't get in till three. Nobody else heard a shot, no commotion, no screams. Wanna grab some lunch?"

He checked his watch. One-thirty, and he hadn't eaten. "Sure, but someplace close. We've got to watch the hotel security videos, remember?"

"Yeah. That'll be hours of fun. Better get me some Murine."

He closed his cell and headed for the Eighth District Station. The first forty-eight hours of a murder investigation were crucial, and they had no leads.

What they had was a long list of people who might want Peterson dead.

CHAPTER 3

She stepped out of the stairwell and sauntered down the hallway.

A floppy broad-brimmed hat hid her face, but the grainy black-and-white video couldn't conceal her athleticism, striding along in spike heels, a small purse slung over her shoulder. The spaghetti straps on her low-cut dress revealed well-toned arms, and the short skirt displayed her long muscular legs.

She stopped at Room 635 and tapped on the door.

Frank glanced at Miller, who mouthed: *Bingo.*

Standing behind the Hotel Bienvenue security chief, Frank asked him to pause the tape. Seated on a padded swivel chair, Stephen Taylor hit a button on the video control board. A balding man in his fifties, Taylor wore a dark business suit and reeked of cologne. The scent was overwhelming inside the eight-by-six-foot cubicle. Crammed with equipment, the viewing room sported three tape decks, two sixteen-inch flat-screen monitors, a heavy-duty computer on a metal desk and an ink-jet printer on a stand beside it.

Frank noted the timestamp. At 10:14 P.M., the woman had entered Room 635, Arnold Peterson's room. Moments ago, they had watched Peterson enter the room at exactly 10:00 P.M.

"Okay, Mr. Taylor. Start the tape."

The video sprang to life, the door to Room 635 opened and Ms. Incognito stepped inside. An adrenaline-fueled buzz hit his gut. They had something, but he didn't want to get too excited.

"Could you fast-forward the tape, Mr. Taylor?"

Taylor hit a button and images of the hall whirred by on the monitor. No one entered the hall from the stairwell. No one got off the elevator. No one entered or left any of the rooms. The tape kept rolling.

Antsy with anticipation, Frank focused on Room 635. At last, the door opened. Ms. Incognito stepped into the hall and closed the door. Taylor paused the tape and Frank noted the time. 11:30 P.M.

"She was in there more than an hour," Miller said.

"Shall I continue the tape?" Taylor asked, without turning his head.

"Not yet. Can you print out a freeze-frame when she leaves the room?"

Taylor got on the computer. Seconds later the printer spewed out a sheet of paper with a black-and-white nine-by-six-inch image.

"Thanks," Frank said. "We'll want more, but for now let the tape roll. I want to see what she does."

They watched her walk down the hall. She didn't appear to be in a hurry. Sashaying past the elevator, she opened the door to the fire stairs and disappeared. Frank toted up his impression of her. Sexy. A long-legged stride. Confident. Athletic. Was she a hooker? The dress had a short skirt and a low-cut neckline, but the outfit was classy, not chintzy-looking. The shoes and the purse looked stylish. Expensive. Maybe she was Peterson's girlfriend. If she was a hooker, she was a high-priced hooker.

"Let's fast-forward the tape," Miller said, his voice a low rumble in the cramped cubicle, "see if anyone else leaves the room."

Images of the hallway whirred past on the monitor. No one left Peterson's room. No one appeared in the hall until 12:17 A.M. when a security guard left the elevator and trotted down the hall to Room 635.

"We've seen enough for now," Frank said. "Could you rewind the tape to where she comes out of the stairwell and print some freeze-frame photos?"

Taylor hit Rewind, paused the tape when the woman appeared and printed a photo. Frank examined it. Only the lower part of her face was visible. The rest was hidden by the hat brim, and she was wearing sunglasses. Ms. Incognito was taking no chances, wearing a floppy hat and shades, walking with her head angled away from the security camera. As though she knew it was there.

Girlfriend or hooker? A tough call. If she was Peterson's girlfriend, she might not want her face on a security video for any number of reasons.

Taylor handed them three more shots of the woman. Miller studied them a moment and said, "Long hair. Looks light colored, maybe blonde."

"Could be a wig," Frank said.

"Nobody else in or out of the room." Miller looked at him, deadpan, but his eyes had a familiar mischievous look.

Frank waited for the zinger. Miller made a terrific partner. A former LSU middle line backer, Kenyon was a mean presence on the job: six-foot-six, two-forty, all the more menacing because of his dark skin and shaven pate. Not only that, he was well-educated and street-smart. But the best part was his wickedly warped sense of humor, a welcome asset in a job that often involved revolting sights and smells. And dangerous situations.

"Frank," Miller said, "did you check under the bed last night?"

He cracked up. Humor didn't erase the many horrors they encountered, but it often allayed the tension. "No," he said, "did you?"

"Well," Taylor said, swiveling his chair to face them, "actually . . ."

Instantly alert, Frank said, "What?"

"There's a fire escape outside the window of Room 635. That's why Mr. Peterson rented it. He said he didn't want to be trapped on the sixth floor if there was a fire."

Miller rolled his eyes. "Great. Let's go see it."

Five minutes later Taylor let them into Room 635. The room was cool now, but a faint unpleasant odor lingered. Only a box-spring remained on the four-poster double bed. The forensic techs had taken the mattress and bedding. The hotel wouldn't be renting this room anytime soon.

Frank went to the window and pulled back the drapes. Two latches on either side of the casing were open. "It's unlocked. Kenyon, you got a pen?"

Miller handed him a felt-tipped marker. Using Miller's marker and his own ballpoint pen, he eased open the window. It slid up smooth as silk, without a squeak. He leaned out and took a look.

A wrought-iron fire escape bolted to the backside of the hotel zigzagged down to the second floor. Below it was an alley lined with green dumpsters.

He backed away so Miller could take a look.

"Better get the techs to come back and dust for prints," Miller said.

"Can I close the window?" Taylor asked.

"No, leave it," Frank said. "We'll need to take that security video."

"Yes, sir. Did you want to watch the other tapes now?"

Miller shot Frank a look that said, *No way.* Aloud Miller said, "Let's watch the tapes for the lobby, do the rest tomorrow."

After Frank put in a call for the forensics technicians, they watched the videos that covered the hotel entrance. Several women entered and left the hotel between ten P.M. and one-thirty A.M., but none wore a floppy hat and a dress with a mini-skirt and spaghetti straps. Frank bagged and tagged the tape with the mystery woman, told Taylor they'd be back tomorrow and they left.

Inside the elevator they took turns yawning. Neither of them had gotten much sleep last night. Now it was four o'clock. Almost seventeen hours since Ms. Incognito with the confident long-legged stride entered Peterson's room and did whatever she did. If she shot Peterson and left the hotel, she wasn't on the security tapes that covered the entrance. Another puzzle to solve.

"Man, the fire escape was a curveball," Miller said. "Maybe Peterson's wife hired her so she could blackmail him. Maybe the shooter used the woman to get Peterson in a compromising position."

Frank thought about it. Most widows begged him to find their husband's killer, but not Corrine Peterson. The spouse was always the prime suspect, but her anguished expression when he asked why she hadn't filed for divorce remained an after-image in his mind. At forty-five, Corrine figured her options were limited. Maybe she was right. Would he date her? Doubtful.

They were almost the same age, but she was angry and bitter. He figured he had a lot of good years left. Besides, he had Kelly, a woman he cared deeply about, and they still had great times in bed. This morning he'd woken up with a hard-on. He was looking forward to seeing her on Friday. But if they didn't get a lead on the Peterson case, he might have to work. Bummer.

"She's not your typical grieving widow, but I don't get the sense she killed him. Peterson had gambling debts. Maybe he didn't pay the vig."

"Frank, you really think Peterson told some mobster to go fuck himself, and the guy shot him?"

"Hey, right now anything's possible."

"My money's on the woman. Coulda had a mean little gun in that fancy purse she was carrying. Mm, mm, mm. A female hitter. That's a first for me."

"Me, too. Maybe she's Peterson's girlfriend. It's obvious she didn't want to be seen, used the stairs instead of the elevator to avoid running into anyone. But the fire escape opens up a whole new scenario. We can't discount the possibility that someone else got in and out of the room that way."

"Frank, you're making it too complicated. Did you see *The Last Seduction*?"

"Yeah. Great flick. Linda Fiorentino was something."

"No kidding. She was hot, before it was hip to be hot." Miller nodded, then said, "She also knew how to use a gun."

———

He left the Holt residence at 5:30 and got in his car. According to Linda Holt, Fenwick had come home at seven Wednesday night, after which they ate dinner, watched TV and went to bed. Pictures of Jesus and religious statuary decorated the Holt living room. Linda wouldn't lie to him in front of the Virgin Mary, would she?

Cross Mr. Self-important off the suspect list. Unless he'd hired a hitter.

Frank toyed with that scenario. The woman was the hitter. Dressed like a hooker. Flirts with Peterson, goes up to his room and pops him.

He shook his head, unable to picture it. A female hitter? In the movies maybe, but in real life? Doubtful.

Another possibility. The woman was a hooker or paid to look like one. She goes in the room, unlocks the window while Peterson's in the bathroom, gets him hot to trot and the hitter comes in through the window.

He didn't like that scenario much better than the first one.

Miller was right. He was over-thinking the case, conjuring complicated scenarios. The woman went in the room and killed Peterson. Simple. Over and out. But why?

Walking away from Peterson's room she didn't act like a killer. She acted nonchalant, like she didn't have a care in the world.

A new possibility hit him. What if Peterson wasn't dead when she left the room? What if the hitter was still in there with Peterson? What if she didn't know Peterson was about to get whacked?

21

Overtaken by weariness, he yawned. Man, if he didn't get some sleep tonight, he'd never make it to the weekend. He dug out his cell and hit the speed-dial for Kelly's home phone.

"Hey, Frank, how're you doing?" she said in her low husky voice.

The husky voice that always turned him on. "Wasted and I'm not talking alcohol. How about you?"

"Hold on, okay? I need to shut off the torch."

After her NOPD workday his lover fired up her creative side. She made jewelry in a workshop in her garage, not tacky little trinkets, not chintzy beads strung into necklaces like you'd buy on Bourbon Street. In addition to being a smart detective and sexy as hell, Kelly O'Neil was a master welder. She fashioned small pieces of brass into elegant earrings, brooches and bracelets, which she then painted with various shades of enamel.

She came back on the line and said, "Looks like you've got your work cutout for you, huh? The Peterson murder is the lead on all the local channels. All kinds of wild rumors and speculation."

"Yeah. I'm meeting with Vobitch first thing tomorrow. He's under the gun, all kinds of politicians crawling up his ass."

"Nothing new there. How's it going? Any leads?"

"Got leads up the wazoo. The guy was a ruthless son-of-a-bitch. He was also screwing around on his wife. And then there's the mysterious woman on the security video . . ."

"Ooooh," Kelly crooned. "Tell me more."

"I would but I gotta go back to the office and prep for the meeting and then I better crash. Are we on for dinner tomorrow night?" They always had dinner together on Fridays.

"Sounds great. I'll get the takeout. You've got enough to worry about."

"Thanks. I'm not sure what time. I'll call you around five and we'll figure it out." He flipped his cell shut and smiled.

Talking to Kelly always put him in a good mood.

If he wasn't so tired he'd go over there right now and jump her.

CHAPTER 4

Friday, 25 July

When Frank entered his boss's office at nine o'clock, the look in Morgan Vobitch's slate-gray eyes said it all. F-bomb explosion coming right up. He took the chair in front of the desk and kept his mouth shut.

"Fuckin politicians." Detective Lieutenant Morgan Vobitch swiped back his thick mane of silvery hair, his face dark with fury. "They think we just wave a magic wand and grab the killer, slam-bam, end of story."

Prior to joining NOPD fifteen years ago, Vobitch had spent ten years with NYPD. Now he supervised the homicide detectives in Districts One, Three and Eight. He was built like a Sherman tank and often behaved like one, steamrolling anyone or anything that got in his way. He resembled Detective Sipowitz on *NYPD Blue* and spoke a Bronx patois laden with F-bombs. If he didn't want TV reporters to quote him, he dropped the F-bomb on camera. On purpose. Frank loved the guy. They had the same take-no-prisoners attitude: *Nail the fuckers and put 'em in jail.*

"Take a look at this." Vobitch tossed him a copy of the *Times-Picayune*.

A front page headline said: **Babylon East executive murdered in French Quarter hotel.**

He scanned the story, zeroing in on the quotes from outraged politicians.

"Our great and glorious city is a tourist destination!" said the councilman whose district included the French Quarter. "People come here from all over the world to enjoy the sights and sounds of the French Quarter. How can they do that when a man is murdered in one of our finest hotels?"

French Quarter business owners and the bigwigs running the Babylon casino and Hotel Bienvenue were equally outraged, saying the publicity was ruining their image and costing them business.

Then, a quote from the New Orleans mayor. "I understand Mr. Peterson was shot execution-style in the head." Great, Frank thought. Leaks about the crime scene were already spawning rumors, rumors that were certain to multiply. He scanned the rest of the article.

The final quote was the kicker. "I've asked the Attorney General to assign

23

their most experienced prosecutor to the case, District Attorney Roger Demaris," said NOPD Superintendent William Atkins.

Bad news. Roger Demaris was a pit-bull. He was also a royal fucking pain in the ass, demanding daily updates from the lead detective on the case.

He set the newspaper on the desk near the pink message slips that littered a green blotter dotted with coffee mug stains.

"Roger Demaris is on the case," he said.

"Correct. Now we got the number-one prick in the DA's office breathing down our neck." Vobitch's lip curled in a sneer. "Thanks to our fat-fuck NOPD Super and his Slick-Willie media manipulation."

Superintendent William Atkins, a jumbo-sized black man, had won the position due to his ability to sweet-talk the media, not his crime-fighting skills. He was quick with a quote and reporters loved his suave articulate demeanor. But Atkins had far fewer fans within the ranks of the NOPD.

"No mention of the Hotel Bienvenue security video. You think that will leak to the media?"

An icy stare from Vobitch. "Are you kidding? No way that stays under wraps. Sure as shit some bigwig's assistant will blab to a reporter to score some brownie points."

"Maybe the Super will give us more bodies to work the case."

"We don't need more bodies," Vobitch griped. "We need a solid lead."

"A lead would be great, but I need help. I need to interview the hotel guests, check Peterson's financials, eyeball every security video from the time Peterson left for work on Wednesday till the security guard found his corpse. Jesus, if I watch 'em all myself, I'll go blind."

"I'll get some District-One detectives to help you. Let's talk about the autopsy." Vobitch flashed a sardonic smile. "Which, thanks to the VIP victim, was completed in record time. Christ, we got dozens of homicides this year, none of 'em made a ripple. I'm still waiting for autopsy reports on two of 'em."

But those victims weren't VIPs found in a posh French Quarter hotel, Frank thought.

"According to the coroner," Vobitch said, reading from the report, "marks on Peterson's wrists and ankles suggest that he was tied up. No defense wounds to indicate he fought the killer."

"We didn't find any ligatures or cuffs in the room, but the killer could have taken them with him."

"No semen stains on the body or the bedding. Significant?"

"I talked to the hotel housekeeping director. Peterson had a standing order for the maid to leave fresh towels and change the sheets every day."

"Frank, every murder comes down to means, motive and opportunity."

"We searched the hotel for the murder weapon and didn't find it, but the killer could have ditched it in a storm drain or a trash barrel. Plenty of those in the French Quarter."

"So that leaves motive and opportunity. You said Holt seems pretty comfortable sitting in Peterson's chair. Big job, big bucks, that's motive."

"True, but his wife swore he was home with her all night and I believed her. You want motive? How about Peterson's gambling debts? And his wife knew he was cheating on her."

"You think she killed him?"

"She said she was home with her kids and right now I can't prove she wasn't. I'll ask around, see if anyone saw her near the hotel. But she's not the woman on the video. You saw it. Wrong build. She could hide her face and wear a wig but she couldn't change her height and weight."

"She had to be pissed about the girlfriends, might have been pissed about the gambling, too. Killing him wouldn't solve the financial problem, but at least he couldn't run up more debt betting on the ponies or whatever fuckin thing he was putting money on."

"But we don't know if she knew about the debts. And if he borrowed money and didn't pay, there's another addition to the suspect list."

"Christ on a crutch!" Vobitch exploded. "The guy didn't get along with his co-workers, couldn't keep his dick in his pants, couldn't stop gambling . . ."

"Maybe I'll get something from the men on the Peterson enemies list." He checked his notes. "Ken Volpe and Ivan Ludlow."

"Lean on Peterson's wife about the gambling debts, too. Christ, we got no leads and a shitload of suspects: his wife, his enemies, throw in the angry spouse of some woman he was screwing . . ." Vobitch smiled his killer smile. "And then, of course, there's my all-time favorite, the Big Bad Bogyman."

Vobitch's phone rang. He glanced at it, but didn't answer. "Frank, I think the woman on the video is the hitter. We got tape of her entering and leaving the room. She could've had a gun in that fancy purse. A snub-nosed .38 would fit into it easy."

"She's got attitude, I'll give you that. She walks like Linda Fiorentino."

A blank stare. "Who's Linda Fiorentino?" Vobitch didn't watch TV crime shows or violent movies. His wife, a former ballet dancer, hated them.

"She played a gun-toting sexpot with attitude in a movie."

"I don't give a shit about her attitude. What we need is motive. Did someone hire her or did she have her own agenda?"

"She looked pretty relaxed after she left the room. Maybe Peterson wasn't dead yet."

Vobitch lowered his head and gave him his steamroller glower. "Frank, we got enough complications already. Let's not invent more."

"I don't want to assume the woman on the video killed him. She might look like our best bet now, but I'm not going to exclude other possibilities. It's too soon."

"She had means and opportunity. All we need is motive."

"Kenyon thinks Peterson's wife might have hired her to blackmail him. If she had pictures of him in bed with a hooker, she'd have power over him."

"So who took the pictures? Forget Spiderman climbing the fire escape. And if his wife hired the woman so she could blackmail him, why kill him?"

"I don't know. The coroner didn't find any tape residue near his mouth. No attempt to keep him quiet."

"She had a gun. That'll keep a guy quiet."

"I still don't buy your female hitter theory. We don't know she had a gun. We don't have the murder weapon. Who is she? Why did she kill him?"

"I don't know, but we got tape of her entering and leaving the room. She goes inside, disables Peterson somehow and cuffs him so she can question him. That's why she didn't tape his mouth."

"Question him about what?"

"Hell if I know. She pops her questions, doesn't like his answers and kills him. Frank, we gotta find her."

"Yeah. Piece of cake."

Vobitch gave him an icy stare. "That's our job, Frank. And that's exactly what that prick Roger Demaris is gonna tell me every fuckin chance he gets. We don't solve this case fast, heads are gonna roll and I don't want one of 'em to be mine. Find the woman in the video and get her in here."

3:30 P. M.

She checked out of the Sunshine Inn, a low-budget hotel two blocks away from the French Quarter, and towed her suitcase around the corner to her rental car. The three extra-strength Excedrin she'd taken had done nothing to ease her blinding headache, and the sweltering heat didn't help. The air was thick with humidity, and leaden clouds hung low in the sky, hinting at rain. Although she'd dressed in a T-shirt and shorts, she was already sweating.

June Carson had paid cash in advance to rent the room for a week. On her fake documents, she liked to use names of birds, like Robin, or the names of months, like June. She was saving April for the Main Event.

She locked her suitcase in the trunk. Leaving it in the car was risky, but the Circle K was only three blocks away. One more errand and she'd be ready to leave New Orleans. Maybe that would get rid of her headache. Hop in the car, hit the highway, put on some music and relax.

As she strode up the street two dragonflies flitted across her path, chasing each other. A good omen. Dragonflies brought good luck, and if last night was any indication, her luck was holding. Thanks to her meticulous preparations everything had gone without a hitch. Exhilarated, she had returned to the Sunshine Inn. Unable to sleep, she'd curled up in bed and listened to the night sounds—honking taxis, muted laughter, snippets of conversations—just as she'd done as a child.

26

Killing Peterson had been essential to her plan and it had succeeded beyond her wildest dreams. Now she had his words on tape. The incriminating words she would use to complete her mission.

Then she would be free.

Intent on her errand, she rounded the corner onto Esplanade Avenue. For years her life had been a long dark tunnel with no light at the end. Along the way there had been a few good times—befriending Gabe, living in Paris, even loving Willem had been wonderful for a while—but a series of ordeals had brought pain, sorrow and years of hard work that brought her no joy and little reward. For years her goal had been simple: Avenge her mother's murder.

It had taken her years to track down the killer. Now there was no doubt. Now she was ready take revenge on the monster who'd killed Mom. For years, this overwhelming sense of obligation had consumed her, ruling her life. Soon the crushing burden that rode her back like a demon from hell would be lifted.

But then what would she do? Who would she be?

An image of Arnold Peterson's terrified eyes flashed into her mind, the moment before she'd shot him. The recurring image had kept her awake most of the night. Peterson was a rich man with powerful friends, accustomed to being in control. But last night he wasn't. She was. At that moment she'd felt an awesome sense of power. Even now the memory revved her heartbeat.

Peterson wasn't the monster that murdered Mom, but he had aided and abetted the man who did. Mom had waited twenty years for her murder to be avenged. Soon the wait would be over. But she had to get out of New Orleans. Now. Peterson's murder was all over the news.

Avoiding the twisted slabs of cement heaved up by the roots of giant oaks, she lengthened her stride, ignoring the relentless pain in her temples. The Circle-K convenience store was on the next corner. Her rental car was gassed up and ready to go, but she needed supplies. Once she got on the highway, she wouldn't stop for at least two hundred miles. Rest areas had security cameras, and she couldn't afford to leave any trace of her departure from New Orleans.

A bell dinged as she entered the Circle-K. Unlike the air outside, the store was cool. The sudden chill made her head throb. Glass-front coolers in the rear of the store held refrigerated items. She took out a large bottle of chilled Aquafina and small packets of ham and cheese. Moving along the grocery aisle, she heard the bell ding as another customer entered the store.

She tucked a box of Triscuits under her arm and continued down the aisle. Gallon jugs of bottled water lined the bottom shelf. She stooped to take one off the shelf, straightened and froze. Someone was watching her.

The back of her neck prickled, a creepy sensation, as though a swarm of spiders were crawling over it. Her sunglasses were in her tote. Should she put them on? No, too obvious. *Leave the store, get back to the car and go.*

Ducking her head, she edged down the aisle toward the register. In her peripheral vision, she spotted the man but didn't look directly at him. "Never look into the eyes of a grizzly bear," one of her American clients had told her over dinner at a fine Parisian restaurant. "If you do the bear will charge and kill you." She didn't know if this was true or not, but it seemed plausible.

She pretended to examine a can of mixed vegetables, but her entire being remained focused on the man who was watching her. Not just watching, staring at her, the way a wild beast stares at its next meal.

She gathered details: A white man. A dark beard. A cowboy hat.

Her heart hammered her chest and her palms grew slick with sweat. She slid the gallon jug of water and the other groceries onto a shelf. The pain in her temples made her nauseous. She should never have come to the store, should have gotten in her car and driven away. Cursing her mistake, she fingered the good-luck talisman that hung from her neck.

How could this happen when she was so close to escaping?

She strode to the register. The clerk, a young black man with a friendly smile said, "Find everything you wanted?"

"Yes, thank you." She gave him two dollars for the bottle of Aquafina.

Her heart was ready to jump out of her chest.

Off to her left, Cowboy Hat was still staring at her.

The clerk gave her the change and said, "Have a nice day."

"Thanks, you too." She sidestepped to the door, opened it and lunged outside into the heat. She wanted to run to her car as fast as her legs would carry her, but that would be stupid. Cowboy Hat was watching her for a reason. He was a predator like the grizzly bears, and grizzlies could run faster than humans. Or so she'd heard.

Extending her legs, she strode along the sidewalk, ignoring the blinding pain in her temples. Could she outrun Cowboy Hat? Maybe he was wearing cowboy boots too. That would slow him down. To calm herself, she tried to think positive. She was imagining things. Jumpy after all the stress and tension from last night. Tired from lack of sleep. Cowboy Hat liked her looks and wanted to ask her out for a date.

No need to panic. No one in New Orleans knew her.

She glanced behind her.

Fear clawed her chest like a ravenous beast.

Cowboy Hat had long legs too, and he was gaining on her.

Clutching the bottle of Aquafina in her sweaty hand, she turned the corner and broke into a trot. Her car was a half block away. Almost home free.

"Hey, Natalie," called a nasal voice. "Wait up."

CHAPTER 5

Poised to attack, she turned to face him, legs flexed, arms by her sides.

Her mind, shocked into paralysis when he called her name, had gone into preservation mode. He knew her. Knew she was in New Orleans.

Who was he? How big a threat?

Cowboy Hat trotted toward her. No cowboy boots. He was wearing Nikes and a broad smile. "Hey, Natalie, great to see you. Don't you remember me? Tex Conroy. We went to school together in Pecos."

Tex Conroy. His face was fuller now and the dark beard made him look different, but she felt the same panicky breathlessness she'd felt whenever she'd been around him in school. She pushed the feeling down to her midsection and summoned a smile. It took every bit of acting skill she had.

"Oh. Hi, Tex. I didn't recognize you." And desperately wished he hadn't recognized her.

"You look different, Natalie. Your hair's shorter. I like the new color." He looked her up and down, eyeballing her breasts, then her bare legs. He smiled and leaned closer. For a disgusting instant she thought he was going to kiss her. She backed up a step.

"But when I saw that bird hanging around your neck I knew it was you."

Involuntarily, she touched the firebird pendent. Her good luck talisman.

Not this time. This time it had betrayed her.

"Hot damn!" Tex exclaimed, chortling like a teenager. The obnoxious teenager she'd known in high school. "Wait till I tell the guys you're here. Are you on vacation or do you live here?"

Wait till I tell the guys you're here. Her heart slammed her chest. If he was here with his friends, this could be a huge problem. She breathed down to her diaphragm, part of her taekwondo skill set. No way could she allow anyone to know that Natalie Brixton was in New Orleans when Peterson was murdered.

Not when she was so close to her goal. Mom had waited too long.

"I'm here on a work assignment," she said. "How about you?"

"I live here. Left Pecos five years ago after my Daddy died. I'm bartending at a beer joint down on Decatur Street."

"Sorry to hear about your father." Speaking platitudes as she fought to overcome her fear. Old fears and new ones. She was afraid to talk to him, equally afraid not to.

Leering at her, he said, "How 'bout we have dinner? We can catch up on old times."

Old times. Had he forgotten his ugly taunts about her mother? Her mind churned with alternatives, all of them bad. Dinner was impossible. She had to leave New Orleans now. But if Tex called his football player buddies, he'd tell them she was here. He would also tell them what she looked like.

"Gee, Tex, I can't. I'm off to another assignment." She mustered a friendly smile. "Tell you what. I've got one more chore to do before I leave. If you come with me, I'll buy you a beer afterwards."

He grinned, baring crooked yellow teeth. "Well now, that sounds like a mighty fine proposition. What's the chore?"

Walking along beside him, she fell into familiar habits, honed to perfection after all these years. Be what he wants you to be, use your imagination and bamboozle him. "I work for *Golf Magazine*. My boss sent me here to photograph the golf courses. There's a big tournament coming up."

"Yeah? I ain't heard nothin about a golf tournament."

She doubted he'd ever played a round of golf in his life. Tex was a macho man with a cop for a father. Golf was for sissies. Real men played football.

"The magazine has a long lead time. Do you have a car?"

"Sure do. It's parked right around the corner, near my apartment."

A chill ran down her spine. For a week she'd been staying at the Sunshine Inn and all that time Tex had been living in an apartment two blocks away.

"Great," she said as they turned the corner. "Why don't you drive? The golf course is in City Park near the art museum. There's a nice lounge in the clubhouse."

"Sounds good to me," Tex said, and stopped at a powder-blue Cadillac.

"Wow, you must be doing okay, Tex."

"Not really. I bought it in Pecos. The sheriff's department was auctioning off some cars they confiscated." He gave her a sly wink. "I think some Mexicans drug runners were using it."

She gritted her teeth. Tex and his football buddies had thought it was great fun to taunt her about Gabe. *How's your wetback boyfriend, Natalie?*

Tex unlocked the door and opened it for her. Sir Galahad to the max. Did he think she was going to sleep with him? The car stank of beer, and balled-up Burger King wrappers littered the floor on the passenger side. Tex got behind the wheel, took off his cowboy hat and tossed it on the back seat.

He pulled away from the curb and wheeled right onto Esplanade Avenue. She set her tote in the foot-well and clenched her hands in her lap, knowing what she had to do, but unsure of where or how to do it.

Moments later as they drove north toward City Park, he pulled out a cell phone. Her stomach spasmed in fear. "What are you doing?"

He looked over and grinned. "Calling my friend Tommy."

One of his football buddies. Her heart hammered her chest. "Now? Let's wait till we have a beer. I'd love to talk to Tommy. It would be fun." She held her breath. If he called Tommy now it would force her hand.

After an agonizing pause, he slipped the cell back in his pocket. "How long is this photo shoot gonna take? I'm mighty thirsty."

Of course. Tex had always been thirsty, thirsty enough to get smashed at his graduation party, drive home drunk and kill his girlfriend on the way.

"Not long, Tex. Ten minutes tops." She touched his arm, an intimate gesture promising future intimacies. "Then we'll have a nice cool one."

———

The Riverside Hilton Security Director's office was on the eighth floor. When Frank got off the elevator at four o'clock Ivan Ludlow loomed in a doorway across the hall. He looked like Killer Kowalski, six-foot-eight with massive shoulders that swelled the jacket of his tailored business suit.

"Detective Renzi?" Ludlow said, and extended his hand. No smile.

"Thanks for seeing me on short notice, Mr. Ludlow." They shook and he gave Ludlow points for not crushing his hand. The far wall of his office was floor-to-ceiling glass, yielding an expansive view of the Mississippi River and beyond. A polished-oak desk faced the door, completely bare except for two items. An old-fashioned metal spindle with pink memo slips impaled on it, and a plastic mini-roulette wheel full of peppermint candies.

In a corner near the door, two leather chairs stood on either side of a low table. Ludlow took one and Frank took the other. Ken Volpe, the first man on Peterson's enemies list, worked for Bally's Riverboat Casinos; he'd been in Las Vegas all week, attending a conference. Frank sized up the second man on the list. Coarse black hair combed straight back from his face fell to his shoulders. His most prominent feature: Gila monster eyes, large and heavy-lidded.

Expressionless, Ludlow gazed at him without speaking, a clear message: *Talking to an NOPD homicide detective doesn't intimidate me.*

"You're here about Arnold?" Ludlow said at last. His face was like a Cezanne painting, all planes and angles. Although his appearance suggested European ancestry, his speech had no foreign cadence or accent.

"Yes. Someone suggested you might have had a beef with him."

Ludlow flicked a massive hand as if swatting away a fly. "I have no quarrel with Arnold."

"Let bygones be bygones?"

31

Ludlow blinked his Gila eyes. "Detective Renzi, I have an excellent job, an office with a splendid view and no hassles. The people who manage the Riverside Hilton treat me very well. Ken Volpe found an equally good job. I assume someone told you Arnold muscled us out of Babylon East."

He couldn't imagine the man he'd seen on the Hotel Bienvenue bed muscling Ivan Ludlow around. Ludlow would have broken him in half.

"Where were you between ten o'clock Wednesday night and two the next morning?"

"Home with my wife." Ludlow took a framed photograph off the table between them and held it out. Dressed in ski attire, Ivan had his arm around a striking raven-haired woman in similar attire. Beyond them were snowcapped mountains. The woman was a foot shorter than Ivan and she was smiling. Ivan wasn't. Maybe he never smiled.

"Nice picture," he said. "Where was it taken?"

"In Switzerland last year. We went there for our vacation."

"I'll need to interview your wife to confirm your alibi."

Ludlow shrugged. "As you wish. She teaches German at Metairie Country Day School."

"Did Arnold Peterson have a gambling problem?"

"If he did, it's news to me. A group of us went to the Fairgrounds a few years ago--"

"People who worked at Babylon East? Or was it a social event?"

Two Gila eye-blinks. "Arnold and I never socialized. I may have met his wife at a Christmas party. No, this group was from the Babylon marketing department. Arnold and some of the others placed a few bets. I didn't. I'm not much of a gambler."

Ludlow's pager buzzed. He glanced at it and returned it to his pocket. "My men get anxious during hurricane season. No more vertical evacuations, so if the mayor orders everyone to leave the city, we must be ready to evacuate our guests."

Frank nodded. He'd seen the horrors of vertical evacuations first hand. Prior to Katrina some New Orleans residents had booked rooms in high-rise hotels. During the dark desolate days after the storm they had been stranded in rooms without electricity. No food, no water and no toilet facilities.

But that was then. Now he had a hotel with a different problem.

"Do you know anyone who might have wanted Arnold Peterson dead?"

"No. What did you get from the security cameras?"

A sucker punch question, one he didn't intend to answer. Ludlow was a security director and had assumed the Bienvenue had security cameras.

"Do you know if Arnold Peterson ever used call girls?"

A tiny pause, but no change of expression. "He never mentioned it, but it's possible. Arnold was a heavy drinker. Moderation was never Arnold's strong point." Ludlow gazed at him expectantly. Blinked predictably.

32

"Thanks for your time, Mr. Ludlow." Ludlow was no dummy, had surmised, correctly, that they had something on videotape.

But he wasn't going to tell Ludlow about the woman on the video. And Ludlow wasn't going to tell him anything more about Arnold Peterson.

————

When they stopped at the traffic light opposite the New Orleans Art Museum, she could see people strolling along the tree-lined drive that led to the museum. She told Tex to turn right. No way did she want anyone noticing the distinctive powder-blue Cadillac with a young couple inside.

"Where y'all off to next?" Tex asked.

"Arizona. There's lots of golf courses out there."

"A bunch of sissies must live there. Golf is for faggots."

Good old Tex, as bigoted as ever. She told him to take the next left and drive into the park. The golf course was nearby, but she had no intention of going there. She needed a secluded spot with no people around.

A minute later she saw it.

"Park here," she said. "The golf course is just beyond those trees."

"Why can't we park at the clubhouse?"

"My boss wants me to get some shots of the back nine." She faked a laugh. "You wouldn't believe how finicky these pro golfers are."

He pulled onto the shoulder beside a grove of trees with picnic tables. She got out and slung her tote bag over her shoulder. Without waiting for Tex, she forged past the picnic tables into the stand of trees.

Behind her, Tex griped, "I don't see any golf course. Where is it?"

Her stomach knotted with tension. It was after four. Would people come here this late for a picnic?

"Beyond those big oak trees. Go ahead and see for yourself." She waved him ahead of her and looked back. The road was no longer visible and she heard no passing cars. Now or never.

She let him get a few steps ahead of her and reached into her tote.

He stopped suddenly and turned to look at her. "What are you doing?"

She smiled brightly. "Getting out my camera. For the pictures."

It was like déjà vu. Taking pictures of Randy beside the Pecos River.

Seemingly satisfied, Tex turned and kept walking.

The familiar cold hard iceberg formed inside her. She took the .38 Special out of her tote, pressed it against her leg and hurried to catch up, her heartbeat an anxious rat-a-tat against her ribs. When she was five feet behind him, she glanced over her shoulder to make sure no one was around. She saw no one.

Listened for sounds of a car. Heard nothing.

Two long silent strides brought her closer. She raised the revolver and fired one shot into the back of Tex Conroy's head.

His head jerked, his body lurched forward, and he toppled to the ground.

His legs twitched for a moment and lay still. With frantic haste, she knelt down and dug his wallet out of the back pocket of his jeans. Felt for his car keys. Didn't find them. Where could they be?

She had to find them. To get away fast, she needed a car.

With a mighty heave, she rolled him over. His face was a bloody mess, his eyes open and staring. Bile rose in her throat. She swallowed it down.

Her heart pounded like a wild thing. *Focus. Concentrate. Get the keys.*

She found them in his front pocket. Holding the gun against her right leg, she ran back to his Cadillac.

When she emerged from the grove of trees, the picnic area was deserted.

Relieved, she got in the car, cranked the engine and glanced in the rearview mirror. Her heart almost stopped.

A blue-and-white NOPD cruiser was approaching the car.

Panic clawed her stomach. Had someone heard the shot?

She looked again. No flashing lights on the cruiser. But the distinctive powder-blue Caddy belonged to the dead man someone would eventually find in the woods. And the cruiser was almost upon her.

She grabbed Tex's cowboy hat off the back seat, jammed it on her head and turned as though she was looking at something on the passenger seat.

Moments later the cruiser passed her, continued down the narrow road and disappeared.

Sour bile flooded her mouth. She opened the car door, leaned out and vomited on the grass. Panting, she opened the bottle of Aquafina, rinsed her mouth and spat on the ground. Her hands were shaking, her whole body wracked with tremors. She did a U-turn and drove out of the park.

Ten minutes later she drove down Esplanade Avenue at the edge of the French Quarter. Her insides were still shaking. Two blocks over she parked the Cadillac in a strip mall near where it had been parked before. She took a packet of alcohol-soaked baby wipes out of her tote, used one to clean the steering wheel and door handles, got out and walked away.

On the way back to her rental car she dropped Tex's keys in a trash bin on the sidewalk, jogged to her car, got in and opened Tex's wallet. And found two hundred dollars in cash. Maybe he'd just gotten paid. When he spotted her in the Circle K, he'd seen the girl he used to intimidate in high school and got excited, thinking she might give him a tumble. What a joke. No, not a joke, a disaster. He'd followed her outside. Forced her to talk to him. Prevented her from leaving. Which left her no choice but to kill him.

Tex had always been a shit, but did he really deserve to die?

She blinked back tears.

Her years of living dangerously were catching up to her.

Last night after she shot Peterson, she'd felt triumphant. She enjoyed the risky parts: the hunt, the deception, the challenge of reeling him in. Most of all, she enjoyed the anger.

Anger made her feel powerful. The gun made her dangerous.

She was no victim, she was an avenger.

But fifteen minutes ago she had killed an innocent man in cold blood.

Killing Tex was an unforeseen complication, unforeseen and dangerous.

Arnold Peterson and Tex Conroy shot with the same gun. Sooner or later the cops would figure that out. She had to ditch the gun someplace where it would never be found.

She pocketed the two hundred dollars, polished the wallet with another baby wipe and cranked the rental car. She didn't know how long it would take for someone to find Tex's body and call the police, but with no ID on him, it would take a while to figure out who he was. By then she'd be gone.

As she pulled away from the curb, raindrops splattered the windshield. Her mouth still tasted sour, but the monumental iceberg inside her was gone. She pulled over beside a trash bin on the sidewalk, dropped Tex's wallet into it and kept driving. Two blocks later she stopped at a traffic light.

The entrance to the interstate was one block away. She glanced at her wristwatch. 4:35. Rush hour. Traffic would be heavy on the I-10.

The nail that sticks up is hammered down. Her favorite Asian proverb.

Her maroon Toyota Corolla would be one car of many, just another drone headed home to Slidell after work. She'd love to stop on the twin-span that arched over the eastern edge of Lake Pontchartrain and toss the gun, but that would be impossible during rush hour.

She would have to stop in Slidell and dump the gun. Then she'd get back on the I-10, head east and dump June Carter, too.

June had served her purpose. Time to be someone else.

Hey, Natalie, great to see you. Tex's voice, jolting her. Haunting her.

She closed her eyes, willing the voice to stop.

When I saw that bird hanging around your neck I knew it was you.

A horn blared behind her. She opened her eyes. The light was green.

She stomped the gas, gritted her teeth and thought about her mother, visualizing the disgusting crime scene photographs.

Mom in a sleazy hotel room. Beaten and strangled by a monster.

CHAPTER 6

"How'd your meeting with Morgan go?" Kelly set containers of Chinese takeout on her kitchen counter and drank from a bottle of Bud Light.

"It was ugly." Frank relaxed into his chair and guzzled some Heineken. Nothing like a cold one after a long day. No, two long days. Twenty-two hours ago he'd been eyeballing Peterson's corpse. But his headache was gone, and for the next few hours he could enjoy the company of his smart, sexy lover.

Slim and trim in shorts and a scoop-neck jersey, she brought the takeout to the table. "How bad was it? Any F-bombs?" After Katrina, she'd worked Homicide for a while, got to know Vobitch's explosive style first hand.

"A meeting with Vobitch without F-bombs? Be serious." He rose from his chair and put his arms around her. "How hungry are you?"

"Hungry enough to eat dinner before we get into mischief."

Mischief. Sounded good to him. He was tired, but not that tired. He gave her his Robert Mitchum bedroom-eyes. "Eat your dinner. You'll need the energy later."

She gave it back to him, a femme-fatal stare. She had the sexiest sea-green eyes he'd ever seen and a gorgeous bod to go with them. Not to mention a bawdy sense of humor. She took the chair opposite his, dumped sweet-and-sour sauce over her egg roll and set the plastic container on the table. "Who's the woman on the security video?"

"Hell if I know," he said, eyeing the half-empty sweet-and-sour container.

She grinned. "Oops. You need more? I might have some in the fridge."

"Nah, I'm in the mood for hot." He dumped the remaining sweet-and-sour on his plate, added mustard sauce and stirred it with an egg roll.

"Eeeew. How can you eat that?"

"Like this." He took a big bite, chewed and swallowed. "How was your day?" Kelly worked Domestic Violence now and that could be brutal.

"Good, actually. Remember the woman I told you about that got her nose broken by her so-called boyfriend?"

"Yeah. We should put these guys on a desert island without any water."

"Nah. That's too good for them."

"She got kids?"

"A five-year-old boy, which makes it worse. He sees what his father's doing to his mother. That's what I told her. I think it convinced her to leave the asshole. I got them a temporary placement at the New Orleans Women's Shelter. She'll do okay." Kelly brushed tendrils of dark hair away from her face. "Come on, Frank, tell me about the mystery woman on the video."

"Not much to tell. She was smart enough to conceal her face with a floppy hat and sunglasses, so we can't even put out a picture. I think I'd recognize her if I saw her though. She's got a very distinctive walk."

"Yeah? Sexy?" Kelly arched an eyebrow. "Nice bod?"

He pretended to consider the question. Kelly worked out at a gym three times a week, ate whatever she wanted and never gained an ounce: five-seven, long legs and a great ass. Her upper endowments weren't bad either.

"Well, not as nice as yours."

"Very good, Detective Renzi. That is the correct answer. Did you get the autopsy report?"

"Oh, yeah. Big rush on this one. One .38 caliber slug to the head, ligature marks on the wrists and ankles. Whoever shot him tied him up first."

"Maybe he was into S & M. Maybe the woman's a dominatrix."

"No way. The purse she was carrying wasn't big enough to hold whips and chains."

"You think she killed Peterson?"

He gnawed on a boneless sparerib. "That's what Miller and Vobitch think. I'm not convinced." He dug into his Kung Bao Chicken.

After a while Kelly set her plate aside and gave him a speculative look. "One shot to the head. You think it was a hit?"

"If it was, we got plenty of suspects. His wife knew he was screwing around, and Peterson's flunky told me he had gambling debts. How's that for possibilities? One shot to the head makes it look like a hit. But maybe somebody wants to con us into thinking that. There's a fire escape outside the window. Somebody else could have got in and shot him, got out the same way." He finished his chicken and leaned back in his chair.

"Maybe the woman was his mistress. Maybe she asked him to leave his wife and marry her, he said he wouldn't, and bam, one shot to the head. Never underestimate a woman scorned."

"True." He'd experienced that first hand, had an ugly divorce to prove it. "But I don't think so. She was too calm and collected when she left the room."

"So who is she? A high-class call girl? Plenty of those around."

"Yeah. The Canal Street brothel was the tip of the iceberg."

He carried their plates to the sink and ran hot water over them. After two years, he felt comfortable in the house Kelly had once shared with her husband. Terry O'Neil had been a cop, too. Five years ago, driving home one rainy night, he stopped to help a disabled motorist in the breakdown lane on the I-10 and got hit by an eighteen-wheeler. Terry died instantly. The motorist and the truck driver survived. End of story. Except for the widow.

Kelly wrapped her arms around his waist and said in the sexy voice he loved, "You don't have to clean up, Frank. I'll do it later."

He pulled her close, savoring the feel of her body. "Have I told you lately that I think about making love to you at least three times a day?"

She moaned low in her throat and kissed him hard and deep.

His cell phone rang. Damn! He didn't dare turn it off. A break in the Peterson case could come at any time. "Sorry. I need to take this."

"Yo, Frank," said Kenyon Miller. "Hate to bother you on a Friday night, but I think we just caught a break. One of the District-Three uniforms called me a half hour ago, said they found an unidentified body in City Park. White male, mid-thirties, one shot to the head."

"One to the head," he repeated for Kelly's benefit, saw her eyes widen.

"I'm at the scene now. Looks to me like it might be the same caliber slug as the Peterson hit."

"I'll be there in ten minutes." He shut his cell, dreading Kelly's reaction. Every time they were set to hop in the sack, he'd get a call and have to leave.

"It's okay, Frank. I know you're under the gun. This might be a lead."

Relieved, he embraced her and did his Arnold Schwarzenegger imitation. "I'll be baaaack."

"Oooh. The Terminator. I can't wait." In a seductive drawl, she said, "In that case, I guess I'd better slip into something more comfortable."

He grinned. "How about bare skin? That'd be good."

———

Slidell, Louisiana

Getting to Slidell, normally a forty-minute drive, took her an hour and a half, the rush hour traffic slowed by wind-driven rain. The panic she'd felt when the NOPD cruiser drove past Tex's Cadillac was gone, but her mouth still tasted sour. Shooting Tex with the gun she'd used to kill Peterson was a huge problem. She had to ditch the gun where no one would find it.

She stopped at a convenience store and bought some granola bars and a liter of bottled water. Alternately munching a granola bar and swigging water, she got on a secondary road and drove toward Lake Pontchartrain. On a map the lake looked like a big bite taken out of the Louisiana boot. A twenty-three-mile causeway bisected the lake, ferrying north shore commuters to New Orleans. Slidell was on the eastern end of the lake near the Mississippi border.

A sign directed her to the lakefront. She took the turn, felt relieved when no cars followed her. A steady rain drummed the car roof. Scrub pines lined the dark narrow road. No street lights. Her headlights pierced the foggy gloom, wipers sweeping the rainwater off the windshield.

Two minutes later she drove into a gravel landing overlooking the lake. She killed the headlights and windshield wipers. Two wooden docks jutted out into the lake, barely visible in the fading light. The landing appeared deserted, not a soul in sight, no vehicles, no lights. Creepy. Silent and still.

She rolled down her window and raindrops spattered her arm. A sudden *caw* startled her. A blackbird swooped up to a nearby tree and perched on a gnarled limb, scolding her. The *caw-caw-caw* pierced her like a primal scream. Was it a sign? A warning? Birds had always been her lucky charms.

But not today. Tex had recognized her firebird talisman. She closed her eyes. Pictured his bloody face and his crumpled body. Opened her eyes. Slowly counted to three hundred to make sure no one came along to observe her.

Satisfied that she was alone, she pulled the hood of her windbreaker over her head and left the car. Windblown rain pelted her face as she strode to the lake. A ghostly mist hovered over the water, and the air smelled briny. Like a scene from a horror movie, thick banks of impenetrable fog rolled toward her. The closest dock was ten yards away. A small dingy was tied to a stanchion with thick coils of rope. The other dock had no boat, but it was thirty yards farther away. Unwilling to stray too far from the car, she chose the dock with the boat. She wanted to dump the gun and get out of here as fast as possible.

She walked to the end of the dock where it jutted out over the water. Twenty yards from shore it was eerily quiet. The mist over the lake was like a live thing, rolling waves that dampened her face. Spooked by the gloom and the sinister fog, she dug the .38 Special out of her pocket, dropped it in the water and felt a huge sense of relief. She couldn't imagine anyone finding it.

She turned to retrace her steps and her heart almost stopped.

Twenty yards away someone in a yellow rain slicker stood at the other end of the dock.

She was surrounded by water. The only way back to the car was along the dock. To quell the panic-stricken thump of her heart she took deep breaths: in through the nose, out through the mouth. Mustering her courage, she strode toward the shore. And the yellow rain slicker.

As she drew closer she realized it was an older man, not tall, maybe two inches taller than she was, but husky enough to bulk out the yellow slicker. Visible inside the hood was a pale doughy face. Inside the dough, the man's beady hamster-like eyes were fixed upon her face, glaring at her.

"This is private property." A deep voice-of-doom.

"I'm sorry. My friend's house is near here and I can't find it."

"I been watching you," he said, eyes fixed on hers. "You been here ten minutes. That's plenty of time to figure out your friend doesn't live here."

Her heart jolted. Watching her. Had he seen her drop the gun in the lake?

"I thought I might be able to see her house from the end of the dock."

"What's your friend's name?"

39

"Valerie Duncan," she said, conjuring a name from her past, Val, her dancer-girlfriend in New York. She edged toward her car. "Sorry I disturbed you. I'll call her and get directions."

Keeping his body between her and the car, Beady-Eyes put his hand in the pocket of his yellow slicker.

Sweat dampened her palms. Did he have a gun? Then a more ominous thought. Maybe he was a cop.

"I got no use for people who think they can just waltz onto my property, missy. Had one-a-my boats stolen last year."

"That's terrible. But I'm not interested in your boat."

He licked his bottom lip and his eyes roved over her body, assessing her. She knew that look. If she didn't do something fast, he would jump her.

"I'm leaving now," she said firmly, and set out for her car with long determined strides.

Behind her, footsteps crunched the gravel. She didn't dare turn and look. She reached the car and yanked open the door. Climbed behind the wheel and locked the door. Looked out the window.

A looming presence in his yellow slicker, Beady-Eyes stood by the car, his face clenched in a scowl.

She started the car and slammed it into reverse, heard the wheels churn the gravel, throwing bits of dirt against the undercarriage. She did a U-turn and drove off, rocketing along the dark narrow road, gripping the wheel with her sweaty hands. A heart-pounding minute later she reached the main street.

The headlights of other cars reassured her, but she was exhausted. Atlanta was 400 miles away and she didn't dare stop at a motel. June Carson had to disappear without a trace. She got on the I-10 headed east and assessed the damages. If Beady-Eyes had seen her drop the gun in the lake, he'd have said so. He was just another powerful man who enjoyed hassling women. If he'd made a move on her, she'd have knocked him on his ass.

Now that she'd dumped the gun she could focus on her next task. Get to Atlanta and get on a plane. To keep herself awake, she put on Joan Jett's *Runaways* album, singing along as she barreled down the highway. She knew the lyrics by heart.

Two hours later she stopped to buy gas and use the restroom. Back on the road, she put on a Bon Jovi album, singing along at the top of her lungs.

She loved the titles: "Runaway" and "I'll Sleep When I'm Dead."

And best of all: "Work for the Working Man."

The lyrics were perfect: *I ain't living, just to die.*

That's for sure.

Natalie

October 1988

My mother was a prostitute.

The policewoman didn't say so that day, the worst day of my life. She said Mom worked for an escort service. But I knew what that meant. Six nights a week I sat at home after Mom went to work. My favorite TV shows were *Dallas* and *48 Hours*. One time I saw a prostitute in a miniskirt and a skimpy top and white knee-high boots. She had a hard-painted face and chewed gum. Mom never let me chew gum. She said it made me look cheap.

Mom didn't wear mini-skirts or skimpy tops and she didn't own any knee-high boots. How could she be a prostitute? I told the policewoman Mom was a hostess at Commander's Palace, a fancy restaurant.

She put her arm around me and said, "Honey, your mom didn't work at Commander's Palace." Her face had a pained look and her eyes were sad. "We found her in a hotel room."

Mom. Found dead in a hotel room. The policewoman didn't say how she died and I was afraid to ask. A big dark cloud twirled me up into a corner of the ceiling with the cobwebs. My heart was beating hard and fast. I couldn't breathe. But I didn't cry.

"Did your mom have any boyfriends?"

And I thought: That's what prostitutes do, right? Have boyfriends. It hurt me to think about it. The part of me that wasn't up near the ceiling said, "No. She didn't have a boyfriend."

The cop gave me a fake smile. "Who takes care of you while your mom is working?"

"Nobody. I take care of myself."

That made her frown. "What about your relatives?"

At first I thought it was a test. Talking about my relatives was complicated. I didn't know where my father and his parents were, and Mom doesn't get along with *her* parents so I don't know where they were, either.

"Mom's got a brother in Texas."

41

That seemed to make the policewoman happy. "What's his name?"

"Brixton, same as me." After the divorce, Mom got her maiden name back and changed my name too. She didn't want people thinking we were foreigners. My father's name is Thu Phan. Thu means Autumn in Vietnamese. He was born in October. His father, Bao Phan, was born in Vietnam but his family moved to France back in the 1950s. Mom said Bao Phan met my grandmother, a Frenchwoman, in Paris. I don't know what her name was. But I didn't say this to the policewoman. She had too much on her mind already, frowning and clenching her jaw like she was angry about something.

"What's your uncle's first name?"

"Jerome. He lives in Pecos. We got a Christmas card from him last year." Thinking about Christmas almost made me cry, but I didn't.

Christmas wasn't going to be very merry this year without Mom.

———

Living with the Brixtons in Pecos was okay at first. As far back as I could remember it was just Mom and me. After never having a family, it was nice to live with one. Uncle Jerome said to call him Uncle Jerry. He's five years older than Mom. "I was her big brother," he said. He smelled of pipe tobacco and had thick muscular arms, probably because he drove a UPS truck and had to lug heavy packages into people's houses.

Aunt Faye didn't talk to me much. I got the feeling she wasn't happy having another kid around. She already had two of her own. Faye's got bottle-blond hair that she poofs out with metal tines. She's almost as skinny as the tines. She never ate much, but she always said a prayer before dinner. That seemed weird. Mom wasn't religious, but most everyone in Pecos was. All the kids went to Bible school in the summer.

My cousin Randy's twelve. He's got dark reddish hair and a temper to match. Ellen's eight. She's a bookworm, always reading, hardly ever speaking. At least not to me. Ellen and Randy had rooms on the second floor. Mine was on the third floor in the attic. It only had one window so it was hot and stuffy, but at least I could cry in private.

One night Jerry sat me down on the sofa and told me a story about Mom. I think he did it to cheer me up. But thinking about Mom made my stomach hurt. I missed her a lot. Never again would we buy ice cream cones and walk along the Mississippi River talking about books and movies and clothes.

Mom was dead. Murdered. In a hotel room.

"Your mom was a terrific dancer," Jerry said, and told me a story about how she went to New York after high school. Mom's dream was to dance with the Rockettes at Radio City Music Hall, but then she met my father and got pregnant. Jerry smiled when he said this, like it was supposed to make me happy. I don't think it made my father happy. Otherwise, he wouldn't have left when I was two.

After he finished the story, Jerry said I would always be welcome in his home. Then he went in the kitchen and got a beer, like he was relieved about something. I was glad he didn't say anything about Mom being a prostitute. Maybe he didn't know. But I think the lady cop probably told him.

———

At school all the Mexican kids hang out together, chattering in Spanish, which I don't understand. I can speak French, though. Mom taught me. She learned it from my father, who spoke French fluently. Mom and I used to speak French when we went for walks in the French Quarter.

Another fun thing we'd never do again.

All the girls in my class listen to country music. I'm into rock. At night in my room I listen to a radio station that plays Guns N Roses and Elton John. The boys are into playing football and ignoring girls. But my fifth grade teacher likes me. I always do my homework. In New Orleans, I got A's in English, French and social studies, B's in math and science. In Pecos, the work seems easier. I get A's in everything.

Sometimes Randy called me names like *slant eyes* and *gook*. Not when Faye or Jerry were around. One time I told him to shut up, and he grabbed my hand and bent back my wrist. It hurt a lot, but I didn't cry so he finally let go.

After supper Randy and Ellen and I watch TV in the living room. Randy picks the shows. He loves *America's Most Wanted*. I think he'll grow up to be a criminal someday. He's already sneaky and mean. Sometimes I wondered what it must be like to commit a horrible crime and have to hide for the rest of your life. I love John Walsh. He's handsome. Sometimes I fantasized that he was my father. Except I knew he wasn't. He's not half Vietnamese.

I think Faye's an alcoholic. One time I saw her stuff a Smirnoff bottle in a garbage bag and throw it in the trash before Jerry got home from work. Faye doesn't have a job. She watches soaps on TV every day, chugging OJ and vodka. When we get home from school, she yells us at to go outside. Like she's angry. I'm angry too. Mom's gone, and living with Uncle Jerry and Aunt Faye in Pecos is way worse than staying home alone at night in New Orleans.

Now Christmas is coming. Another Christmas without Mom.

———

After Easter, Faye and Jerry started arguing in the kitchen after dinner. Jerry said, "I'm sick of eating hot dogs and hamburger." Faye said, "Get over it. I don't have the money to buy steak."

And I thought: *If you didn't buy so much vodka, you would.*

One night she screamed at Jerry and accused him of having an affair. It was sort of like *Dallas*, except I couldn't turn it off. I didn't know if Jerry was having an affair or not but it wouldn't have surprised me. Faye never read newspapers or books. What did they talk about?

43

I thought about telling Jerry about Faye's vodka problem but I decided that would be a mistake. In October 1990, Jerry told me the New Orleans policewoman had called. By then Mom had been gone two years. I got excited, thinking she'd found Mom's killer. No such luck. Jerry said she'd called to say she was still working the case. I wanted to ask her why she couldn't find the killer, but when I asked Jerry if I could, he said No.

I should have asked him for her phone number and called her myself. Maybe I will someday. Except I can't remember her name.

Then the most wonderful thing happened. One morning after breakfast I went outside and found a kitten outside the back door, mewing like he was hungry and scared. He was all black except for two white paws and the white muff under his chin. When I picked him up he started purring.

I named him Muffy and I loved him with all my heart.

Muffy was an orphan, like me.

When I asked Faye if I could keep him, she said, "No. Cats are smelly."

But I squeezed out some tears and told her I'd keep the litter box in my room and clean it every day. So Faye let me keep him. I loved the way Muffy lapped up milk with his little pink tongue. The best part was the way he purred when I held him and petted his fluffy black fur.

Whenever Randy tried to pick him up, Muffy hissed and scratched him. I was glad. Randy's mean. He's fourteen now, almost as big as Jerry. He plays on the high school football team. I think Faye's afraid of him.

In September I started eighth grade. The boys are still into football, but now they make smart-ass remarks to the girls in the cafeteria. Not to me. I'm twelve, but I haven't filled out like most of the girls. My bra size is 32 AA.

One day I went to the school library to research my father's heritage. I thought it might help me figure out who I was and who I was supposed to be.

I found a great article about Vietnamese culture in an encyclopedia. Reading it made me feel good, like I finally belonged to something. The parts I liked best were Veneration of Ancestors, Devotion to Study, and the belief that certain animals and parts of nature protect people.

I chose birds and mountains to protect me.

But one part scared me. The Vietnamese believe that people who die a violent death become angry spirits who bring misfortune to family members if they don't avenge their death. That made me think of Mom. Murdered in a hotel room. Was Mom waiting for me to avenge her?

If I didn't, would her angry spirits bring me misfortune?

Sometimes I thought about this late at night in my room.

I still didn't have any friends but I wasn't alone. I had Muffy. He'd snuggle against me and purr while I did my homework or listened to music on the radio. But one day when I went up to my room after school, Muffy didn't chirp and come running to me like always. He was lying on my bed. His body was limp and his eyes were open and I knew he was dead.

A terrible pain burned my stomach. First Mom, now Muffy.

Then Randy barged in my room. "How's your precious kitten, slant-eyes? Fuckin cat scratched me once too often so I wrung its neck."

I wanted to kill him. For a long time after Mom died I felt like something had eaten away my insides and left a big gaping hole. When I felt lonely and sad, I could go up to my room and cuddle Muffy.

But now my adorable kitten with the little pink tongue was gone too.

Somewhere deep inside me an iceberg formed, cold and hard. I didn't know if I would ever be able to love anyone again. But I knew one thing. Someday I would make Randy pay for what he'd done to Muffy.

"Get out of my room," I said. "I hate you."

"Shut up you little gook pussy."

That night at dinner I couldn't eat. When Jerry asked if something was wrong, I shook my head. Faye just sipped her OJ cocktail. Ellen said nothing. Randy bragged about the great play he'd made at football practice.

The next day at sunrise I buried Muffy behind the garage.

———

We still watched TV every night after supper. Now Randy was into *Star Trek* reruns. One night we watched an episode from 1968 called *Elaan of Troyius*. France Nuyen played Elaan. She was so beautiful I thought my heart would stop. The next day in the library I read her biography and found out France Nuyen was half Vietnamese and half French, like me. It didn't make up for losing Muffy, but it made me proud to know that someone like me could be an important actress on a hit TV show.

I made sure not to let Randy know how much I loved her. He couldn't kill France Nuyen like he'd killed Muffy, but he could stop watching *Star Trek*.

That turned out to be the least of my problems.

Right before Christmas I woke up one night and Randy was sitting on my bed, smelling the way boys do when they're hot and sweaty.

"We're kissing cousins," he said, "so kiss me."

The cold hard iceberg formed in my stomach. "Get out of my room, Randy. Get out or I'll scream and wake up Uncle Jerry and he'll smack you."

He grabbed my arm and tried to pull me closer and I bit him.

He jerked away and rubbed his arm. "You bit me, you slant-eyed gook."

He left, but that didn't mean he wouldn't be back, and my door had no lock. That Sunday after church I asked Jerry to put a lock on my bedroom door. I was afraid to tell him Randy had killed Muffy and tried to kiss me. Later that day Jerry bought a lock at the hardware store and put it on my door.

That made me feel safer.

But it didn't stop me from wanting to kill Randy.

CHAPTER 7

Saturday, 26 July

Frank peered through the windshield at the traffic inching down Chartres Street. A mule-drawn tour buggy was four cars ahead of them, the mule clip-clopping along slow as a turtle, the tourists ogling the French Quarter sights. Even with the A/C cranked full blast Miller's car felt like an oven thanks to the brutal noonday sun beating down on them.

"We'd have made better time walking," he said.

"What," Miller said, "you in a hurry to talk to the mobster?"

"Kenyon, if the Conroy hit is connected to the Peterson case, we're in trouble. A high-profile murder in the French Quarter? The politicians are already leaning on Vobitch to solve that case. Be hell to pay if they find out we got another one. His job is on the line."

"Morgan can handle it, he's been through this shit before," Miller said. "How's Kelly? Did I interrupt something last night when I called? Seemed like you were in a big rush to leave once you took a peek at Tex."

Miller was fishing. His partner was the only one that knew he was seeing Kelly. Or maybe the rest of the squad knew and pretended they didn't. He didn't care. He suppressed a smile, recalling Kelly's outfit when he'd returned to her house, a lacy pair of black panties and nothing else.

"Don't see her much since she left Homicide. How's she doing with that jewelry business she was fixin to set up?"

"Still making the jewelry. I don't know about selling it. She does it for fun, says it relaxes her after a hard day at work." The tension in his gut eased as the cars ahead of them moved forward.

"Reason I ask, Tanya just started a business."

"Good for her. I like multi-talented women. Good looking . . . sexy . . ."

Miller grinned. "Cut the jive. What it is, Jason's only twelve but he's already six feet tall, gotta buy him men's size clothes."

"Takes after his dad."

46

"Yeah. But he's got no interest in football, doesn't wanna be a cop either. He wants to be an astronaut. Tanya 'bout flipped when she heard that, knew enough to keep quiet. Next week, he'll be into something else."

"Sure," he said, deadpan. "Racecar driver."

Miller gave him The Look. "Yeah. Lotta black racecar drivers out there."

Traffic stalled again, waiting for the mule to make an aromatic deposit. Irritated, he focused on what to ask the owner of Tequila Sunrise. Conroy's employer. Until Conroy took a slug in the head.

"Tanya got this idea to make hip T-shirts for oversized teens, you know, slap a decal of the computer-game hero-du-jour on the front 'stead of having the shirt be plain, or--" Miller looked over, grinning now. "Some dorky saying might appeal to a senior citizen."

He burst out laughing. "Like, anybody over twenty-five?"

"Twenty be more like it."

"Sounds like a good idea. Just for boys? Or girls, too?"

The traffic jam broke and Miller put the car in gear. "Boys mostly. Tina's fourteen, almost as tall as Jason, but she's into being *an-oh-rex-ic* like her girlfriends, won't put a stick of gum in her mouth, it's got sugar in it. Jason, he eats everything in sight."

"So how's it going?"

"Not bad. Some of my LSU football bros got kids with the same problem. Tanya found a store on the Internet sells a dozen T-shirts for twenty bucks. Kids tell her which hero they want, she buys the decals and irons 'em on the front. But she needs a hip name for the business. Got any ideas?"

He had no idea about hip business names, plenty of ideas about what would happen if they found out the Conroy hit was related to Peterson's.

"How about Hip Duds for Teens, something like that?"

"I dunno, Frank. Duds sounds like spuds. These kids don't need any reminders about food, get enough of that watching food commercials on TV."

Miller didn't need any either. He was in good shape for a guy six-six and two-forty. But when they worked out at the gym, Miller constantly complained about his weight. As a middle-linebacker for the LSU Tigers, he'd eaten whatever he wanted. Now that he'd hit forty it was different.

Miller wheeled onto Decatur Street, parked the unmarked car in a loading zone, plopped an NOPD official-business sign on the dashboard and said, "Let's go see the mini-mobster."

They hustled into the Tequila Sunrise. After the sizzling heat outside, the lounge felt like a freezer. The long narrow room stank of beer, and neon beer signs on the walls provided the only illumination. At the bar, six men were sucking up bottles of Corona, eyes glued to a baseball game on the TV above the bar. Someone got a hit and they let out a cheer.

Frank flashed his ID at the bartender and said they needed to talk to the owner. The barman gestured to a hall at the far end of the bar.

"Nicky's in his office. He's expecting you."

It hadn't taken long to ID the body in City Park. This morning a clerk opening a convenience store saw a car parked in the lot. A posted sign said No Overnight Parking so the kid called the manager to see if he wanted it towed. But when he described the car--a powder-blue Cadillac--the manager said, "No, that's Tex's car," called Tequila Sunrise and found out Tex never showed up for work last night. Having seen a bulletin on the late news about an unidentified man found dead in City Park, the manager called NOPD. An hour later they had a name: Lawrence Conroy.

They walked past the bar and entered a dark hallway. A door at the end of the hall was open. Inside the office a paunchy man in a green-and-white striped shirt sat behind a messy metal desk. His pink scalp showed beneath wispy-gray strands of a comb-over. He glowered at them, owl-eyed.

Frank didn't take it personally. Pissed-off was probably Nicky's usual demeanor. He'd dealt with plenty of Italian lowlifes in Boston. Not that Italians had a corner on the scumbag market. He did the introductions, then said, "What can you tell us about Lawrence Conroy?"

"I can tell you he didn't show up for his shift last night."

"How long did he work here?"

"A year, maybe. I'd have to look it up. We get a lotta turnover."

"Was he a good worker?" Miller asked.

"He wasn't stealing from the till, if that's what you mean."

"Did he have a girlfriend?" Frank asked.

"I got no idea. You'd have to ask the other bartenders."

"We'll need names."

Nicky opened a drawer and held out a sheet of paper. "Here's a list of my current employees."

Miller took the list and began copying names into a small spiral notepad.

"Did Conroy have any enemies?" Frank asked.

With a dead-eyed look, he said, "Hey, everybody's got enemies. The kid was a bartender, not a priest. I think he's from Texas, but I don't ask for life stories when guys come in looking for a job. You wanna see his application?"

"Yes." Nicky needed a dope-slap. And a better hair stylist. Frank scanned the application. "No next of kin listed."

"I guess that means I don't gotta send his last paycheck to anybody."

He glanced at Miller. "You set with the names, Kenyon?"

"Yes, but we need a way to contact them."

Nicky held out another sheet of paper. "Here's their phone numbers."

"You got a copy machine?" Miller asked.

Nicky made a show of looking around the office. "Gee, I don't see one, do you?"

Frank wanted to ram a fist down his throat. Nicky wasn't going to give them squat. At this point they didn't know if the slug that killed Conroy came from the same gun that killed Peterson, but he'd been in law enforcement long enough to know that whatever could go wrong usually did. Vobitch had put a rush on the ballistics tests, no telling when they'd get the results.

"In that case," he said, "I guess we'll have to take this one with us."

"Hey," Nicky said, outrage written large on his jowly face. "I need it. One of 'em doesn't show—"

"We'll return it after we make a copy. Thanks for your time, Mr. Abate."

As they returned to the bar, Miller muttered, "Asshole."

They took seats at the bar and Miller waved the bartender over. "What can you tell us about Lawrence Conroy?"

The bartender, a twenty-something guy with a droopy ginger moustache and a gold ring in one nostril, frowned. "You mean Tex?"

"Is that what you call him?" Frank said.

"Yup. He's a good ol' boy from Texas, wears a cowboy hat all the time, even when he's working."

Frank glanced at Miller, got back a tiny nod. After hearing about the body in City Park, the uniform who'd been on patrol that day reported seeing someone in a cowboy hat in a powder-blue Cadillac parked near where Tex Conroy's body was found. According to the patrol officer only one person was in the car, but other than the cowboy hat he couldn't give a description.

"Were you and Tex friends?" Miller asked.

"Not really." Looking anxious, he said, "Is he okay?"

"Someone found him in City Park last night," Frank said. "Shot dead."

The barman didn't seem too upset, didn't seem surprised, either. Maybe he'd seen the late news last night and put two and two together.

"Did Tex have a girlfriend?" Miller asked.

"Yeah. She came in a few times. Quiet little gal. I don't know her name."

"How about the other bartenders?" Frank asked. "Did anyone know him well?"

The guy sucked the end of his mustache into his mouth and screwed up his face. At last he said, "Ask Benita. She knew him better than anyone."

Miller checked his notepad. "Benita Gonzales. And your name is?"

"Arthur Miller." The bartender grinned. "Not the guy that wrote plays. If I was a bigshot writer like Arthur Miller I wouldn't be working in this dump. And don't be thinking Tex's girlfriend shot him. That little gal's too mousy, wouldn't kill a cockroach if it was crawling up her arm."

Nice image. They left and got in the car quick to escape the brutal heat.

"Wouldn't kill a cockroach," Miller said. "Hell, it's the quiet ones you gotta watch out for."

Frank chuckled. "Like Tanya?"

Miller looked at him, deadpan. "The day Tanya's quiet is the day I'll really start to worry. Let's go see Benita."

———

Her plane landed at Logan Airport at 9:53. During the two-and-a-half-hour flight she'd dozed fitfully, jolted awake by ghastly faces with dead eyes. Bone-weary, she edged into the crowded aisle. Last night at the Atlanta airport she'd bought the last copy of Friday's *Times-Picayune*. The Peterson murder was all over the front page, including his photograph, taken at a business dinner, Arnold smiling broadly as if he'd just closed a lucrative business deal.

No more business for Arnold now.

No more smiles, either.

The cops weren't saying much, but that didn't reassure her. Either they had no idea what happened or they did and they weren't saying. Nothing in the paper about an unidentified man found dead in City Park. Early this morning she had pinned a chestnut-brown fall to her hair and used her Robin Adair ID to board the plane.

Chinese proverb: *All warfare is based on deception.*

The shrill cries of a cranky baby cut into her thoughts, and the crush of passengers in the aisle began to move. Towing her suitcase, she hustled up the gateway and raced through the terminal to the Logan Express bus stop.

Several people sat inside the glassed-in cubicle.

Five minutes later she boarded a bus to Nashua, New Hampshire.

———

They talked to Benita Gonzales at a coffee shop near her apartment. When they told her Tex was dead, she seemed much more upset than the bartender. She didn't cry but her eyes welled up. An attractive woman in her twenties, she had thick brown hair, brown eyes and a gold ring in one nostril.

Was body piercing a requirement for bartending, Frank wondered.

"Do you know if Tex had any enemies?" he asked.

Benita sipped her foamed latte, considering. At last she said, "Not that I know of. But he didn't treat his girlfriend very nice, I can tell you that."

"Anything you can tell us might help us find the killer," Miller said.

Her eyes widened. "Whoa! I didn't mean that I thought she killed him!"

"Of course not." Miller gave her a reassuring smile. "What's her name?"

"Maryanne. I don't know her last name. She only came in a few times when Tex was working. I don't think he wanted her there. He used to flirt with the customers." Benita wrinkled her nose and her nose-ring waggled. "If he'd been my boyfriend, I'd have called him on it, but Maryanne seemed timid. One time she had a bruise near her eye and when I asked how she got it, she said she ran into a door. The usual bullshit."

Benita rolled her eyes. "Sorry for the language."

Frank grinned. "I've heard worse. We need to talk to Maryanne. Was she living with Tex?"

"I'm not sure. He lived over near Esplanade. His landlord might know."

"Did Tex ever mention any enemies?" Miller said. "You know, people had a grudge against him?"

"Not to me. He was always talking about his friends in Pecos. He played football in high school and most of his friends were on the team. He never mentioned any enemies. He said his father was the chief of police."

They thanked her and paid Tex's landlord a visit. He knew nothing about a girlfriend and wouldn't let them into Tex's apartment without a warrant.

Stymied, they went back to the car.

"Tex seems like a peachy-keen guy," Miller said. "Got a bunch of hometown football buddies, no enemies, slaps his girlfriend around and then? Bada-bing, one shot to the head. The *back* of the head, not the front."

"Exactly. We get the warrant to get into Tex's apartment, maybe you can find the girlfriend's name."

Miller raised a quizzical eyebrow. "You taking a vacation or something?"

"Very funny. I'm going to Pecos, see if Tex crossed one of his buddies and they came here and bumped him off."

"Travel budget's tight these days. You think Vobitch will okay it?"

"He will if we find out the slug that killed Tex came from the gun that killed Peterson."

Natalie

1992 - 1994

For my fourteenth birthday in April, Faye made me a birthday cake. I don't know why. Maybe because she knew I'd started my periods. She seemed surprised when I asked to use one of her tampons. I wished I could talk to Mom. I felt so alone. Now Mom had been dead almost four years.

In September I started ninth grade at Pecos High School. Faye and Jerry were still arguing. Randy was sixteen and totally obnoxious, bragging about playing on the high school football team. Ellen was twelve and mousy as ever. I still didn't have any friends, but I liked my classes and the teachers were okay. One day in the library I heard two girls raving about Mr. Adams, the drama teacher. That reminded me of France Nuyen. She's a great actress and I wanted to be like her. The next day I signed up for Drama Club. I figured it would be neat, pretending to be someone else.

Mr. Adams was really cool, but the best part was meeting Gabriel Rojas. Gabe, to his friends. He's a year older than me. He never tries out for any of the parts. One afternoon I stayed late to help him paint the sets for the next play. I didn't want to go home and deal with Randy and Faye and her vodka problem. When I told Gabe my grandfather was born in Vietnam, he seemed impressed. He said his parents had come here from Mexico.

Maybe that's why we hit it off. We were both foreigners.

By then I was five-six and still growing. Faye complained about all the clothes she had to buy me. Gabe's shorter than me, only five-four. His skin is the color of a burnt-umber Crayola. His eyes are dark too, almost black. Mine are tan, the color of light brown sugar. We started hanging out after school. I loved talking to Gabe. He told me neat stuff I knew nothing about, like Pythagoras—Gabe's a math whiz—and computer games and Mexican artists like Frieda Kahlo and Diego Rivera. Gabe said his parents were talking about them one night at dinner.

I couldn't imagine it. Faye and Ellen never said a word at dinner. How could they when Jerry and Randy were going on about football?

Gabe said I reminded him of Joan Jett. "Not your looks, your attitude. Like, you take no shit from anyone."

I liked that. Gabe had no idea of the shit that went on in the Brixton household. I went to the library and found out Joan Jett was a rock star. She started her first band—an all-girl band—when she was fifteen in 1975 before I was born. How cool is that? I loved the name of her band. The Runaways. I often thought about being a Runaway, and it had nothing to do with a band.

Joan had a pretty face and dark shaggy bangs that flopped over her eyes. That night in my room I studied my face in the mirror. My nose is long and straight like Mom's and my lips are average, not fat, not thin. Only my eyes look Asian. They're almond shaped and narrow at the outside corners. I decided I liked them. They made me different. Unique.

Randy still called me slant-eyes, but right then and there I decided to be proud of my Vietnamese heritage. By now my Vietnamese beliefs, Ancestor Veneration and Devotion to Study, were second nature to me. And I liked having birds and mountains to protect me.

I got a job at Burger King, but I hated the greasy-beef-and-cooking-oil smell. Outside where we dumped the trash there were cockroaches. The fourth day, a huge cockroach ran over my foot so I quit and started babysitting for our neighbor, a single mom with two little kids. She worked nights at the local steak house. It didn't pay much but it got me out of the house.

One Saturday in October Faye took me and Ellen to a flea-market. Faye loves bargains. Jerry was at a football game watching Randy. I fell in love with a Japanese print of a bird flying over a snow-capped mountain. One corner had a smudge, so I got it for two dollars. Then I saw this gorgeous pendant: a metal bird with curved wings and a big tail. It was silver, inlaid with red enamel (my favorite color). The lady said it was a firebird, a good luck charm. She wanted ten dollars. I only had five, but she let me have it.

On Monday I wore it to school. Gabe loved it. He said it looked like something his ancestors might use to ward off evil spirits. Then he invited me to his house on Friday to watch a video. He seemed anxious, like I might say no. I think he's got a crush on me. I said yes right away so he'd know that I liked him. But I didn't want him to be my boyfriend. Girls were always breaking up with boyfriends. I wanted Gabe to be my Best Friend for Life.

Gabe rented *The Karate Kid,* the original one from 1984. His mom thanked me for the bottle of Sprite I brought, and Gabe and I sat in the living room to watch the movie. We had fun and the movie was great. Then Gabe walked me home. He told me his dream was to be a video game designer. I said that was cool and he was smart and I was certain he could do it.

"What's your dream?" he said, gazing at me with his almost-black eyes.

For some reason it reminded me of Jerry's story about Mom's dream to dance with the Rockettes. So I said, "I want to be a dancer."

I didn't dare tell him I wanted to kill Randy. Gabe lived in a normal house with normal parents and a normal brother and sister. He had no idea how horrible my family was. Faye was still drinking and Jerry was working long hours for UPS (or having an affair). Ellen's twelve and still mousy, and Randy is still Randy. Now my bra size is 34 D. Sometimes the boys yelled crude comments at me, but I ignored them. I was still an outsider, but I had Joan Jett and France Nuyen to imitate and thanks to my Devotion to Study I still got good grades. Best of all, I had a Best Friend for Life: Gabe.

Watching *The Karate Kid* gave me an idea. The bus I rode to school went past a strip mall with a sign that said Tae-Kwon-Do lessons. I wanted to be strong and flexible like the Karate Kid. After Jerry put the lock on my door, Randy stopped bothering me, but he was big and strong and he still scared me.

So I signed up for taekwondo lessons.

One day when I left the cafeteria after lunch Randy and his football player friends huddled together to block the entrance. My hands got sweaty. Randy and his buddies drove souped-up cars and I'd heard rumors that they had guns. Gun ownership was a big deal in Texas. Even Jerry had guns, a pistol and a rifle that he kept locked in a closet.

When they saw me, Tex Conroy—the police chief's son—yelled in his ugly nasal voice: "Hey Natalie, I hear your mother's a prostitute."

Heat flamed my cheeks. My insides were shaking like the time I got the flu and had a high fever. I rubbed my firebird, hoping it would protect me.

Then Randy said real loud, "Nah, Tex. Her mother *used* to be a prostitute. But one of her customers killed her. She musta been a lousy lay."

They all laughed. I wanted to kill every single one of them.

I kept walking but my thoughts were whirling like debris in a tornado. Mom. Dead in a hotel room. Murdered four years ago.

Waiting for me to avenge her.

Right then and there I made up my mind to do it.

But first I had to kill Randy.

———

1994 -- 1995

My junior year I got a part in the spring musical. We did *Oklahoma*. Joan Jett was my new idol, but I still loved France Nuyen, and now I was an actress, too. Mr. Adams said I was a great dancer and acting was easy. After living with Jerry and Faye six years, I was good at pretending to be who they wanted me to be, and Mr. Adams taught us techniques for faking emotions.

I was good at that, too. Three years since Randy killed Muffy and I never once let on that I wanted to kill him.

By now Randy and his buddies had graduated. Now Randy's a guard at the federal prison. He loves carrying a gun and bossing prisoners around. And having money to spend on girls and cars and beer. I think Tex's father helped him get the job. Chief Conroy has a lot of law enforcement connections.

54

A good thing because Tex got in trouble a lot. A month before graduation, his girlfriend committed suicide. I heard she was pregnant, but I don't know for sure. She took a bunch of pills. The newspaper said she left a note but didn't say what was in it. And after the graduation party, Tex drove his date home and crashed his souped-up Mustang into a tree. The girl died. Tex walked away without a scratch. People said he'd been drinking.

I thought for sure he'd go to jail, but he didn't. His father must have pulled strings or something.

Randy still lived at home, still said nasty things to me when Jerry wasn't around, and Faye was still drinking. Ellen was in ninth grade now, still a bookworm, still colorless and quiet as a mouse. Maybe even quieter.

Thanks to my taekwondo lessons I wasn't as scared of Randy as I used to be. *Tae* means to strike with a foot. *Kwon* means to strike with a fist. *Do* means *way*. My teacher's name is Carlson. That seemed odd because taekwondo is a Korean martial art, but Mr. Carlson's wicked strong and does incredible moves. He's a fifth-Dan (like a fifth-degree black belt) and he taught me a lot.

For instance, the leg is the strongest weapon a martial artist has, and kicks are the best way to disable your opponent so he can't retaliate.

Every eight weeks I passed tests to get to a higher level. Mr. Carlson said I was a fast learner. I advanced to first *geup*, the highest student rank, and got to wear a red belt with a black stripe. Then I studied breaking techniques. Breaking boards requires physical skill and intense mental focus. It was hard, but I mastered it. I wanted to learn the advanced techniques.

I figured I might need them. If I didn't avenge Mom, the Ancestor gods would bring me great misfortune.

Sometimes after the others left (maybe because I'm part Vietnamese) Mr. Carlson would give me a private lesson. First he taught me throwing skills, falls for self-defense and jumping techniques. Then he showed me pressure points. In Korean they're called *jiapsul*. I said I doubted that I'd ever have to use them.

A half-lie. One part of the taekwondo oath said: "I shall be a champion of justice and freedom." I liked that. Justice for Mom. Freedom for me.

Sometimes when I had trouble remembering what Mom looked like I got out my only picture of her. It was taken at her wedding in New York. My father wasn't in it. Mom threw all his pictures out. Mom looked happy and beautiful in her long white dress, but that was a long time ago. When did she start to be unhappy, I wondered. When she realized she'd never dance with the Rockettes? When my father left? But the picture gave me no answers.

Thanks to my Devotion to Study I got inducted into the National Honor Society. Not that I planned to go to college. I had no money and I knew Faye and Jerry couldn't give me any.

I already knew what I was going to do. I was just biding my time.

Gabe was following his video-game-designer dream. Odessa College gave him a scholarship to study computer science. I was happy for him, but Odessa is 75 miles away, so I only saw him on weekends. Gabe worked at a computer store. For my sixteenth birthday he gave me a used computer. I got an email account so we could email each other every night and talk like we always did.

Ellen just turned fourteen. Her eyes have that dead look like Faye's, and she bites her fingernails down to the quick. Sometimes they bled. I wanted to ask her what was wrong. She kept avoiding me, but one night I cornered her in her room. She was lying on her bed reading a book, some fantasy novel about vampires. Her thumb had a big scab where she'd bitten the cuticle.

"Ellen," I said, "what's wrong? Why are you biting your nails?"

She just looked at me with her dead eyes.

"Tell me," I said. "Faye won't help you. She's too buzzed on vodka."

For a minute Ellen didn't say anything, but then her face scrunched up and she started to cry. "Randy," she said between sobs.

My heart turned to stone. "What did Randy do to you?" But part of me knew already. Ellen didn't have a lock on her bedroom door.

"He makes me . . . do things."

"What does he make you do?"

"He makes me give him blow jobs," she whispered. "He's got a gun."

I felt sick, like I might throw up if I didn't drink some water.

The next night after dinner I got Jerry alone and asked him to teach me how to shoot. He seemed surprised. He'd taught Randy how to shoot, of course. Boys were supposed to know how to handle guns. Ellen wasn't interested in guns. She lived in a fantasy world with vampires.

Except when she was giving Randy blow jobs.

So Jerry took me to the gun range and showed me how to shoot his revolver. The first time I did okay. The next time I hit the target every time, not bull's-eyes but close. Jerry was impressed. Afterwards he took me out for ice cream. There were a lot of things I wanted to ask him: Are you having an affair? Do you know Faye's an alcoholic? Do you know your son makes his sister give him blow jobs? But I didn't.

We talked about what I'd do after high school. I told him a bunch of lies.

I didn't want Jerry or anyone else knowing my plans.

The next weekend I made a picnic lunch, and Gabe and I went to this beautiful spot on a bluff high above the Pecos River. Gabe and I are still Best Friends, but not lovers. I think he would have liked us to be, but after I told him I wanted us to be Best Friends for Life, he seemed to understand. Besides, he knows I'm not dating anyone else.

After we ate lunch I told him about Randy and Ellen.

Gabe was shocked and disgusted, like I knew he would be. His face got tight and he clenched his jaw and his dark eyes looked very angry. Then he asked if Randy ever bothered me.

I said no, and told him I had a lock on my bedroom door.

Then I asked Gabe to get me a gun.

CHAPTER 8

Monday, 28 July   Pecos, Texas

At eleven-thirty Frank parked in front of a modest blue ranch house and got out of his rental car. Hot air hit him like a blast furnace. By the time he rang the doorbell he was sweating. Clarisse Conroy opened the door, clutching a tissue in her hand. Her thin face was careworn, her skin wrinkled and brown, like she spent a lot of time in the sun.

"Detective Renzi?" she said, dabbing red-rimmed eyes.

He'd called her an hour ago from the airport in Odessa. She was eager to talk to him, grief-stricken about her boy. The Pecos police had done the notification on Saturday after NOPD called them.

"Yes, ma'am. I'm sorry to trouble you at a time like this."

"I still can't believe my boy is gone. Come in and sit down."

He stepped into the living room and stopped, appalled by the odor. The house reeked of cat piss. A flowered-print sofa faced a wide-screen television.

Three calico cats lay on the sofa. Clarisse shooed them off and gestured for him to sit down. Wondering how many cat hairs would cling to his pants, he perched on the edge of the sofa. Clarisse plucked a fresh tissue from a box on the end table and sank onto a well-worn wingchair beside the sofa.

"Do you know who killed my boy?" she said in a querulous voice.

"That's why I'm here, Mrs. Conroy. I'm hoping you can help us."

Her eyes welled with tears. "Why would anyone want to kill my Tex?"

Two black cats appeared in the kitchen doorway, stared at him and disappeared. How many cats did she have? Judging by the smell, a lot. He tried breathing through his mouth. It didn't help.

"Losing Eugene was bad enough." She pronounced it *You*-gene.

Going with it, he said, "When did you lose *You*-gene?"

"Five years ago. He had a heart attack. *You*-gene was the police chief and that could be very stressful. Tex was all tore up when he lost his daddy. Two months later he moved to New Orleans. I didn't want him to go, but . . ."

"He lived here with you then?"

"Yes. He fixed up a room in the basement, put paneling on the walls and whatnot. It's got a private entrance." Her gaze shifted and settled on a mewing calico cat that prowled the room.

"Did Tex have a girlfriend?"

"Oh, Tex had lots of girlfriends. All the girls loved Tex." But she didn't seem happy about it, clamping her thin lips together.

"Did he go to college after high school?"

"Tex had no interest in college, no interest in being a policeman like his daddy, either. After high school his best friend got a job at the federal prison, but Tex wasn't interested in that, either." She gave him a plaintive look. "Tex never found himself, you know what I mean?"

Frank said he did, and waited. Silence often elicited better results than questions.

"He thought about being a park ranger. For the National Park Service? But he failed the test. I told him to take it again." Clarisse smiled for the first time. "If at first you don't succeed, try try again. But he wouldn't. Tex was stubborn, like his daddy." Her blue eyes welled with tears.

"Did Tex ever mention a man named Arnold Peterson?"

"Not that I recall. When he came to Pecos, he stayed with one of his high school friends." Her lips tightened. "He didn't like my cats."

For the hell of it, he said, "How many cats do you have?"

"Lordy, I don't know. A couple dozen? I just feed 'em and take care of the little ones when they come. They keep me company now that I'm alone."

Dozens of cats. He fought back a shudder. "Did Tex have any enemies?"

"Of course not," she said indignantly. "Ev'body loved Tex. Why would he have enemies? My boy wouldn't hurt a flea."

Except for slapping his girlfriend around. "Did he like to gamble?"

"Not that I know of. He liked to have fun with his friends. And his girlfriends."

"I'll need names. Do you have his high school yearbook?"

"Of course! Tex was co-captain of the football team. Him and Randy. Lordy, that class was jinxed."

"Jinxed? In what way?"

Clarisse rose from her chair. "Let me get the yearbook."

She left the room and he heard her calling the cats by name. Dozens of them. It gave him the creeps. Cleaning the litter boxes, feeding them. Cat hairs all over the place. The overwhelming stench. No wonder Tex moved out.

She returned with the yearbook, sat beside him on the sofa and opened the book to the page with Tex's picture. An average-looking kid, confident smile, open face. The motto beneath the photo said: *Winning beats losing any day.*

"You said something about his class being jinxed?"

"Sure did seem like it. Right before graduation Tex's girlfriend committed suicide. And then the night of graduation . . ." She sighed. "Tex drove his date home from the party and the car went off the road and hit a tree. Lordy, it was awful. Tex was okay, but the girl died the next day."

The police chief's son hits a tree and his passenger dies? Worse than awful. "Did they charge him?"

"Soon as he heard, *You*-gene went over there and drove Tex home. The girl's parents said Tex got drunk at the party." Her lips tightened. "But my boy could hold his liquor." She lapsed into silence, staring into space.

"So they didn't charge him?"

"Well, yes, they did. Negligent driving, death resulting, I think it was. The judge put him on probation for a year. That made it hard for him to get a job."

"Sounds like he had a tough year."

"Yes. His best friend died. Randy and Tex were co-captains of the football team." She flipped some pages and tapped a picture. "That's Randy."

He studied the photo. Randolph Brixton, aka Randy. Unlike Tex, Randy's face had a hard look, no smile, dead-fish eyes. "What happened to Randy?"

"He was having a picnic with his family near the Pecos River. Somehow or another he slipped and fell over the bluff." Her lips pursed. "Randy's friends figured his cousin pushed him."

"His cousin?"

"His cousin Natalie. That girl was trouble, I can tell you that. She came to live with the Brixtons after her mother was murdered. In New Orleans."

Stunned, he said, "Murdered in New Orleans? When was this?"

"Years ago. Natalie was ten when it happened. Back in 'eighty-eight I think it was. That girl was strange. Tex told me her mother was a prostitute."

Surprises galore in Pecos. "Is her picture in the yearbook?"

"Maybe. She was in the drama club." Clarisse flipped to the Drama Club page. "That's her there." Tapping her finger on a group photograph.

Natalie stood beside a short Hispanic boy. Attractive girl, tall and slender with long legs. Nice smile. "Does she still live in Pecos?"

"No. After Randy's funeral she left town, hasn't been heard from since."

"I'd like to borrow the yearbook. The photographs might be helpful."

Clarisse looked at him, horrified. "You're going to take it?" she wailed.

"For a few days. I'll get it right back to you. Do Randy's folks still live in Pecos?"

"Well, his mother does. I'm not sure about the father. Faye lives over near the bus station now."

"Can I use your phone book? I'd like to call and see if I can talk to her."

Clarisse rose and went in the kitchen, cooing to her cats. A calico cat tore through the room pursued by a big black cat, their claws scratching the wood floor as they disappeared around the corner. Clarisse returned with a phone book. "Faye should be home. She watches soaps most of the afternoon . . ."

The only Brixton listed in the phone book was a Gerald Brixton. He wrote down the number and rose to his feet. "Thank you for your help, Mrs. Conroy."

Her eyes welled with tears. "You'll find whoever killed my boy, won't you? And punish him? The coroner's office called this morning and said they're ready to release the body. One of Tex's friends is going to drive to New Orleans and bring him home." She mopped her eyes with a tissue. "Thank you for coming, Detective Renzi. Will you be in Pecos at dinnertime?"

For an instant he had the horrible thought that she was going to invite him to dinner. With her dozens of cats.

"There's lots of Mexican places, but Longhorn Jack's is the best restaurant in town." Her lips tightened. "Natalie used to work there."

He thanked her again and went out to his rental car, wondering if the rumors about Natalie were true. After he talked to Faye Brixton, maybe he'd stop by Longhorn Jack's and see if someone there could tell him more about Natalie. The tall slender girl with the long legs and the nice smile.

————

Unlike Clarisse Conroy, Faye Brixton lived in seedy part of town. Clarisse looked careworn, but Faye looked worse, a gaunt haggard face, pale sallow skin. She let him into the living room and muted the television set. A soap opera was on. He had no clue which one. To him, they all seemed the same: beautiful people arguing and bed-hopping like crazy.

But he didn't smell any cats, for which he was deeply grateful.

"Thanks for taking time to speak with me, Mrs. Brixton."

He sat on an easy chair with faded brown upholstery. No cat hairs.

Faye sank into a well-worn depression in the couch next to an end table with a tall glass of what appeared to be orange juice. "You said something happened to Tex," she said, her voice flat and expressionless.

Her hair, dyed platinum blond, was styled in a sixties bouffant. Her face had a hard look, like her son Randy, and her pale-blue eyes seemed glazed. Maybe there was more than OJ in the glass.

"Unfortunately, yes. Someone shot him in New Orleans. He's dead."

Her mouth gaped open. "Someone shot Tex? Who'd want to kill Tex?"

"I understand your son was a friend of his."

Emotion worked her face, emotions he couldn't identify. Grief wasn't one of them.

"Yes. Him and Randy were co-captains of the football team."

"Mrs. Conroy said your son had an accident."

Faye Brixton took a long pull from the glass of OJ. "Randy fell off a bluff near the Pecos River. As I'm sure Clarisse told you."

He heard a slight slur in her speech. Definitely not just OJ in the glass.

"Can you tell me what happened?"

"I didn't see it happen," she said quickly. Too quickly.

"But you were there?"

"Ellen and I were at the picnic table."

"Ellen?"

"My daughter. Randy's sister." She took another swig of OJ. "Natalie wanted to take Randy's picture so they went around the bend to find a good spot. That's where it happened."

"Where *what* happened?"

Faye gazed at him, expressionless. "I don't know. I wasn't there."

"Mrs. Conroy said Randy fell off a cliff."

"Onto some rocks. Yes."

Her demeanor seemed odd. No grief, just matter of fact statements about the death of her son. "Was Natalie with him when he fell?"

"She told the police that Randy was drunk and he slipped and fell over the bluff. That's what she said."

"What do you say?"

A muscle worked in her jaw. "I say she's right. Randy brought a six-pack of beer to the picnic and drank the whole damn six-pack himself."

"Where's your daughter? Does she live here with you?"

"No."

"And Mr. Brixton?"

Her lips tightened in a grim line. "We're divorced. I had to sell our house and move into this dump. I don't have a clue where the rat-bastard is now."

"Does Ellen live in Pecos?"

"Yes."

"How old is she now?"

"Old enough to get herself a boyfriend and get pregnant. Ellen is a very unhappy person."

"Why is that?"

"I don't know. She's always been unhappy. Then she met this guy and they started dating and she got pregnant. The asshole split, of course." Faye grimaced. "Men."

It seemed like Faye was the unhappy one. Or maybe this was just one big unhappy family.

"Do you have Ellen's phone number? I'd like to speak with her."

"She lives two streets over." Faye checked her watch. "If you hurry you might catch her before she goes to work. She's a waitress at Longhorn Jack's."

Faye gave him the directions to Ellen's place. Before he got to the door, she hit the clicker and a cacophony of voices spewed from the TV set.

Soap time! Soap and OJ. And whatever else was in the glass.

CHAPTER 9

Faye Brixton's place was no prize, but Ellen Brixton's was worse, a run-down duplex with filthy white siding and sagging gutters. When Frank rang the doorbell, a young woman opened the door. Mousy brown hair framed her thin face. Her colorless gray eyes regarded him with suspicion.

"Hi, Ellen? I'm Frank Renzi, New Orleans police. I just spoke with your mother and I'd like to ask you a few questions. Can I come in?"

"What kind of questions?" Her wispy voice was barely audible.

"It's really hot out here. Mind if I come in?"

"Okay," she said, clearly annoyed, "but I have to go to work. If I'm late the manager gets pissed."

Toddler toys littered a threadbare oval rug in her tiny living room. Ellen had on a white blouse and a short black skirt, her work uniform he assumed. She didn't invite him to sit down.

"Your mother said your brother fell off a cliff several years ago. Can you tell me what happened?"

"Randy was drunk." Her voice had an edge to it. "My mother's a drunk, too. As I'm sure you noticed."

Unhappy, and definitely angry. "How'd you get along with Natalie?"

"We got along okay."

"Your mother said you were having a picnic the day Randy died."

"Right, me and Mom and Natalie. And Randy."

"And Natalie was with Randy when he fell?"

She looked at him, no expression in her colorless gray eyes. "I guess."

"What do you think happened?"

"Like Natalie said. Randy was drunk and fell off the bluff."

"Uh-huh. You miss your brother?"

"Not really. Randy was a shit."

"Where's your father?"

"Living in Dallas with his girlfriend. I have to go or I'll be late."

"Does your mom baby-sit while you work?"

63

"Are you kidding? I wouldn't leave Tommy with a drunk. I pay the woman next door a big chunk of my pay to watch him. Mom's useless."

The family was beyond dysfunctional. An alcoholic mother. A father living with his girlfriend. And Ellen had no use for her brother. Dead or alive.

"What are you doing in Pecos?" she said, her eyes wary.

"Tex Conroy has been living in New Orleans. Someone shot him."

"Really?" Her demeanor and body language said she could care less. "Did you talk to the Cat Woman?"

He struggled to keep from laughing. "You mean Mrs. Conroy?"

"Yes. How's Tex doing?"

"He's dead."

"Tex is dead?" She started laughing.

Weird. "You don't seem too broken up about it."

"Tex and Randy were buddies. Good riddance to both of them."

Ellen was angry with her parents, had no use for her brother or Tex. The jury was still out on Natalie. He sure did want to talk to Natalie.

"Did Natalie have any close friends?"

"Yeah, Gabe Rojas. They were friends all through high school."

"Does he still live in Pecos?"

"I think so. Gabe's married now. But not to Natalie."

Not to Natalie. What did that mean? He thanked her, went out to his car and dialed information. A minute later he was talking to an office worker at Pecos High School. When he said he needed to see a yearbook, she said he'd better hurry, the office closed in twenty minutes. He got there in ten.

The clerk, a stout woman in a polka dot dress, asked which yearbook he needed. He told her 1995. When he said he might need to take it with him, she frowned. "We don't let people take our copies out of the building."

He flashed his ID. "This is for a police investigation. I'll sign for it."

Seemingly impressed, she bustled into a closet, came back with the 1995 yearbook. "What sort of investigation is it?"

"Sorry. I can't say." He smiled. "You know how it is. You watch TV."

The woman grinned. "I sure do. I love *Law and Order*."

Sure, where every murder got solved in sixty minutes. He signed for the yearbook, took it to his rental car and looked at Natalie Brixton's photograph. An attractive girl, engaging smile, long dark hair, average features except for her eyes: almond-shaped, angling upward at the corners, hinting at Asian ancestry.

Below the picture was Natalie Brixton's motto: *Freedom and justice for all*.

Was that a quote? He ran through the Pledge of Allegiance in his mind. No, the Pledge ended "with *liberty* and justice for all."

Justice for all. He pictured the woman in the security video walking down the hall with her confident long-legged stride. But how would Natalie know Peterson? And why kill him? It didn't make sense.

But she had been with Randy Brixton when he fell off a cliff. Randy's mother and sister didn't seem too unhappy about his death. Didn't seem upset about the death of Tex Conroy, either.

He flipped to the Drama Club page. In 1995 they'd put on a production of *Oklahoma*. In one photo Natalie stood with a group of dancers. She had a great figure and long legs. Like the woman in the hotel security video. But a single attribute did not a positive identification make.

He got on his cell and dialed information. Moments later he dialed the number for G. Rojas. When a woman answered, he asked to speak to Gabriel Rojas. "I'm sorry, he's at work. Who's calling please?"

"Detective Frank Renzi, New Orleans Police. When will he be home?"

"He's usually home for dinner by six-thirty. What's this about?"

"It can wait till after dinner. Could I stop by around seven-thirty?"

"Eight would be better. Gabe likes to spend time with the boys after dinner."

"Thank you," he said. "See you at eight."

His stomach rumbled. His flight from New Orleans had taken off at 5:25 A.M., arrived in Houston at six-thirty. No food on the plane. His connecting flight put him in Odessa at nine. He'd rented a car and had eaten a raisin bagel with his jumbo black coffee while driving to Pecos, had arrived at the little one-horse town at eleven. Since then he'd interviewed Clarisse Conroy, Faye Brixton and Ellen Brixton. No lunch. A meal at Longhorn Jacks was in order.

The restaurant where Natalie Brixton had once worked.

———

Longhorn Jack's was jammed so he took a stool at the bar. A young bartender in a white shirt came over and said, "What can I get you?"

"A beer and lunch, but I got a question. I know a woman who worked here ten or twelve years ago. Anyone here now that might have known her?"

"I've only been here two years. Lemme ask in the kitchen." The kid disappeared through a door behind the bar. Moments later he came back. "The busboy might know her. Hank's been here forever. He just went outside for his smoke break."

Frank said he'd be back, went outside and circled the building.

A short black man with a white apron tied around his waist leaned against the back wall. A fringe of gray hair encircled his bald head.

"Hi, Hank? You got a minute?"

"Got a ten minute smoke break," Hank said, his dark eyes wary.

"Have your smoke. It won't bother me. Did you know Natalie Brixton when she worked here?"

Hank pulled out a pack of Camels. "You with the police?"

Hank had been around, had made him as a cop even without a uniform. When he lit up Frank noticed thick calluses on his fingers. "I'm a detective with the New Orleans department. And you're a bass player."

Raised eyebrows and a faint smile. "How'd you figure that?"

"The calluses on your fingers. I played a little jazz trumpet years ago."

"Good observation." Hank took a deep drag on his Camel, blew smoke. "But that's what they pay you for, right?"

"That and a few other things. You play with a Pecos group?"

"Every Friday and Saturday. Get off work at six, clean up, go play at a little club near the bus station. What you wanna know about Natalie?"

"You remember her?"

"Oh yeah, pretty girl like that? Nice person, Natalie. Where she at now?"

"I don't know, but I'd like to talk to her."

Hank's eyes got wary again. "This about Randy Brixton?"

"Did you know Randy?"

Hank flicked ash off his Camel and looked away. "Not really."

"How about Tex Conroy?"

"Didn't know him neither. Knew his daddy though. Chief of Police."

"I hear rumors about how Randy died. Do you know what happened?"

"Heard the same rumors as you, ain't gonna add none. Natalie had a tough life, lost her mom when she was ten, lived with the Brixtons eight years." Hank grimaced. "That family's screwed up, you ask me."

"Did Natalie tell you something to make you think so?"

"Told me enough. Told me Randy was an asshole. Didn't have to tell me the mother's a souse. Ev'body in town knows that. No wonder her husband left. I hear he's living with some woman in Dallas."

"You got any idea where Natalie is?"

"Nope. After Randy's funeral, Natalie gave her notice and quit. You wanna find Natalie, talk to Gabe Rojas. Far's I know he was her only friend, used to pick her up after work some nights."

"You know Gabe?"

"Know him by sight. Never talked to him. Good kid though, never in trouble. Last I heard he made it big with them video games." Hank took a drag on his Camel and dropped the butt on the ground. "I best be getting back to work. You find Natalie, tell her Hank says hello and wishes her the best."

"I will. Thanks for your help. What's the name of the club?"

"The Calico Cat. Got a big sign out front, you can't miss it."

Hank returned to the kitchen and Frank reclaimed his seat at the bar. It seemed clear that Hank had no use for the Brixton family, equally clear that he liked Natalie. And Gabe. Her only friend.

He saw Ellen Brixton lugging a tray of food and drinks into the dining room. He hoped she was getting big tips. A single mom with an alcoholic mother unfit to mind her child, Ellen needed every penny she could get.

———

Assuming Mrs. Rojas had told her husband an NOPD cop would arrive at eight, he rang their bell at 7:45. Surprise was often a detective's best weapon. The house, a brick-front split-level with a two-car attached garage, looked expensive. Gabe Rojas must be doing okay.

He heard high-pitch squeals and kids' voices approaching. A short man holding a squirming little boy opened the door. "Detective Renzi? My wife said you called. You'll have to pardon the mess. I was playing hide-and-seek with my boys." He grinned, his even white teeth contrasting with his burnt-umber skin. "Guess who lost."

"Daddeeeeee!" squealed the dark-haired, dark-eyed little boy.

"Looks like you've got quite a handful there. How old is he?"

"This is Carlos. He's six and he's got a twin brother, Jorge."

Frank followed them into the living room where another toddler, the spitting image of Carlos, was building a Lego airplane amidst Lego pieces strewn over the tawny-brown carpet. "Daddy, it's not time to go to bed."

"Yes it is my little friend. Time for both of you to go see Mom." Gabe Rojas mussed the hair on his boys' heads and gave them a gentle shove toward the stairs off the foyer.

"Beautiful kids. When my daughter was that age she never thought it was time for bed either."

"Too many fun things to do," Rojas said. He was five-four at most, rugged but not overweight, and his face bore an amiable expression. "Would you like a cold drink?"

"No, thanks. I had dinner at Longhorn Jack's." No reaction from Rojas.

"Have a seat," Rojas said, gesturing at a chocolate-brown couch opposite a big-screen TV and an entertainment center. "How can I help you?"

The decor reinforced his impression that Gabe Rojas was comfortably well-off, which mirrored his assessment of the man: comfortable in his skin as he sat on other end of the couch, relaxed and cooperative. Outwardly anyway.

"I'm investigating a murder that happened in New Orleans last week."

"Who got murdered?" Rojas said, his dark eyes suddenly full of concern. "Someone from Pecos?"

"Tex Conroy. Did you know him?"

Visibly relieved, Rojas said, "Not well, but I knew him. What happened?"

"Someone shot him." No reaction from Rojas. Strange. "Tex moved to New Orleans five years ago. Do you know if he had any enemies? Anyone that might want him dead?"

A sudden wail came from a distant room. Rojas rose from the couch, went to the hall and called up the stairs, "Everybody okay?"

A woman's voice called, "We're fine, Gabe, just a little soap in the eyes."

Rojas returned to the couch, looking troubled. And not about soap in the eyes. "Tex was in the football clique. Some of them could be ... obnoxious."

"Randy Brixton was Tex's friend, right?"

Rojas tensed and his mouth tightened. "Yes."

"Eight years ago he died under, shall we say, mysterious circumstances."

No longer relaxed and comfortable, Rojas said nothing.

"How well did you know Natalie Brixton?"

"Is that what this is about? Natalie?"

"I talked to some people and they said you were friends."

"In high school we were, yes."

"When did you last talk with her?"

Rojas examined his fingernails as if some alien form of life had taken up residence there. "I haven't talked to Natalie in years. After her high school graduation she left Pecos."

He's lying. "Do you know where she is now?"

"Detective Renzi, I told you I haven't talked to her in years. How would I know where she is?"

"Maybe she sent you a postcard. Where was she the last time you talked to her?"

"I need to say goodnight to my boys." Rojas abruptly rose from the couch and left the room.

He knows something, Frank thought, something about Natalie Brixton.

Five minutes later Rojas returned and sat on the couch, not looking cooperative now, more like belligerent. "I can't help you, Detective Renzi. I haven't seen Tex Conroy in years. Same with Randy Brixton."

"Where do you work?" A diversionary softball to mollify the man.

"I own my own business. I design video games."

Frank gestured at the well-furnished room. "Looks like your business is doing well."

"It was rough at first, but then one of my games took off." With obvious pride, Rojas said, "Six years ago I hired two software engineers and moved my business to Odessa to be nearer the airport. Now that we have a website, we ship worldwide. Last year we grossed twelve million. This year looks even better. Our next generation of games will be out in time for Christmas."

"Good for you. Everyone in Pecos speaks very highly of you. I talked with Ellen Brixton today. She said you were Natalie's only friend."

"Ellen." Rojas frowned, looking troubled. "How's she doing? I haven't seen her in a long time."

"She's working at Longhorn Jack's. She's got a son. But no husband."

"Ellen had it rough."

"Is that what Natalie told you?"

"Yes," Rojas snapped, "that's what Natalie told me. We were good friends in high school. It was not a romantic relationship." He paused, appearing to struggle for control. "The Brixtons took her in after her mother was murdered. But I'm sure you don't need me to tell you that."

"I think you know some things that you're not telling me."

"Maybe I do. Try this. Randy Brixton was making his sister give him blowjobs."

The gut-punch revelation made his skin crawl. "Did Ellen tell you that?"

"No. Ellen told Natalie. Natalie told me."

He thought about what Ellen said when he asked if she missed her brother. *Not really. Randy was a shit.* And Tex? *Good riddance to both of them.* If what Rojas said was true, Randy was worse than a shit. He was a rapist. One who'd died under mysterious circumstances. And the person with him at the time, Natalie Brixton, had chosen a motto that said: *Freedom and justice for all.*

But that didn't prove she pushed Randy off the cliff.

He took out a business card and gave it to Rojas. "If you think of anything helpful, call my cell phone anytime. And if you hear from Natalie, tell her I'd like to speak with her. Wherever she is."

Angry eyes and a clenched face. "I don't expect to be hearing from Natalie. *Wherever* she is."

Maybe Rojas knew where Natalie was and maybe he didn't. But Frank was certain of one thing. Rojas had lied when he said he hadn't heard from Natalie since high school. He'd take that to the bank.

Natalie

1995 -- 1996

The summer before my senior year I got a job at Longhorn Jack's. It was hard work lugging trays of steaks dinners and cocktails around, but the tips were good. I saved as much as I could. I still didn't know who killed my mother, but I figured I'd need money to find out. And do something about it.

Randy went out drinking with his friends every night to pick up girls, so on my nights off I got to watch *N.Y.P.D. Blue*. I still liked the cop shows best. In June the girls in my class got excited when Reba McEntire won a Country Music Award. Big deal. She's not half as good a singer as Joan Jett.

Ellen gave me a graduation present, a true-crime book: *The Journalist and the Murderer* by Janet Malcolm. Sometimes I think Ellen is smarter than she lets on. Gabe took me to the graduation party and told me about the video game he was designing. We had a great time.

One night in July I ate dinner at home on my night off, and Jerry said UPS was sending him to Dallas for five days to learn how to be a supervisor. "Then I'll be making more money," he said. Faye's face got that pinched look. Maybe she thought Jerry was taking his lover with him to Dallas.

Later I got on my laptop and checked the weather forecast. The first four days he'd be gone it was supposed to rain, but Saturday was supposed to be sunny and hot. The next day I told Faye I wanted to treat her and Randy and Ellen to a picnic while Jerry was away. Because they'd been so nice to me all these years. It killed me to say it, but I put on a happy face like I'd learned in acting class. "I know a great place. Randy can drive us."

On Saturday I bought a big order of Popeye's fried chicken and stopped at a bakery for an apple pie. Randy loved fried chicken and apple pie. At 4:30 I had him drive us to the place where Gabe and I had our picnics near the bluff above the Pecos River. It was hot but we sat at a redwood picnic table under a shade tree and ate dinner as the sun went down.

Faye and Ellen didn't eat much but Randy ate like a pig, as usual. He also polished off a six-pack of beer. Faye drank the OJ cocktail she'd brought in her thermos. Nobody was talking and thinking about what I planned to do made me nervous. The fried chicken sat in my stomach like a lump of lead.

70

After Randy pigged out on apple pie, I took out my camera. "Wow, look at that beautiful sunset. Let me take your picture, Randy."

"Here?" he said, and scrunched up his face like an idiot.

"No. Over by the bluff." I left the table and waved for him to follow.

Randy kept grumbling that he was hot, but I kept walking until we went around a bend. When I looked back, Faye and Ellen were out of sight.

I pointed to a clump of bushes up ahead. "That's the best spot."

The best spot to do what I had decided to do, the place where you could look over the bluff and see the jumble of rocks piled up beside the river.

"Stand over there near the bluff and look handsome."

What a joke. His Harley-Davidson T-shirt had yellow sweat stains in the armpits and his legs were fat and hairy below his cutoff jeans.

But I had to get him in the right position.

He went over to the bluff and faced me.

"Closer to the edge, so I can get the sunset and the river in the picture."

He backed up three paces. Better but still not close enough.

I let the camera dangle from the strap around my neck and took the .38 Special Gabe got me out of the pocket of my jeans. It's small and easy to hide and it felt good in my hand. Especially when I thought about the day Randy broke Muffy's neck and felt the iceberg, cold and hard, inside me.

"What's that, you little gook? You got yourself a pea shooter?"

Randy looked nervous—he'd left his gun in the glove compartment of his car—but not worried. Yet. I gripped the gun with both hands and aimed it at his chest. "You killed Muffy."

That wiped the smile off his face. "Cut the shit, Natalie."

"Back up, Randy." Now he was two feet from the edge of the bluff

"You're crazy. I always knew it. Your mother was crazy too."

I wanted to shoot him, but that would be a mistake.

And I didn't intend to make any mistakes. Not today.

"Does it make you feel important when you make your sister give you blow jobs?"

"Shut up, you gook bitch. I never made—"

"Yes you did. She told me. You're disgusting, Randy. Back up."

"Put the gun away." He clenched his fists and took a step toward me.

I pulled the trigger. He yelped and grabbed the lower part of his leg. I hadn't intended to hit him, but I had to make him understand that I'd shoot if he didn't do what I said. "Back up or I'll shoot you in the heart."

Now there was real fear in his eyes. He held up his hands, palms out. One had blood on it. "Don't shoot. I didn't mean it."

"Yes you did. You meant to hurt me when you killed Muffy and you meant to hurt me when you told your friends my mother was a prostitute. And what you did to Ellen was worse. You made your own sister give you blow jobs." All the while I kept the gun aimed at his heart. "Back up or I'll shoot."

He backed up a step. Now his heels were at the edge of the bluff, no place to go but down. "Please," he said. Now he looked terrified.

I loved it. Now I was in control.

I fired a shot over his head to scare him and it worked just the way I'd planned. He lost his balance and windmilled his arms to keep from falling.

But he couldn't. He screamed as he fell over the bluff.

My hands were shaking and my heart was beating faster than it did after a taekwondo workout. I crept to the bluff and looked down.

Fifty feet below me, Randy lay on the rocks. I had hoped that he would bounce off the rocks into the river and float away. He hadn't, but I was pretty sure he was dead.

And I was glad. *Justice for Muffy and Ellen.*

I did one of my taekwondo spin moves and hurled the gun out into the fast-flowing river. Then I ran back to Faye and Ellen.

When I got to the picnic table I was gasping for breath.

"Randy fell!" I shouted. "He fell over the bluff!"

Bleary-eyed from her vodka-and-OJ cocktail, Faye looked at me, mystified. Finally she said, "I think I heard shots."

Ellen looked at me with her pale gray eyes. Her dead eyes.

"I didn't hear a thing," she said.

———

Three officers from the Reeves County Sheriff's department questioned me for hours, asking the same questions six different ways. But I stuck to my story. I told them Randy was fooling around near the edge of the bluff and he'd had a few beers (which was true) and he slipped and fell over the edge. Then I squeezed out some tears and they let me go.

Faye didn't seem too upset about Randy. I think she was glad he was dead. I know Ellen was. I don't know how Jerry felt. Texas men don't cry so Jerry kept up appearances at the funeral. He never asked me what happened. I figured the cops told him what I'd said.

A week after Randy's funeral I quit my job at Longhorn Jack's and brought my laptop to Gabe's house. Gabe says that even if you delete files on a computer, people can retrieve them. I told him I was leaving and gave him the laptop and asked him to make sure the hard drive got erased.

He said he would. Then we got in his car and went out for a beer.

Gabe looked sad, but I think he'd always known that I would leave Pecos someday. When I asked how his courses were going, he shrugged, like that wasn't something he wanted to talk about right now.

When we went out to his car, I hugged him. "I love you, Gabe."

"I love you too, Nat. I'll miss you."

His voice was husky and his eyes were wet. Mine were too.

"We'll always be best friends," I said. "I'll email you."

Gabe nodded, but I could tell he was working hard not to cry.
He didn't ask where I was going.
And he didn't ask about Randy.
Two days later I got on a Greyhound bus bound for New York City.

_____

1996 -- 1997

Two weeks after I got off the bus I took a one-week class at an exotic dance studio: Pole Dancing, Exotic Dance and Lap Sinsations. When the class ended I asked the teacher (her name was Val) if I could take the Professional Program. I said I was running out of money and I needed a job.
Val put her arm around me and said, "Honey, you are gonna be HOT."
Like we were girlfriends. I was amazed. I'd never had a girlfriend. The next day Val took me shopping. I bought two pairs of 5-inch stiletto heels and a bunch of glittery pasties and G-strings and took the Intensive Professional Course. My bra size was 36-D now, but my breasts were small compared to some of the girls. When I mentioned this to Val, she winked and said, "Honey, it's what you do with 'em that counts."
At the end of August she helped me get a job at an entry-level club. "Not a dive. A club where you can get experience and make decent money."
And did I need money. I was renting a room at a boarding house and my savings were almost gone. I auditioned for the manager of Cheetahs, a club in Manhattan near a subway stop, and got a job dancing topless from three to seven. After my dinner break I danced from nine until two AM.
I called it dancing in the dark. Dancing topless in front of strange men didn't bother me. I was proud of my body. It was strong and supple, and my legs were slim and muscular from taekwondo. My long hair was an asset, too. I draped it over my breasts to make my strip sexier. The tips were good: lots of dollar bills, fives for a good dance, ten for a lap dance.
Val warned me never to go home with a client. I think she worried because I was young. Val was twenty-eight. I was eighteen, but I told her I was twenty-one. She also warned me not to get into drugs. As if I would. I had to stay healthy and strong and focused. Mom had been waiting eight years for me to avenge her. Every October on the anniversary I did my Veneration of Elders ritual. I'd light an incense stick and sit in front of Mom's picture and chant my taekwondo oath: *I shall be a champion of justice and freedom.*
Then I'd promise Mom that I'll find her killer and punish him.
I sent Gabe an email from an Internet Café to let him know I was okay. I didn't say where I was or what I was doing. At the end I wrote: I LOVE U, IRS. Our private joke. My birthday is April 15, tax day. I wondered if he'd finished designing his video game. I missed Gabe a lot.
The boarding house where I lived had a kitchen, but it stank of stale food

so I ate at a cafeteria two blocks away. That's how I met Darren. One Sunday it was crowded and he asked to sit at my table and we got talking. We started meeting for breakfast every day. Darren was an actor, but he didn't get many acting jobs. To support himself, he modeled for clothes catalogs. He showed me his page in a Sears catalog. He had dirty-blond hair and an average face, but he looked great in a suit. I don't know if he was a good actor or not, but he took a lot of auditions. The second week he asked me out to a movie.

I liked him. Not as much as Gabe, but he was fun to talk to, so I went.

Darren loved foreign movies. We saw *The Full Monty*. It was hilarious, a bunch of unemployed Brits turned themselves into male strippers. Afterwards we ate pastrami sandwiches at a deli, and I told Darren I worked at a strip club. He didn't seem shocked. "We do what we gotta do to survive," he said.

I was thrilled when Dennis Franz won an Emmy for *N.Y.P.D. Blue*. He's great. He takes no shit from anyone. That's what Gabe said about me: *You take no shit from anyone, Natalie.*

In October Darren invited me to his apartment. I knew what that meant, but I was eighteen and tired of being a virgin. I didn't know what to expect. I mean, I knew how it worked, but Mom never got a chance to talk to me about sex. I still missed her terribly. I couldn't tell her about Gabe or Darren, couldn't ask her advice about how to dress. Or what to do when I was about to lose my virginity. I figured I'd just close my eyes and endure it, but Darren was gentle and considerate. He seemed surprised that I was a virgin but didn't question me about it.

His apartment was tiny, but it didn't stink of food. The next time I went there I asked how much the rent was. When Darren told me, I mentally divided it in half to see if I could afford it. I could, but I wanted him to suggest it. Six weeks later I moved in. It worked out great. Darren was cheerful and affectionate and very clean. He didn't leave hairs in the bathroom sink and he loved movies. On Thanksgiving we went to see *LA Confidential*. Kim Basinger played a call girl and two cops fell in love with her. I wondered if any of Mom's customers had fallen in love with her.

I also wondered if anyone would ever fall in love with me.

Darren was nice, but I wasn't in love with him. When we saw France Nuyen in *Angry Café* I didn't tell Darren she was my idol. I didn't want him asking about my heritage. Joan Jett was still my idol too. After I got the job at Cheetahs I bought a Walkman so I could listen to her CDs.

One night in April I was partying outside the Cheetah's employee entrance with three other dancers. They'd bought me a cake to celebrate my birthday. They thought I was twenty-two, but I'd just turned nineteen. Alexa, another dancer, brought a customer outside. Some men take the girls outside to ask them for extras. But I wasn't going to give blow jobs in an alley or get in a guy's car, not even if they flash fifties and hundreds. It's too dangerous.

That night, Alexia went with this customer. I don't remember what he looked like. I never noticed what they looked like.

This wasn't about looks, it was about money.

The next day the cops found Alexia's body in the East River. Val called my cell that morning, hysterical, and warned me not to go back to Cheetahs. She said the cops would find out Alexia worked there and question all the dancers. She knew a club with better clientele. She told me to call the manager and say she'd recommended me. That's how I wound up working at the Platinum Plus Gentlemen's Club.

It was way better than Cheetahs. I worked the lunch crowd from eleven to two, took a long break and danced from seven to midnight. That was great. I got home earlier and got up earlier. During my break I worked out at a taekwondo studio to make sure I didn't lose any of my moves.

I also started looking for my father. He and Mom had met in New York so I thought he might still live here. One day I went to a community center in an area where many Asian-Americans lived and told a lady I was looking for a Vietnamese man named Thu Phan. She gave me directions to a church where a Korean group met. Useless. Some people think all Asians are alike.

I looked in the phone book and found four numbers listed for Phan. But no Thu Phan, not even a T. Phan. When I called the numbers, no one spoke English. I couldn't think of another way to find my father so I stopped looking. That made me sad. I wondered if I would ever meet him.

But not knowing who murdered my mother made me feel even worse.

One day I found an ad in the Yellow Pages for Private Investigators. It said: *Discreet Inquiries*. I was hoping to hire a PI to go to New Orleans and find out if the police had any suspects. I dialed the number and right away this gruff voice said: "Scanlon Investigations, can I help you?"

Startled, I blurted, "I'm trying to find the person that murdered Jeannette Brixton."

After a pause the voice said, "When and where was she murdered?"

"New Orleans, in 1988. They never found the killer, but they must have had suspects and I need to find out who they were."

My heart was thumping like mad.

"And you want me to find them?"

"No. I don't want you to find them. I want you to find out their names."

"Uh-huh. Well, that's different. I'll give it a shot, but it's gonna cost you."
"How much?"

"First off, there's my daily rate, which isn't cheap. I gotta fly to New Orleans and find a cop willing to get me the file. That might cost you a grand, maybe two. And I got my plane fare and living expenses . . ."

As his voice droned on I started to feel sick.

"Bottom line," said the gruff voice, "it might cost you four or five grand. I'll need three grand up front."

Three thousand dollars. Most of my clients at Platinum Plus were stock brokers and lawyers, and the tips were great, but living in New York was expensive. After working there three months I had saved four hundred dollars.

It would take me years to save three thousand dollars.

Tears filled my eyes and ran down my cheeks. I closed my cell and put my head down on the kitchen table and cried.

How could I avenge Mom if I didn't know who killed her?

I made myself a cup of green tea, but it didn't make me feel any better.

I got out Mom's picture and thought about the day I brought home my fourth grade report card. I thought it was pretty good. All A's except for the B in math. But Mom said, "How come you got a B in Math?"

"It's the word problems. They're hard. Who cares where two cars meet up if one starts from Boston and the other one from San Francisco, and they tell you how fast they're going? It's stupid."

Mom gave me one of her stern looks, the kind that made her green eyes extra-green. "Natalie, you're a smart girl. Don't be a quitter. Bring the math workbooks home and I'll help you with them after school." So Mom helped me, and she was right. The word problems weren't really that hard.

On my next report card I got an A in Math, too.

I kissed Mom's picture and decided I would never give up.

I wasn't a quitter. No matter what it took, no matter how long it took, I would find Mom's killer and punish him.

———

The second week of December a distinguished-looking man in a charcoal pinstriped suit came in the club and asked me to sit at his table. "You are a wonderful dancer. Have you studied karate?"

I just about fell off my chair. Judging by his eyes, he was part Asian, but I couldn't tell where his ancestors were from. When I told him about the taekwondo, he smiled. "I would like to hire you for my business. You are much too good to waste your talents in here. Compared to the other dancers, you stand out like a red flare against the night sky. What is your name?"

"Lorelei," I said. That was my dancer name.

He shook his head. "No, what is your real name?"

I was afraid to tell him. Even Val and Darren didn't know my real name. Darren's name was on the apartment lease and I paid cash for everything, including my new Social Security number and the fake ID I'd bought from the guy at the pay-as-you-go cell phone store. I didn't want anyone to be able to trace me through my tax returns and figure out where Natalie Brixton was.

"What's *your* name?" I asked.

He smiled and gave me his card. "Just call me Lin. My last name is hard to pronounce."

He was right. His last name was twelve letters long with only one vowel.

"Are you hiding from someone? Are you in trouble with the police?"

I thought about Randy. But the cops never charged me so that didn't count. "No. I just don't like to give my real name."

"As you wish, Lorelei. But you are too intelligent for this mindless dancing. Most of these men would like to have sex with you. But what they really want is a girlfriend, someone to listen to their problems and make them feel important. And maybe have sex, maybe not. The men who patronize my business are quite wealthy. For one hour of your time they would pay me two-thousand dollars."

My mouth fell open. $2,000 an hour? It took me a *month* to make that much. "My name is May," I said. "May Hargrove. How soon can I start?"

Lin laughed. He seemed cultured and intelligent, and my instinct said to trust him. I don't know why. Sometimes I just went with my gut.

"Do you by chance speak any language besides English?" he asked.

"I speak French pretty well."

His eyes went wide like he'd just won the Powerball.

"Wonderful. How would you like to go to Paris?"

CHAPTER 10

Tuesday, July 29, 2008   New Orleans

"Natalie Brixton." Frank set the Pecos High School yearbook on Vobitch's desk and pointed to a photograph. He'd already told him what he'd learned from Tex Conroy's mother, Randy Brixton's mother and sister, and Natalie Brixton's friend Gabriel Rojas.

After studying the photo for several seconds, Vobitch nodded, smiling now. "I like it. Looks like we know who the woman in the security video is. Her cousin fell off a cliff, and she was the only witness. So. Did he fall or was he pushed?"

"The cops questioned her and let her go."

"She knew Conroy, maybe she knew Peterson, too. Ballistics report says the bullets that killed Conroy and Peterson came from the same gun."

"But that doesn't prove she shot them. And don't forget the fire escape. Maybe the shooter got in the room while Peterson was in the bar."

"And hid where? And don't tell me the bathroom. Most guys have a drink in a bar, first thing they do when they get to the room is take a leak. Frank, Spiderman didn't climb up the fire escape to a room on the sixth floor."

"Maybe Spiderman was one floor down in Room 535."

"Fuck!" Vobitch raked stubby fingers through his silvery hair. "The techs lifted prints off the window casing, some Peterson's, some not. Coulda been the cleaning lady for all we know. I think the woman's the shooter, but we better find out who rented rooms with access to the fire escape that night."

"If you think Natalie's the shooter, what's her motive?"

"Looked like a hooker to me." Vobitch glanced at a 5-inch mini-TV on the file cabinet beside his desk. A commercial was on with the sound muted. "We already know Peterson couldn't keep his dick in his pants. Maybe she had a peashooter .38 Special in that fancy little purse she was carrying. Maybe Peterson asked her to do something she didn't like, so she popped him."

"That's one possibility. But Peterson was in debt. Maybe he borrowed money from a loan shark and didn't pay—"

78

"Frank. Be serious. He didn't pay the vig, those guys wouldn't send a woman to take him out."

"Okay. But if you like the hit theory, we need motive."

"Maybe she killed him at someone else's behest."

"Behest," he said, half-smiling.

Vobitch jutted his jaw. "Yeah, *behest*. You think I don't know what it means?" Glaring at him. "You think I'm from Texas or some fuckin thing?"

They both cracked up. Vobitch often used sarcasm to burn off stress. And the media drumbeat was louder now than when he left for Pecos.

"Okay," he said, "but if the woman was a hired gun, who hired her?"

"I'd start with the wife. Nine times out of ten the spouse is the killer."

"I can't picture Corinne Peterson hiring a hitter. Hell, she wouldn't know where to find one."

Vobitch grinned. "I know a certain family in this town she could call . . ."

"Yeah, yeah," he said, knowing the *certain family* his boss referred to was Italian. Vobitch loved jiving him about his heritage. He dished it right back, busting Vobitch about Jewish guys who married beautiful black women, like his elegant ballet-dancer wife.

The phone rang. Vobitch glanced at it and made a face. "Gotta take this one. I give the mucky-mucks my hotline number so I know to answer it. The rest get my regular number, have to leave a voicemail message." He picked up, barked his name and listened silently.

Restless with energy, Frank rose and paced the room. It was half the size of the homicide office. The window behind the desk looked out on the area where the NOPD motorcycles parked. The desk and two visitor chairs took up half the space. File cabinets lined the pale green walls. Above a two-drawer cabinet was a framed photograph: Vobitch in his NYPD uniform shaking hands with the Mayor of New York. Frank smiled, recalling the day they'd met five years ago.

"We'll get along fine, Renzi," Vobitch had said. "I'm a New York Jew, you're a Boston wop. The good ol' boys down here hate us Yankees. They're still fighting the Civil War. But we know who won."

Since then they'd had a few disagreements, but two years ago when he'd shot and killed a deranged stalker, Vobitch had backed him to the hilt.

Vobitch slammed down the phone. "Fuckin asshole."

Frank returned to his chair. "Who was it? Donald Trump?"

"Worse. DA Roger kiss-my-ass Demaris." Vobitch drew a finger across his throat. "While you were gone, Miller talked to Peterson's wife, asked if the name Tex Conroy rang any bells. She said no, but I'm not writing her off as a suspect. She's pissed at hubby, hired the woman to take care of it. These days you can get anything on the Internet, including a hitter."

"Maybe she hired Conroy to set up the hit. The woman kills Peterson, gets worried that Tex will blab and pops him, too."

"Frank, everything we got points to Natalie Brixton. She knew Conroy--" Vobitch glanced at the TV, grabbed the clicker and sound blared from the TV set. The weather channel.

He'd forgotten about the hurricane churning into the Gulf, a common occurrence in the summer. Hurricane Gail had been upgraded to a Category 3 and it's projected path included New Orleans. When the report ended, Vobitch hit the mute button and looked at him expectantly.

"Maybe she's Peterson's mistress," he said. "Maybe she asked him to get a divorce and he said no."

"So why'd she kill Conroy? Frank, you hit the jackpot in Pecos. Natalie Brixton knew Conroy. The bullet that killed Conroy came from the same gun that killed Peterson. Why make it complicated?"

Was he? Maybe the woman in the video was Natalie Brixton. But for some reason he didn't want to believe it. She'd had a rough life, but why kill Arnold Peterson? Or Tex Conroy, for that matter?

"What about Fenwick Holt?" he said. "He wants Peterson's job so he can make the big bucks."

"Forget Holt. Why kill Peterson if he was gonna get fired because of his gambling problem. Frank, we need a plan. Right now all we got is the woman in the video. Gimme something to feed the fuckin media."

"I'll have an artist make a sketch from the Brixton yearbook picture, adjusted for age. You can send it to the newspapers and TV stations, say we're looking for a person of interest, have 'em call the tip line."

"I like it." Vobitch jotted notes on a yellow legal pad. "How about you talk to some of the helpful hookers around town, shake that tree for info."

"Okay." And after a beat, "Twenty years ago Natalie Brixton's mother was murdered in New Orleans. October 1988. I checked the files. The case was never solved. Ring any bells?"

"What the fuck! Why didn't you tell me that before?"

Good question. Maybe because he didn't want to believe Natalie was the killer. But he sure did want to solve the case. Then he'd have time to see Kelly. Their romp in the sack last Friday seemed like eons ago.

"Saving the best for last."

"Where'd you get it?"

"From Tex Conroy's mother. She heard the mother was a prostitute."

"Murdered prostitutes don't make much of a splash in New Orleans. October of '88? That's before I got here. You think Peterson killed the mother and the daughter popped him for revenge?"

"That's what I thought at first, but Peterson was working in Chicago in 1988. His wife said they got married that year. I want to talk to the lead investigator on the case. Jane Fontenot. You know her?"

"Yeah. Good detective. She retired last year. I'll give her a call, set up a meet. While you were gone, Miller talked to Conroy's girlfriend." Vobitch grimaced. "All upset, don't know nothin."

"Did he find anything in Conroy's apartment?"

"Nothing helpful, but plenty of beer. Three cases of Bud stacked in the kitchen, a six-pack in the fridge, guy probably drank 'em while he watched football. Kenyon said there were Dallas Cowboys posters taped to the walls and a foot-high stack of *Sports Illustrated* magazines in the living room."

"Conroy doesn't strike me as the sharpest knife in the drawer."

"Frank, he was from *Texas.*"

But not all Texans were dumb, Frank thought. Gabe Rojas was smart enough to run a million-dollar computer-game business. Savvy enough to hide whatever he knew about Natalie, including her whereabouts.

"Conroy knew Natalie Brixton," Vobitch said. "We need to find out if she knew Peterson."

"Right," he snapped, irritated. "When I find her, I'll ask her."

"Frank, the fuckin DA just threatened me. If we don't solve the Peterson case soon, he'll put someone else on it. I'm fifty-seven. You know what that means? Early retirement. And I'm not ready to retire. Find Natalie Brixton and get her in here."

There was anger in Vobitch's eyes, but also a hint of melancholy. Vobitch lived for the job, and now his job was on the line. Hell, Demaris might be looking to get Frank Renzi fired too.

"I'll do my best," he said. But he had no clue how to find Natalie Brixton. And he still wasn't convinced she was the woman on the video. "Call me after you talk to Jane Fontenot. I'll get an artist to do a sketch of Natalie."

"Do it quick," Vobitch said. "They're hyping Hurricane Gail as the Next Big Blow. If the mayor   decides to evacuate the city, forget finding Peterson's killer. We'll all be pulling traffic duty."

———

Boston   2:30 P.M.

Girl Dies in Murder Bust said the bold front page headline on a *Boston Globe* dated November 29, 2000, one of several she had requested from the librarian in the Boston Public Library periodicals room.

Yesterday on NOLA.com she'd read an article about a man found dead in City Park, identified by police as Lawrence "Tex" Conroy. Hinting the cases might be related, it said NOPD Homicide Detective Frank Renzi was the lead investigator on the Conroy case and the Arnold Peterson murder.

She knew what that meant. They knew both men had been shot with the same gun. Then the article noted that Renzi had joined NOPD in 2002 after a twenty-year stint with Boston PD. Scary.

81

She was living near Boston. Renzi might be looking for her in New Orleans, but she had to be careful. *Know your enemy.*

That's why she'd come to the library. The only other researchers in the periodicals room, two college-age women, sat at a long wooden table four rows ahead of her. Antique lamps with green-glass shades and gold pull-chains stood on each table. She turned hers on and read the article.

Shortly before dawn Boston Police detectives Franklin Sullivan Renzi and John Albert Warner had gone to a public housing project to execute a warrant for the arrest of Thaddeus "Whacko" Lewis, age 20. Lewis was wanted for the murder of a rival gang leader, Andre "Kingpin" Jackson, on July 4, 2000. Both men were African-American.

What happened next was in dispute.

According to Renzi and Warner, when they entered the apartment Lewis came out of a room at the end of a hallway brandishing an Uzi and began firing. Renzi and Warner returned fire. Investigators collected forty-five bullet casings. In the midst of the firefight, a girl came out of a room mid-way down the hall. Janelle Robinson, age 11, died. Lewis was wounded and taken to a hospital where he later died. Renzi and Warner were unhurt.

A front page story in the next day's *Globe* said Renzi and Warner had been put on paid administrative leave while the Boston PD Internal Affairs unit investigated the incident. A sidebar offered conflicting views. Several black ministers commended Boston police for trying to rid the project of drug dealers. Others questioned why more care wasn't taken to capture a known criminal with a long police record. The dead girl's mother was outraged.

"Them cops went in there guns blazing and killed my girl," said Mrs. Robinson. "I'm gonna sue their ass."

She set the paper aside. Eight years ago Detective Frank Renzi had been embroiled in controversy. Was that why he moved to New Orleans?

She leaned back in her chair and gazed at the high arched ceiling. Thanks to her Devotion to Study, she loved libraries. The BPL, as Bostonians called it, had excellent research facilities. Conveniently located in Copley Square, it was near Copley Place, an upscale shopping center with a parking garage. New York had a great library, too. She'd been there many times. She loved the stone lions, named "Patience" and "Fortitude" by Mayor Fiorello La Guardia, that guarded the entrance.

For the last twenty years she had needed plenty of patience and fortitude.

She had chosen birds, not lions, to protect her. Unfortunately, her firebird pendant had betrayed her. But meeting Tex was a fluke. It would never happen again. No one in Pecos knew where she was, not even Gabe, though they'd stayed in touch over the years. She smiled, picturing his mischievous grin, dark-skinned face and almost-black eyes. What did he look like now? she wondered. Now he was married, with two kids.

Twin boys!!! his email had said.

She opened the next item in her stack, a *Boston Globe Magazine* dated March 2001. Amanda Kondraki, a Globe staffer, had written an in-depth profile of Franklin Sullivan Renzi titled: **Good Cop, Bad Cop?**

Facing the text were two photos. In one Renzi gazed into the camera with dark smiling eyes. Despite his hawk-like nose, he was undeniably attractive, an angular face, high cheekbones, a sensuous mouth. The other photo was a different: hard eyes, a grim slash of a mouth and a jagged scar visible within the dark stubble on his chin.

She took a surreptitious sip of bottled water, thinking: Who's the real Frank Renzi, the handsome smiling man or the hard-eyed hunter? The profile might not provide the answer, but it might offer some helpful clues.

After an Internal Affairs investigation cleared Renzi and Warner in the November 2000 incident, Renzi resumed working as a homicide detective. Warner retired and moved to Florida to live with his daughter. Kondraki had interviewed one of Warner's friends, who said Warner had been distraught over the girl's death and the intense scrutiny that followed.

The next two paragraphs contained some eye-openers. The year 2000 had been difficult for Renzi. First his mother died. Then his wife filed for divorce citing adultery and a bitter court battle followed.

Then came The Incident, as Kondraki termed it, and the resulting public furor. After summarizing what happened, Kondraki inserted several quotes. Renzi's supervisor, Lieutenant Harrison Flynn, called his work exemplary, saying, "Detective Renzi has the highest clearance rate of any Boston PD homicide detective in the previous ten years."

That gave her pause. Her hunter-adversary usually got his man.

Then came a quote from Renzi's father, Appellate Court Judge Salvatore Renzi: "My son did the job he was hired to do, take vicious criminals with no regard for human life off the streets."

She turned the page and three photos leaped out at her. One filled the left-hand page: Renzi playing basketball on a playground, surrounded by black teens. Below it was a quote from Reverend Horace Denton, minister of the Mission Baptist Church where, ironically, Janelle Robinson's funeral had been held: "Officer Renzi has served the black community well. Without seeking the spotlight, he goes beyond the call of duty, mentoring many of our at-risk youth, especially boys without fathers. Officer Renzi is a fine role model."

Two photos on the facing page were starkly different. One showed a grim-faced Renzi, besieged by reporters and television cameras, captioned: "BPD Homicide Detective Frank Renzi leaves police headquarters after giving testimony to Internal Affairs."

Beside it was a photo of Janelle Robinson's mother, captioned: "That man's a killer. He murdered my girl in cold blood."

Quoting unnamed sources, Kondraki said several police officers believed Janelle Robinson had been romantically involved with the murder suspect, Thaddeus Whacko Lewis.

In a brief interview, Kondraki asked Renzi about this and also why he had attended the girl's funeral. His response: "I don't know why Janelle Robinson was in the apartment or why she chose to step into the hall at that moment. All I know is she didn't deserve to die."

When asked if Janelle Robinson's mother was a crack addict, he refused to speculate, saying: "Mrs. Robinson is grieving for her daughter." Noting that Renzi also had a daughter, Kondraki asked about his ugly divorce battle and the adultery charges. At that point Renzi terminated the interview, saying, "My private life is nobody's business."

Kondraki's conclusion: "Homicide Detective Frank Renzi remains an enigma to many, including his police department colleagues. While many admire his work ethic, they say they don't know him well. Good cop? Bad cop? You decide."

Good question. She set aside the article. She now knew more about her adversary, but it didn't reassure her. Renzi was an intelligent man, a detective with a high clearance rate. It was clear that he knew the gun that killed Arnold Peterson was also the gun that killed Tex Conroy. How long would it take him to dig up the dirt on Tex?

A chill iced her spine. What if he went to Pecos and found out Tex and Randy were best friends?

That could lead to other, more dangerous discoveries.

CHAPTER 11

At five o'clock she left the library and walked around the corner to the Copley 222, a boutique hotel with a comfortable lounge. Later it would be crowded but it wasn't now. She loved the ambiance: lush green fern plants in the corners, muted lighting from wall sconces along dark wood-paneled walls. It reminded her of a bar in Paris where she used to go with Willem. But she refused to think about Willem, or lament about what might have been.

Now that she'd done her research, she wanted to relax with a glass of fine wine and plan her moves. A grand piano stood in the corner with its lid closed. At seven, there would be a jazz trio. Too bad she couldn't stay. She loved jazz, but she had too much to do. In three weeks she would be in New Orleans for the Main Event. Her endless twenty-year journey was almost over.

Vengeance is coming soon, Mom, I promise.

Three singletons—two men and a woman—sat at the square bar in the center of the lounge. Keeping her distance, she slipped into a padded-leather swivel chair at one corner of bar. The barmaid, a thirtyish woman with spiky blond hair, came over and smiled at her. "What can I get for you?"

"How about a glass of red wine? A good Merlot."

"The 2003 Estate Merlot from Napa Valley is good. Want to taste it?"

"No, I trust you." *Always make friends with the bartender.*

Lori, according to the name-tag pinned to her white shirt.

"I love your glasses," Lori said.

"Thanks. They're Vera Wang." Set in thin silver titanium frames, the rectangular nonprescription lenses made her appear studious, a ploy she used to convince bartenders she wasn't a hooker.

Lori delivered her wine, waited as she took a sip, smiled when she said it was great and left her alone. She dug a Sharpie and a small notepad out of her tote bag. In tiny printed letters, the kind she used in her diary, she made a list.

1) G, NH. Massachusetts gun laws were far more strict than those in New Hampshire. That's where she'd bought the .38 Special that now sat at the bottom of Lake Pontchartrain. She needed a new one, but she didn't want to buy it at the same shop. Last night on the Internet she'd found another one in Hookset, New Hampshire.

2) Buy Car/Register in A's name. After finding the gun shop, she had trolled EBay for reasonably priced late-model cars. She'd saved a substantial amount of money to finance the Main Event, but half of it was gone, and the final part of her mission would be expensive.

April was her last fake ID. But after the Main Event, she wouldn't need one. Then she could live life as a normal person.

Whatever that was. Her life had never been normal.

She took a sip of wine and relaxed in her chair. She loved being in a bar with people around. Sometimes a deep loneliness welled up inside her, a visceral longing that made her want to talk to someone. She still missed Gabe. Sometimes when she watched TV she even thought about Darren, half-expecting to see him in some sitcom. She never did. And she missed Willem terribly. She had been so certain that would work out . . .

Resolutely, she banished thoughts of Willem and focused on her target. He often traveled on business, but during the third week of August he would be in New Orleans to open the latest addition to his chain of swanky clubs.

She became aware of a faint masculine scent, a presence near her left elbow. Startled, she glanced at the man, then away.

Lori was already upon him, beaming as she set a cocktail napkin on the bar in front of him. "Hi, Oliver. The usual?"

"Thanks, Lori. That would be great."

Lori added ice cubes and liquor to a metal shaker. "Rough day?"

The man emitted a low rumble, part laugh, part groan. "Rough doesn't begin to describe it." He appeared to notice her for the first time. "I'm sorry. Did I take someone's chair?"

She sized him up: Mid-thirties, dark curly hair, and a mouth that might be cruel if he wasn't smiling. No wedding ring, but men often removed them when they went on the prowl. Still, he was attractive and his suit was well-tailored. She hadn't come here to meet a man, but she wasn't averse to interesting encounters.

"No. Be my guest. You've had a bad day." Letting him know she had overheard.

Lori set a long-stemmed glass garnished with a cherry in front of him and discreetly moved away.

"Maybe it'll get better now that I've got my Manhattan," he said, gazing into her eyes, his obvious but unspoken words being: *Now that I've met you.*

She slipped her pen and notepad into her tote and raised her glass in a mock-toast. "Here's to a fine evening. My day wasn't that great either."

He sipped his Manhattan, regarding her steadily, his eyes Azure-blue, like the sky on a calm summer day. Inviting eyes. Sexy.

"Are you visiting or do you live here?"

"Visiting, sort of." She turned on the seductive smile that men found so alluring and spun him a story. "I'm a freelance writer. This afternoon a woman was supposed to give me the inside scoop for an article." She paused, aware that he was hanging on her every word. "But she stood me up."

He brushed her forearm with his fingers, a quick touch that made her body tingle. "How annoying," he said. "There you were, all set to get some crucial information and the woman ruined your day. Sounds a bit like mine."

"What happened?"

"A man was supposed to authenticate a piece of art for me. The provenance of an artwork can determine whether it's worth millions or worth nothing," he explained.

Thanks to the art lessons provided by her Parisian employers, she already knew this. But never mind. "And it was worthless?"

His mouth quirked. "Worse, actually, but let's not talk about my problems. I want to know more about you." He hesitated as though making a difficult decision. "I'm Oliver James."

She hesitated too. Should she give him her name? She went with her gut. "Robin Adair."

He took her hand as if it were delicate porcelain china and held it in his. The warmth of his palms against hers felt wonderful. When he let go, she felt as though she'd lost something precious.

"Happy to meet you, Robin Adair, writer extraordinaire. Are you staying here at the hotel?"

She gave a rueful laugh. "No. Too rich for my blood, I'm afraid. I've got a room at the Lennox." She didn't, but Oliver didn't need to know that. "This one has a much nicer bar."

"Would you care to join me for dinner? I've got a reservation at the Top of the Hub." He smiled, a boyish smile that revealed even white teeth. "Sorry. We've only just met and you may be meeting someone else for dinner. But I hope not."

She returned his smile. "I hadn't thought about dinner. I'm still trying to figure out if I can salvage my article. The Top of the Hub sounds lovely. I've never been there."

Oliver waved to Lori, told her to put both drinks on his tab and gave her a credit card. When Lori returned with the credit card slip, he signed it with a flourish and stood. "If you've never been to The Top of the Hub, we should stroll the Skywalk. Then we'll have a drink and, *voila*, it will be dinner time."

"Enchante, M'siur. Votre idée est tres bien."

He stared at her, clearly impressed. No, not impressed, captivated.

"You speak French," he said. "And with such a charming accent."

Be who they want you to be. She smiled, enjoying the moment, the thrill of seduction and the delicious anticipation of what might happen next.

"I lived in Paris for a while."

———

New Orleans

They zoomed at him like bubbles on a 3-D screen-saver, but they weren't bubbles, they were appalling images: the hole in Peterson's forehead; Corrine Peterson's tears when he asked how the kids were doing; Tex Conroy's grief-stricken mother; Morgan Vobitch, his eyes melancholy.

After he and Kelly made love he usually felt fantastic. Now his body was sated, but his mind was spinning like a cement mixer.

He had to find Natalie. But how?

"Hey, Spaceman," Kelly said. "What are you thinking about?"

"Thinking you're the best wench in the whole wide world."

"Well, I am enjoying my postcoital bliss, but now I'm hungry. Are you?"

"You always make me hungry." He kissed her lips. "Hungry for more."

"Same here, cowboy, but if I don't eat soon . . ."

"Want to go out?" He traced his fingers over her well-muscled stomach.

"Nah. I've got a barbequed chicken in the fridge."

"Should be plenty. We already had the main course."

She tousled his hair and gave his cheek a love-tap. "Hey, wise-ass, I'm a cop, remember? I know a deceptive statement when I hear one. You'll probably eat the whole chicken."

"I might. That'll give me plenty of energy for dessert. Round Two."

They got dressed and went in the kitchen. While he opened bottles of Bud Light, Kelly put the chicken in the oven. She looked gorgeous, white shorts contrasting with the tan on her long legs, legs that felt fantastic wrapped around him. Already he wanted dessert. His dark mood was gone. Goofing around with Kelly always made him feel better.

"Fill me in on the Peterson case," she said. "You know, the stuff you're not telling the media."

"Morgan likes the hit theory. Peterson's wife is one possibility."

"You think she hired someone to kill him?" Kelly asked, gazing at him, her sea-green eyes intent.

"Actually, I don't. She seems angry but beaten. She knew her husband was screwing around, but I don't think she'd hire someone to kill him. When I asked how the kids were doing, she started to cry. Man, I hate it when women cry. I never know what to say."

Kelly gazed at him, somber-eyed. "You knew what to say when I told you what happened to Terry."

"That was different. You lost your husband in a senseless accident, and he wasn't screwing around on you."

Her eyes got a faraway look in them. She shook her head, as though banishing a bad memory. "Peterson's assistant is another suspect?"

"Right. He's a self-important asshole, yap, yap, yap, like a little dog. I like big dogs. They give you a nice deep woof. All the little ones do is yap."

"Yeah, but the bigger they are, the more they eat."

When they began dating two years ago, she'd told him her husband used to bring stray dogs home. Too many, she'd said. A touchy subject. Time to lighten up. "Dogs are better than cats. When I interviewed Conroy's mother, I go in the house and this awful stench hits me. She must have two dozen cats. It was horrendous, fur balls on the floor, cat hairs on the furniture. I had to take my slacks to the cleaners."

"Must be an animal hoarder." Kelly went to the oven and took out the chicken and a foil-wrapped loaf of garlic bread. His stomach rumbled as delicious aromas filled the room.

"Let's eat in the living room. I've got a surprise for you. I had a copy made of the hotel security video."

"The mystery woman? Great! Go set it up. We can watch it while we eat." Kelly sipped her beer. "Did you see *Romeo Is Bleeding*?"

"I don't think so. What's it about?"

"Lena Olin plays a Russian assassin, outwits a bunch of Italian mobsters that put out a contract on her. She sleeps with the hitman and he falls for her."

"Hey, whadda you expect? Good-lookin broad like dat? Well-hung?" When Kelly rolled her eyes, he said, "When did this female assassin thing start? Kenyon and I were talking about *The Last Seduction*. I forget when it came out."

"Mid-nineties maybe? Did you see *Nikita*? Or the remake with Bridget Fonda, *Point of No Return*?"

"Nope. More female assassins, right? I better check them out."

"Frank," she said firmly, "go set up the video."

He took his briefcase in the living room. An Ansel Adams print hung on the wall above the sofa, a wide vista of snow covered mountains below a cloud-filled sky. Kelly said she attributed her success as a detective to her creative side. She'd said it as a joke, but he thought she was right. Sometimes you had to line up the facts in a creative way to solve a difficult case.

But creativity wasn't going to help him find Natalie Brixton.

He took the security video out of his briefcase, put it in the tape deck and turned on the TV. It was tuned to the Weather Channel and they were updating Hurricane Gail, which had strengthened to a Category-4. When the meteorologist put up the cone of possible land strikes, New Orleans was smack dab in the middle of it.

Kelly arrived with a tray of barbequed chicken, garlic bread and a dish of potato salad and set the tray on her coffee table. He gestured at the TV screen. "Morgan was right. If the mayor mandates an evacuation, forget the Peterson and Conroy murders. We'll all be pulling traffic duty."

"And that'll be a nightmare, four-hundred-thousand people trying to get out of town."

He sampled a chicken leg and the garlic bread while Kelly switched to the video. She handed him the clicker. "You know the parts to skip."

He fast-forwarded to where Peterson entered his room and hit Pause. "See the time stamp? Ten o'clock. The woman shows up ten minutes later." He fast-forwarded the tape until the door to the fire stairs opened and hit Pause. "Heeeeere's Johnny!"

Kelly laughed. "Frank, you are so bad." But when he hit Start, she leaned forward, gazing at the screen as the woman stepped into the hall. He let it run until the woman entered Peterson's room and hit Pause.

"You can't see her face at all," Kelly said. "The hat. The sunglasses."

"I figure she knew about the security camera, which means she was up to no good, and I'm not talking criminal solicitation."

But was it Natalie?

Kelly polished off a chicken wing while he forwarded the tape to where the woman came out of Peterson's room. He hit Play, let it roll until the woman disappeared into the stairwell and stopped the tape.

"No one else goes in the room until the security guard shows up."

"Can you roll it back to where she comes out of the room? I think I spotted something."

He rewound the tape and ran it again. The woman left the room and began walking toward the fire stairs. "There," Kelly said. "Stop the tape."

He hit Pause and the grainy image quivered on the screen.

"What? I don't see anything."

"See the inside of her left ankle? Looks like a tattoo near her ankle bone."

He squinted at the screen. "Man, how did you spot that? Kenyon and I watched this tape a half-dozen times and we didn't notice it."

"Of course not. You were too busy admiring her other endowments."

"Yeah. Well . . ." Maybe she was right. And maybe he didn't want to believe it was Natalie because he felt sorry for her. "It's too small to see what kind of tat it is."

"I bet if a crime lab tech enhanced it and blew it up, you'll could."

"Very good Detective O'Neil. Just for that, you get an extra-special treat tonight."

She made her eyes go wide, her lips twitching as she tried not to smile. "And what might my extra-special treat be, Detective Renzi?"

He grinned. "Round two in your bedroom. But I've got something else to show you first."

CHAPTER 12

He dug the Pecos High School yearbook out of his briefcase and showed her Natalie Brixton's photograph.

"Beautiful girl," Kelly said. "Exotic looking eyes, part Asian maybe."

"In 1988 her mother was murdered in New Orleans. Natalie was ten."

"Wow. She had a rough life, but you'd never know it from her picture. She seems very self-confident, smiling, looks right at the camera. You think she's the woman in the video?"

"Maybe." Everyone else seemed to think so, but he wasn't convinced. He flipped to the Drama Club page and showed her the photo of the dancers.

"She's tall, like the woman in the video," Kelly said. "Too bad you can't see her ankle. If she had a tat, it would clinch it."

"True, but nothing about this case is simple. I want to talk to the lead detective on the mother's murder case. Jane Fontenot. Vobitch knows her, but she retired last year. Unfortunately, when Vobitch called to set up a meet, he got a voicemail message saying she's in Africa. On safari."

"An adventurous woman."

"I wish she'd chosen some other time for an adventure. She won't be back till the twelfth of August."

"Bummer."

"I'll read the case file, see if anything leaps out at me. Call Ellen Brixton and Natalie's friend Gabe Rojas, too, and ask if Natalie had a tat on her ankle in high school." But would his two reluctant witnesses tell him?

"She doesn't look like a killer to me," Kelly said, "not in these pictures."

"No, she doesn't." Was that the problem? In the photograph she looked young and innocent, just another pretty teenager. Now she was thirty. Was she the woman on the security video? Was she a killer?

He tapped the motto below the picture. "Freedom and justice for all."

Kelly stared at him. "You think she killed Peterson because he killed her mother?"

"No. In 1988 Arnold Peterson was living in Chicago."

"So why would she kill him?"

"Good question. If I find her, I'll ask her. The DA leaned on Vobitch today, said he'd pull us off the case if we don't solve it soon. Vobitch wants me to bring her in, but nobody in Pecos knows where she is."

Except for Gabe Rojas, who claimed he didn't.

But he was pretty sure Rojas had stayed in touch with Natalie after she left Pecos. The week after she witnessed her cousin Randy fall off a cliff.

———

Boston

As they strolled around the Skywalk Observatory, Oliver laced his fingers in hers as though they were lovers. Maybe they would be. So far she liked everything about him: his rugged looks, his easy banter, his obvious intelligence. Did she dare to hope? It had been a long time since she'd enjoyed a lover with these qualities. Too long.

The Skywalk on the fiftieth floor of the Prudential Center offered breathtaking views of Boston. Oliver pointed out landmarks: the Charles River, Fenway Park, the Hatch Shell where the Boston Pops played on the Fourth of July for the fireworks.

When she said she'd seen this on television, he said, "Being there is better. If you're here next July, maybe we'll watch it together. Where do you live? You don't have an accent. Except for your delightful French."

The question caught her flat-footed. He knew her name, but she didn't want him knowing where she lived. "I grew up in the Midwest, but I live in upstate New York now." Lies, but she had driven through upstate New York and could talk intelligently about it if he asked. But he didn't.

On the north side of the Skywalk, he said, "On a clear day you can see New Hampshire from here. The border is only forty miles away."

She knew that. She lived there. But Oliver wanted to show off and play tour guide. *Be what he wants you to be. Make him feel important.*

When they entered the restaurant the Maitre-d greeted him by name. "Hello, Mr. James. Follow me."

Flanked by tall windows, their corner table included a stunning view of the sunset. They ordered drinks—another Manhattan for Oliver, a glass of red wine for her—and she sank back in her chair. This was much nicer than being home by herself. After the stress and anxiety in New Orleans, it felt wonderful to be able to relax and enjoy the company of an interesting man.

He sipped his Manhattan, set the long-stemmed glass on the white linen tablecloth and gazed at her. "Tell me more about your writing career, Robin. Did you go to journalism school?"

"No, but writing always came easily to me. My high school English teacher said I'd probably write a best-selling novel and become rich and famous." She shook her head and laughed. "Didn't happen. Where did you go to school?"

"I majored in business at Harvard, and art history." He grinned and tiny lines crinkled at corners of his eyes. "I couldn't decide what I wanted to be when I grew up."

"I still can't," she joked. He laughed and drew a "one" in the air.

Oliver James was exceedingly charming, a very attractive man. A bit like George Clooney without the gray hair. She was enjoying herself immensely. Dangerous. She had to keep her eyes on the prize. After all the suffering and heartache she had endured, nothing was going to prevent her from completing her mission. Two weeks from now she would appease the angry Ancestor gods and avenge her mother.

The waiter came and took their order and departed.

"What were you doing in Paris?" Oliver said.

Her heart jolted. How did he know? Then she remembered. She'd told him in the bar. "Studying art. Good thing I didn't give up my day job."

"What was your day job?"

She recited her usual story. "I clerked at Shakespeare's Bookstore. Back then my French was terrible, and mostly English speakers go there."

"An interesting shop. Smells musty though, all those books crammed floor to ceiling. Pity I didn't meet you then. We could have had fun in Paris."

"Yes. It's a beautiful city." A lump formed in her throat. She and Willem had enjoyed many wonderful times in Paris, until everything fell apart.

"We have remarkably similar interests. I gather art didn't turn out to be your calling?"

"No. After a year of lessons it was clear that I wasn't destined to be a famous artist, either. By then my French had improved, so I got a job waitressing at a nice restaurant."

"Which one?"

She waved her hand. "I doubt you'd know it. There are a million great restaurants in Paris." If you don't lie about details, you don't have to remember them later.

"How long did you live there?"

Why all the questions, she wondered. It was making her nervous.

"Five years." Five long years that ended in heartbreak, with many traumas along the way. "What sort of art dealer are you?"

He studied her for a moment, blank-faced, then sipped his Manhattan. The silence went on so long her antenna went up. Was he concocting a story? She knew the symptoms. She'd done it often enough herself.

At last he said, "I deal in antiquities."

"Interesting. I know nothing about ancient art. I like modern paintings. I love the Orsay Museum."

"So do I. Any favorite artists?"

"I love Manet, especially The Pfeiffer. You can almost hear the boy playing his little flute."

"The Olympia is my favorite. She looks so imperious, lying there naked, confronting the viewer."

Correct. Olympia lying there naked like the courtesan she was, accepting a bouquet from a client from a maid. She loved the painting too, but it hit too close to home. "Did you ever use your Harvard business degree?"

"Oh, I used it all right. Used it to make a lot of money."

She made her eyes go wide. "Really? How?"

"Remember the one-word answer Dustin Hoffman got in *The Graduate*?"

"Plastics." She'd watched the video three times. She loved Ann Bancroft.

"Correct. For me, it was stocks. Playing the market is risky. You can lose your shirt if you don't know what you're doing, and I didn't have a lot of shirt to lose. I made a fortune, but after a while I didn't find it very satisfying, so I got out and began dealing in European and African antiquities."

"That sounds complicated. Tell me about it."

"I got stiffed a few times at first. That's when I started tracking down people who deal in stolen art."

Tracking down people. A frisson of fear prickled her skin.

Oliver smiled his George Clooney smile. "Don't worry. I don't work for the feds. But I'll have to report the 10th-century Greek urn I saw today. Beautiful piece. Unfortunately, the provenance was an obvious fake."

She digested this as the waiter arrived and served their dinners. A moment ago, she'd been ravenous. Now, the odors wafting up from her plate nauseated her. Oliver James might not work for the feds, but it sounded like he had law enforcement connections. Her stomach cramped.

She picked up her fork and forced herself to eat, even managed to chatter about inconsequential topics. When she set her plate aside, Oliver said, "How were your scallops?" Gazing at her with his oh-so-seductive eyes.

"Delicious." Despite the tense knot in her stomach, she'd managed to eat most of them. She gestured at the window where the sun was a huge red ball hovering over the horizon. "And the view is spectacular."

"Gorgeous," he agreed. "What's your article about?"

Blindsided, she froze and her brain seized up. Unable to think of an answer, she joked, "About to go up in smoke if I don't find another expert to give me a quote."

He nodded and said nothing, gazing at her expectantly.

His question was perfectly legitimate, and she cursed herself for not preparing an answer. Then she remembered an article she'd seen in one of the newspapers at the library.

"It's about electric-powered cars and the problems owners might have recharging them. The expert that stood me up teaches at MIT." She flashed her charming smile. "But that's boring. Tell me more about your antiquities. I don't know much about early art, and I'd love to hear about it."

Be what they want you to be. Oliver James was a successful man who'd made a fortune, got bored and decided to do something he considered altruistic.

Nabbing crooked art dealers. She was playing with fire.

But taking risks were nothing new to her. Since her mother's murder twenty years ago, she had taken dozens of risks: in Pecos, New York, Paris, and most recently in New Orleans.

Oliver patted his lips with a napkin. "Most of what I do is rather boring, but when I get a hot tip, it gives me a rush." He grinned and the corners of his eyes crinkled. "The thrill of the hunt."

The thrill of the hunt. That she understood perfectly.

Under her prodding, he told her about other art objects he had acquired, ones that weren't fakes. And forgot about electric cars.

After the waiter cleared the table, Oliver leaned back in his chair, gazing at her. "Robin, I've enjoyed our time together more than I can say. I find most women boring, but you've had some interesting experiences."

You have no idea. "Thanks, but no more than you have."

"It strikes me that we're a lot alike. You hunt for experts to add authenticity to your articles. I hunt for art objects and authenticate them for myself or other buyers."

"The thrill of the hunt," she said, smiling at him.

"Exactly." Gazing at her with his sexy sky-blue eyes, a look that made her body tingle. "I'm staying in town tonight. Would you like to have a nightcap?"

He didn't say *in my room* but she knew that's what he meant. And she knew how to play the seduction game. First came the flirtation, then they tried to close the deal. And she knew the best response.

Never act eager. Make the man pursue you. The thrill of the hunt.

"This has been a wonderful evening, Oliver. I've enjoyed it tremendously, but I'm afraid I have to pass. I have an early appointment tomorrow."

She smiled to soften the rejection, a genuine smile. Her interest in Oliver James went far beyond simple attraction. It had been three years since she'd slept with a man she cared about.

He took out a business card and gave it to her. "The top number is my business phone, but my cell number is below it. I hope you'll call me the next time you're in town."

She put the card in her purse and pushed back her chair, a move that took considerable self-discipline. She wanted to go to bed with Oliver James. Every inch of her body yearned for it. But it wasn't going to happen tonight.

She had to keep her eyes on the prize.

Tomorrow she had to buy a gun.

Natalie

1998

Before I could work for The Service, I had to take some blood tests, including one for AIDS, and a physical. Lin said he was sure everything would be fine. The week before Christmas, I took the exam and the tests.

Three days after New Years Lin called my cell. "Our limo will pick you up tomorrow at noon. Tell the Platinum-Plus club you're moving out of state, pack your things and say goodbye to your boyfriend."

I'd told Lin about Darren, but I wasn't going to tell Darren anything. The next day after he went to work I wrote him a note. *Dear Darren, I have to go to Iowa. Big medical emergency in my family! Love, Jennifer XOXO.*

Then I called Val and thanked her for being such a great friend. I said I'd found a new job in California and wouldn't be seeing her for a while.

Probably never, but I didn't say this.

Val said: *You're so talented, Jennifer. I wish you the best. Keep in touch.*

The limo drove me up along the Hudson River to a secluded estate near Tenafly. At the end of a long winding road lined with fir trees, we stopped under the portico of a big three-story mansion. Lin opened my door and said with a big smile, "Welcome to The Service. Let's go over some details."

The Service would pay me $500 a week for my training. "When we think you're ready," Lin said, "you'll fly to Paris for more training. You can brush up on your French, Laura." He handed me a New York state driver's license with my photo on it. The name on the license was Laura Lin Hawthorn.

"Laura Lin is the name you will use with your clients. Lin is my brand name for the girls I recruit. Clients know they will have a satisfying girlfriend experience with my girls. Never give them your last name."

I nodded. Changing names was nothing new for me.

"I need your old identification papers." He held out his hand and waited while I took out my driver's license and Social Security card. "And your cell phone, please. I have a new one for you."

So I gave him my cell. In a way, that was a relief. I didn't want Darren or Val calling me. If they did, I'd have to lie and make up a story. Now I would have a new cell with a new number. And a new name.

Laura Lin Hawthorn. I liked it. Laura Lin, to my clients.

Then Lin took me to meet Madame Romanov, a petite woman with raven-black hair, ivory skin, small dark eyes and thin lips slathered with crimson lipstick. She reminded me of Ann Bancroft in *Point of No Return*. But I wasn't going to Paris to kill anyone. I was going to be their girlfriend.

Later when I asked Lin if Madame Romanov was from Russia, he said, "She would like everyone to think so." He was wearing smoke-tinted glasses. I never saw him without them, indoors or out. I could barely see his eyes. I wondered if he was trying to hide his Asian heritage, but I didn't ask. Maybe he was from Russia. I didn't ask about that, either.

Madame—that's what I always called her—gave me a list of what I would learn. Her haughty manner made me anxious at first, but she was extravagant with her praise when I got something right. My makeover began with the beauty stylist. Ellen raved about my long glossy-black hair. After she trimmed it to shoulder length, she said, "You have beautiful eyes, Laura. Sometimes you may want to downplay the Asian look. Other times you may want to enhance it." She showed me how to do this with makeup.

Next came lessons in table manners and proper etiquette while eating and drinking. I was already way ahead of Bridget Fonda in *Point of No Return*. I didn't chew with my mouth open, and I knew about place settings and wine glasses from working at Longhorn Jack's. Even so, I learned a lot about fine wines and which ones went best with certain meals.

Then came lessons on how to walk gracefully. That was easy. Even in my six-inch spike heels I could walk with confidence. Madame was impressed. By then I was starting my third week of girlfriend training. For two days, Madame quizzed me on current events. Thanks to my Dedication to Study, I did very well. I still read a newspaper every day and surfed the Internet, which was great for breaking news and politics.

But Madame said I was weak on sports. The only teams I knew about were in New York. She told me to always study the sports pages. "Even cultured men are gaga about sports," Madame said.

I had to use all my willpower not to laugh when she said *gaga*. I was certain this word did not come easily to her. But Madame prided herself on being *au courant* with slang.

Then she sent me to a young woman with stunning green eyes and a radiant smile. Lisa asked what my sex preferences were. I wasn't expecting that! Lisa said The Service wanted a list of what I would and would not do with clients. Her questions were very specific. I said I wanted nothing to do with whips and chains or bondage, threesomes or anal penetration. Then Lisa showed me how to fake an orgasm. At first I didn't know what she meant. I had never had an orgasm. But thanks to my acting skills, I caught on fast.

In my free time I read newspapers and magazines, watched TV and used my laptop to surf the Internet. For my fourth week Madame sent me to the gym. Mr. Takagi, the instructor, was taller than most Japanese men, six feet at least. He had shiny black hair and appeared very fit in his shorts and T-shirt.

He led me to a padded mat and positioned me opposite him.

"What will you do if a client asks you to do something you do not want to do?" he asked, and grabbed my shoulders with both hands. Without thinking, I elbowed him hard in the ribs, spun away, did a taekwondo spin move, kicked him in the chest and knocked him on his ass.

I thought he'd be angry, but when he rose to his feet he was smiling.

"Which *dan* have you achieved in taekwondo?"

"First *geup*," I said proudly. "My teacher in Texas was a fifth-*dan*."

Mr. Takagi made a nice face to show he was impressed. Politeness is very important in Asian cultures. "You have mastered your spin and kick moves very well. Did your teacher also show you breaking and jumping techniques?"

"Yes, and falls for self-defense." I didn't mention the pressure points Mr. Carlson showed me. Or my TKD oath: *I shall be a champion of freedom and justice.* Sometimes it's best to keep certain things to yourself.

Mr. Takagi bowed and said, "You do not need any further instruction from me. I will tell Madame that you have passed the physical training. If you would like to work out in the gym, I will leave a note at the desk that will admit you whenever you'd like."

The next morning Lin called me to his office. When I got there he smiled and said, "Your flight to Paris leaves JFK tomorrow at noon. Take only a few belongings and clothes. We will help you buy whatever else you need in Paris. I'm very pleased with your progress, Laura."

His compliment barely registered. *Your flight to Paris leaves tomorrow.* I used my TKD focus to keep my face blank, but my heart was hammering my chest.

He gave me a U.S. passport with Laura Lin Hawthorn's name and my photograph. I thanked him and left the office in total panic. Tomorrow I would fly to Paris, but I had to make an important phone call. I had been meaning to do this, but I was too scared. Now I didn't have a choice.

In my room I called the New Orleans Police Department, not 911, the main number. My stomach felt like snakes were crawling around in it. When a male voice answered, I said I wanted to speak to someone about a cold case. I knew the lingo from watching the cop shows on TV.

He asked what type of case and when was it.

"A murder," I said, "on October twenty, 1988."

He put me on hold and transferred me to Homicide. My insides were shaking. Mom had been waiting almost ten years for me to avenge her, and I hadn't made much progress. That made me feel ashamed.

A new male voice said, "Homicide, Sergeant Daily."

When I told him what I'd told the first man, he said, "Hold on while I look it up on the computer."

He sounded bored, like people got murdered everyday and it was no big deal. More waiting. More heart pounding. My hand was sweaty on the phone.

"Okay," Sergeant Daily said, "I found the case file. The lead detective was Jane Fontenot, but she doesn't work homicide anymore, she's in Sex Crimes. I think she's working today, let me transfer you."

I cringed. Sex crimes? Is that what they thought Mom's murder was?

The phone beeped a few times and a woman's voice said, "Lieutenant Fontenot."

I was so flustered I couldn't speak.

"Hello? Sergeant Daily said you had a question about a cold case?"

"Yes. About the Jeannette Brixton murder, October eighth, 1988."

After a short silence Lieutenant Fontenot said, "Who are you?"

I could hardly breathe. I spoke the first name that came into my head. "Mary Brown. I'm calling on behalf of Natalie Brixton, Jeannette's daughter."

"Natalie. How's she doing? She must be all grown up now."

Her voice sounded warm, like maybe she cared about me. Then I realized she was the woman who came to the apartment that day, the most terrible day of my life. I couldn't remember what she looked like. All I remembered was the horrible sick feeling inside me when she told me Mom was dead.

"Natalie's fine," I said. "She asked me to call because she's in Australia and calls from there are expensive."

"Uh-huh. And what did you want to know?"

"Um, Natalie wants to know if you have any leads."

"Okay, you'll have to bear with me, because I'm not working Homicide anymore, I'm in Sex Crimes. And it's been a few years—"

"Almost ten," I said. "Ten years in October."

"Right. I don't have the file in front of me but as I recall we got no forensic evidence from the body, no DNA, no semen on or inside the body." She cleared her throat. "Sorry, but some of this is, uh, rather unpleasant. We collected some fibers from the room, but we never found a match. We didn't have much to go on. No one saw anyone go into the room. Or leave it."

"Does that mean you never had any suspects?"

"We had the names of men known to frequent that particular hotel for, uh, sexual encounters with women. I interviewed them and got nowhere."

I wanted to scream. Ten years, and this was all I was going to get? Mom had died a violent death. I *had* to find her killer and punish him. My

Vietnamese heritage required it. If I didn't, Mom's angry ancestor spirits would haunt me forever and bring me great misfortune.

"Please," I said. My voice was shaking, but I couldn't help it. "Can you give me the names of the men you checked out?"

"Sweetheart, I can't give out names to a voice on the phone. If you came to New Orleans—"

"I can't come to New Orleans."

"Okay. Tell Natalie . . ." Long pause, then a heavy sigh. "Tell Natalie I had a gut feeling about one guy, but his wife said he was with her that night. I didn't believe her, but--"

"Why didn't you arrest him?"

"Because he's a very powerful man, and if I arrested him and couldn't make the murder charge stick my boss would sent me to Siberia."

A powerful man. That was one clue. "Can you tell me his name?"

"No, I can't."

I wanted to kill her. "Can you tell me why he was so powerful?"

"Let's just say he had plenty of clout then, and he's got even more now."

Another clue. The man was still alive. "How did he kill her?"

"I don't think Natalie needs to know that."

Yes, I did.

"You can tell me," I said. "If it's too awful, I won't tell Natalie."

There was a long pause. Finally she said, "He hit her with something. The coroner said it might have been a flatiron, but we didn't find one in the room." Another pause. "The cause of death was manual strangulation."

My stomach heaved. The monster had strangled Mom.

I swallowed the bile that rose in my throat and said, "Okay."

But it wasn't okay, it was horrible.

"Does this man still live in New Orleans?"

"Honey, this guy ain't going nowhere. Men like him don't leave town, they just grab more power. He's a wealthy bigshot with powerful friends."

"How did he get to be so powerful?"

"The same way all these muttonheads get power. Make big bucks, spread it around and collect powerful friends. I'm sorry I can't help you, sweetheart. When you talk to Natalie, give her my regards and tell her I'm sorry we couldn't close the case."

I thanked her and hung up. The familiar iceberg invaded my gut.

A vile monster had murdered my mother. A despicable man, a wealthy man with powerful friends. And a wife to give him an alibi.

Not much, but it was a start.

CHAPTER 13

Wednesday July 30, 2008 Nashua, N.H.

To prepare for the gun buy she put on a beige linen suit, pulled her long dark hair into a ponytail and left her second-floor apartment. *Look professional but non-threatening.* The way to her car went past the swimming pool. Her next door neighbor, a public school teacher with wiry chest hair and a flabby white belly, lay on a plastic chaise beside the pool, soaking up the sun.

"Hi Robin," he said. "Going to work?"

"Yes," she said, smiling as she passed him. "You do what you gotta do."

George owned the unit next to hers. The day she moved in he'd offered to help her. She thanked him and declined. The less people knew about Robin Adair the better. Whenever she encountered other residents, she smiled and spoke but otherwise kept to herself.

She got into her Honda Civic. To ward off the glare of the midday sun, she put on her Raybans, got on the Interstate and settled in for the half-hour drive. The gun shop in Hookset was twenty-five miles away.

Three years ago when she returned from Paris she had chosen not to live in New York. She didn't want to run into anyone from her previous life: Val or Darren or men who'd frequented Cheetahs or the Platinum-Plus Club. Or her father. But after five years in Paris, she didn't want to live in a little hick town.

Boston had great cultural offerings and sky-high rents to match. Then she found a listing for a rental in Nashua, New Hampshire. Nashua was only fifty miles from Boston. The state motto clinched her decision. *Live free or die.*

Perfect. It was on the license plate of her car, registered to Robin Adair.

As the Honda ate up the miles, her mind flirted with Oliver James.

She couldn't stop thinking about him. His good looks, intelligence and charm entranced her. The attraction appeared to be mutual. He had asked her to call him. Maybe she would. But she couldn't allow Oliver to divert her from her goal. Mom had been waiting too long.

She left the Interstate at Exit 11, paid the toll and drove to the gun shop. According to the website, Gerry's Sport Shop sold firearms, ammunition and

101

accessories of all kinds. The store had 1500 new and used guns in stock, and a wheelchair ramp for the disabled. She didn't expect any problems. Buying a .38 Special at the gun show in Nashua last year had been easy. Anyone over twenty-one could buy a handgun in New Hampshire, as long as they hadn't been convicted of felony or a crime of domestic violence. That let her out.

A mile down the road she pulled into a gravel parking lot in front of a one-story building with rustic redwood siding. Gerry's Sport Shop looked like a well-fortified log cabin. Iron bars protected two small windows. A wheelchair ramp led to the front door. She parked several yards away from a battered green SUV. The only other vehicle, a Ford-250 pickup with Harley-Davidson decals on the rear window, stood at the rear of the store, shaded by pine trees. The owner's truck, she assumed.

A bell dinged as she entered the store. The odor of gun oil permeated the shop. Twenty feet ahead of her, a man with an eye patch stood behind a waist-high counter talking to a customer in a red-plaid shirt. Behind the counter, floor-to-ceiling cubbies held boxes of ammunition. Engrossed in conversation, the men ignored her. Good. She'd make her move after the buyer left the store. The fewer witnesses the better.

Along the wall to her right, rifles and shotguns stood butt down in wooden racks, their muzzles resting in grooves to separate them. She went to a six-foot-long glass display case on the opposite wall and pretended to look at the handguns with red price tags dangling from their triggers.

Ten minutes later, the man in the plaid shirt left with a double-barreled shotgun and two boxes of ammunition.

"Help you with something, Missy?" called the owner.

She went to the counter. The man stank of cigarette smoke, and a black patch covered his left eye. "I'd like to buy a handgun."

"You licensed to drive in this state?" he asked, glowering at her as if she were a criminal.

"Yes."

He held out his hand. "Lemme see it."

She took it out of her wallet, conscious of his breathing, sucking air through the dark hairs sprouting from his nostrils. He held the license close to his good eye, frowning as he examined it. "Okay, DOB makes you over twenty-one so we got that over with. Ever been convicted of a felony?"

"No." Going for some humor, she added, "Never been convicted of a domestic violence charge, either."

"Men ain't the only ones beat on their spouses, Missy! Women do, too."

So much for humor. "I'd like to buy a handgun—"

"Hold it." His visible eye bored into her like a laser beam from hell. "No use telling me what ya want till I check to see if I can sell it to ya. State law requires me to do a background check. Hold on while I go out back. Don't touch nothing while I'm gone. I got video cameras all over the store."

The comment hit her like a shotgun blast. Video cameras recording her face, clearly visible with her hair pulled back in a ponytail.

"You don't behave, Beauty'll take care of ya, ain't that right, Beauty?"

A low menacing rumble made her neck hairs stand up.

A huge German shepherd rose to its feet behind the counter, fixed its yellow eyes on her and drew back its lips in a snarl.

She tried to swallow. Couldn't. Her mouth felt like sawdust.

The owner smiled, revealing pointy yellow teeth. "Beauty won't do you no harm, long as you don't touch nothing." He opened a reinforced steel door beside the counter and disappeared.

Her heart pounded so hard she feared the dog would hear it and attack her. Dogs could smell fear. She took a series of deep breaths, trying to calm her racing heart. Hoping to hide her face from the security camera, she slowly squatted--no sudden moves--and pretended to look at the hunting knives in the display case below the counter.

A menacing rumble came from the dog. Her legs trembled. Using every ounce of her willpower, she maintained her squat. But why bother? If a security camera was behind the counter, it had already recorded her face. Her mind scrabbled for a solution. But how could she think when every fiber of her being was focused on the dog? And what it might do to her. With people, she felt confident that her taekwondo moves would save her in dangerous situations, but they would be useless against a trained attack dog.

Beauty's sharp fangs and menacing snarl effectively imprisoned her.

Extending her arm to expose the wristwatch under the sleeve of her jacket, she checked the time. What was taking so long? What was he doing back there? Where was the security camera? Correction. Cameras. The store probably had several. She cursed her stupidity. Fearing she might look suspicious, she had left her Raybans in the car.

Two endless minutes passed. She imagined the dog's powerful jaws clamped on her arm, fangs piercing the skin, imagined those fangs at her throat, imagined blood spurting on the floor. Her leg muscles ached. Tucking her chin to her chest, she eased to her feet. Flexed her shaky legs.

Another menacing snarl. The dog impaled her with its baleful yellow eyes.

She was desperate to leave but too afraid to move. If she did, the dog might attack. And the owner had taken her driver's license. Panic sat on her chest like a rhinoceros. Fearing she would vomit, she swallowed the bile that rose in her throat.

Another agonizing minute passed. Finally, clutching her license in his ham-like fist, One-Eye returned and trained his good eye on her. "You bought a handgun at a gun show in Nashua last year. What happened to that one?"

"My boyfriend stole it."

"Yeah," he snorted, "and my mother's the Queen of England." Picking up on his belligerent tone, the dog resumed its menacing low-throated rumble.

"He did! Last week we had an argument and the next day while I was at work he stole my gun. I'm afraid he'll come back and kill me!" She didn't have to feign fear. Her chest felt like a gigantic hand was squeezing it.

"He live with you?" One-Eye ostentatiously examined her license and said, "Robin."

"No, but he has a key. I changed the locks, but I'm afraid he'll come back and break down the door."

"You got a license to carry?"

"No." New Hampshire gun owners weren't required to register them, but anyone intending to conceal a loaded gun on their person or in a vehicle needed a license to carry. This year she'd done both, *without* a license to carry, and she had no intention of applying for one. To get it, she would have to submit an application to the police. No way was she giving information about Robin Adair to the cops.

"You know how to shoot?" One-Eye asked, curling his lip in a sneer.

I can shoot well enough to kill someone and you might be next.

"I go to a gun range once a week."

"What kinda gun you lookin to buy?"

"A .38 Special, like the one my boyfriend stole. I've still got ammo for it."

His implacable one-eyed stare bored into her. The silence lengthened.

She wanted to kill him, might have if she'd had a gun in her hand. But then the dog would attack, and she would have to kill it, a serious violation of her Veneration of Nature code.

A fulminating fury rose inside her. There were other places to buy a gun.

"Give me my license. If you don't want to sell me a gun, I'll go somewhere else."

"Heh, heh, heh," One-Eye chuckled, showing his pointy yellow teeth. "Don't get excited. I got just the gun you want right over here. Beauty, stay!"

The dog sat, eyeing her with its menacing yellow eyes. The owner went to the glass case with the handguns, unlocked it and took out a .38 Special. Ten minutes later she left the stop minus four-hundred dollars and a thirteen-ounce Smith & Wesson 637 Airweight .38 Special with a stubby barrel in her handbag. Unloaded. She didn't need more ammunition. The box in her apartment was almost full and it would only take one bullet to kill her target.

———

New Orleans

Seated at his desk in the Homicide office, Frank opened the case file on Jeanette Brixton. Murdered October 20, 1988. The crime scene photos were brutal, blood-matted hair, gobs of blood on her face, her lips pulled back in a grimace, her eyes bulging. Even so, she clearly attractive.

He wished she was still alive so he could talk to her. What had driven her to become a prostitute? Was that the only way she could support herself and her daughter? Did she take Natalie out for ice cream, take her to movies? Did Natalie know her mother was a prostitute? He hated to judge the woman, but couldn't she have found another way to support herself? Apparently not. And even if Jeanette Brixton was a prostitute, she didn't deserve to be murdered.

He skimmed the autopsy report. Cause of death: manual strangulation. Deep bruises but no identifiable prints on her neck. He flipped pages, searching for Jane Fontenot's notes. Most cold case files contained the lead detective's notes, but not this one. Nothing to indicate what Jane's take on the case was. Another dead end. He slammed the folder down on his desk.

Jane wouldn't be back from Africa until August 12th. Today was July 30.

Thirteen days. An eternity. He didn't know if there was a connection between the death of Jeanette Brixton in 1988 and the murders of Arnold Peterson and Tex Conroy last week, but one thing was certain.

The pressure to solve those cases would only get worse.

———

Portsmouth, NH   6:45 PM

Still shaken by her experience at the gun shop, she sought solace at The Press Room, a popular hangout in downtown Portsmouth. She slid onto a bar stool and the bartender came over, mid-twenties and energetic with a full dark beard and a friendly smile. "Hi! What can I get for you?"

"A glass of your house red, please. Will there be live jazz tonight?"

"Not tonight, but we got a great sound system. That's McCoy Tyner playing now." Moving with practiced speed, he grabbed a bottle, poured wine in a glass and set it in front of her. "Want to run a tab?"

"No, thanks. I'll just have one glass." She'd been desperate for some live jazz to calm her nerves after her ordeal with One-Eye. A McCoy Tyner CD playing on a sound system wasn't the same.

"Suit yourself." He set the tab in front of her and moved down the bar to chat with two college students in T-shirts with UNH stenciled on them.

She took a sip of wine. Not bad, but nothing like the wines she was accustomed to in Paris. She set the glass on the cocktail napkin, pleased that her hand wasn't trembling. Her legs no longer felt weak and rubbery either, but she was still cursing her stupidity. Why hadn't she disguised her face?

But last year when she'd bought the gun at a Nashua gun show, there were hundreds of people milling around. No attack dogs, no security cameras. And breaking into Gerry's Sport Shop to steal the videotapes wasn't an option. Before she left, One-Eye had said: "Beauty sleeps here. Anybody breaks in they'll get their throat ripped out."

Badly-shaken by Beauty's ferocious snarl, sharp fangs and menacing eyes, she had driven to Hampton Beach, seeking solace from the sea. The beach was jammed, sun-lovers of all ages enjoying the fine summer day, frolicking in the surf. The ocean breeze and the salt water scent had soothed her.

But the razor-sharp pains in her gut had returned.

One-Eye knew she'd bought a gun in Nashua last year, which meant there was a record of it. And by now the NOPD would know that Tex and Arnold Peterson were shot with the same gun. She'd dumped that gun in Lake Pontchartrain, but what if Beady-Eyes found it? And this morning Hurricane Gail had dominated the news on NOLA.com. Another worry.

She flinched as "Agitation" came over the sound system, Miles Davis spewing notes into the stratosphere. She knew it well. Willem adored Miles, saying he was a musical magician. Willem wove his own brand of magic.

On the verge of weeping, she massaged her temples and assessed the damages. Robin Adair's face captured on a security video while buying a gun, but so what? One-Eye probably recycled the tapes. Next week her face would be replaced by someone else's. Even if he saved all the tapes, why would anyone look for her in a gun shop in Hookset, New Hampshire?

The bartender interrupted her litany of worries. "How's the wine? Would you like another glass?"

Startled, she saw that her glass was almost empty. "No, thanks." She paid the tab and surveyed the room. The bar was far more crowded now than before. A slow-burn of acid churned her stomach. The gun buy had gone badly because of her sloppy preparation. From now on, she would take more care with her research and stay aware of her surroundings.

From now on, she would.

Music sabotaged her resolve. Miles Davis playing "The Maids of Cadiz."

The haunting ballad brought tears to her eyes. And memories of Willem. She pictured his craggy face. They could have been so happy. Unwilling to cry, she dug her nails into her palms. She had shed too many tears over Willem. And this was no time to think about the past. She had to focus on her target.

She left the Press Room and went to her car. The air smelled fresh and clean, and the .38 Special was locked in the trunk. She had bought it for one purpose. To avenge her mother. Three weeks from now she would.

Then she could get on with her life.

Memories of Oliver swirled in her mind like wisps of smoke: his sexy smile, his seductive blue eyes, his intoxicating scent. She got in the Honda and took out his card and punched his number into her cell. After one ring he answered in his sexy low-pitched voice.

"Hi Oliver, this is Robin Adair."

"Robin! I'm so glad you called. Are you in Boston?"

"No, Portsmouth, New Hampshire, staying with friends."

"Any chance you can come to Boston Friday so we can have dinner?"

Her body tingled, a delicious hint of sexual arousal to come.

"I think that could be arranged."

CHAPTER 14

Friday, 1 August

"Sorry I didn't have these for you sooner," Monica said, brushing frizzy carrot-colored hair away from her face. "It's the hurricane. Three of my clients called yesterday wanting to pick up their orders early."

Cursing the hurricane, Frank nodded, as though it wasn't a big deal, but Vobitch was pissed. He'd wanted to publish them yesterday. "It's only two o'clock and the traffic's already crazy. The gas stations are mobbed, everybody topping off in case the mayor orders an evacuation."

"The supermarkets are worse. Everyone's stocking up on bottled water and non-perishable food. Even if there's an evacuation a lot of people won't leave. They'll just hunker down and ride it out."

The odor of printer's ink and paste-up glue filled Monica's first-floor studio. She was the graphic artist NOPD hired to do their composite sketches. Her shop was on Frenchman Street near the French Quarter.

"How about you? Are you leaving?"

"I doubt it. This place is on fairly high ground. I don't want looters to come in and trash the place." She went to a gun-metal gray desk in the corner, opened a folder and showed him a computer printout.

He studied the sketch. It was based on Natalie Brixton's yearbook photo but altered to what she might look like at age thirty. Monica had made her face thinner to highlight her well-defined cheekbones and altered her mouth. Unlike the photo, Natalie wasn't smiling. The image was striking.

"Great job." He'd love to compare it to the video. But the hat brim and dark glasses had hidden the woman's face.

Monica gave him another sketch. "I did a three-quarter view to show her profile."

"Excellent!" Natalie's chiseled jaw and slender nose were clearly visible.

"I did another one," she said, hesitantly handing him another printout. "I don't know if you'll like it."

He stared at it, amazed. Monica had added sunglasses to the first likeness. Now it looked eerily like the woman in the video. He'd shown Monica a still from it but warned her not to talk about it. Over the years, he'd found her to be trustworthy. He hadn't said where he got the still, but Monica watched TV and read the newspaper. She knew he was working the Peterson case.

"This is perfect!" he said. "Great idea."

Monica beamed. "That's what my clients pay me for, Frank. Great ideas."

"You got an invoice? I want to get these on the early news."

"I only put two on the invoice. I wasn't sure you'd want the other one."

"I want it. Can you print an invoice for all three?"

"Sure." She sat down at her computer and got to work.

While she redid the invoice he wandered the shop. Colorful brochures, company logos, letterheads and poster board signs hung on the walls. One had a red arrow at the top pointed both left and right. Below it, red letters said: **Parking for Italians Only**. He'd seen such signs in Boston's North End, an Italian neighborhood where old women sat on stoops chattering in Italian and white-haired men played bocce in Paul Revere Park. The mobsters hung out at Café Pompeii, plotting dirty deeds over cups of espresso. But most of them were in jail now, and gentrification had brought more affluent residents.

Monica gave him the invoice. He thanked her, went out to his car and called Vobitch. "I just picked up three sketches from Monica. They're great."

"About time," Vobitch growled. "This fuckin hurricane is headed right at us. Bring 'em in so I can fax 'em to the TV stations."

"You think the mayor will order an evacuation?"

"Hell if I know. The TV stations are running a crawl line about the mayor's news conference at three. If he mandates an evacuation, the sketches won't be worth shit. Only thing you'll see on TV will be the mayor and live shots of stalled traffic on the Interstate. Even if they run the sketch, nobody'll see it. Most people have already left."

Frank said nothing. Vobitch was right. In this town, a hurricane in the Gulf trumped everything, including VIP murders, pit-bull politicians and asshole DA's like Roger Demaris.

———

For her Friday night date with Oliver she wore her favorite silk dress, an Yves St. Laurent with a long skirt, boat neckline and red dragons on a black background. She had banished her worries, for the moment at least.

Time to relax and have fun with an attractive man.

He took her to Ristorante Abate, an Italian restaurant in Boston's North End. When they arrived at seven, the Maître d' greeted Oliver by name and said he had a superb table for two on the second floor.

Beyond the foyer, a well-dressed couple sat at a bar watching a national weather report. On the screen Hurricane Gail was a huge orange swirl in the

Gulf heading for New Orleans. Pretending to adjust the strap on her shoe, she read the crawl line at the bottom of the screen: the New Orleans mayor had ordered a mandatory evacuation. She straightened and smiled at Oliver, but the news dampened her mood. If New Orleans took a major hit from Hurricane Gail, the city might not get back to normal for weeks.

But she'd worry about that tomorrow, along with all the other things she had to worry about.

Their table had a fabulous view of Boston harbor and twinkling lights on buildings along the waterfront. Once they ordered their drinks—a Manhattan for Oliver, red wine for her—she stopped fretting about the hurricane. She wanted to enjoy the company of a man she found enormously attractive. Tonight Oliver had on a charcoal-gray Armani suit—she'd know that tailoring anywhere—and a pastel-blue shirt that favored his sky-blue eyes. He sipped his Manhattan and smiled. "Have you ever been in a hurricane?"

Sometimes it seemed like he could read her mind. Dangerous.

"No, have you?"

"Yes. When you hear about 150-mile-an-hour winds on TV, it's just a number, but it's downright terrifying when you're in the middle of it."

"When was this?"

"Years ago, in Barbados."

"What were you doing in Barbados?"

He did his George Clooney bit, leaning forward and giving her a sexy smile, his eyes crinkling at the corners.

"If I told you," he said quietly, "I'd have to kill you."

She laughed dutifully, but his comment scared her. He'd said it as a joke, but it might have been a ploy to avoid answering her. She did that sometimes when she didn't want to answer inconvenient questions.

"I lived in New Orleans as a kid, but I don't remember any hurricanes." Back then hurricanes had been the least of her problems.

"Really?" Oliver said. "I thought you grew up in the Midwest."

She sipped her wine, buying time to concoct an answer. Why did she say she'd lived in New Orleans? Because for the first time in weeks she was having fun. From now on, she'd think before she opened her mouth.

She was saved by their waiter, who recited the specials.

"I recommend the Zuppetta di Cozzi for the first course," Oliver said. "Sautéed mussels in a garlic and tomato broth. It's a delicious."

"That sounds wonderful. I love mussels."

The waiter wrote down their order. While Oliver chose a bottle of wine she glanced around Ristorante Abate. An intimate restaurant, one suited for romance, not business discussions. She wondered when he'd been here, and with whom. A woman, probably.

After the waiter left, Oliver said, "You were about to tell me about where you grew up. New Orleans and then the Midwest? Whereabouts?"

In addition to charm and intelligence, Oliver had an excellent memory. She cursed herself for mentioning the Midwest. She'd never been there.

"We moved around a lot. One little Midwestern town looks pretty much like another. Where did you grow up?"

He said nothing for a moment. At last he said, "Connecticut until I was ten. Then we moved to Washington, D.C. My father was a low-level diplomat in the Foreign Service."

"That must have been interesting. Did you travel abroad?"

"No. I didn't get to Paris until after I graduated from college. Where did you go to college?" He sipped his Manhattan and looked at her expectantly.

Her hands dampened with sweat. All these questions about her past were unnerving. "I didn't," she said, truthfully. "My parents had no money. I took a few courses here and there at community colleges. None that you've ever heard of, I'm sure."

"Where did your parents come from?" he asked, smiling at her.

Another question she wasn't prepared to answer.

Again the waiter saved her. After putting a basket of garlic bread on their linen-draped table, he set tureens of steaming soup in front of them. The spicy aroma made her mouth water. The waiter opened their wine and poured a sample for Oliver, who nodded. The waiter filled their glasses and left.

Oliver gestured at her Zuppetta di Cozzi. "I hope you like it."

"I'm sure I will. It smells fabulous."

For a time they were silent, enjoying the soup and the warm buttery garlic bread. Finally, Oliver said, "Seen any good films lately? I'm a big movie fan."

Movies? She'd been far too busy to see movies. She couldn't even think of a current title. "Not lately. I used to, but now that I'm busy writing . . ."

"Let's compare favorites. What's yours?"

At last, an easy question. "I loved *The Full Monty*."

"Hmm. I didn't see that one. What's it about?"

"A bunch of unemployed Brits are desperate for money." She laughed. "So they go and stand in the unemployment line buck naked."

"Sounds hilarious. Where'd you see it?"

"I forget." Next he'd ask who she'd seen it with. That reminded her of Darren and another film they'd seen together. "I liked *L.A. Confidential*, too."

"Yes. Kim Basinger was great, but I hated the Hedy Lamar look. Sad movie."

You have no idea how sad it is to be a prostitute.

"What's your favorite?" she asked. Make him talk about himself and stop asking questions. But before he could answer, the waiter came to clear their first course. After he swept crumbs off the tablecloth and left, Oliver said, "Last week in New York I saw *The Departed*. I love Scorsese films."

"Me too," she said. "I loved *Goodfellas* and the *Cape Fear* remake."

"You must be into crime," Oliver said.

Another disturbing statement. He smiled, his eyes dancing with mischief. She decided he was joking. "Isn't everyone? Crime *films*, I mean."

He nodded but his smile was gone. "You're very feminine, Robin, but you have an aura of toughness about you. Where did that come from, I wonder?"

And you'll have to keep wondering. She launched into a story about her visit to Monet's house in Giverny outside Paris, describing the magnificent gardens. That led to a discussion about art and painting that continued throughout dinner. When they finished, Oliver said, "Would you like dessert?"

"No thanks. Everything was delicious, but I couldn't eat another thing."

"Good. I was hoping we'd go to my hotel room." Gazing into her eyes, he caressed her hand. "I want to make love to you."

———

Two hours later she lay beside him in his king-sized bed, lulled into satisfied stillness by his lovemaking. Oliver's foreplay, by turns tender and passionate, had brought her to a shuddering climax. Not only was he an intelligent man and a fine conversationalist, he was a marvelous lover. Her best ever, except for Willem. She wasn't in love with Oliver, but this had been a wonderful evening, one she desperately needed. For a few hours, she'd been able to relax and forget the heavy burden of responsibility she carried.

He rolled onto his side and caressed her cheek. "You're an amazing woman, Robin. I can't imagine why some guy hasn't married you so he can have you all to himself."

"I could say the same about you. You're not married, are you?" After this delightful evening, she didn't want to find out he was married. Over the past ten years, she'd met enough married men to last a lifetime.

"No, I'm not married. Never got around to it. And you?"

"Same here. I'm still trying to figure out what I'm going to be when I grow up, remember?"

"I remember everything about you, Robin. It's been ages since I felt this comfortable with a woman. Would you like a drink of water?"

"That would be perfect."

He went to an alcove where the bathroom was located. Naked, he looked even better than he did in a suit, his body trim and muscular. Moments later she heard the toilet flush. He returned to the bed with two glasses of water. They drank deeply. Then Oliver lay down beside her and pulled her close.

"Tell me about your parents. Are they still living?"

Why did he have to spoil things with all these questions? Questions that brought back bitter memories, long-ago traumas and more recent ones. She caressed his wiry chest hair. "Oliver, my family is not something I care to discuss right now. Not when I'm feeling so relaxed and happy."

Gazing into her eyes, he caressed her cheek. "Unpleasant memories?"

"Yes." She glanced at the clock radio on the bedside table. Almost one A.M. Time to leave before he skewered her with more questions. "This has been a magnificent evening, Oliver, but I should go now."

"Really? Why not stay the night? I hate to think of you driving to New Hampshire at this hour."

"I'll be okay. I need to get back. I have a lot to do tomorrow." She rose from the bed and began putting on her clothes.

"Working on another article?"

Aware that he was watching her, she said, "Oh, various things."

Worrisome things that were now at the forefront of her mind. Hurricane Gail and the evacuation. Detective Renzi investigating two murders. Most of all, worries about her target. Was he in New Orleans now or watching the storm from another city in one of his swanky bars?

When she finished dressing, Oliver rose from the bed and came to her. She put her arms around his neck. "I enjoy your company very much, Oliver. Thank you for making this such a wonderful evening."

He raised her hand to his mouth and kissed it. "The first of many, I hope. How long will you be staying with your friends in New Hampshire?"

"I'm not sure." She wanted to see him again, but she had to keep her eyes on the prize. The countdown to the Main Event had begun. "I may have to fly to Chicago to wrap up my article."

"If you do, I hope you'll call me. Do you have a cell phone?"

He was angling for her number, but she wasn't going to give it to him.

"I'll call you in a few days, I promise."

He smiled and his eyes crinkled at the corners. "You better. I've grown quite fond of you, Robin Adair. If you don't call me, I might have to track you down."

Track you down.

The words sent a frisson of fear down her spine.

She brushed his lips with a kiss and left.

CHAPTER 15

Saturday, 2 August 1:15 P.M.

A fine mist blurred the windshield of his squad car, a hint of the deluge Hurricane Gail would bring. Frank tried to get comfortable, but his uniform, which he seldom wore, had too much gear strapped to the belt. For more than an hour he'd been parked underneath the Pontchartrain Expressway a block west of Lee's Circle. Traffic was sparse, almost nonexistent.

Most of the evacuees had already gone. The governor of Louisiana had declared a state of emergency and activated 2,000 members of the National Guard. The mayor had announced a dusk-to-dawn curfew. After six o'clock, he'd be flagging down any car not deemed essential. All NOPD officers below supervisory rank were pulling twelve hour shifts. He'd drawn noon to midnight. Kelly had midnight to noon. He wouldn't see her for a while.

A black Ford Explorer barreled down the St. Charles Avenue exit ramp and slewed to a screeching halt at the red light when the driver spotted his cruiser. During evacuations people drove like maniacs, running red lights and gridlocking intersections.

Evacuation of the parishes on the Gulf had begun yesterday, assisted by contraflow lane reversals, outbound-only on all highways going north, east, and west. Unwilling to repeat the Katrina debacle that stranded thousands of residents, the state had mobilized 700 buses to drive evacuees to shelters north of Lake Pontchartrain. Others had been put on trains at the Amtrak station.

The light changed and the black Explorer lurched forward. Frank eyeballed the driver, a long-haired white male. The guy was probably up to no good, but he wasn't here to stop suspicious drivers. He was here to make sure traffic didn't get snarled so that any last minute stragglers could evacuate.

A half hour ago Maureen had called. Hearing her voice and her parting words--*Love you, Dad. Be careful*--had gotten him through the first hour of his shift, but now he was bored. He'd forgotten to bring some CDs. No music on the radio, the stations were all-talk, people calling in to bitch about traffic and whatever else was on their mind. Many were angry that tomorrow's Saints game had been moved to Cincinnati. Others were furious that Mississippi Governor Haley Barbour had closed the I-10 east-bound lanes at the Mississippi border. Barbour said he didn't want Mississippi residents to get stuck on a clogged Interstate. This forced Louisiana evacuees headed east to Georgia and Florida to drive north on I-55. Now I-55 was a parking lot.

His cell buzzed, Vobitch calling him. "What's doing, Frank?"

"Nothing. I'm parked in a cruiser near Lee's Circle. What's happening at the station?"

"Bedlam. Everybody's bitching about something. Did you see the T-P this morning?" T-P was Vobitch's polite term for the *Times-Picayune*, his more colorful moniker being *fucking local rag.*

"I didn't have time, caught a few winks before I came in for my shift."

"No sketch in today's paper. When I called they said they had to cover the hurricane to, and I quote, *Serve the needs of the public.* Christ, first they crucify us for not solving the Peterson case, then they screw us because of a fucking hurricane. The TV stations ran the sketch at the end of the news, but who's watching? Everyone's gone, only ones left are the nogoodnicks and desperadoes."

"Take it easy, Morgan. After Gail blows through and people come back, we'll have 'em run it again. By then people will be paying attention."

"I hope so. Only thing we got going for us is the Babylon Casino bigwigs are more worried about losing money because they're closed than they are about the Peterson case."

"Be grateful for small favors," he said, eyeballing the intersection. "Man, this place is a ghost town."

"You'll get some action later. The drug pushers come out after dark like the roaches they are. You don't think the little maggots desperate for their next fix are gonna evacuate, do you?"

"Probably not. Where's Juliana? Did she stay or go?"

Twenty years ago, Juliana, a tall willowy black woman, had been a ballet dancer in New York City. One night after a show Vobitch rescued her from a mugger. Not love at first sight, but close. For all his salty language, Vobitch had a cultural side few people saw. One night over a beer, Vobitch told him his parents had fled Russia to escape the pogroms rounding up Jews. His father, a professor of Fine Arts in Russia, was reduced to selling men's clothes at a Manhattan department store. But he'd taken his son to symphony concerts and art museums on a regular basis.

"She decided to stay. She's stubborn too." Vobitch chuckled. "That's why we get along."

He smiled, imagining the spirited debates that enlivened the Vobitch household.

"Nathan's South is still open. You want a sandwich?"

Vobitch claimed he maintained an office in the Eighth District Station in the Quarter because he wanted to be where the action was. Bullshit. Nathan's South, which made New York-style deli sandwiches, was two blocks away. They'd named one The Vobitch: pastrami and Swiss on rye with spicy Dijon mustard and a big dill pickle.

Frank figured Vobitch felt guilty about being in the station while he was out patrolling. "Hell yes. Get me The Vobitch, spicy brown mustard, no tomato. With fries. It might be a while before I see another meal."

"Okay, I'll call in the order, bring it over in half an hour or so."

He shut his cell and eyeballed the area. No cars and no pedestrians.

But then a skinny black man on a fancy trail bike whipped through the underpass, pedaling like mad, and disappeared down St. Charles Avenue. Fancy bike for such a scruffy-looking guy.

His cell rang and he grabbed it when he saw the ID.

"Hey, Frank, how are things?" Kelly said. "Any problems?"

"Not a one. I'm bored as hell. How bad was your shift last night?"

"You don't want to know. Why do people turn into idiots when they get in cars?"

"Because they got the idiot genes. Where were you?"

"Slidell. It was chaos, a gazillion people trying to get on I-10 east."

"And couldn't because the Mississippi governor got the idiot genes, too."

"He sure did. I don't know what he was thinking. Instead of getting on a four-lane highway, they had to go north on a two-lane. I hear there's a twenty mile backup on I-55."

Hearing her stifle a yawn, he said, "Better get some sleep. Another long night tonight."

"I'm going to bed as soon as I hang up."

Lowering his voice to a sexy murmur, he said, "What are you wearing?"

"Don't you start, Frank Renzi. I saw *Sea of Love*, too."

"Ellen Barkin was great, wasn't she?"

"Yeah. Walks in a grocery store bare-ass-naked under her trench coat and Al Pacino's waiting for her in the produce department squeezing the melons."

"One of my all-time favorite scenes. So? What have you got on?"

But then his radio handset erupted: *Renzi, you still near St. Charles Avenue?*

"Hold on," he said to Kelly, "Dispatch calling."

He keyed his radio. "Renzi, what's up?"

"Armed robbery in progress at the Walgreens, corner of St. Charles and Jackson."

"I'm on it." He dropped the handset on the passenger seat, slammed the car into gear and said to Kelly, "Gotta go. Armed robbery at a Walgreen's."

"Ah, geez. Be careful, Frank."

"I always am."

"Liar. Call me when it's wrapped."

"I will." He turned onto St. Charles and hit the lights but not the siren.

Three minutes later he slowed at the Jackson Avenue intersection. Walgreen's was across the street beyond the neutral ground with the streetcar tracks. He hooked a U-turn and parked. The store was closed, but the drive-up window was open so people could fill prescriptions.

He unholstered his weapon and crept to the front window. The front of the store was dark, but lights were visible in back near the pharmacy window. He edged along the front of the store, stopped at the corner and took a quick peek. And saw the scruffy black guy straddling the fancy bike at the drive-up window. He was holding a gun on the clerk inside the drive-up window.

"Police!" Frank shouted. "Drop the gun and get on the ground!"

But the guy didn't drop the gun. He whirled and shot at him.

———

Nashua, New Hampshire

At two o'clock she took a taxi to the Super Stop & Shop near the highway exit closest to the Massachusetts border. Last night she'd found the car she needed on EBay. The owner lived in Billerica, twenty miles from the New Hampshire border. After some haggling Bobby Oakes had agreed to sell his metallic-brown 2002 Ford Focus to her for thirty-five-hundred dollars in cash. He'd just finished his junior year at U-Mass-Lowell and needed money to pay his tuition in the fall. She'd promised him an extra hundred if he would drive to Nashua to complete the transaction.

Bobby wasn't due until two-thirty, but she wanted to be there when he arrived to make sure he didn't look dodgy. She bought a bottle of iced tea in the Stop & Shop, went outside and sat on a shaded bench in front of the store.

The parking lot was jam-packed with cars and shoppers wheeling grocery carts out to their cars. An elderly woman with wispy white hair pushed a cart out of the store and sank onto the bench beside her. "Pretty soon I'll be eating Alpo meatloaf. I swear they raise the prices every week."

She nodded in commiseration. "It does seem like it."

The woman smiled at her. "What a cute hat. Where did you get it?"

Earlier, she'd bought the broad-brimmed beach hat at a Dollar Store. "Thanks. I got it at Hampton Beach. Have a nice day."

Unwilling to get into a conversation lest the woman remember her, she rose from the bench, went inside and stood at the community bulletin board by the front window, pretending to read the flyers. A minute later a yellow taxi stopped in front of the bench. The elderly woman got in the cab and the driver loaded her groceries into the trunk. As the taxi drove away a metallic-brown Ford Focus entered the lot, trailed by an ancient yellow VW Bug.

The Ford pulled into a space near the Stop & Shop marquee and the Bug parked beside it. A pudgy kid in cutoff jeans and a Red Sox T-Shirt got out of the Ford Focus and looked around.

She left the store and walked over to him. "Hi, Bobby?"

"Yes, are you Angela?"

"I am. Thanks for driving up to meet me. Do you have the title?"

He waved an envelope. "Got it right here. You got the money?"

"Yes, but I'd like to see the title first, to make sure it's in order."

She reached for the envelope, but Bobby pulled it away. "Show me the money." A broad grin appeared on his pudgy face. "Man, I love that line."

Irritation gnawed at her stomach. She had no time for this. She had too much to do and too many things to worry about. "This isn't a movie, Bobby. Come on, I'll count out the money for you."

She went to the trunk of his car, took out her wallet and peeled off hundred-dollar bills. "There's the thirty-five-hundred for the car, plus the hundred I promised you for driving up here. Show me the title."

He showed her the title but kept a firm grip on it. "I deserve two hundred for driving up here. Gas is expensive. I hadda fill Jimmy's tank to get him to follow me here and drive me home. Besides, you won't have to pay sales tax if you register it in New Hampshire."

She had no intention of registering the car in New Hampshire, but he didn't need to know that. "We made a deal, Bobby. An extra hundred. That's what I brought."

"But thirty-five-hundred only covers tuition. Textbooks are expensive."

"You've got your problems and I've got mine. Let's do a walk-around."

She circled the car to check for damage. The driver's side had a few dings, nothing to get excited about, but the right front fender had a big dent and a long scrape where the paint was missing. She gave Bobby a stern look.

"You didn't mention the dent and the scratched paint on the phone last night. Take the thirty-six hundred and give me the title and the keys."

Avoiding her gaze, he called, "Jimmy, take the plate off my car, will ya?"

Jimmy, a string-bean with a long dark ponytail, got to work on the plate. Bobby counted the money again and handed her the title. "The car runs great, Angela. I just changed the oil a week ago."

"That's good, but I need keys to drive it."

"Oh yeah, I almost forgot." He handed her the ignition key, took a spare key out of his jeans pocket and called to his friend. "Are we set, Jimmy?"

Jimmy held up the license plate. They climbed into the yellow Bug, and drove off. She climbed in the Focus and cranked the engine. The car reeked of cigarette smoke, and the gas gauge was riding on empty. Thanks a bunch, Bobby. She'd better fill the tank. Another chore, one of many on her Do-list.

Be prepared. Leave nothing to chance. She pulled a rectangular piece of cardboard out of her tote--her makeshift temporary plate--and placed it in the rear window, hoping a cop wouldn't stop her on the way home. Her condo complex had a large parking area to accommodate visitors, and the metallic-brown Ford Focus was innocuous-looking. That's why she'd chosen it. The Ford would be just another car among many.

———

4:30 P.M. New Orleans

"What do you mean, just a scratch? Jesus, Frank! You could be dead!"

"Yeah, but I'm not." Rather than call Kelly from his office, he'd gone out to the cruiser and used his cell. Booking the robber had taken a while and he'd promised to call so she wouldn't worry. But when he told her what happened, she'd pitched a major hissy fit. To lighten things up, he said, "Can you believe it? This old guy pedals a stolen bike to a Walgreen's drive-up window and tries to rob the place. You can't make this stuff up."

"Don't joke, Frank. He had a gun didn't he? He shot at you, didn't he?"

So much for humor. "Yeah, well, I was scared shitless for a second, but he only got off one shot, a wild one at that. The slug ricocheted off the side of the building and a piece of brick hit me in the face." He peered into the rearview at the Band-Aid on his cheek. "It's fine, no stitches, nothing. Hell, by the time I see you, there won't even be a scab."

"Well," she said, somewhat mollified, "if you say so. Damn, I am sick of this hurricane shit. Sick of working the overnights, too. I can't sleep in the daytime."

"I can't either. It screws up your body clock. When I get off at midnight I'm too wired to sleep." Like a lot of cops, he often had trouble sleeping. Working homicide he'd get calls in the middle of the night, work twenty hours, nap for three and go back to work. He slept fine at Kelly's house though.

"Damn, I miss you."

"I miss you too. Now that I know you're okay I better catch a few winks before I go to work."

"Where are you patrolling tonight?"

"Gentilly and the St. Bernard Housing Project area."

A tough neighborhood. He rubbed the jagged scar on his chin, a habitual gesture when he was worried. "Be careful. All the gangbangers come out after midnight. That's when they do their dirty deeds."

"I know, but I'm riding with Ben Washburn. He's tough. We'll be fine."

A rugged black man with plenty of street smarts, Ben was an experienced cop, fifteen years with NOPD. But that wouldn't protect Ben or Kelly, from the 'bangers. The drug dealers carried heavy fire power.

"Be careful," he said again. By now this was their ritual term of endearment, meaning *I love you and I don't want anything to happen to you.*

"I will, Frank. You be careful too."

Natalie

1998 -- 2000 Paris

Living in Paris was scary at first, but like Mr. Carlson said, I'm a fast learner. New Yorkers think they live in the greatest city in the world, but Paris has many cultural attractions too, and people seemed to appreciate them more. They weren't gaga over sports and TV shows and pop stars, and most of the women wore stylish outfits with chic accessories and high-heels.

The day I arrived Lin picked me up at the airport and drove me to a flat they'd rented for me on the Left Bank. "Near the Sorbonne where many students live," Lin said. We passed dozens of outdoor cafes and bistros and clothing stores. I couldn't wait to explore them. Lin said I could take a nap if I was jet-lagged, but I was too wired to sleep, so he gave me a Metro map and showed me the nearest stop: St-Michel.

Then we drove to the 16th Arrondissement. The Service had a gorgeous office there, a suite of rooms on the fifth floor of a high-rise. The National Theatre of Paris was only blocks away. I couldn't wait to see a performance, but I first had to finish my training. They said my French needed work.

It sure did. People in Paris spoke so fast I could barely understand them. A tall elegant-looking Frenchwoman named Monique took me to Yves St. Laurent to buy clothes. Monique paid. That surprised me, but I didn't say anything. She wouldn't let me speak English, only French. Then we went to Vera Wang and bought four silk scarves, a pair of sunglasses and two fancy purses, one silver, one with black sequins.

"You can buy more when you start working," Monique said.

My pay was in US dollars, which they wired into the bank account they'd set up for Laura Lin Hawthorn in Switzerland. They gave me French francs for spending money. When I got back to my apartment I fell into bed, exhausted. But I tossed and turned most of the night.

In the morning I went to a cafe and had a Café Grande (a large coffee with milk) and two croissants. **Then I walked to Shakespeare's Bookstore,** the famous shop that sells books in English. It smelled musty, and I had to squeeze through aisles packed floor to ceiling with books.

119

I bought two paperback thrillers and kept walking to Odeon, a big square with many movie theaters. Some films were French, but most of them were American. I missed seeing movies with Gabe and Darren. But I was too exhausted to watch a movie. That night I slept like the dead.

The next day Monique asked me what I wanted my specialty to be. I figured she meant sex. My disgust must have showed because Monique smiled and said, "The Service has a high-class reputation. All of our girls are cultured and well educated." Then she asked what my special interests were.

This reminded me of Mom's calendar with the Vermeer paintings. One for every month. The Girl With the Pearl Earring was on the calendar when Mom was murdered. I decided this was a sign. Mom loved art and Paris had a zillion art museums, so I said art.

For the next week a little Frenchman with a pencil-thin mustache taught me about art history. He was a great teacher and very patient when I asked him to repeat things (because he spoke French so fast). I learned a lot.

Monique took me to museums to test my comprehension. We went to the Musee d'Orsay, the Rodin and Picasso museums, the Pompidou Center, the Modern Art Museum and the L'Orangerie for the Impressionists. The Monet murals on the curved walls downstairs were unbelievable. Monique said if I liked them, I should take a train to Giverny to see Monet's flower gardens and the arched bridges over the lily pads.

Early in March, Monique said I was ready for my first client. That scared me. When she said he was from Uganda, I freaked out. For my high school social studies class I had written a paper on Uganda. What I remembered most: Idi Amin had been Uganda's military-dictator president. He was big and fat and rumored to be a cannibal. He wasn't president of Uganda anymore, but that didn't make me feel any less terrified.

My client was a diplomat, a huge black man, and fat like Idi Amin, but he seemed pleased with me. When we met, he took my hand and said, "So happy to meet you, Laura Lin." In English.

He had an unpronounceable name, so I called him *Honey*. When he asked what my interests were, I said art, but that was the end of that conversation. He went on about politics in his country and how difficult his job was. I smiled and said I understood. This was while we had dinner at L'Arpege, a ritzy restaurant. The food was fantastic and so was the wine, but I could barely eat. I was too worried about what would happen when we went to his hotel.

We didn't get there until midnight. Right away, he asked if I'd mind taking off my clothes.

I smiled and said, "Of course not, honey," and took off every stitch.

He gazed at my body but didn't take off his clothes.

"Come here," he said. When I stepped closer he said, "Would you mind if I touch your breasts?"

I said, "Of course not, honey." *Be what they want you to be.*

That's what Madame taught me. But I was thinking: If this 300-pound giant jumps on top of me, he'll crush me.

Then I remembered what Ann Bancroft told Bridget Fonda in *Point of No Return*: If you run into a problem, just smile and say: *The little things never bother me.* That's what Bridget did when Harvey Keitel killed her helper. She smiled and said: *The little things never bother me.* And Harvey didn't kill her.

Little things? No problem, but men built like Idi Amin?

But then the strangest thing happened. He petted my breasts and ground himself against my crotch and came right away. Sort of like a standup lap dance. "You are so beautiful, Laura Lin. When I come back to Paris next month, I would like to take you out for dinner again."

I said I would love that and told him to arrange it with The Service. Then I went home. The girlfriends never handled money. Clients paid The Service directly. I don't know how much my Uganda client paid for five hours of my time, but they said he added a $500 tip to show his appreciation. All together I made $2,500. They wired $1,500 into my bank account and gave me the rest in francs. They also said I would now be responsible for buying my own clothes and paying the rent on my apartment.

The next day I signed up for lessons at a taekwondo studio. I couldn't believe how rusty my skills were. The teacher must have been disgusted, but he made a polite face the way Asians do. Even so, I knew how out of shape I was. From then on I went there three times a week to work out.

All my clients weren't as easy to please as the diplomat from Uganda, but every time I got home from a "date" I added up the numbers in my bank account and reminded myself why I was doing this. To avenge Mom.

But first I needed to find out who killed her. I knew it would cost a lot, thousands of dollars, according to the PI in New York. And after I found out his name, I would have to figure out how to punish him. That would cost money too. A lot, probably.

I accumulated several regulars—generous tippers—who saw me three or four times a month. In my spare time I went to movies. Parisians were gaga over Hollywood movies and my French clients loved to discuss them. I used *Pariscope,* a weekly magazine that lists what's happening each week, to choose which films to see. Early on I figured out that *vo* in the listing meant *Version Original,* meaning it was in English with French subtitles. I always saw the *vo* version. Most of the subtitles were idiotic.

To celebrate my twentieth birthday on April 15th, I sent Gabe a coded email: *P is fantastic. E-tower is great. I love you, IRS.* I was sure Gabe would figure it out. I missed him a lot, but I didn't miss Pecos. I wondered how Ellen was doing now that Randy wasn't around to make her give him blowjobs.

One day in the office I met a girl and we got talking. Her name was Amanda Lin. None of us ever revealed our last name. Amanda was tiny, only five-two, but she had a gorgeous face and big boobs. We went to a café and chatted in English over a Café Grande. We didn't talk about our previous life, so I don't know where she's from.

I hoped she'd be my girlfriend like Val in New York, but Amanda spent her free time with her boyfriend. Now and then we went out for lunch. Her specialty was jazz. When I said mine was art, we swapped information. Being *au courant* in two areas was better than one. Some clients just want a pretty girl to talk to at dinner and have sex with afterwards, but many of my clients were wild about jazz. I started going to jazz clubs and fell in love with the music.

It made me feel free, the way I used to feel when I was in New York, dancing in the dark.

Every day I watched the news on TV to keep up with current events. That's how I found out about the Columbine shootings. It happened April 20, 1999, five days after my twenty-first birthday. Two high school kids brought guns to school and killed several of their classmates; then they killed themselves. It reminded me of Randy and his football-player friends in Pecos.

I wished I could talk to Gabe about it, but I didn't dare call him.

When I felt lonely, I'd go to an upscale bar just to be around people. I liked hearing their murmured conversations. Sometimes I'd fantasize that I was with a man, but then I'd give myself a dope-slap.

Forget romance. I had to avenge Mom's murder. *I shall be a champion of freedom and justice.* Justice for Mom, then freedom for me. Freedom to live my life however I wanted. Which didn't include working for The Service.

One day I went to the Pompidou Center. The modern art collection is remarkable. Afterwards I went to the gift shop and noticed a tall carrousel that displayed many postcards. I spun it around. When it stopped, my heart jumped into my throat and my hands got cold as ice.

Facing me at eye level was a photograph of the gargoyles perched on the facade high above Notre Dame Cathedral. They were hideous, gaping mouths, angry eyes, long sharp talons gripping the cement facade.

This was what I imagined the angry Ancestor spirits looked like.

A violent shudder wracked me. I was certain this was no accident.

Mom's ancestor spirits had sent me a message. Tears filled my eyes.

Mom had been waiting for me to avenge her for eleven years and I had done nothing. I felt so ashamed. I went home, took out Mom's photograph, lit some incense and chanted: *I shall be a champion of freedom and justice.*

By the end of August 1999 I had saved 6,000 dollars. I figured that was enough to hire a detective. On the Internet I found a directory for private investigators in the United States. I didn't want to use anyone in Louisiana so I called a man in Tennessee. Closer than New York, but not too close.

He answered in a southern drawl. "Nicolas Hart Investigations, how can I help y'all today?"

"I need information about a murder in New Orleans. October 1988."

"Waahl, that's a while back. I take it the cops didn't solve the case?"

"No, but they had some suspects and I want to know who they were."

"Why don't y'all call the New Orleans police and ask them?"

"If I wanted to do that, why would I call you?"

He laughed. "Ya got me there. Call me Nick. What's your name?"

This time I was ready with my fake name. "Virginia Smith," I said.

"Smith, huh." He paused and I heard him light a cigarette. "Okay, Virginia. Tell me what you want me to do and I'll tell if I can do it."

So I gave him Mom's name and the date of the murder. Jane Fontenot had said her prime suspect's wife had given him an alibi. I couldn't imagine why. Didn't she know he was a monster? But I didn't say this. I gave him Jane's name and said I wanted a copy of the file to see who her suspects were.

Another pause. "Is your name on the list of suspects, Virginia?"

I had to pinch myself to keep from laughing. "I wasn't even old enough to drive in 1988."

"Okay, Virginia, but it's gonna cost you. I gotta drive down to N'Awlins and find a friendly cop without too many scruples. Probably have to pay him a bundle to copy the file."

"No problem. How much do you think you'll need?"

"To bribe the cop? A grand, maybe two. I'll do the best I can for ya."

"And how much will your services cost?"

"I need three grand up front as a retainer. Hard to say about the rest. Depends how long it takes me."

"Okay, but how do I know you'll get me the file?"

"Don't you worry 'bout that, Virginia. Might take me a while, but I'll get it. Once I do, I'll give you an itemized account of my expenses and send you a bill for the balance."

So I agreed to wire 3,000 dollars into his bank account.

What choice did I have? Jane wouldn't give me the names of her suspects and I needed them to find Mom's killer. I gave Nick my cell number and said I was in Paris so he'd know how to reach me. He gave me his bank information so I could wire the money and said he'd call me when he verified that it was in his account and that was it.

I slumped in my chair, my shirt damp with sweat. But my heart was singing. At last someone was going to help me find Mom's killer. I got up and did a dance around my kitchen. Nick had said it might take a while, but I felt like I had taken the first step in my journey. An important step.

I called my Swiss bank and told them to wire the payment to Nick. It cost extra to keep my name and account number off the transfer. Then I poured myself a glass of good red wine and got to work on my plan.

Unfortunately, most of it involved money. A lot of money.

I allowed 6,000 dollars for Nick, including the bribe for the NOPD cop. To accomplish my goal I would need fake IDs. I figured I'd need at least three. I had bought a fake ID in New York, so knew how much they cost. To be on the safe side, I wrote: *Four fake IDs ($4,000)*. I couldn't take a gun on a plane. After I flew back to America I would have to buy a gun *($1,000)* and a car, maybe two or three.

Clearly I would need a lot more money than I had in my bank account. I didn't allow myself to get discouraged, but I didn't forget the gargoyles either. I put a Joan Jett CD in my walkman and sang along with it as I drank my wine.

Soon I would have the name of a suspect. Soon it would be October 1999. Almost eleven years Mom had been waiting.

I'm going to find the man that killed you, Mom. And make him wish he hadn't.

———

Servicing clients almost got to be routine. *Be who they want you to be.* Smile and laugh at their jokes. Flatter them. A surprising number of them had no interest in sex. Most of them were older men. I think they were ashamed of their flabby bodies. But they liked being seen with a beautiful young woman, implying they were hot stuff in bed when they weren't. It was all for show.

But what did I care? It made my job easier.

Two weeks before Christmas Nick called. He said he needed an operation to fix a double hernia. He apologized and said he'd be back on his feet soon. "After Mardi Gras I'll go to New Orleans and get the file you want, Virginia."

This was a big disappointment. Another frustrating delay. Mom had been waiting for me to avenge her since October 1988.

But at least I was doing something about it. Nick was going to get me the names of the suspects and my bank account was getting fatter.

I was looking forward to April 15, 2000. My twenty-second birthday.

But in February The Service called to say I had a new client. His country of origin was France, but he lived in New York. He was in Paris on business.

This was the sort of information they always gave me about new clients.

Then they told me his name. Thu Phan.

When I heard this, I felt like a boxer had punched me in the stomach.

Thu Phan. Born in France. A businessman from New York.

Visiting Paris. Using an escort service.

Thu Phan was my father. This I knew with absolute certainty.

I couldn't decide what to do.

124

CHAPTER 16

Sunday, 3 August

Frank dragged himself out of bed at ten A.M. and took a shower. It didn't help much, didn't get rid of his dull headache. Last night after work he was too wired to sleep so he zapped a frozen pizza and ate it while he watched a movie on TV. Slim pickings at that hour, but he stumbled upon an old Francois Truffaut film, *Love on the Run*. Good flick, but he dozed off, had woken at three A.M. and stumbled into bed.

He shaved dark stubble off his face, put on his uniform and drank a double shot of espresso while he watched an update on Hurricane Gail on TV. The meteorologist predicted fierce wind and heavy rain; the Louisiana governor and the New Orleans mayor were pleading with residents to get out of town. Nothing about the Peterson case. Nothing about Tex Conroy.

And no sketch of Natalie Brixton.

He scooped his keys off the kitchen counter and left. On his way to the station he stopped at a convenience store to buy a *Times-Picayune*, had to wait in line behind people buying bottled water and whatever else remained on the shelves. He took the paper out to his squad car. Buried on Page 3 of the Metro section was the composite sketch of Natalie, the full face version without sunglasses, and a brief article with a number to call if anyone had information.

As if anyone would. People who had evacuated wouldn't see it, and the ones who'd stayed were worried about the hurricane, praying their electricity wouldn't conk out and the wind wouldn't rip off their roof. He wheeled the squad out of the parking lot and headed for the station. Kelly was still working her midnight to noon shift, probably as irritated and burned out as he was.

Maybe he'd call her later, catch her in the shower and ask her what she had on. Damn, he couldn't wait Hurricane Gail to blow through.

Then he could spend some quality time with Kelly.

And continue his hunt for Natalie.

———

Nashua, NH

She got up at noon, slipped on her blue silk bathrobe and wandered into the kitchen. She was still catching up on sleep after her date with Oliver on Friday. She brewed herself a pot of green tea, enchanted with sense memories of his touch and how marvelous she felt after they made love.

Exquisite memories. Except for his parting words.

If you don't call me, I might have to track you down. But that was macho posturing. He was annoyed that she wouldn't give him her cell phone number. Besides, how could he track her down? He had no idea where she lived.

She poured steamy green tea into a mug and took a sip. She couldn't allow Oliver to become a distraction. She had to focus on her mission. Hurricane Gail was approaching New Orleans. She set her mug of tea on the kitchen table next to her laptop and got on the Internet.

Fantastic! The National Weather Service forecasters had narrowed the cone of possible land strikes. They now believed Hurricane Gail would make landfall as a Category-3 storm three hundred miles east of New Orleans. It was unlikely the city would suffer any major damage. Once the residents returned, everything would return to normal.

After all her worry and anxiety, her plan was falling into place.

A shiver rippled through her.

In two weeks she would be in New Orleans.

She put a cinnamon-raisin bagel in the toaster and leaned against the counter. After her endless twenty year journey, she was about to avenge her mother's murder. Then she could think about having a life. With Oliver James? A tantalizing thought. She sipped her tea, enjoying the light, fresh taste.

Oliver was a world traveler and an art connoisseur. They could visit the art museums in Paris, dine at first-rate restaurants, drink fine wine and make mad passionate love afterwards. It had been three years since she done that with Willem. Three years of solitude.

Like sneaky jackals, visions of her first true love had infiltrated her dreams last night, images that jolted her awake. Willem taking her on a boat trip down the Seine. Willem seated opposite her at a swanky restaurant, handsome and sexy in his Armani suit. Willem in a nightclub, making love to her with his eyes, a prelude to their lovemaking at home.

Willem saying he loved her, but . . .

The odor of something burning filled her nostrils. She whirled and pulled the smoldering bagel out of the toaster. She threw it in the garbage. Given her experience with Willem, she didn't dare get too excited about Oliver. What did she know about him, really? Not much. After graduating from Harvard, he'd made a fortune in the stock market. Then he'd became a dealer of ancient art.

Or so he said.

But she had told him a pack of lies. What was to say he wasn't lying too?

She sat down at the table and set her chin on her palms. Why couldn't life be simple? Hers had been a series of ordeals. Her mother's murder. Eight nightmarish years with a toxic family in Texas. And then, the killings.

Randy. Arnold Peterson and Tex Conroy.

She massaged her throbbing temples. Was she a monster like Randy? Did a killer gene run in the Brixton family? Her mother had turned to prostitution to make money and so had she. And her father was no prize. Embracing her Vietnamese heritage had brought a sense of belonging and a certain amount of comfort. But ever since her mother's murder, the vindictive ancestor spirits had inflicted terrible trials upon her.

Randy, killing her beloved Muffy. Even after she left Pecos, the misery continued. Dancing half-naked in New York for men who lusted after her body. Having sex with wealthy men in Paris who paid her to do their bidding in bed. If she didn't punish Mom's killer, the angry ancestor spirits might inflict worse punishment.

Already she had done terrible deeds that would haunt her to her grave.

But after she avenged Mom's murder, her life would improve.

It had to, or there was no hope.

She had to stop thinking about Oliver and focus on business. She'd been so relieved about Hurricane Gail she'd forgotten to check NOLA.com. She got on her laptop and navigated to the website. Yesterday it had been full of evacuation procedures. Nothing about the Peterson murder or Tex Conroy.

Today, the front page was still about Hurricane Gail, but under the Metro Section a headline said: **Police seek person of interest in Peterson murder**.

She clicked on the article and saw the sketch of a woman's face.

Her heart almost stopped. Natalie Brixton's face. Impossible! She had hidden her face from the security camera in the hall outside Peterson's room.

Her head throbbed as she read the article.

New Orleans police are seeking information about a person of interest in the murder of Arnold Peterson. If you recognize the woman in the sketch, call Homicide Detective Frank Renzi at the Eighth District station. Police describe her as a slender woman between the age of twenty-five and thirty. They also believe she has a tattoo on her ankle.

A tattoo on her ankle. Bile rose in her throat. Fearing she would vomit, she clamped a hand over her mouth. The tattoo on her ankle was tiny. How could they have seen it on the security video?

Willem had one too, exactly like hers.

"It will be our secret," he'd said. "Ours alone, just you and me."

Tears pricked her eyes. Did Willem still have his raven tattoo, she wondered. Did he ever look at it and think of her?

Thanks to her study of Vietnamese culture she had come to believe that birds would protect her. But Tex had recognized her because of her seabird pendant, her good luck charm. Now the New Orleans police were seeking a woman with a tattoo on her ankle, a woman who looked like Natalie Brixton.

Detective Frank Renzi, the relentless hunter, was hot on her trail.

An icy waterfall of fear chilled her to the bone. After all the disgusting acts she'd done to earn money to avenge Mom, would Renzi thwart her?

She straightened her spine. No one was going to thwart her. She would execute her plan, avenge her mother's murder and disappear. But how did they get her picture? She massaged her aching temples. Had Tex fingered her from the grave? What if Renzi went to Pecos and talked to Tex's mother?

What if Mrs. Conroy told Renzi about Natalie Brixton? And Randy.

Then a more ominous thought hit her. Oliver knew her as Robin Adair, but he had commented on the tattoo last Friday as they lay in bed.

"What a delicate ornament for your beautiful ankle," he'd said, smiling as he caressed her thigh.

But why would Oliver read the *Times-Picayune*? He didn't know Natalie Brixton from a hole-in-the-wall. She shut down the laptop. Nothing was going to prevent her from completing her mission. Nothing.

Her phone rang. Distracted, she answered without checking Caller-ID.

"Hello Robin." Oliver's deep distinctive voice. "I'm so happy to hear your voice."

She felt like she'd been hit by lightning. She wanted to scream *How did you get my number?* She dug her fingernails into her palms.

Stalling for time, she said, "Oliver?"

"Yes. Am I interrupting something?"

"No. I'm just surprised to hear from you. How did you get my number?"

He chuckled. "There are ways to get a phone number if you want it badly enough."

Her neck prickled. Ways to get a number, if you had the wherewithal to do it, and obviously Oliver James did.

"How's work going?" he said. "You said you had a lot to do."

"It's going okay." Well, some things were, but not phone calls like this.

"I called to see if we could have dinner tonight. Since you live in Nashua, it shouldn't take long to drive to Boston. Traffic won't be bad on a Sunday."

Her stomach went into freefall, a sickening lurch that brought more bile to her throat. He knew her phone number, knew where she lived.

What else did he know?

She forced herself to smile. *Be what they want you to be.*

"Hold on while I check. I have an appointment today."

She stood by the counter with the phone clenched in her hand, her mind reeling. She closed her eyes, forced herself to focus.

And everything became clear. Oliver was no longer a mere distraction.

Oliver was a serious threat. Oliver knew too much.

"I won't be free until seven, but I could meet you at nine for a drink."

"Excellent. Come up to my hotel room. I'll chill a good bottle of wine and we can chat for a while. I've got a couple of questions for you."

A couple of questions for you. She no intention of answering any questions, from Oliver or anyone else.

"Fine. See you then," she said, and hung up. Oliver wanted her to come to his room for a drink. So they could chat.

A disgusting echo of her father's words eight years ago.

She ran to the bathroom and vomited into the toilet.

———

New Orleans 6:10 P.M.

Stifling a yawn, Frank forced himself to concentrate as he patrolled the deserted streets near the Interstate entrance in eastern New Orleans. Low hanging iron-gray clouds loomed in the sky and rain spattered the windshield. Six hours and he'd seen only four cars, last minute stragglers leaving town.

Before he left the station, Vobitch had buttonholed him, furious at the TV stations for not running the Natalie sketch, only slightly mollified that it had run in the newspaper. "Page three of the fucking Metro Section," Vobitch had said. "I'll stay in my office in case any tips come in, but the city's a ghost town. Only people gonna call are the nutcakes and weirdoes."

Frank drove under the massive I-610 overpass and turned left. Gusty winds buffeted the cruiser and rain beat on the roof. A scruffy-looking man stood by the traffic light at the end of the I-610 off-ramp. Dressed in torn jeans, he held up a cardboard sign asking for spare change. Never mind that no cars were coming, and no cars were going to be coming.

The guy probably came here every day to beg for change, no matter what. Hell or high water or Hurricane Gail.

He pulled up beside the panhandler, a dark-skinned man of indeterminate age, a weather-beaten face and gray-speckled beard, could be anywhere from forty to sixty. Frank rolled down his window, saw fear blossom in the man's eyes. Fear of cops not hurricanes. "You got someplace to stay?"

"Mm-mm," the man mumbled, avoiding Frank's gaze.

"It's almost dark and it's raining. You best get inside. It's going to be a nasty night." He pulled out a five-dollar bill and held it out the window.

The man snatched the bill and bobbed his head. "Thank you, sir. You have a blessed day."

"You too, but I don't want to see you here when I come back in half an hour. The convenience store up the street is still open. Go buy some food, get inside and stay there till the storm passes."

"Yessir, I will," the man said, and trudged off in the direction of the store.

Frank hoped he would, hoped he'd buy food, not crack, and stay safe during the storm.

He took out his cell and called Kenyon Miller. Miller was patrolling near the Convention Center. "Hey, Kenyon, what's up? Any trouble?"

"All quiet at the Convention Center." Miller rumbled a gleeful chuckle. "Got the Saints game on the radio, Saints up by twelve. Where y'at, Frank?"

"New Orleans east. Nothing doing here either. Call me if anything happens." For Miller's benefit, he signed off with "Go Saints!" and checked the time: 6:20. The minutes crawling by like cold molasses from a teapot.

Maybe he'd call Kelly. But then he thought: *No, she's probably sleeping.*

His cell rang. For a moment he thought it was ESP, Kelly calling because he was thinking of her. That happened sometimes. But it wasn't Kelly, it was Vobitch. "What's doing, Frank?"

"SOS, Morgan. You know the drill. Police work is ninety-five percent boredom, five percent piss-your-pants terror."

"Well, for me it's been ninety-eight percent boredom, two percent bullshit. Two calls on the fuckin tip line, both of 'em bogus. One guy swears the woman in the sketch is his ex-girlfriend. She works at a bar over in Algiers. He's got a hair up his ass for God-knows-what-reason, wants us to go arrest his former beloved. He also said she's got tattoos all over her arms."

"Forget that one. How about the other one?"

"Some old woman," Vobitch said, his voice oozing exasperation. "Says it's her long-lost daughter who disappeared twenty years ago. The daughter was forty-five then, which would, according to any first-grader's calculation, make her sixty-five now. Like I said, Frank. The nutcases are the only ones calling. I'm heading home. Jim Whitworth's covering the tip line. I told him to call you if he gets any tips that light up the all-time-spectacular thrill meter."

Frank grinned, enjoying his boss's trademark sardonic humor.

Until Vobitch said in an ominous voice, "Watch your back, Frank. After dark it's a fucking jungle out there."

CHAPTER 17

Boston 9:25 P.M.

She backed her Honda Civic into a slot on the down ramp near the exit of the Copley Place garage. In case she had to leave in a hurry. Her long dark hair was pulled into a ponytail to go with her beach outfit: white culottes and a sleeveless pastel-blue top, with a matching scarf loosely tied around her neck. She put on her floppy beach hat and sunglasses, and got out of the car.

The garage was hot and stuffy and stank of gasoline and car fumes. A sick-ache invaded her stomach, one that matched the pain in her heart. She had no idea how her tête-à-tête with Oliver would go, but she had prepared for the worst.

A deep longing welled up inside her. She had hoped their love affair would continue, but judging by their phone conversation, it might not.

Her Frye Oxfords didn't go with her outfit, but she could run in them if she had to, and the heels were reinforced with steel. She went to the trunk and took out a large Neiman Marcus shopping bag. Averting her face as she passed the cashier's cage, she went up a short ramp. One fork veered right to exit on Huntington Avenue. To her left, a doorman was unloading luggage from a yellow taxi parked in the circular drive in front of the Marriot Hotel.

A revolving door dumped her into the air-conditioned lobby near an escalator that descended from the Copley Place Mall. The lobby was deserted, but to her right, fifteen yards beyond the escalator, a desk clerk was checking in an older couple with expensive-looking luggage.

With her head down, she walked straight ahead to the recessed alcove with the polished-brass elevator and hit the call button. A bell pinged. Her heart fluttered, an anxious thrum in her chest. But the doors opened on an empty car. She stepped inside and punched the Level Three button. Using her taekwondo focus, she breathed deeply to calm her racing heart. Holding the Neiman Marcus bag in one hand, she pulled the hat brim lower to hide her face from the security cameras that awaited her in the Level Three hall.

A flesh-colored Band-aid covered the tattoo on her ankle.

131

Earlier she had called a tattoo parlor in Nashua to see if she could get it removed. The man asked what color it was and how big. When she said it was black and very small, he said he had the laser equipment to do it, but it might take four or five treatments. She'd thanked him and hung up.

When the elevator stopped, she got out and turned right. Oliver's room was at the far end of the hall. With long purposeful strides, she lowered her head, walked down the hall to Room 226 and tapped on the door. Oliver opened it right away and smiled at her. "Great to see you, Robin. I'm sorry we couldn't have dinner, but at least we can have a drink and talk for a bit."

She beamed him a big smile. *Be who they want you to be.* "I'm sorry, too. I have to go to Chicago tomorrow, and I may be there for a while."

He looked at her, blank-faced. "I love your hat. Looks like you've been to the beach."

"The woman I interviewed lives near Revere Beach so we met there." Holding up the Neiman Marcus bag, she said, "I brought a change of clothes, but the interview ran long and I didn't have time to change."

She set the bag on the floor beside the royal-blue sofa and lay her beach hat over the top. Hidden under a lightweight denim jacket at the bottom of the bag was her new .38 Special, fully loaded.

She sank onto the sofa and crossed her legs. "What did you do today?"

He gazed at her, expressionless. "Would you like a glass of wine? I chilled a bottle of Chardonnay." He smiled, a genuine smile, or so it seemed.

The sleeves of his white shirt were rolled up to the elbow, exposing tanned sinewy forearms. He looked so handsome her heart almost melted. Almost. Somehow, Oliver had obtained Robin Adair's phone number and address. He knew she had a tattoo on her ankle. Frank Renzi was hunting for a woman with a tattoo who looked like Natalie Brixton. She couldn't imagine why Renzi would contact Oliver. Then again, she couldn't have imagined running into Tex Conroy in a New Orleans convenience store, either.

Being on her own all these years had taught her to trust no one. Rely only on yourself. While Oliver poured the wine, she focused on her goal.

Find out how he got your information. Find out who he really is.

He returned with two wine glasses, handed her one and sat down beside her. She got the impression he was waiting for her to question him.

She wasn't. Let him make the first move.

At last he said, "You're very quiet tonight, Robin."

She shrugged. "It's been a long day."

"Did you hurt your ankle?" he asked, gesturing at the Band-aid.

Her heart sank. Why had he zeroed in on the one thing she didn't want to talk about? "Just a little scrape. It's nothing, really."

"I'm disappointed that you didn't tell me you live in Nashua."

"Why be disappointed? Now you know. So what?"

He looked at her, blank-faced, but she saw anger in his no-longer-seductive eyes. "Sometimes I like surprises. Other times, I don't. I like you a lot, Robin, but you're a bit of a phantom. That got me curious."

Her scalp tingled as though her hair wanted to escape the ponytail and stand on end. She shifted her position, turning to face him. "Curious?"

"Three years ago Robin Adair rented an apartment in Nashua and registered a silver 2004 Honda Civic there. You said you've never been married, right?"

"True," she said, gazing at him steadily. "So?"

"So I wondered if you changed your name. Because prior to 2005, Robin Adair doesn't seem to exist."

She stared at the floor. Pictured her Japanese print of the snow-covered mountain. Heard a distant crack. Saw slabs of snow cascade down the mountain, snowballing into a deadly avalanche of ice and snow.

Oliver had collected a deadly avalanche of facts.

"You've been checking up on me," she said coldly. "I don't like that. Did you pay someone to investigate me?"

He did his George Clooney act, smiling at her. Even his eyes were smiling. "Chalk it up to my profession. I deal in antiquities that may or may not be authentic. It's my job to verify the facts. When you buy a used car, you have your mechanic check it out first, don't you?"

She stared at him. Used car? Had he been following her? Her cheek muscles felt stiff and wooden. "And did you find anything incriminating?"

He touched her hand. "No. But it puzzles me that until 2005, Robin Adair seems to be a phantom."

"That isn't my birth name. The night we met I told you my family isn't something I care to discuss. My childhood was . . . difficult."

"What's your real name?"

She gave him an icy look. "None of your business. Should I hire a detective to dig up your secrets? I'm sure you've got them. Everyone does."

"I'm sorry. I didn't realize this would upset you so much."

"Well, it does," she said, truthfully.

Oliver knew too much about Robin Adair. If only he didn't. If only their love affair could continue. But now Oliver was *The Man Who Knew Too Much*. And she had to decide what to do about it.

"My father was a cruel man. When I was young, he abused me." Not entirely true, but close enough. She gazed at the rug and summoned her acting skills. Conjured a memory of Randy coming into her room to kill Muffy. Tears filled her eyes. "So did my cousin. It took me years of therapy to get over it. Even then, my therapist said I might have flashbacks for the rest of my life."

A tear ran down her cheek. She brushed it away.

And became aware of a terrible stillness.

She looked at Oliver. His eyes were cold, and his lips were set in a cruel line. "Don't con me, Robin, or whatever your name is. Don't lie to me."

In an instant she made her decision. "I don't have to listen to your insults. I'm going home." She rose and stepped away from the couch.

His lips parted in shock. Before he could move, she did a taekwondo spin and kicked the side of the head with the heel of her shoe. He lurched sideways and collapsed on the floor. She grabbed the shopping bag, took out the plastic cuffs and studied him. He lay on his back, slack-jawed, eyes closed.

Working rapidly, she fastened his right wrist to one leg of the sofa, cuffed his right ankle to the other one. But when she reached for his left wrist, he grabbed her arm in a fierce grip, his angry eyes focused on hers.

She kicked him in the kidney, jerked free and took out her .38 Special.

With his free hand, he rubbed his side where she'd kicked him. Then his eyes focused on the gun.

She aimed the steel-blue muzzle at his forehead. "Who are you?"

With a faint smile, he said, "Isn't this is a bit over-the-top, Robin?"

His cocksure attitude infuriated her. Just like Randy, thinking she had a gun but wouldn't use it. "No. Who are you?"

"I told you. Oliver James, antique art dealer extraordinaire."

She flicked the gun, an impatient gesture. "Who did you hire to investigate Robin Adair?"

His smile disappeared and his eyes grew crafty. "If I tell you, will you put the gun away?"

"Maybe. Tell me. Then I'll decide."

"I have friends who do that sort of work. One of them did me a favor."

An icy chill ran down her spine. Someone else knew about Robin Adair. "Who is he? A cop? FBI?"

"Please, Robin. Put the gun away. I won't hurt you."

She laughed, a bitter laugh laced with panic. "Hurt me? You've already hurt me. More than you could possibly know. What agency does he work for?"

"The CIA."

Stunned, she stared at him. "How do you know people in the CIA?

He glared at her silently, his formerly-captivating eyes narrowed to slits. With grim determination, she aimed the gun at his forehead and stepped closer. But not too close. Thanks to her TKD training, she knew not to get close enough for his free arm or leg to harm her.

"Tell me who you are. Tell me your real name. Tell me about your CIA connection. If you don't, I will shoot you. Believe it."

"I believe you." His chest rose and fell rapidly. "After I graduated from Harvard, two CIA agents recruited me. I figured it would be exciting. But most of it was boring. I got out after two years. That's it. End of story."

"Who's your CIA friend?"

His lips tightened. "CIA operatives never give up names."

Jagged pain pierced her heart as enchanting memories flitted through her mind: Robin and Oliver bantering at the bar, Robin and Oliver eating dinner at the Top of the Hub, Robin and Oliver making love in this very room last Friday. And worst of all, the fantasy she'd conjured about their future together.

But Oliver James and his quest for authenticity had smashed her fairytale to smithereens.

"It didn't have to be this way," she said, avoiding his gaze.

She couldn't bear to look at his eyes.

She didn't want to shoot him, but what choice did she have? Oliver, a former CIA agent, still had CIA connections. If she allowed him to live, he would track her down, just as he had tracked down Robin Adair. And she would never avenge her mother's murder.

Focusing on the center of his forehead, she took a deep breath, let part of it out and pulled the trigger.

The gunshot reverberated through the room.

Involuntarily, she reeled back. Her ears hurt, but the ache in her heart was far worse. She forced herself to look at him. His eyes were open but unfocused, his lips pulled back in a grimace. In the middle of his forehead, blood oozed from a small circular hole.

A sob wracked her, an involuntary spasm that shook her entire body.

Why couldn't you just enjoy our time together and look forward to more, as I did?

But she had no time to mourn what might have been. She had to get out.

She grabbed the Neiman Marcus bag and her wine glass and ran to the alcove. The bathroom door was ajar. She elbowed it open, set the glass on the white-marble vanity next to the sink and pulled a long blond wig out of the shopping bag. With frantic haste, she stuffed her ponytail under the wig and checked herself in the mirror to make sure no dark strands of hair were visible.

Her ears were still ringing, though not as badly as before, and her head pulsed with a demonic throbbing pain. She shoved the gun to the bottom of the shopping bag, dumped the wine down the sink, dropped the wineglass in the bag and left the bathroom.

A terrible tableau confronted her. Oliver, sprawled on the floor, eyes vacant and staring. Beneath his head a bloodstain soaked the off-white carpet. Nauseated, she clenched her teeth against the bile that rose in her throat. Someone might have heard the gunshot. She had to get out.

Jamming the beach hat on her head, she went to the door and used her neck scarf to turn the knob. Ever so slowly, she pulled the door open an inch. And heard voices in the hall. Her heart accelerated into a runaway gallop.

She elbowed the door open two more inches and poked her head into the hall. To her right, a security guard in a navy-blue uniform stood outside the room next door. All the air left her lungs in a whoosh. She couldn't breathe. To reach the elevator she would have to walk past the guard.

Was there a fire escape outside Oliver's bedroom window? But if she went down the fire escape, someone might see her and grow suspicious.

She sidled into the hall, used the scarf to pull the door shut and walked toward the elevator with a confident stride as Madame had taught her.

". . . heard a shot. I'm positive." A woman's querulous voice.

The guard noticed her and turned. She kept going, marching past him with long-legged strides toward the elevator.

"Miss?" he called in a gravelly voice. "Did you hear a shot?"

"No." She kept walking, reached the elevator and stabbed the call button.

"Hold it, Miss. I want to talk to you." Walking toward her now.

She reached in the Neiman Marcus bag. Slid her fingers around the .38 Special. She didn't want to shoot him, but if she had to she would. Every muscle in her body was rigid with tension.

A ping sounded and the elevator doors opened.

She lunged inside. Stabbed the Door-Close button. Heard footsteps running down the hall.

"Hey, lady! Don't leave. I want to—" The elevator door slid shut.

———

12:20 A.M. New Orleans

Frank let the hot shower spray beat on him for ten minutes, got out and toweled off. It had been a backbreaking day, twelve hours on patrol, and tomorrow would be no different. He pulled on a pair of briefs, grabbed his radio handset and went in the kitchen. At seven o'clock, he'd eaten the sandwich Vobitch brought him. He wasn't hungry enough for a meal, but he needed a snack. The hurricane was screwing up his appetite, his sleep patterns, and his love life. He checked the time: 12:27. He wondered where Kelly was.

He took a stick of extra-sharp Cheddar out of the refrigerator, set it on the counter and opened a cupboard. And remembered he had no crackers.

As he mulled the alternatives his radio handset erupted: "Officer down! Officer down!" He upped the volume, heard Dispatch say, "What's your 20?"

The response was garbled. Dispatcher: "I don't read you. Say again."

He held his breath. *Don't let it be Kelly.*

After an eternity, a weak voice said: Elysian Fields and Filmore. Hurry.

Kelly's voice. Then, loud and clear over the radio handset: Pop-pop-pop.

Gunshots. He clenched his fists. "Damn it to hell!"

Dispatcher: "Attention all units. Officer down at Elysian and Filmore. Unit twelve, please report." Unit twelve. Kelly's patrol car.

His heart was a machine gun inside his chest. Pulling on jeans and a T-shirt, he listened for a response on the radio.

Nothing. Kelly was in trouble.

He jammed his SIG-Sauer in his holster, grabbed his car keys and left.

CHAPTER 18

As the elevator descended she tore off the beach hat and the blond wig and stuffed them into the Neiman Marcus bag. Her head throbbed in rhythm with her racing heart. Every minute was precious. By now the guard might have called the police and Boston Police Headquarters was only two blocks away. She had to get out before the cops got here. She yanked off the scrunchie that held her ponytail and shook her head, letting her long dark hair fall to her shoulders. The elevator eased to a stop and the door slid open.

Panic gored her like an ice pick. Beyond the plate-glass windows in the lobby, blue lights pulsed in a strobe-like effect. The cops had already sealed off the exit from the parking garage. She would have to escape on foot.

But she couldn't get out this way. The cops outside would see her.

She heard sirens. More cops. Tonight had been a disaster. Oliver was dead and the guard would have described a blond woman in white culottes who refused to stop when ordered. She dug a blue denim jacket out of the bag and put it on. No more blonde wig, but she couldn't hide the white culottes.

The sirens grew louder and went silent as two cruisers jolted to a stop outside the hotel, lights flashing. Four uniformed officers jumped out, guns drawn. She thought her heart would stop. If they came in the hotel, they would see her. Her heart relentlessly slammed her chest. She felt light-headed. Afraid she would faint, she dug her nails into her palms. Saw the four cops run to the squad cars guarding the parking garage exit.

Any minute they would come in the hotel. If she left the elevator alcove, the clerk at the check-in desk around the corner would see her. To her left, centered in the wood-paneled wall of the alcove, a sign on a door said: *Employees Only*. Without hesitation, she opened the door and entered a long narrow room. To her immediate left, white curtains dangled from three vacant changing stalls. Beyond them, gray-steel lockers lined both walls.

At the far end was a metal door with a red *Exit* sign above it.

But to reach it she would have to pass the half dozen wooden benches in front of the metal lockers. A small dark-haired man, Hispanic by the looks of him, sat on one bench lacing a pair Nikes.

137

She composed her face in a neutral expression and walked toward him.

"You work here?" he said in a thick Spanish accent, frowning at her.

In rapid French, she said, "I'm meeting Angela outside. I'm late and she's waiting for me!" And kept walking toward the exit.

"Wha'?" he said. "I don' understand you."

She reached into the Neiman Marcus bag.

If he tried to stop her, she'd shoot him.

———

Frank got on the I-10 and headed for the Elysian Fields exit. His cell phone rang. He grabbed it and Kenyon Miller said, "Yo, Frank. Where y'at?"

"On the I-10 headed for Elysian Fields. What's happening?"

"I'm at the scene." A pause, then a deep a sigh, Miller clearly struggling for control. "Fucking maggots shot Ben in the head. He's gone. Kelly's in an ambulance on her way to City Hospital."

"Christ! How bad is it?"

"EMT said she took a slug in the left side near her heart."

His chest felt like a gigantic hand was squeezing it. After spending two years with Kelly, a woman he'd grown to love, he didn't want to lose her.

"I said you were on the way, held her hand and told her to hang in there."

"Did they get the shooters?"

"Got two of 'em. One got away. You going to the hospital?"

"Heading there now."

"Me, too. Vobitch is already there. He got pretty fond of Kelly, you know, when she was working Homicide. And so did I."

"Thanks for calling me. See you at the hospital."

He took the next exit, got back on the I-10 headed west and hit the lights and sirens, recalling the case he and Kelly had worked together two years ago. Kelly had survived that one. Now she was in a hospital, fighting for her life.

———

She burst through the exit door into the dark humid night. More sirens. She looked right. A security guard in a blue uniform was running toward Huntington Avenue. If he turned and saw her, it was all over. She vaulted a low brick wall onto St. Botolph Street and ran to the opposite sidewalk. No shouts. No shots. She took off at a dead run, her feet pounding the pavement.

Two blocks later, gasping for breath, she leaned against a telephone pole and vomited in the gutter. She wiped her mouth, her thoughts in a whirl. The Colonnade Hotel was around the corner on Huntington Avenue one block away. She ran to the corner and paused to get her breathing under control.

She put on her dark glasses and walked to the entrance. Swinging her Neiman Marcus bag, she sauntered past the desk and entered the hotel gift shop. She grabbed a Boston Red Sox cap off a display and went to the register.

A sleepy-eyed woman and smiled at her. "Last minute souvenir?"

She smiled back. "Yes. My brother would kill me if I didn't get him one."

She paid cash for the cap, hurried to a rest room. She put on the Red Sox hat and studied her image in the mirror. What did people notice about you, really? Your skin color: white, black or brown. Your hair: long, short, light or dark. And your build: tall or short, fat or thin.

Now she looked like a college student who'd been shopping, carrying a Neiman Marcus bag, a baseball cap set at a rakish angle on her head. But she had to get to Nashua before the cops found Robin Adair's car in the parking garage. Oliver James and the CIA operative he'd refused to name knew Robin's address. Oliver was dead, but the CIA man wasn't. And Robin Adair's address was on the Honda's registration.

She returned to the hotel lobby and went outside. Miracle of miracles, a yellow cab was coming down Huntington Avenue. She stepped off the curb and waved. When the cab pulled over, she got in the back seat.

"Hi, could you take me to Logan Airport?"

————

City Hospital, New Orleans

Surrounded by antiseptic odors and the hiss of oxygen, he stood beside Kelly's bed. Hooked up to tubes and beeping monitors, she looked utterly defenseless, face ashen, eyes closed. Two years ago she had held an armed killer at bay until backup arrived. Tonight she'd held off three thugs, had even managed to wound one of them.

The thought of her standing alone against her attackers tore him up. His throat thickened and he turned away. The nurse had said Kelly would probably wake up soon and he didn't want her to see his anguished expression.

He conjured a vision of her mischievous sea-green eyes and the sound of her low-throated laugh. When was the last time they'd shared a laugh? The night he'd shown her the security video when they were talking about female assassins. Three nights ago. Eons ago.

Her eyes fluttered open and settled on his face.

"Hey," he said softly. "You're okay. You're going to be fine."

Speaking the words he'd want to hear if their situation were reversed.

She tried to smile. "I'm still out of it, Frank. But I'm glad you're here."

He kissed her forehead. "Where else would I be? The doctor said after some rehab, you'll be fine. Did he talk to you?"

"Yes, but I was too woozy to catch most of it. Tell me what he said."

"The slug bounced off your clavicle, chipped off some fragments. That's why the surgery took so long."

He didn't mention what else the doctor had said. She was lucky the slug hadn't hit a major artery. If the path had been four inches lower it would have hit her heart and she'd be dead.

"How's Ben?" Kelly asked, her eyes fixed on his.

The question he'd been dreading. He took a white Styrofoam cup on the bedside table, pulled the tab off the straw. "Here, have some water."

She waved it away. "Tell me about Ben. They shot him, didn't they."

He took a deep breath and let it out. "Yes."

"So? How is he?" Her sea-green eyes seemed darker than usual, dark as the ocean depths. When he didn't answer, her eyes welled with tears. "He's dead, isn't he." A tear spilled over and ran down her cheek.

Fighting for control, he kissed her forehead again. "The most important thing right now is for you to rest and get better."

He took a tissue out of the packet on the nightstand and wiped the tears away. "Kelly, I know you and Ben were tight. He was a great guy and a great partner. But you did what you could. You shot one of those maggots and—"

"Did you get them?" she whispered.

"We got two. The other one got away, but we'll find him, I promise."

She closed her eyes, and he knew she was processing the information.

"Kenyon Miller and Morgan Vobitch are waiting down the hall. They're worried about you."

Her eyes fluttered open. "Aw, what sweethearts."

He forced himself to smile. "They want to come give you a kiss, but I don't want to leave you alone with 'em while I'm not here."

She gave him a weak smile. That made him feel better. If he could make her smile, maybe they would get through this. "Want me to call your dad?"

Her eyes widened. "Jesus! I didn't even think about that. Would you?"

"Sure. Give me the number."

She spoke it aloud and he wrote it on his palm with a pen. He caressed her cheek. "I'll tell Kenyon and Morgan they can't stay long. You need to rest. I'm gonna go call your dad, but I'll see you tomorrow bright and early, okay?"

She gave him a sleepy, dreamy-eyed smile. "Okay, Frank. Be careful."

His throat tightened. Terms of endearment. "You're gonna be fine, Kelly. I'll see you tomorrow."

He walked down the hall to a bench where Miller and Vobitch sat side by side, talking in low voices. They saw him coming and rose to their feet.

"How is she?" Vobitch asked, his face knit in the mother of all frowns.

"Damn lucky to be alive according to the doc, but she'll be okay."

"Thank God for that," Miller said, relief plain on his face.

"I told her you guys want to say hello. She seemed happy about that."

Vobitch clenched his jaw, his eyes somber. "Does she know about Ben?"

"Maggots." Visibly upset, Miller clenched his fists. "I'm gonna find the fuckhead that shot Ben and tear him a new asshole."

"I didn't want to tell her," he said, "but she guessed. I want you to go in there and tell her she's brave as hell and she did everything she could, 'cause right now she's got survivor's guilt, you know?"

"We will," Miller and Vobitch said in unison.

"Thanks. Now I gotta go call her father and tell him what happened."

———

She sank lower in the backseat of the taxi, stomach churning. Traffic on Huntington Avenue was at a standstill. Twenty yards ahead of the cab, police cars with flashing blues were parked helter-skelter outside Copley Place and the Marriott Hotel. She hugged her ribs, trying to quiet her racing heart.

"Where you headed?" asked the driver, eyeing her in the rearview mirror.

She met his gaze, forced herself to smile. "Australia."

His face registered amazement. "You're going to Australia without any luggage?"

For some reason his question calmed her. Focus. Invent a story. Don't think about that police officer over there directing traffic who might notice you in the backseat of the cab and arrest you.

"My brother waiting for me in Terminal E with my luggage. Our flight leaves at six and we don't want to miss it." She mustered another smile. "I can't wait to get to Sydney."

Seemingly satisfied, he put the cab in gear and inched forward. Traffic was moving now as the cop waved his flashlight in jagged swoops, directing vehicles around the squad cars. She held her breath as the taxi drew even with the cop, her palms damp with sweat. But the cop waved the taxi along with his flashlight and focused on the car behind them. Weak with relief, she unclenched her fists. She was free. For the moment, anyway.

Once they cleared the traffic jam it took only fifteen minutes to get to Logan Airport. The cabbie drove her to Terminal E, the departure and arrival point for international flights. When they entered Departures, a State Police cruiser stood outside the Aer Lingus entrance to the terminal.

She had the cabbie drop her at the Air France entrance fifty yards beyond the cruiser, paid him in cash and added a generous tip. Fighting a desperate urge to run, she sauntered into the terminal and went to the nearest rest room. Most of the State cops she'd seen at Logan were men. She doubted one would follow her into a women's rest room. She splashed cold water on her face, cupped her hands and swished water around her mouth to get rid of the disgusting taste. Her insides had stopped shaking, but her legs hadn't.

And her mind was going seventy miles an hour. An express bus ran from Logan to Nashua, but not this late. She would have to wait here overnight. Dangerous. State police officers patrolled the terminal round the clock, and the cops at the airport, train and bus stations would be especially vigilant.

Assuming Boston PD had put out a description of the woman leaving Oliver's room, they'd be looking for a blond woman in white culottes. She'd ditched the wig but not the culottes. If only she'd bought a pair of Red Sox pants to go with the cap. But she'd been too desperate to escape.

She used the toilet and returned to the departures area. Terminal E was deserted. No passengers. No shops open. No clerks at ticket counters. She felt conspicuous. Visible through the plate-glass windows facing the roadway was the French-and-electric-blue State Police cruiser. A trooper in a distinctive State Police hat sat behind the wheel. Monitoring his radio, no doubt.

For all she knew, he was listening to her description right now.

It was almost midnight, but a few flights might still be leaving Terminal B. A shuddering yawn wracked her. She was exhausted, her legs shaking with fatigue. She needed someplace to rest where the cops wouldn't find her. Shuttle buses circled the airport roadway 24/7 to transport passengers and workers between terminals, but to get it she'd have to wait outside and that would attract the trooper's attention. She began walking toward Terminal B, her footsteps echoing in the deserted glassed-in corridor.

Five minutes later she trudged into Terminal B. And saw a State trooper inside a glassed-in area facing the airport roadway.

She ducked into a rest room. A tall woman with pecan-brown skin stood at the sink, washing her hands, an airport worker, judging by her green coveralls. "Excuse me, do you know if any stores are open in this terminal?"

"Try Hudson News," the woman said, not looking at her. "It's a couple doors down on the right."

"Thanks." She left the rest room, spotted the Hudson News sign and hurried to the store. Perched on a stool inside a kiosk, a slender Hispanic woman with silver hoop earrings was reading a paperback. The only other customer, a young man in jeans and a T-shirt, stood at the magazine rack, leafing through a *Sports Illustrated*.

She picked out a souvenir T-shirt and a pair of navy sweatpants with a Red Sox logo. At the back of the store, she took a bottle of Aquafina out of a cooler and grabbed a package of trail mix from a wire rack. Then she noticed the knapsacks hanging from hooks along one wall. Perfect. She needed to hide the Neiman Marcus bag. And the gun.

She chose a black knapsack and took everything to the register.

The woman stifled a yawn. "Find everything you wanted?"

"Yes, thank you." She paid cash and returned to the rest room.

Now it was empty. After changing inside a handicapped stall, she came out and studied herself in the mirror. She looked like a different person: a white T-shirt with **BOSTON** emblazoned across the front, navy sweatpants and a Red Sox baseball cap. She strapped the black knapsack over her shoulders. Inside was the Neiman Marcus bag. At the bottom of the knapsack, hidden by the clothes she'd removed, was the .38 Special.

She went downstairs to Arrivals, walked past two baggage carrousels and went out to the glassed-in cubicle where the bus passengers waited. No one waiting now. Taped to the glass was a schedule. The first bus to Nashua departed Terminal A at 8:10 A.M, stopped at Terminal B two minutes later.

Another yawn wracked her. She was exhausted, but she had to stay alert until she got on the bus. Seven long hours from now, provided a State cop didn't stop and question her. If he did, she was done for.

Our Lady of the Airwaves, a Catholic chapel, was on the ground level between Terminals B and C. During the day, a priest said Masses there. The chapel was open 24-7 for people to pray if they so desired. She didn't intend to pray, but she desperately needed a place to rest.

Ten minutes later she sank onto a wooden pew at the rear of the dim-lit chapel and set her knapsack beside her. Ten rows ahead, a circular light fixture cast a rosy glow over the altar. Two spotlights lit up large statues on either side of the altar, but the rest of the chapel was dark. Fearing she'd fall asleep, she prioritized her tasks. If she could get to her condo without being arrested, Robin would disappear. She already had a car. But she had to decide what to take with her.

She closed her eyes and pictured her clothes closet.

A horrific image blindsided her: Oliver lying on the carpet, blood pooling under his head, eyes vacant and staring. Accusing eyes. Chills wracked her, and tears stung her eyes. What sort of person was she?

An evil person, with no regard for human life. Because of a chance encounter, Oliver had taken a fancy to Robin Adair. And now he was dead.

She bit her lip and made her mind go blank. *Think about Mom. Think about the freedom you'll have after you avenge Mom. Think about anything but Oliver.*

Two weeks from now April West would be in New Orleans. Where Detective Frank Renzi was stalking Arnold Peterson's killer. A woman with a tattoo on her ankle who looked like Natalie Brixton.

A chill skittered down her spine.

CHAPTER 19

Thursday, 7 August   New Orleans

Frank stopped outside Kelly's hospital room and looked in the window. Seeing her sitting on the bed with her legs dangling over the side took the edge off his dark mood. He'd just come from Ben Washburn's funeral, a somber ceremony attended by hundreds of police officers. Ben's wife had been stoic, but their three kids clung to her, weeping. Other eyes were leaking, too. Ben was a popular guy, much-loved by his many friends and colleagues. Now he was dead. Shot by a worthless scumbag. It could just as easily have been Kelly.

He pushed through the door. "Hey, gorgeous, you look like you're raring to go." Her face was still drawn and pale, but the tubes in her nose and arm were gone. The doctor had said she could go home tomorrow.

"Ready to get out of here, that's for sure. How was the funeral?"

He didn't want to talk about it, but he'd been expecting the question. "Kenyon gave one of the eulogies. Ben and his wife lived right down the street from him. Their kids play together."

Kelly nodded. Her desolate expression and sad eyes tore him up.

"I said a few words too. I didn't know Ben well, but he was a good man. I said you were lucky to be alive--" His throat thickened and he broke off, overcome with emotions he'd managed to fight off at the funeral. He couldn't imagine not having Kelly in his life.

"That night on patrol," Kelly said, her lips quivering, "that night Ben told me his wife was pregnant."

"Damn. I didn't know that. Sometimes life just isn't fair."

"I don't think he told many people. She's not very far along. I'll go see her as soon as I get out of here."

"Well, let's get you get back on your feet first." *And get your mind off Ben.* "How's the physical therapy going?"

"They had me try some new exercises today. My shoulder muscles are so weak it's pathetic. The therapist will come to my house for two weeks. Then I can go to the gym."

144

"I'll go buy you some groceries tonight. Got any requests?"

A glimmer of a smile. "What a guy. You gonna buy me chicken soup?"

"Whatever it takes to make you better." He gave her a big smooch on the lips. She put her arms around him and nuzzled his neck.

"Well, well, what have we got here?" said a female voice.

Startled, he pulled away. A tall gray-haired nurse smiled at him. Mary Halloran, according to the name tag on her starched white uniform. Her blue eyes twinkled. "It's okay. We allow kissing, as long as it makes the patient feel better." Clipboard in hand, she went to Kelly and held out a small paper cup.

"I don't need any more pain meds," Kelly said. "I'm fine."

"That's good, but you better take them. The doctor will let you know when to stop. You're his poster-girl, you know. Quick recovery and all."

Kelly made a face and swallowed the pills. Halfway to the door, the nurse turned and said, "Take good care of Kelly, you hear? We've gotten very fond of her."

"Don't worry. I will."

After she left, Kelly said, "She's been so sweet. Everyone has."

"You're a hero," he said, and wished he hadn't when he saw her sorrowful eyes. He didn't want her thinking about Ben. The bastard who'd shot him was in the lockup, unable to make bail. To distract her, he said, "No major flooding from Hurricane Gail so most of the evacuees are back. I've been working my butt off on the Peterson and Conroy murders."

Vobitch had pulled strings to get him off patrol duty so he could visit Kelly twice a day.

She sucked up some water from a Styrofoam cup. "Any leads?"

"I showed the Natalie sketch to the Hotel Bienvenue bartender, but he said she didn't look familiar. Nothing helpful from the tip line, either."

"Now that the evacuees are back maybe you'll get something."

"I hope so. I'm sure Corrine Peterson didn't go to the hotel that night. I showed her picture at the parking lots near the hotel and checked the cab companies, got zilch."

"What about Peterson's enemies? Any luck?"

"Nothing. Ivan Ludlow's wife said he was home all night, and Ken Volpe was in Las Vegas that week. And why would they hire a hitter? They both landed good jobs after they left The Babylon. Which leaves Morgan's favorite suspect. The big bad bogyman."

"He's so sweet." Seeing his incredulous expression, she laughed. "Morgan, I mean. He brought me some chocolate chip cookies his wife made, and Kenyon came in with pecan pie from Tanya. Everybody's being so nice." Her smile faded. "I'm not looking forward to testifying though."

"That's months away." He leaned closer, gave her another kiss. "I think it's about time we got into some mischief."

She brushed tendrils of short dark hair away from her face. "Yeah. After I get home and wash my hair and make myself a tad more alluring."

"You look fine. I don't mind those skuzzy hanks of hair."

She swatted his arm. "Did you call the people in Pecos about the tat?"

"Aw shucks. Here I was thinking we were about to have a little verbal foreplay."

She flashed her sexy smile. "Tomorrow, cowboy. Tell me about Pecos."

"Right. Pecos. I called Ellen Brixton and asked her if Natalie had a tat on her ankle in high school. Ellen said definitely not. Then I called Rojas." Rojas had been openly hostile. "He said Natalie had no tat on her ankle, also said he didn't want to talk to me, pretty much told me to fuck off."

"You think he knows where she is?"

"If he does, I can't force him to tell me unless we get a grand jury with subpoena power to make him talk. And we're nowhere near that."

"So you're back to square one," Kelly said. "Bummer."

"Looks like it." He checked his watch. "I better get back to the office."

His cell rang. He silenced it quickly. Cell phones were verboten inside the hospital, but he didn't want to miss a crucial call. When he answered Vobitch said, "Frank, we got a call on the tip line. The desk clerk at the Sunrise Inn near Esplanade said the woman in the sketch might have stayed there."

Adrenaline upped his heart rate. "Great! I'm on my way."

———

Ithaca, New York

Her neck prickled as an odd sound penetrated her second floor window. After her narrow escape in Boston, any atypical noise put her on alert. She went to the window, peeked through the Venetian blind and saw the landlady dragging a large green trash barrel out to the sidewalk.

Two days ago she had rented the room for a week, saying she was apartment hunting for her fall semester at Ithaca College. The landlady, a pleasant middle-aged woman with a friendly smile, glanced at April West's Vermont license and asked no questions. Vermont was one of the few states in the country where a photograph was not mandatory on a driver's license.

She sank onto the cheap futon that filled one wall of the room and sipped from a bottle of iced tea. To her left, a tiny alcove had a hot plate, a microwave and a mini-refrigerator, a far cry from her Nashua apartment, but she'd lived in worse places. At the boardinghouse in New York her room had no kitchen, just a lumpy bed and a tiny bathroom, so she'd moved in with Darren. Was he still auditioning for the soaps? she wondered. No. He was probably married with two kids, working as a floor manager at Nordstrom's.

She massaged her neck to ease the tense knots. Yesterday at the Ithaca Registry of Motor Vehicles she'd stood in a line that shuffled forward inches at a time. When she reached the counter, she gave April West's license and the title for Bobby's Ford Focus to the clerk. On the registration form she'd listed the rooming house as her current address.

The woman got on the computer. That made her nervous. Computers could access all sorts of information. What if Bobby had unpaid parking tickets? But after an endless wait, the clerk printed out the registration and said the plates would be mailed to her current address. "You should have them within five days," the woman had said.

Four more days to wait. She stifled a yawn. She was still exhausted, her mind endlessly replaying her escape. After the Logan Express bus dropped her in Nashua, she'd taken a taxi to her apartment. Fearing the cops might arrive any minute, she tossed a few items in a suitcase, grabbed her laptop, took the back way to the parking lot to avoid other residents and fled in the Ford Focus. But in her haste, she had left the apartment without taking the time to erase her fingerprints.

That worried her, but there was nothing she could do about it now.

Two grueling days later she had arrived in Ithaca, exhausted but unable to sleep. Last night she had jolted awake again, heart pounding, hands sweaty, reliving a familiar nightmare in vivid color. Oliver's bright red blood seeping into the carpet. His sky-blue eyes staring at her, full of reproach.

A feeling of desolation overwhelmed her. Tears filled her eyes, brimmed over and rolled down her cheeks. Oliver had been in the wrong place at the wrong time, treated Robin Adair to dinner and wound up dead. Because she was a monster who killed innocent people. First Tex, now Oliver.

Would she ever find happiness with a man? Four years ago she had been certain that Willem was the man of her dreams. Wrong.

Gritting her teeth, she rose from the futon and went to a small card table just outside the kitchen alcove. Her laptop was on the table beside her cell phone. She dialed a number and waited.

"Parades-A-Plenty! Mrs. Reilly speaking," a voice squalled.

The voice ran across her ear like an ugly rasp, high-pitched and shrill as a banshee. Madame would have sent the woman to the voice coach immediately.

"Do you have a room available on Friday, August fifteenth?"

"August? There won't be any Mardi Gras parades then, you know," the woman said sharply.

"That's okay. I'm not coming to see the Mardi Gras parades. I have a job interview at Loyola."

"You're a student? I don't rent rooms to students anymore. A bunch of hooligans stayed here two years ago for Mardi Gras and got drunk and trashed my best room."

"But I'm not a student—"

"One of them peed on my sofa. Can you imagine?"

147

She could imagine strangling the woman if she didn't shut up. "Mrs. Reilly, I'm not a student. I'm interviewing for a teaching position at Loyola."

Silence on the other end. Blessed silence. Then, "You don't sound old enough to teach at Loyola. How old are you?"

"I'm thirty-two." Or so the DOB on April West's license said.

"What will you be teaching," asked her relentless inquisitor.

"Comparative Religion." Like many New Orleans residents, the woman was probably Catholic, or Baptist perhaps, like the people in Pecos.

"Well. I'm Catholic myself and I don't have much use for those weird religions. Buddhists and Hindus and whatnot. Hold on while I check to see if I have a room available."

Grateful for the silence, she conjured an image of Mrs. Reilly, a scrawny old woman with a neck like a turkey probably. She'd deliberately chosen a B&B upriver from the French Quarter, away from the Sunshine Inn. That place had bad karma. Tex had lived two streets away. Parades-A-Plenty was on the opposite side of the Quarter, conveniently located on a side street one block from the St. Charles Avenue streetcar line. Convenient, but the owner was obnoxious enough on the phone. In person she might be worse.

"You're in luck," squawked the Banshee. "I have a beautiful room on the third floor with a single bed and a private bath for seventy dollars a night."

"How much would it cost for a week?"

"A week? Well. I'll give you a discount. A week will be four hundred."

"I'll take it. My name is April West. I'll pay you cash in advance."

"Oh no you won't! I need a credit card to hold the room. In case there's any damages."

She dug her nails into her palms to keep from screaming. She couldn't use a credit card. They were too easy to trace.

"Credit cards are against my religion. I'll send you a money order."

Silence. Then, "Against your religion?"

"Yes. If you give me your word *as a Catholic* that you'll hold the room, I'll mail you a money order for *five hundred* dollars. Otherwise, I'll find someplace else to stay."

"Well. All right, I guess. You have the address?"

"Yes. I'll send it overnight express and call to make sure you got it."

She closed the cell and massaged her throbbing forehead.

Not a very auspicious beginning for the Main Event.

————

New Orleans

When Frank arrived at the Sunshine Inn, the clerk was waiting behind the check-in desk. A wiry clean-shaven black man, Rasheed Cooper appeared to be in his mid-thirties and he had a zillion tattoos, multi-colored swirls and curlicues that covered every visible inch of skin on his arms and neck. Did he have tats on his Yankee Doodle? Frank wondered.

He flashed his ID and said, "Mr. Cooper? I got a message that you called about the sketch of the woman."

"Yes, sir. Woulda called sooner, but it took me two days to get back from the evacuation. Me and my girlfriend went to Jackson, Mississippi. Man, traffic was a bear, bumper to bumper the whole way."

"So I heard. What can you tell me about the woman?"

"Didn't look much like the one in the sketch. She wore sunglasses and her hair was shorter, light brown, but I'm pretty sure she stayed here. The article said the woman had a tat on her ankle. One morning when she was having coffee in the breakfast room, I noticed the tat on her ankle."

"Easy to see why. You look like you're a tat connoisseur."

Rasheed beamed. "Got a few, for sure. You want her name?"

"I do. Her name and anything else you can tell me about her."

"She registered as June Carson on July seventeenth, stayed here a week, checked out on the twenty-fourth." Rasheed shrugged. "That's about it."

Frank liked the dates. June Carson had checked out the day Tex Conroy was shot in City Park, the day after the Peterson murder.

"Did she have a car?"

"We got no parking on the premises, you know, so we don't ask our guests give us plate numbers. But I saw her drive past the Inn one day."

"Can you tell me the make and model? Even the color would help."

"Looked like a Toyota Corolla. Maroon. Couldn't tell you the year."

"Great, that's a big help. Anything else distinctive about her?"

"Not really. She kept to herself. Only time we spoke was when she checked in and out."

"Did she sound like she was from here? Or somewhere else?"

"Couldn't say for sure. Didn't seem like she was from around here, but she didn't have no twangy Texas accent or nothing." Rasheed gazed at him expectantly.

Clearly, Rasheed had been following the Peterson and Conroy cases on the news. By now it was public knowledge that Tex Conroy was from Texas.

"Thanks for the tip, Mr. Cooper. I'll be in touch."

Buoyed by the lead, he left the Sunshine Inn. Now he had a name. It might be fake, but it was better than nothing. Was June Carson the woman on the security video? That woman had a tat on her ankle and so did June Carson.

Coincidence? He didn't think so. Now all he had to do was find her.

And if June Carter turned out to be Natalie Brixton, he'd finally get some answers.

Natalie

2000   Paris

For my date with Thu Phan I prepared with great care.

I was certain he was my father.

Accepting him as a client brought great emotional turmoil and conflicted feelings. Part of me felt ashamed of myself for becoming a prostitute, a high-class escort to be sure, but still a woman paid to have sex with men. Another part of me felt ashamed that my father paid women for sex. Yet another part of me felt enormous curiosity. Veneration of Ancestors was now second nature to me. I wanted to meet him and see what he was like. Still another part of me wanted to confront the man who had abandoned us.

But as I prepared for our date my dominant emotion was fear. I was afraid he would recognize me, equally afraid that he wouldn't. Most of all, I was afraid I would not find the courage to confront him and tell him I was the daughter he had forsaken so many years ago.

Using the makeup tricks I had learned, I emphasized my Asian eyes with eyeliner and glittery eye shadow. I brushed my long black hair until it gleamed. Then I chose my outfit, an elegant ankle-length silk dress with red dragons embossed on a black background. A slit on one side showed off my leg. I put on shiny-black spike heels, a dab of jasmine perfume and studied myself in the mirror. Then I put on my favorite earrings, the ones shaped like seagulls. The birds would protect me. Or so I hoped.

To give myself courage, I took out Mom's picture and I chanted my TKD oath. *I shall be a champion of freedom and justice.* Three times I chanted it.

———

When the taxi stopped in front of Thu Phan's hotel on the Champs-Élysées, my palms were sweaty and my heart was racing. Not even my TKD focus could calm me. But I strode into the lobby with my head held high, walking with the smooth confident stride Madame had taught me. As instructed, I went to an in-house phone and dialed Thu Phan's room number.

"Bon soir. C'est tu, Laura Lin?"

Goosebumps rose on my arms at the sound of his low pitched voice and melodic French, using the familiar *tu*, not the more formal *vous*.

"Oui," I said. "C'est tu, Monsieur Phan?"

"It is," he said in English. "You have a lovely voice and a charming accent, Laura Lin. Please come up so we can have a drink and get to know each other before we go out for dinner."

Two minutes later I knocked on his door, aching with anticipation but also filled with dread. I had no idea how this night would end. The door opened and my father appeared. I thought my heart would stop.

He was very handsome, glossy black hair swept back from a high forehead, full lips and dark-brown Asian eyes. After surveying me from head to toe, he smiled, a generous smile that exposed gleaming white teeth. "Come in, Laura. You are every bit as beautiful as Lin said you would be."

I said nothing. I hated being weighed and measured against some sort of beauty yardstick. He gestured at a cozy loveseat and I sank onto it, grateful I didn't have to stand. My legs were shaking. I barely noticed my surroundings. My entire being was focused on my father. He was tall and slender, moving with easy grace in his bare feet. He wore tailored black slacks and a ruffled dress shirt with gold cufflinks.

"Can I get you a cocktail?" he said. "A glass of wine?"

"A glass of wine, thank you." I smiled. "I'm a little bit nervous." My usual opener to put the client at ease. Tonight it was for me. I was terrified.

"Don't be nervous, Laura Lin. I can tell that we will have a lovely time."

I said nothing. *A lovely time? Not after you hear my big surprise.*

He filled two glasses from a bottle of chilled white wine, set them on the Italian-marble coffee table in front of the loveseat and sat beside me.

"I was told that you live in New York," I said. "That must be exciting."

"Paris is just as exciting and much more beautiful. I was born here."

My heart did flip-flops inside my chest. "How interesting! I would love to hear about it. Did your parents always live Paris?" Even as I said this my mind was estimating his age. Mom would have been forty this year, and my father was four years older than she was. This meant Thu Phan was forty-four. Twice my age. I tried not to think about that.

"My father's family had to flee Vietnam in the 1950s. Because of the political upheavals. They settled in Paris. He met my mother here."

"Is your mother also Vietnamese?" I knew she wasn't, but I wanted to learn more about my heritage.

"No, French. She died years ago. But enough about me. I understand that you also have Asian ancestors. Tell me about your parents, Laura Lin."

I couldn't believe my ears. Here was an opening as big as the Empire State Building, but it was too soon. I wanted to know more about my father before I delivered my surprise. If I found the courage to do it.

151

"Later, perhaps. I'd love to hear about your work. Are you a professor at an important university?" By now I knew all the tricks: Flatter a man and he will tell you all about himself, the good parts anyway.

He waved a dismissive hand. "Teaching does not interest me. I own real estate in Manhattan, apartment buildings and retail stores. It took years of hard work to make them pay off, but now my business does quite well." He looked disgustingly pleased with himself. "So I get to travel and see the world."

And spend obscene amounts of money on call girls.

"Have you ever been to Vietnam?"

"No." He moved closer on the love seat, close enough for me to smell his spicy aftershave lotion, close enough for him to put his hand on my thigh. "You have beautiful eyes and skin, Laura. How did you happen to begin working for The Service?"

"I needed money." That was the truth. Never mind why I needed it.

He nodded. "You seem quite young. That is why I asked."

"I'm twenty-two." I dug my fingernails into my palms. "I was born on April 15, 1978."

But this announcement of my birth date did not bring the response I had hoped. My father looked puzzled for a moment, then took my hand and ran his fingers down my forearm. "Would you like to make whoopee before we go out for dinner, Laura Lin?"

I sat there, stunned, and my stomach clenched in a painful knot. I had not expected his request to come so soon, and his ignorance of my birth date, willful or not, hurt me deeply. A seedling of anger took root inside me.

"My name isn't Laura. My name is Natalie."

He frowned. "I don't understand. What has this to do with anything?"

"It has to do with Jeanette Brixton."

A shocked look rippled over his face. "Jeanette? I don't understand."

"Yes, you do. I am Natalie Brixton, Jeanette's daughter."

I don't know what I expected. I guess I wanted him to embrace me and tell me how thrilled he was to have found his long lost daughter. But he sprang to his feet, hands fisted at his sides, and glared at me. "You are not. Why do you pretend to be someone you are not?"

My cheeks flamed with anger. "Why are you using an escort service?"

His Asian eyes narrowed to slits. "This is not what I paid for, to have some slut berate me."

"Who are you to call me a slut?" I shouted, unable to keep my voice low and well-modulated as Madame had taught me. "You pay women half your age for sex. You abandoned me when I was two, and you never paid my mother a dime for my support."

"I don't have to listen to this." He pointed to the door. "Get out."

Tears flooded my eyes. Once again my father was casting me aside just as he had twenty years ago. I rose and faced him. In my spike heels I was almost as tall as he was. "You think women are your playthings? Do you know what your wife had to do to support herself and her child? *Your* child?"

Something flickered in his eyes and quickly disappeared. His implacable gaze remained locked on mine, but a muscle jumped in his jaw, a telltale sign of his discomfort.

"My mother was a prostitute. That's what your ex-wife had to do to survive. She had no money and no skills." I smiled, not my charming smile, the smile I used to convey displeasure and defiance. "Her brother told me she was a great dancer, but not great enough to get a job that would support us."

He stalked to an antique writing desk and picked up his wallet. "How much do you want? Name your price."

If I had been holding a gun in my hands I would have shot him.

Fear spilled down my spine like ice water. Not for my physical safety. Thanks to my TKD skills, I felt confident I could disable most men. It was the Vietnamese Ancestor gods I feared. This man was my father. If I killed him, the angry Ancestor spirits would haunt me forever, seeking to avenge my father's violent death, as I sought to avenge my mother's.

I had no gun, of course. I had only words. But words are also powerful.

"Name my price? No price that you could ever pay, Mr. Thu Phan. You never cared about me. If you cared about me, you wouldn't have abandoned me. In all the years after you left, twenty years, you never tried to get in touch with me. Not once. Ever."

"I was working, trying to make a living." He waved a dismissive hand. "But why should I explain? You wouldn't understand."

"Don't you want to know what happened to my mother?"

Clearly annoyed, he said, "Okay, what happened to her?"

The moment of truth. My truth.

"In 1988 we were living in New Orleans. I was ten. Mom worked six nights a week from nine o'clock until whatever time she got home. While she was at work, I stayed in our crummy little apartment. Alone. And then one day she didn't come home." Bitter memories swirled in my mind, sharp and clear.

Tears welled in my eyes and rolled down my cheeks.

Thu Phan remained stone-faced. "What happened?"

And I thought: *Why sugarcoat the pill? He's a grown man. He can take it.*

"A policewoman rang the doorbell and told me she was dead."

His mouth gaped open. "How terrible! You must have been—"

"Don't give me your fake sympathy!" I wanted to twist the knife and make him feel every bit of the guilt he had avoided for twenty years. "The police found her body in a sleazy hotel room. Naked. In bed. One of her johns punched her and hit her. And strangled her."

Thu Phan took a deep breath and blew out his cheeks. "I'm sorry. Give me your address. I will send you a check every month."

"I don't want your money," I said coldly.

He looked puzzled. "What do you want then?"

"Is that what you think life is about? Money? You're rich enough to buy whatever you want. If you want someone to love you . . ." I smiled my terrible smile. "To *pretend* to love you, you call The Service and they send you a woman who makes you feel important and provides you with sex. That's all women are to you, playthings to use and discard when you're done with them."

"Natalie," he said in a low voice.

My heart surged when he said my name, acknowledging at last that I was his daughter.

His shoulders slumped like a deflated balloon. "I'm not like that. I've been hurt, too."

It was a very good thing I did not have a gun. "Don't try to weasel out of this by saying some woman fucked you and dumped you."

Seeing the shock in his eyes as I said this was priceless. "Want to know how I spent the rest of my so-called childhood? Living with Mom's brother and his screwed-up family in Texas. My cousin Randy tried to fuck me, but I wouldn't let him. So he made his sister give him blowjobs."

My father gaped at me. "Why didn't his parents stop him?"

"Because his mother was a drunk and his father was having an affair." All of a sudden I felt exhausted. My insides were shaking. "I'm leaving now. If you care about me at all, Mr. Thu Phan, you will tell no one about this conversation. You will tell Lin and everyone else at The Service that you were absolutely thrilled with the service provided to you by Laura Lin."

He had the grace to look shamed at least. "I will do that, of course. I wish you would allow me to send you a check . . ." He trailed off when he saw the look on my face.

I grabbed my purse and strode past him. But at the door, I stopped. It took all my willpower not to turn and take one last look at him. Part of me wanted to memorize his face. Another part of me still wanted him to hold me and comfort me, the little girl he had abandoned so long ago.

But that would be a mistake, because I knew that what I had said was true. Thu Phan was rich and powerful like the man who murdered my mother. Like many powerful men, my father used women. He might not beat them or kill them, but what he did was just as bad: Use their bodies for sex and dismiss them. These ugly thoughts churned through my mind as I rode the elevator down to the hotel lobby.

When the elevator stopped, I ran to a restroom and vomited into a toilet.

CHAPTER 20

Friday, 8 August

"Two minutes and the swordfish should be done." Frank glanced at Kelly, seated at her kitchen table, her shoulders hunched, her arms hugging her body. He went to the table. "You don't look so hot. What's wrong?"

"I'm okay. Just a little cold, that's all."

"I'll get you a sweater." He pulled the chain on her ceiling fan to turn it off, took foil off the plate of chocolate chip cookies on the counter and gave her one. "You're hungry. Eat a cookie."

"I don't want to spoil my dinner. I'll be okay."

"Eat the cookie," he said sternly. For two days in the hospital she'd been unable to keep any food down, a normal reaction to the anesthetic the nurses had said. But to him Kelly looked painfully thin.

He went to her bedroom closet, found a white cardigan and returned to the kitchen. The cookie was gone. Kelly gave him a guilty grin.

"Hey, don't look guilty. The doc said to fatten you up."

"He did not."

"Well, words to that effect." He helped her put on the sweater. "Hold on while I check the fish."

He opened a slider door, stepped onto her deck and raised the lid of the gas grill in the corner. The swordfish looked great, toasty brown on the top, smelled even better. He plopped it on a platter and cut into the middle to make sure it was done. Perfect. He took the fish inside and set it on the table.

"Wow," Kelly said, "it smells great. I guess I really am hungry."

He took two baked potatoes out of the oven, set them on dinner plates and brought them to the table, went back for a dish of fresh-steamed broccoli and sat down opposite Kelly.

"Dig in," he said. "Oops, we need butter for the potatoes." He got a stick of butter out of the refrigerator, put it on a saucer and brought it to the table.

"Frank, you're working too hard. Sit down and eat."

"Working too hard? My favorite woman needs nourishment!"

She tried the swordfish. "Fantastic. You've been lying. You told me you don't know how to cook."

He waved a hand. "Push comes to shove I can."

"Dad and Michael are flying down from Chicago for the weekend."

He was glad the two cops in her family were coming to lend their support but it might cause complications.

"Guess I won't be staying here over the weekend, huh?"

"Mmm, probably not. But Dad wants to meet you."

He paused with a forkful of potato halfway to his mouth. "Is that good or bad?"

"I wouldn't worry about it, if I were you. Dad can be rather possessive but he said he was glad you were here to look after me."

He was still trying to figure what that meant, when his cell rang. He answered without checking Caller ID.

"Heyyy, Franco, what's doing?"

A visceral jolt ran through him down to his scrotum. Only one person ever called him Franco. Gina.

Aware that Kelly was listening, he said, "Hey, whaddaya know?" The greeting he'd used during the nine years he and Gina had been lovers.

"Got something juicy for ya. Are you busy?"

He glanced at Kelly. She was toying with a lock of hair, watching him.

"Sort of, but it's okay. What's up?"

"Last week I caught an AP wire story about the Peterson case," Gina said. "I've been following it online. We just got a similar case up here. A VIP murdered in a posh hotel."

His heart rate kicked into high gear. Gina covered the crime beat for the Boston *Herald* and had connections with a few cops. "What the guy's name?"

"Oliver James. One shot to the head."

"One shot to the head?" he said for Kelly's benefit. Kelly's eyes widened.

"Yeah," Gina said. "Just like Peterson. They found him in the Marriott Hotel near Copley Place."

"Who is he? You got any background?"

"Recently he's been dealing in art antiquities. Before that he made a shitload of money in the stock market. Before that he worked for the CIA."

"CIA?" He looked at Kelly, who gazed at him wide-eyed. "When?"

"It's a long story. Bottom line, a woman in the next room heard a shot and called hotel security. A guard went up to talk to her. While they were talking, a woman came out of the room where they found the body."

"Jesus. Just like Peterson. Did they get her?"

"No," Gina said. "But they got her car and her name."

Kelly's doorbell rang. She started to get up but he flapped his hand at her and said to Gina, "Hold on a second, I'll be right back."

Pressing the phone to his leg, he said to Kelly, "This is a Boston reporter I used to know. She's covering another murder that might be connected to ours. Eat your dinner. I'll get the door."

He dashed through the living room and opened the door.

Kenyon Miller stood there with a foil-covered pan. "Yo, Frank. Got a pan of lasagna for Kelly. Tanya made it. Also got some good news."

"Me too," he said, waving his cell. "Do me a favor. Go sit with Kelly while she eats. I got a line on a case in Boston that might tie into ours."

As Miller ambled toward the kitchen Frank went down the hall to Kelly's room. He hadn't spoken to Gina for two years, and he wanted to talk to her without monitoring every word that came out of his mouth. He sat on the bed and murmured into his cell, "Sorry, Gina, I'm with some people, had to find a quiet place so we can talk. How you doing? It's good to hear your voice."

"Same here." And after a pause, "I'm doing okay, I guess."

"What's going on? Is something wrong?"

"Long story, Franco. Listen, this is case is a hot potato, and I can't get much from my police sources."

"What about the woman? You got a name?"

"That's the problem. They won't tell me." Gina chuckled, a low throaty sound. "But if you come up here, they'll tell you."

He had mixed feelings about going to Boston. If the case was related to the Peterson and Conroy murders, Vobitch would send him up in a heartbeat, but he didn't want to leave Kelly alone too long while she was convalescing.

"You know how the budget scene works. But I'll get up there someway or other. Any chance we can get together for a drink or dinner?"

After his ex-wife filed for divorce and called Gina the "other woman," his life had gone in the toilet. Gina's husband also filed for divorce. Then the little girl died in the Fuckup and he'd moved to New Orleans. He and Gina had kept in touch for a while, but two years ago, Gina had remarried. They hadn't spoken since.

"Sure we can, Franco. Just call my cell and tell me when you're coming."

He wanted more details on the murder, but he was more concerned about Gina's reaction when he asked how she was doing. "What's going on, Gina? Are you okay?"

"I've been better, Franco. Tell you all about it when I see you. Call me."

She clicked off and he sat there, lost in thought. He was happy to hear from her, even happier to know she was thinking of him. But something was definitely wrong. Gina had the most bombastic personality of any women he'd ever known. Today she sounded sad. Almost melancholy.

When he returned to the kitchen, most of Kelly's dinner was gone. Seated opposite her with a bottle of Bud, Miller started to get up, but Frank waved him off. "Don't get up. I'm too wired to sit. This might be the break we need."

"You got a lead?" Miller asked.

"You first. You said you had good news."

"They found June Carson's car at the Atlanta-Hartsfield airport. We checked the registration, tracked down June Carson's license through DMV, got a copy of a New Jersey license with her picture."

"Fantastic," he said. "We're finally getting somewhere."

"Well, sort of," Miller said, looking glum. "I searched every damn data base I could for June Carter, came up empty. Vobitch put out a nationwide BOLO. Somebody spots her, we'll get her."

"Don't count on it. The June Carter ID might be bogus."

"What makes you think so?" Kelly said.

He didn't answer immediately. He prided himself on his analytical skills. He didn't often make mistakes, but this time he might have. At first he'd been unwilling to believe the woman on the video was Natalie. In fact, he still had a hard time believing a woman had killed Peterson in cold blood. But that might be a mistake. He pictured the video, visualizing the woman's confident stride. Now Boston PD had similar case, a prominent man found murdered in a first-class hotel, a woman seen leaving his room. Two men murdered in two different cities. Both times the woman had escaped. The odds were looking better and better that Natalie Brixton was the killer.

"Natalie left Pecos in nineteen-ninety-five," he said, "hasn't been heard from since. She probably picked up a fake ID. If she bought one, she could have bought half a dozen."

He told them what he knew about the Boston case.

When he finished, Kelly asked, "Why is she killing all these men?"

"Good question," he said.

"A former CIA agent?" Miller said. "Far out, man. You got connections with Boston PD, right?"

"Yes. I'll go up and check it out. But I wouldn't count on it solving our cases. I don't think she's done."

Kelly gazed at him wide-eyed. "You think she's got more targets?"

He cupped her face in his hands and kissed her.

"That's my girl. Always a step ahead of the band."

CHAPTER 21

Monday, 11 August Boston

Frank parked his rental car in the Boston Common underground garage at noon and strolled through the grassy park. Taking advantage of the sunny day, teenagers in shorts were playing Frisbee, while people of all ages, some walking dogs, carefully avoided several scruffy-looking panhandlers.

He walked to the Boylston Street T-stop and got a jumbo iced coffee at Dunkin' Donuts. During his stint with Boston PD, he'd downed gallons of their coffee, hot or iced, depending on the weather. When he moved to New Orleans, he was amazed to find only one Dunkin' Donuts in the entire city.

Perched on a low cement wall beside the park, he sipped his iced coffee, enjoying the rich flavor. His appointment at Boston Police Headquarters was at one. He should eat lunch, but he didn't feel like it. His stomach was too jumpy. No telling what kind of reception awaited him.

Would they greet him with open arms and say *Welcome back, great to see you?*

Or would some asshole say *Shot any innocent little girls lately?*

The whap of a skateboarder landing on the cement sidewalk snapped him back to reality.

Two young Asian women wandered past him, giggling and talking. Then two young black men came along, one with a knapsack strapped to his back, the other hobbling along on crutches. A sports injury, Frank wondered, or a drive-by shooting? Plenty of those in Boston. A portly middle-aged white man in a striped polo shirt marched up to a green-painted bench, plopped his gym bag on it, dropped to the sidewalk and began doing pushups. Frank couldn't help counting. After fifteen pushups, the man hesitated, did four more, struggled to his feet and walked off with his gym bag.

A siren whooped a warning, and a police car with flashing lights bulled through two lanes of traffic. Some things never changed. People of all ages and colors, weird characters exhibiting odd behavior, lights and sirens.

Damn, he missed Boston, missed the action and the people.

Well, he missed some people. Others, not so much.

————

When he walked into Headquarters a welcoming committee was waiting in the lobby, seven men in uniforms and two detectives in street clothes, guys he'd played hoop with. Amid the hustle-bustle of the station, his former colleagues asked how he was doing and how did he like New Orleans? And the inevitable question: Are you up here working a case?

Unwilling to explain, he said, "If I told you, I'd have to kill you."

They all laughed, but Rafe Hawkins didn't. A hulking six-foot-four wide-body with ebony skin and dark menacing eyes, Rafe had played center on the hoop team. Trash-talking Rafe mock-punched his arm and growled, "Better than your usual *No comment*." Then he smiled. "Great to see you, Frank."

He was glad to see them, but in the midst of the reunion, two detectives hurried by, avoiding his eyes. Not men he'd worked with, but they'd been with Boston PD when The Fuckup happened. He and his partner had been cleared, but they didn't want to risk being tainted by scandal, wouldn't even come over and say hello.

Fuck 'em, he thought. Friends like that he could do without.

The welcoming committee walked him to the elevator. He rode it to the second floor and went down the hall to the Assistant Superintendent's office, now occupied by Lieutenant Colonel Harrison Flynn. Hank to his friends. Frank had known him for twenty years. Eight years ago when the murder-bust blew up in his face, Hank had been one of his strongest supporters.

Seated at a gunmetal gray desk in front of a window with a great view of the Copley Square skyline, Hank said, "Welcome back, Frank. Say hello to Clint Hammer."

In front of the desk, a man sat on a padded visitor chair. Hammer didn't stand, nor did he offer his hand. His name didn't fit his appearance. He was maybe five-six, acne scarred cheeks, pale yellow hair cropped in a buzz cut. His eyes were chilling. Hard gray-granite eyes. Angry eyes.

Frank took the other visitor chair. Hank gave him a heads-up stare. "Clint flew up from Washington two days ago. He works for the CIA. He and Oliver James were friends."

"I understand you might have a lead for us," Hammer said.

"I'm working a case in New Orleans with a similar M.O. A prominent businessman shot in the head in his hotel room. The next day a bartender named Tex Conroy was found dead in City Park, shot once in the head. Both men were shot with the same gun, a .38 Special."

Hammer stroked his weak chin. "How'd you find out about Oliver?"

"Read about it online in the Boston *Globe*. It sounded similar to ours." Never give up your sources, get as much information as possible. "How did you know Oliver?"

One by one Hammer cracked the knuckles on both hands, then said in a rapid-fire monotone, "We went to Harvard together, joined the CIA after graduation. We did a few ops in Central America, watched each other's back.

Oliver got out after two years. I stayed. Oliver's a smart guy and his physical skills were top notch. I can't figure out how the woman did him."

"Well," Frank said, "she had a gun."

Hammer waved his hand. "Oliver would have disarmed her."

"Clint," Hank said, his blue eyes frosty, "I think it would be best to share what information we have. Tell Detective Renzi what Oliver asked you to do."

Frank fought down a smile, imagining the pissing contest when Clint Hammer, CIA spook, tried to play hardball with Lieutenant Colonel Harrison Flynn. Hank knew how to play tough-guy games.

"Oliver asked me to gather Intel about a woman named Robin Adair."

"Why would he ask you to do that?"

"He was dating her. He said she wouldn't talk about her family."

"Ever do that kind of favor for Oliver before?"

"That's not relevant to the discussion."

Riffing on Hammer-speak, he said, "What sort of *Intel* did you gather?"

"According to the background check I did, prior to 2005 Robin Adair didn't exist." Without consulting any notes—maybe he had a photographic memory—Hammer reeled off Robin Adair's phone number, street address in Nashua, New Hampshire, and her driver's license stats: brown eyes, brown hair, DOB, January 10, 1978. In 2005 she registered a used 2004 Honda Civic in New Hampshire, had also purchased a .38 Special at a gun show in Nashua.

"Oliver told me her eyes looked Asian," Hammer said. "We even joked about it. When I told him to watch out, she might be Tokyo Rose, Oliver laughed. And now he's dead."

"What did he say when you gave him the information?" Frank asked.

"He seemed surprised. I got the feeling he liked her."

"Did you talk to him again after that conversation?"

"No."

Frank took the Natalie Brixton sketches out of his briefcase and showed them to Hammer. After studying them, Hammer said in a toneless voice, "That's her. She killed Oliver."

"Maybe. But why?"

"She was up to no good. Her ID was bogus. Maybe Oliver blew the whistle on her. When he told her what I'd found, she killed him."

"But that doesn't explain *why* she killed him," Frank said.

Hammer skewered him with his granite-gray eyes. "I don't give a shit *why*. I'm going to get that bitch and make her wish she'd never been born." He rose to his feet and said to Hank, "Keep me informed. You've got my cell phone number." Holding himself ramrod stiff, CIA Agent Hammer left the office.

Frank looked at Hank. "Can he do it?"

"Do what?"

"Find her and deliver his CIA brand of justice."

"Your guess is as good as mine. He gave us some useful information, but our discussions haven't exactly been cordial. I said I'd keep him informed, but that seems to be a one-way street. I don't know where he's staying. Only contact info I've got is his cell phone number."

"Can we compare the ballistics reports to see if she used the same gun?"

Hank's eyes crinkled in a smile. "I'll have my people talk to your people."

"I'd like to see her apartment. It might help me get a handle on her."

"Sure," Hank said. "Want to do it now? I'll drive you up there."

"Yes. I've got a couple of errands to do later." He wanted to call Kelly and see how she was. Then he had to talk to Gina and find out what was wrong. For nine years they had been lovers. More than lovers. Best friends. On the phone she'd said she was okay, but her tone of voice said otherwise.

———

They grabbed a couple of subs and hit the road. Traffic headed north out of Boston was light at this hour. While they ate their subs, they hashed over the James case. Another thing he missed. Hank was a sharp investigator.

"She parked her Honda Civic near the garage exit," Hank said, "so she could make a fast getaway. Like she planned it. But the cops got there before she could get to her car."

"How'd she get out of the hotel?"

"The security guard saw her get in the elevator, but when we interviewed the desk clerk and two guests who were in the lobby at the time, they didn't recall seeing her. But a door beside the elevator opens onto an employee dressing room, with an exit door so the workers can go outside to smoke."

"Was there a guard on the door?"

"Outside there was, but he heard sirens, ran up to Huntington Avenue to see what the fuss was about. If she came out then, he'd have missed her."

"Did you get prints off the Honda?" Frank asked.

"Yes, and they matched the prints we got from her apartment." Hank drank from a bottle of water and set it in the cup-holder between the seats. "When we interviewed her neighbors, they barely remembered her. The guy that lives next door said he never had a real conversation with her. No one saw her the day after the murder. If she went back and took something, it wasn't obvious."

"Nothing about this woman is obvious. We see what she wants us to see." He looked out the window as fields of grass and scrub pines flashed by. It seemed certain that she'd killed former CIA Agent Oliver James. But why?

"Hank, a woman named Jeanette Brixton was murdered in New Orleans in 1988. Her daughter Natalie was ten at the time, got shipped to Texas to live with relatives. She graduated high school in ninety-five, split town and nobody's seen her since. I think she killed Peterson, the VIP businessman, but I can't figure out why. Tex Conroy went to school with her."

"So Natalie runs into Conroy," Hank said as he took the exit for Nashua, "and he recognizes her."

"Right, but Natalie was posing as June Carson, had Carson's DL, drove a car registered to Carson. I figure she didn't want anybody knowing Natalie was in town, so she killed Tex and split."

"And you think she's the Robin Adair that lives in Nashua."

"Correct." Frank drank from his bottled water. "And here's the best part. June Carson rented a room at the Sunshine Inn in New Orleans. The desk clerk said June had a tat on her ankle. So did the woman on the security video that went in and out of Peterson's room."

"Now there's a helluva clue." Hank drove into a large condo complex and parked. "So your June Carson, our Robin Adair, was dating Oliver James. But his buddy Hammer checked up on her, found inconsistencies, and James called her on it. But why not make up a story? Seems like she planned to kill him. Otherwise, why bring the gun?"

Frank opened his car door. "Put that in the I-don't-know column. Followed by Where-is-she-now?"

Viewing Robin Adair's apartment didn't help much. The medicine cabinet held a box of tampons and a typical assortment of over-the-counter headache and cold remedies. Shampoo and conditioner in a wire rack over the showerhead. A bedroom closet with assorted tops, slacks and a long silk dress with an Asian dragon on a black background. A bunch of shoes on the floor.

They returned to the living room. Frank said. "No computer, huh?"

"Correct," said Hank, "which, now that you mention it, seems odd. Seems like anyone traveling all over the country would have a computer. Maybe she's got a laptop. We didn't find one in her car."

Frank noticed a small Japanese watercolor on one wall. He went over and studied the eight-by-ten-inch painting. Delicate brush strokes depicted birds flying around a snow-capped mountain under puffy white clouds. One corner had a stain on it. Not something a person put on their wall unless it meant something to them. Why didn't she take it with her? he wondered.

"What?" Hank said.

"I think she came here, grabbed what she needed and split. She was in a panic, figured the cops were hot on her trail, didn't take time to wipe her prints. But how did she get here? Can you check the Boston cab companies?"

"Good idea," Hank said. "If she paid a cabbie to drive her to Nashua, they'd have a record of it."

Frank nodded, but he didn't expect it would help them. This case was like a roller coaster: chug up a steep hill, perch on top, then a heart-stopping plunge. Troll for a lead, get excited and have your hopes dashed.

Natalie Brixton was gone.

Natalie

March 2000

Ten days after Mardi Gras on March 17, 2000, the call I'd been eagerly awaiting came. "I got the copy of the file," Nick said. "Sorry it took so long, Virginia. But I said I'd get if for ya and I did. How do you want me to send it to you?"

Mom's murder file, with a list of Jane Fontenot's suspects.

I wanted to shout and scream and jump for joy. But I decided to wait until I was holding it in my hand. "Could you fax it to me?"

"Sure can, dawlin. But we need to settle up first."

"Of course. How much do I owe you?" I didn't care what it cost. I couldn't wait to see the file.

"Wahl, first off, I hadda pay the New Orleans cop two grand. He was afraid he'd get fired, said he hadda bribe the guy that signs out the files to let him take it out and bring it back without putting his name on the log book. And then there's my travel expenses and--"

"How much is it all together?" My heart was jumping in my chest like a jackrabbit running from a Texas hound dog. I didn't want to haggle over money. I wanted to see the file.

"You already paid me three grand, Virginia, and I gave you a break on account of it took me longer than it should've to get it, what with my hernia operation and all. So all's you owe me is fifteen hundred."

"Fine. I'll have my bank wire the money into your account. I don't have a fax machine but I know a store that does. I'll call you back in an hour. By then the money should be in your account."

I arranged to have my Swiss bank execute the transfer. Then I went to a print shop two blocks from my apartment and got their fax number. When I called Nick back, he said everything was all set, so I gave him the fax number.

"I'll include an itemized account of my expenses," he said. "I hope this gets you what you need, Virginia. You ever need anything else, gimme a call."

I thanked him, hung up and danced around my kitchen. My heart was bursting with joy. At last I was about to get some answers.

Thirty minutes later I was holding the file in my hands. My hands were shaking. I raced back to my apartment and began to read. The autopsy report was disgusting. The black-and-white photographs were worse. Mom, sprawled on a bed naked, her eyes vacant and staring, her face smeared with blood where the monster had hit her.

Tears filled my eyes. What was Mom thinking when that monster put his hands around her throat? Was she thinking about me?

I flipped several pages and found Jane's notes. On the third page there was a list of names. Nine men known to frequent the hotel with prostitutes. I clenched my teeth and kept reading. Four of the men had alibis. They could prove they'd been out of town, either with boarding passes for plane flights or receipts from hotels in other cities. That left five names. Two of them were single. Forget them. Jane Fontenot had said that her prime suspect's wife had provided him with an alibi. I studied the last three names.

Roger Monson. Albert Honeywell. Beau Beaubien.

I was certain one of them had killed my mother.

Jane interviewed the men first, then their wives. Roger Monson said he'd been gambling that night at a casino in Pas Christian, Mississippi. He'd come out ahead and had a dated receipt for his winnings. Albert Honeywell said he and his wife had attended a Louisiana Philharmonic concert that night. His wife confirmed this and showed Jane the ticket stubs. I turned the page.

My hands felt tingly, the way they did when I slept on my arm all night. Jane had put a check mark beside the next name. Beau Beaubien, also known as BoBo, claimed he was home that night with his wife Joereen. Joereen confirmed this. Beside her name was a big question mark and a scribbled word that started with the letter B. I couldn't decipher the rest of it.

Unable to calm my racing heart, I paced my kitchen. I was almost certain BoBo was the monster that killed Mom, but I didn't dare call Jane Fontenot and ask her. I couldn't say I was Natalie, and if I pretended to be Natalie's friend again, she might get suspicious.

That night I didn't have a client so I got on my laptop. First I used Internet search engines to find information about BoBo. Like Jane said, he was an important man and my search turned up many articles about him.

I learned a lot. Some of it surprised me. His family was poor, so BoBo grew up in a housing project. He quit school when he was sixteen and got a job at a supermarket. Later he became a bartender. That gave him the idea that led to his success. When he saw how the men in the bar ogled busty woman, he decided to open a bar with go-go dancers. Not strippers or hookers, he was adamant about that. His bar would feature women dancing in scanty outfits to show off their sexy bodies. It took him a while to get the money.

One article hinted he got it from a mobster and remained beholden to him. It didn't give the mobster's name. To celebrate his twentieth birthday in 1975 BoBo opened his first GoGo bar. Not in the French Quarter. Bourbon Street had many bars with strippers. BoBo's GoGo Bar was in the Central Business District and featured plush seating, fancy appetizers and fine liquors and wines to attract wealthy businessmen.

That year he married his high school sweetheart, Lurleen. Soon they had a son, Beau Junior. BoBo doted on him. But he didn't neglect his business. His first bar was so successful he opened one on the west bank, a third in Baton Rouge and started making obscene amounts of money. In one article, he told the reporter that if people had to pay higher prices, they figured they'd get better quality.

That part made me laugh. He was right, of course. The men who used The Service figured they were getting the best women in Paris because of the outrageous prices they had to pay.

By then it was midnight. I was hungry, but I didn't want to stop to cook a meal. I wanted to learn more about the man who murdered Mom. I poured myself a tall glass of iced tea, put a frozen dinner in the microwave (something I hardly ever did) and continued my research while I ate.

Like most wealthy men, BoBo liked to show off. He bought expensive cars—Lamborghinis and Alfa Romeos, BMWs and Audis—and put them in a showroom with big windows for everyone to see. For the Carnival parades he sponsored spectacular floats and paid glittery gals in skimpy costumes to toss Mardi Gras beads and coconuts with BoBo's GoGo Bar logos to spectators.

But in 1980 Lurleen filed for divorce and asked for sole custody of Beau Junior. BoBo called him Chip, as in Chip-off-the-old-block. A photograph showed them at a Little League baseball game. Chip was only five but he already looked a lot like BoBo: blonde hair, big blue eyes and a cocky grin. No way was BoBo going to lose his cherished son. Ugly charges and countercharges followed. I'd have given anything to know what they were, but the judge sealed the divorce papers. One article said BoBo paid Lurleen a huge settlement and serious alimony to win custody of Chip.

I got up and poured myself another glass of iced tea. My mind was in a whirl, my neck had a crick in it, and my eyes felt gritty from staring at the computer screen. But that didn't deter me. I got on my laptop and read the next article the search engine delivered. Two years after Lurleen divorced him, BoBo married his second wife. Her name was Joereen.

Did he ever get confused, I wondered. Lurleen? Joereen?

Then I thought: He probably calls her *honey*. That's what I called all my clients. It saved me the trouble of remembering their names.

A low-flying plane scattered rose petals over their wedding ceremony in City Park, and the New Orleans Symphony played the music. Joereen bore him two daughters, but BoBo ignored them. He took Chip everywhere, surfing in Hawaii, skiing in Aspen, trips to Europe, including a visit with the Pope. Without Joereen. By the time BoBo turned thirty in 1985 his chain of GoGo Bars had expanded to Houston, San Francisco and Chicago.

Despite its fairy-tale beginning, BoBo's second marriage also fell apart. He didn't care about losing his daughters, but he hated parting with his money. When Joereen accused him of domestic battery, he accused her of adultery. Seven years after their spectacular wedding, the divorce became final.

The date sent shivers down my spine. January 20, 1989.

Three months after Mom's murder. If Joereen was fooling around, maybe BoBo was too. And if he was beating Joereen, maybe he was also beating up women he saw on the side. Like Mom.

I flipped back to the page where Joereen said BoBo was home with her the night Mom was murdered. I studied the scribbled word that began with B.

Bullshit? Bully?

Did Jane think BoBo beat up Joereen to make her give him an alibi?

I went to the *Times-Picayune* website, NOLA.com, and searched for more articles about BoBo. First I concentrated on 1989. Joereen's lurid accusations hadn't damaged BoBo's carefully crafted image one bit. One article praised his philanthropy, saying he donated thousands of dollars to the Santa Fund every year and gave ten needy teenagers scholarships to the University of New Orleans. Another described an extravagant party he threw at his house, hundreds of guests dancing to disco music until the wee hours. When his neighbors complained about the noise, BoBo dismissed them as cranks.

BoBo attended all the important social events. One color photograph showed him in an elegant white suit, looking tanned and youthful. I studied his face. He was handsome enough. Thick blond hair crowned his head like a golden halo, but he had a cruel-looking mouth. He also had a beautiful young woman on his arm. That made me want to puke. Like some of my clients, BoBo used sexy young women to proclaim his sexual prowess to the world.

A feature article hinted at his ruthless business tactics. One man, who wouldn't give his name, said two thugs came to his club and threatened to break his legs if he didn't sell it to BoBo. Three months later the club became a GoGo Bar. But that wasn't the most interesting part.

The *Times Picayune* had obtained copies of the financial statement BoBo had filed during his divorce from Joereen. In 1989 his net worth was $210 million; his annual income was $10 million.

What could one man do with that much money? Then I remembered what Jane Fontenot said: Spread it around and become even more powerful.

I sank back in my chair and drank some iced tea. When he murdered Mom in 1988, BoBo was thirty-three. Having seen the disgusting photographs in the murder file, I found it hard to believe someone that young could be so cold-blooded. Now it was 2000, twelve years later.

Did he ever think about it? Did he regret it? Did he have trouble sleeping at night? Probably not. BoBo was a monster.

Next I focused on what he'd been doing since his divorce in 1989.

One article said that after playing the field for six years, BoBo had married wife number three in 1995.

Playing the field for six years. Bullshit.

Paying women to have sex with him was more like it.

His third wife's name was Helena. After their wedding at St. Louis Cathedral in the French Quarter, some questioned why the twice-married-and-divorced BoBo rated a Catholic wedding. But a church spokesman said his first wife had died, and his marriage to Joereen had not been consecrated in a Catholic ceremony. Apparently having an airplane scatter rose petals over their wedding in City Park didn't impress the Catholic church officials.

I checked the recent social events on NOLA.com to find out what BoBo looked like now. And there he was at a Mardi Gras Ball last month with his third wife. Helena looked much younger than BoBo, drop-dead gorgeous in her swanky dress and sparkly jewelry. BoBo looked a bit like Donald Trump: Blonde, blue-eyed, a toothy self-satisfied smile. His eyes had bags under them, as though he had been burning the candle at both ends for years.

Maybe as far back as 1988. When he became a monster.

When Chip graduated from Archbishop Rummel High School in 1993, BoBo threw him a big party. He expected Chip to manage his business empire someday. Unlike BoBo, Chip had graduated with honors. He was all set to major in marketing at Loyola. To become rich and powerful like his father.

Exhausted but content, I leaned back in my chair, looked out the window and saw the faint pinkish glow of sunrise. I'd been up all night.

But I didn't care. Now I knew who my target was. BoBo Beaubien.

And he still lived in New Orleans. A prominent resident who drew plenty of attention in the *Times Picayune* and elsewhere.

Now that I knew his name I could monitor his activities while I saved enough money to punish him for murdering Mom.

CHAPTER 22

Frank entered the Surf and Turf at six-thirty and stopped short. Beyond the foyer Gina sat at the bar, working on a glass of Chablis.

Seeing her gave him a visceral jolt.

During their nine year affair this had been their favorite haunt, a local restaurant with stunning ocean views where they could talk without running into anyone they knew. Several times a month they would meet in the bar and gab over a drink before dinner. Now he felt an overwhelming sense of regret.

He hadn't seen Gina in five years. A hollow feeling formed in his gut.

If he'd stayed in Boston, would things have been different?

Now a spectacular sunset sprinkled orange-gold rays over the shimmering sea. Almost like old times. But after his wife named Gina the "other woman" in their divorce case, Gina's husband had also filed for divorce. Two years ago Gina had remarried, happily this time. Or so she'd said when she called to tell him. But she didn't look happy now.

In fact, she didn't look well. Her skin was pale and her face, framed by ringlets of curly dark-brown hair, looked gaunt. He went in the bar, kissed her cheek and slipped onto the barstool beside hers.

Gina hugged him. "What's the scoop, Franco?"

"I'm glad to see you. That's the scoop."

She smiled, but her brown eyes were tinged with sadness. She touched his hand. "I'm glad to see you too. It's been a while."

"Push comes to shove I could tell you exactly how long it's been. How you doing?"

"I'm okay." She fished a pecan out of a dish of mixed nuts on the bar. "Tell me what you found out today. I hear there's a CIA agent involved."

He laughed. "Still got your sources at Boston PD, huh?"

She gave him a sly look. "Not as good as you, but I've got a couple."

A journalist with attitude, Gina Bevilaqua—she used her maiden name on her byline—was one of the feistiest women he'd ever met. She'd graduated from Boston University with a journalism degree, but rather than apply for work at the *Globe*, the grand dame of Boston newspapers, she got a job at the

Herald, the *Globe's* tabloid rival. Thanks to her smarts, her quirky writing style and her Boston PD contacts, she won a promotion to cover the crime beat.

That's how they'd met.

He ordered a glass of Chianti and told her what he knew about Natalie Brixton, recapped his meeting with Hank Flynn and Hammer and asked what she thought. Back in the day they had often kibitzed on murder cases.

"Seems like you're looking for a phantom." Gina twirled a lock of curly dark hair around her finger. "Natalie left Texas thirteen years ago, disappeared, surfaced in New Orleans and murdered a wealthy businessman." She grinned and did the quote-thing with her fingers. "Allegedly. Then she pops a guy she went to school with in Texas and splits."

"Ever think about being a homicide detective?" He was only half joking.

"Nah. The shit these dumbbells pull? It's more fun writing about it."

Now that they were talking about work she seemed like her usual happy, dynamic self. He was glad. Seeing her look sad and forlorn made him ache for her. That had happened a few times, back in the day. Bad times for both of them, months of emotional turmoil. If he'd stayed, maybe things would have worked out. But he didn't want to think about that.

"Okay, Sherlock," he said. "Why did she kill Oliver James?"

Gina sipped her Chablis and adopted the pensive look she got when she was concentrating hard. "From a woman's perspective? I'd say she was pissed that he dug up dirt on her. Seems like he must have told her, or gave her a clue at least. Otherwise, she wouldn't have brought the gun to the hotel."

"But why worry about him knowing she wasn't who she pretended to be? He didn't know about the murders in New Orleans."

"Maybe he did," Gina said.

"Damn. I told Hammer I read about Oliver James on the *Globe* website. But the *Times-Picayune* has a website, too. Maybe Natalie was afraid he might read it. But why would he? How would he know? Hammer didn't."

Gina munched another pecan. "I don't know. Anything interesting in her apartment?"

"No. Nothing in the fridge, no prescriptions, clothes still in the closet."

"No birth control pills?" Gina asked.

Appalled that he hadn't thought of that, he stared at her. This was why he loved hashing over cases with her. One reason anyway. Mostly, he just liked talking to women. "No. You think we could trace her through a prescription?"

"Maybe. But nowadays you can get birth control pills over the Internet. Maybe she had her tubes tied."

"I'll have Hank check the birth control angle. Her apartment looked like a transient lived there, no books or personal items, just an old Japanese print of birds flying around a mountain."

"A Japanese print. You said Natalie Brixton's part Asian, right?"

"I don't know for sure, but her eyes look Asian in her yearbook picture. Listen, do you know anything about French fashion?"

"Ha!" Gina said, beaming. "Ask me anything. I'm into fashion big time."

Enjoying her gleeful response, he grinned. Gina was five-four and wore spike heels to appear taller. She also haunted fashion outlets for clothes that would flatter her short chunky body. Not that she was overweight. Her body was gorgeous. But he didn't want think about her body, didn't want to remember how fantastic it was when they made love. Already his groin felt hot and achy, not an erection, but close. Time to focus on the case.

"Okay, Ms. Fashion Bug, I found a silk dress in her closet with a label that said Yves St. Laurent, Paris. Mean anything to you?"

"Yeah. Expensive. Did you like it?"

He stroked her forearm with his finger. "Gina, the only way I can tell if I like a dress is when there's a woman inside it. Could she buy a dress like that here, or did she get it in Paris?"

"Paris. Yves St. Laurent won't sell dresses here with labels that say Paris."

"So she's been to Paris."

"That'd be my guess."

"You want to order dinner?" he said. "You look like you need fattening up." She gave him an odd look and her eyes got shiny. He touched her hand. "Hey. What's wrong?"

"I guess I might as well tell you. I've avoided it long enough." But she didn't say more, just drank some wine and looked at him.

"Avoided what?"

"For my thirty-ninth birthday last year I got an interesting present."

His gut twisted. A not-so-good present, judging by the look in her eyes.

"Got a bad mammogram." She flashed a quick smile. "I had a couple of scares before, but this time it was bad. Biopsy said cancer. Stage three."

It hit him like a flash-bang. His throat closed up. Forcing himself to maintain a neutral expression, he rubbed her back, doing slow circles with his hand. "That sucks. Where'd you go for treatment? Someplace good, I hope."

"Yeah. The doctor was good." Her mouth quirked, painful to watch. "They gave me chemo to shrink the tumor. Then he did a mastectomy and took two lymph nodes. To make sure it hadn't spread."

He had a million questions, but now wasn't the time for questions.

He leaned close and murmured, "You feel like eating or you wanna go sit in the car and neck?"

She burst out laughing. "That's my Franco, always the wiseass. Let's go sit in the car."

———

They rolled down the windows of her Mazda 626 to catch a breeze off the water. Lights from the Boston skyline twinkled at them through the windshield, another reminder how much he missed Boston. And Gina.

He pulled her close and kissed her. She responded with her usual passion. Just like old times, nine years of savoring the precious moments they spent together, Gina vibrant and alive, dark eyes flashing as she talked about her work. Her flair for personalizing a story had won her a journalism award after she interviewed the grandmother of a shooting victim, a young black teenager killed by a stray bullet in a turf war that had nothing to do with him.

Feeling her soft pliant lips against his, he wanted her as much as ever. For nine years he'd loved Gina with all his heart, nine years when, except for work and spending time with his daughter, he'd lived to be with her. During the devastating days after the little girl died and the endless Internal Affairs investigation, Gina had gotten him through the times when his wife looked at him every morning with eyes that said *How could you?* As if he'd planned it.

The same reaction when Evelyn's girlfriend saw him with Gina and told Evelyn. "How could you?" Evelyn had said. What he wanted to say, but didn't: *If I wanted to stay celibate all my life, I'd have been a priest.*

But now he felt torn, like an old snapshot ripped in two. He was deeply involved with Kelly, had felt sheer panic when she got shot, desolated at the thought that he might lose her. It would be easy to take Gina to a hotel and make love to her. He sure as hell wanted to. If he and Gina made love tonight, Kelly would never know. But he would. And it would tarnish their relationship in a way that he couldn't bear. Reluctantly, he pulled away.

"What's going on at home? Are you and Greg okay?"

Her eyes grew distant, like she was reliving an unhappy memory. "We were until I got breast cancer. Since then things haven't been so hot."

"Such as?" He had an idea, but he didn't want to say it.

"Bed. Greg's not so hot to trot these days."

He traced a finger along her cheek and down her jaw.

"It's the scar, I guess. He doesn't . . . he can't deal with it. We tried to talk about it but . . ." She shrugged. "Before the diagnosis we were talking about having kids. But that's not something I want to think about right now."

Kids. He'd never pictured Gina with kids. She was too gung ho about her career. Until she got a birthday present with a bitter twist. He stroked her cheek. "You need to take care of yourself, Gina. That's the important thing. Make sure you're healthy and feeling good. Greg needs to understand that."

What he wanted to say but didn't: *Greg needs to understand that you don't love a person and when she gets sick decide you don't want to deal with it.*

When she remained silent, he said, "You want me to talk to him?"

She gave him a look: *Are you crazy?*

"Okay," he said. "Stupid idea."

Gina touched his cheek. "You're just trying to help. I know that."

172

"Yeah. You want me to go punch his lights out?"

They dissolved in laughter.

"It's still fun, isn't it, Franco."

"Yes," he said in a husky voice. Still fun and he wanted her as much as ever. Maybe more.

They were quiet for a while, gazing at the sunset and the ocean.

"Gina, I'd love to—"

"You don't have to say anything. I figure you've got somebody else now. Why shouldn't you? I got married and—"

"That doesn't mean I don't care about you."

Her eyes glistened with tears. "I care about you, too, Franco. You deserve to be happy after what you went through with . . . how's she doing?"

Meaning his ex-wife. "Panic attacks in the middle of the night every so often. She calls me. I calm her down."

Gina nodded, then smiled. "How's Maureen?"

"Great. She's an orthopedic surgeon now, joined a group practice in a Baltimore suburb last year. We're having lunch at the airport before I leave tomorrow. She's up here visiting her mother."

He felt a twinge of guilt. Maureen had wanted to have dinner with him tonight, but he'd told her he was busy working a case. All these complicated loyalties were eating him up.

"I wish you'd called me when you got the diagnosis, Gina. You held my hand a few times when I was hurting. After my mother died. The fuckup with the little girl."

"That's what friends are for. We were never just lovers, Franco."

"Right. So next time *call me* if you've got a problem. Call me any time. I want to know how you're doing." It took every once of willpower he had not to take her in his arms and say: *To hell with dinner, let's go to a hotel.*

"I will." Her eyes took on a steely look. "Greg and I will work it out. One way or the other." Then she smiled, the smile he remembered so well, the smile that said *I love you and we're okay.*

"I'm ravenous, Franco. Let's have dinner."

———

Tuesday 12 August

Delectable aromas permeated the Legal Sea Foods inside Terminal B at Logan Airport. The restaurant was busy, not a vacant table anywhere. He and Maureen had claimed two stools at a high table in the corner. His daughter was all grown up now. Looking at her, he felt proud, but sometimes he missed the little girl he'd played catch with and drove to riding lessons and read to at bedtime. She had inherited his build, tall and rangy, but she had Evelyn's green eyes and auburn hair. She'd changed her hairstyle since he'd last seen her.

Now it was shorter, tendrils of hair falling over her ears. A gorgeous young woman devouring her fried clams with gusto.

He was pretending to eat a bowl of fish chowder. Gina's bombshell had killed his appetite. He couldn't stop thinking about her. And how much he loved her. Seeing her had filled him with an overwhelming feeling of loss, pain that he'd buried for years. Pain that was sharper than ever.

Maureen set her fried clam plate aside and licked her fingers. "Mom wants me to start a practice up here, but Jeremy doesn't want to move. His dental practice is doing great. He just opened a second office."

Alarm bells clanged in his mind. For three years Jeremy had been her steady boyfriend. Like Maureen, he was into horses and show jumping. Maybe he'd better go down there and meet the guy.

"But I'm a little worried about Mom."

Inwardly groaning, he put on his blank face. Mo had voiced her concerns about Evelyn before, saying she should be dating. Not a subject he cared to discuss. He didn't care whether Evelyn was dating or not. And he didn't want to talk about his own love life, either. Too complicated. Especially now.

Maureen gazed at him with troubled eyes. "She's not paying her bills. She showed me a second notice for the real estate taxes on the house."

"That's crazy! I send her a check twice a month for the taxes and other expenses." Checks that ate up a considerable amount of his salary.

"I know, Dad. But I think she's been using it for something else." Mo gave him a guilty look. "I hope you won't be mad, but after she went to bed last night I looked through the file cabinet where she keeps her credit card statements and found some of the bills."

For a moment it shocked him. But even as a child Maureen had been independent and self-reliant. When it came to problem solving, she took after him, not her mother. Evelyn could think of a million reasons why a problem had no solution. So he could fix it.

"And? What did you find?"

"She's been sending money to some charismatic Catholic group. I found a charge for three hundred dollars on last month's Visa statement. And the one before that and the one before that."

Acid pains ate at his gut. Three hundred a month. More than enough to pay the real estate taxes. He popped a Roll Aid and counted to ten. He didn't begrudge Evelyn the money. She'd been a good mother at least. But damned if he was going to let her piss his money away on charity and get in trouble with the taxes on the house he'd paid for.

"I'll call her tomorrow. Do me a favor, Mo. Mail me the real estate tax bill and I'll send them a check." Seeing relief flit across her face, he squeezed her hand. "You shouldn't have to deal with this. I'll handle it."

But a rising tide of anger swelled inside him. Raised by strait-laced Catholic parents, Evelyn adhered to their ways, attending Mass each Sunday

174

and all the holy days. He believed her strict Catholic upbringing was the cause of their abysmal sexual relationship, which had essentially ended after Maureen was born. He couldn't recall Evelyn giving big chunks of money to the church before, but now he wasn't there to pay the bills. Another problem to solve.

His cell phone vibrated against his leg. He checked the ID--Vobitch--and answered.

"Frank," Vobitch said, "we checked the flights out of the Atlanta airport. June Carter, the mystery woman with the ankle tat, wasn't on any of them. Anything new on your end?"

"Yes. Find out if a Robin Adair flew out of Atlanta during that time period. Focus on flights to Boston. She's the prime suspect in that murder."

"Robin Adair. Okay, will do. What time do you get back?"

Vobitch sounded edgy, his voice tense and strained. Was DA Demaris pressuring him? "Not till seven-thirty. You want me to come in then?"

"No. Meet me in my office first thing tomorrow."

Aware that Maureen listening, he said, "How's the patient?"

"Juliana and I brought her a homemade dinner last night. She's looking good." A dry chuckle. "Now that her dad and her brother are gone she can't wait for you to come back."

He smiled. "Good to hear. See you tomorrow." He closed the phone.

Maureen looked at him expectantly. "A lead on a case?"

"Yes. We've got a female suspect with at least two aliases, maybe more."

"Who's the patient?"

Trust his daughter to zero in on the one thing he didn't want to discuss.

"A police officer got shot during the evacuation last week."

She stared at him, aghast. "That's awful. On the Weather Channel they said another hurricane might be headed for the Gulf. If there's another evacuation, you better be careful."

"Don't worry, I will."

But another hurricane was the least of his problems.

Every woman in his life was in crisis: His current lover recovering from a near-fatal gunshot wound; his former lover dealing with breast cancer and an asshole husband; his ex-wife sending money to Catholic charities instead of paying her bills; his daughter seriously involved with a guy in Baltimore.

Meanwhile, a woman he'd never met was roaming the country killing men. And he had no clue where she was or who she might kill next.

CHAPTER 23

Wednesday, 13 August

Seething with anger, Frank stalked down the hall toward Vobitch's office. Before coming to work he'd called his ex-wife, got sent to voicemail and left a message asking her to call him. Where the hell was she? During the school year Evelyn worked for the local school system, but not in the summer. He wasn't looking forward to discussing her spending habits, but he wanted to get it over with. When he got to the station, he had a voicemail message from DA Roger Demaris who wanted to talk to him ASAP. Another unpleasant conversation. Screw that. He'd call Demaris after he talked to Vobitch.

When he entered the office, Vobitch, looking equally aggrieved, gestured at the man in the visitor chair in front of his desk. "CIA agent Clint Hammer. You two have met, right?"

Hammer glowered at him, had a bug up his ass about something. Great. Problems swamping him like waves in a hurricane.

"Yes," he said, taking the visitor chair next to Hammer's. "In Boston."

"Why didn't you tell me about the security video?"

"I didn't think it was relevant to the discussion." Mimicking Hammer's reply when he'd asked if Oliver James had asked him to investigate his other girlfriends.

"Not relevant? You got a possible suspect on a security video and it's not *relevant?*"

Ignoring the irate response, he said to Vobitch. "I got a message from Roger Demaris. Have you talked to him?"

"Not lately," Vobitch said, steely-eyed and deadpan. "But I got a couple of other interesting calls."

Interesting calls from some federal agency in Washington, Frank figured, leaning on Vobitch to cooperate with Hammer.

"I'll let you tell Agent Hammer about June Carter." Vobitch said.

"We got a tip from the sketch we ran on the local TV stations and newspapers." He gave Hammer a pointed look. "The sketches I *showed you* in

Boston. A hotel desk clerk said he was sure the woman in the sketch had stayed at the Sunshine Inn. It's near the French Quarter."

"He recognized her?" Hammer said eagerly. "She looked like the woman in the sketch?"

"Actually, he said she didn't. But she had a tat on her ankle. We included that information with the sketches we published."

"How'd you know she had a tat on her ankle?"

"We spotted it on the security video."

"Jesus Christ! You didn't say anything about a tat in Boston. You didn't think that might be *relevant*? You didn't think that might be *helpful*?"

As though Hammer hadn't spoken, Frank said evenly, "The clerk said he saw her driving a maroon Toyota Corolla."

"We put out a BOLO," Vobitch said. "Atlanta PD found the car in long-term parking at the airport."

Visibly angry, Hammer clenched his jaw. "When was this?"

Ignoring the question, Vobitch said, "We checked the flights out of Atlanta for June Carter and got nothing." His gaze flicked to Frank.

Frank said nothing. If Vobitch wasn't going to tell Hammer they were now checking the flights for Robin Adair, he sure as hell wasn't going to. Fuck Hammer and the CIA.

"Who's the clerk?" Hammer asked. "I want to talk to him."

"Rasheed Cooper. I questioned him at length. I doubt he'll give you anything else."

"Rasheed Cooper." Hammer frowned. "What's he, a jungle bunny?"

Frank saw Vobitch stiffen. Oblivious, Hammer went on, "You gotta lean on these jungle bunnies or they'll just dick you around."

In a quiet voice Vobitch said, "Get out of my office."

Hammer's head jerked up. "What?"

"Get out. Now."

The scary part wasn't the murderous look in Vobitch's eyes. It was his utter stillness and the way he spoke without raising his voice.

Striking a belligerent pose, Hammer raised his chin. "Who the hell do you think you're talking to?"

"I'm talking to you, asshole," Vobitch said in the same quiet voice. "Nobody comes in my office and uses racist language. No one."

Frank couldn't take his eyes off Vobitch, bold upright in his chair and stiff with rage, red-faced, neck corded.

"Get out now, before I rip you apart with my bare hands. You think you scare me because you work for some fucking alphabet-soup agency in Washington? Get your federale pals to lean on me? From here on out you get nothing from me or anyone else in my department, understand? Not one fucking word. Don't call me and don't call Frank or anybody else in the New

Orleans police department. People like you are scum. You make judgments about people you don't even know." He pushed back his chair and stood.

Vobitch wasn't that tall, five-nine or so, but his compact body was brawny and muscular. Hammer stared at him, bug-eyed.

"Hey, I didn't mean to upset you—"

"Upset me?" Vobitch came around the desk, looming over the CIA man now. "*Upset* me? You didn't *upset* me, you little prick with a two-inch dick. You pissed me off so bad I am using every fucking ounce of willpower, every ounce of self-discipline to stop myself from breaking you in half. Get out of that chair, asshole, and get out of my office."

Hammer's face turned beet red. Clenching his jaw, he got up and left.

Vobitch went to his desk and plopped into his chair with a heavy grunt. He raked his fingers through his silvery-gray hair, pinched the bridge of his nose, then looked at Frank. "That guy is scum."

"You want to talk later? I can wait." He'd never seen his boss so angry.

"No. I'm okay." Vobitch gave him an evil smile. "Well, I'm not, but that asshole is in worse shape than me right now. You believe it? I get three calls from the feds yesterday, telling me Hammer's a good guy and let's share our information, yadda, yadda, yadda. Fuckin make-nice bullshit like that."

"That's what happened in Boston. Before Hammer left Hank's office he said he was going to get the woman that killed his friend. His exact words were: *I'll get that bitch and make her wish she'd never been born.*"

"Well, he won't be getting anything more from us."

"Did you check the Atlanta flights for Robin Adair?"

"Yeah." Vobitch smiled. "You notice I didn't mention it to Asshole?"

"I did. And?"

"Robin Adair bought a one-way ticket to Boston, flew out of Atlanta on Friday, July 25th."

"Gotta be the June Carter woman. Robin Adair was living in Nashua, New Hampshire. The prints Boston PD got from her apartment matched the prints in her car. Hank drove me up there. Lots of clothes and toiletries still there, but I think she might have gone there after the Boston hit."

"You're sure she offed this guy, Oliver James?"

"All the evidence they got? There's no doubt. But who is she now? Robin Adair or somebody else?"

"And where is she?" Vobitch said.

"Who is she, where is she and the biggest question of all. Who's she gonna kill next?"

———

When he got back to the homicide office, Kenyon Miller looked up from his computer. "Roger Demaris called. I said you were in a meeting. He wants you to call him right away."

"Figures. He already left me a voicemail message. Roger's shitting his pants, probably getting all kinds of pressure from the VIPs and politicians. And I'm not ready to tell him about the Boston case."

Miller grinned. "Or the nice CIA man that paid us a visit."

"That too."

"What I do when I don't want to talk to Demaris? Call him when I figure he's out of his office." Miller glanced at the clock. "Give it a half hour, he'll probably be in court."

"Good idea." He didn't want to talk to Demaris, but he sure did want to talk to Jane Fontenot. He dialed her number. Yesterday Jane had presumably arrived home from her African safari. He'd given her a day to recuperate. But now he needed answers, now more than ever.

Two rings and she answered. "Hi, Jane? Homicide detective Frank Renzi. I got your number from Morgan Vobitch. How was your trip?"

A low chuckle. "Fantastic. What can I do for you?"

"I've got questions about a cold case, a murder in 1988, heard you were the lead detective. You got any free time this afternoon?"

"I have to take my dog to the vet for some shots early this afternoon, but later is okay."

In the background, he heard ferocious barking. "Settle down, Mischief!" Jane yelled. "It's only the mailman." To Frank, she said, "Sorry. Doberman's are great, but Mischief thinks anyone that comes to my door is a demented killer."

"Good to know you got protection. Can we meet at four o'clock at Rue de la Course?"

"Sounds good, Frank. See you there."

Relieved, he cradled the phone. Maybe Jane would enlighten him about Natalie and her mother's murder. And why her notes weren't in the case file. He glanced at Miller, tapping hunt-and-peck style on his computer keyboard. He wanted to talk to Kelly, but not in front of Miller.

"I'm heading to Café Beignet for coffee. You want one?"

"Yeah, the usual." Miller looked up, grinning now. "Tell Kelly I said hi."

Frank laughed—Miller knew his ploys—and left. The break room had a coffeemaker, but the pot was usually half-full of rotgut coffee. Most Eighth District cops got their coffee at Café Beignet next door. The place opened at seven and served breakfast and lunch. Their coffee was always fresh.

He went out the main door that faced Royal Street and turned left at the foot of the stairs. Café Beignet had tables inside, but when the weather was clear, as it was today, patrons could sit on a small patio adjacent to the station. Several tourist-types sat at round wrought-iron tables, enjoying chicory-laced coffee and beignets laden with powdered sugar. This end of Royal Street was a popular tourist destination because of all the antique stores.

A cement bench stood below a large air-conditioner jammed into one window of the station. He checked for pigeon droppings, sat down and hit the speed-dial for Kelly's number.

She answered right away. "Hey, Frank, how you doing?"

"Hard to say. Lotta shit going on, some good, some not. How are you?"

"Better. I get the stitches out tomorrow."

"Great. Sorry I couldn't talk long last night. I had to call my ex-wife about something." He also needed to get his head together and decide whether to tell Kelly about Gina.

"Hmm. Did you talk to her?"

Still thinking about Gina, he said, "Talk to her?" Had she read his mind?

"Evelyn. You said you had to call her."

"Oh. Right. No. She's avoiding me. How'd it go with your dad and your brother?"

"We had a great time. Dad cooked enough food to last a month and froze it for me. He was sorry he couldn't meet you. I told him you were in Boston working a case. How'd that go?"

"I got a lead on the mystery woman. Her name's Robin Adair. At least that's the name she was using up there. I'll tell you about it when I see you. How about dinner tonight? I'm meeting with Jane Fontenot at four, but I can pick up some takeout, be there by six."

"Don't get takeout. I've got tons of food in the freezer. Who's Jane Fontenot?"

"Lead detective on the Brixton murder back in eighty-eight. I want to see if it's related to the Peterson case. The shit's hitting the fan. Now we've got a CIA agent on our back."

"Whoa! CIA? Why?"

"He knew the Boston murder victim. When I went to Morgan's office for our meeting, he was there. He's pissed that I didn't tell him about the security video. Morgan threw him out."

"Jesus, why? What happened?"

He checked his watch. "Tell you all about it later. I'm getting coffee for me and Kenyon. Then I gotta call Demaris."

"Damn it, Frank, I feel like I'm out of the loop. You better give me a full report tonight."

"I will," he said. "I missed you."

After a pause, she said, "I missed you too." But her voice sounded odd. No warmth, no nothing. Just what he needed. More trouble.

Should he tell her about Gina? Maybe not. Let sleeping dogs lie.

———

But when he called Demaris, the DA wasn't in court, he picked up right away. After a moment of shocked silence, Frank said, "Hi, Roger, how you doing? I got your message." He glanced at Miller, who rolled his eyes.

"What have you got for me on the Peterson case?" Demaris said.

"Got a tip on the woman in the sketch. A clerk at the Sunshine Inn said he was sure she stayed there--"

"I know. Vobitch told me they found her car in Atlanta, but the ID on the registration was bogus. What about the murder in Boston? Is it connected to ours?"

He sipped his coffee, which aggravated the acid burn in his stomach. Demaris knew he'd been to Boston. What else did he know? "I'm not sure. I've got a name for the suspect, but they don't know where she is."

"Which means you've got nothing. Listen up, Renzi. If you don't have a suspect in custody by next Wednesday, I'm pulling you and Vobitch off the case. We got two murders possibly related to a murder in Boston. Interstate connection like that? I'll put the State cops on it, let them solve the case."

A click sounded in his ear, then a dial tone.

He slammed the phone in the cradle. "Fuck."

"Roger got a porcupine up his ass?" Miller said.

"Worse. He just gave me a week to solve the case. If we don't deliver a suspect by next Wednesday, he'll turn the case over to the State cops." He pushed back from his desk. "I'm going for a walk."

Miller took a look at his face and knew enough to remain silent.

To relieve his frustration he did a fast power-walk down to the river. Ignoring the tourists, he mounted the steps to the Moonwalk and stared down at the churning water of the muddy Mississippi.

Churning and muddy, just like his thoughts. Three weeks ago he had two murders to solve. Now he had another one in Boston, one that appeared to be connected to the New Orleans cases. He also had an ultimatum: Capture the killer or Demaris would yank him off the case.

He conjured an image of Natalie Brixton's yearbook photo.

Was she the killer?

He added up what he knew about her. Jeannette Brixton had been murdered in New Orleans in 1988. Another unsolved case. Ten-year-old Natalie moved to Pecos, Texas, to live with her uncle, Jerome Brixton. In the autopsy photos Jeanette Brixton's eyes didn't look Asian, but Natalie's did. Natalie's last name was Brixton. Maybe Jeanette never married the father. Or maybe she got a divorce and took back her maiden name. But Natalie had a father somewhere. So who was he? And where was he?

He stared into the fast-flowing waters of the Mississippi.

No answers there.

Natalie had lived in Pecos until she was eighteen, eight years dealing with a dysfunctional family. An alcoholic mother, a father who was having an affair, and their two children, Randy and Ellen. Randy had died under suspicious circumstances. The only person who saw it happen was Natalie. According to Gabe Rojas, Randy had sexually assaulted his sister. Ellen, now a single mother with a young son, seemed unmoved by the death of her brother and his best friend, Tex Conroy. *Good riddance to both of them.* Hank, the man Natalie worked with at Longhorn Jacks, had said: *If you talk to her, tell her Hank says hello.*

Did Natalie kill Tex Conroy? Was she the woman who'd stayed at the Sunshine Inn near Conroy's apartment? The woman with an ankle tat, like the woman in the security video leaving Arnold Peterson's room.

If so, it led to only one conclusion. Natalie had killed both of them.

He gazed at the mighty Mississippi, where a three-block-long tanker was plowing upriver with millions of gallons of crude oil in the storage tanks. Large white letters painted on the top deck said: NO SMOKING.

Why didn't he want to believe Natalie was the killer? Or the woman on the video? Kelly had jived him, saying he missed the tat on her ankle because he was busy admiring her other endowments. Still, over the years he'd collared plenty of good-looking women, hauled them in on dope or burglary charges.

But never for murder. He pictured the woman on the video. Sexy? Yes. Good-looking? Who knows, her face was hidden. But confident? Definitely, striding along like she knew exactly what she was doing.

He thought about Kelly's comment when he showed her the yearbook picture. *The girl had a tough life. But you'd never know it from the picture, smiling, looks right at the camera.* In the Drama Club photos Natalie had long legs like the woman in the video. And her motto? *Freedom and justice for all.*

None of this proved Natalie was a killer, but if Natalie was the woman at the Sunshine Inn, the odds were high that she was Robin Adair, who'd flown from Atlanta to Boston the day after Tex Conroy was murdered.

Why didn't he want to believe it? Natalie would be thirty now, only five years older than his daughter. Did she remind him of Maureen? Not really. Then he remembered Maureen's anxious expression when she told him about Evelyn not paying the tax bill, her look of relief when he'd said: *You shouldn't have to handle this. I'll take care of it.*

Maybe that was it. After her mother was murdered, ten-year-old Natalie was on her own, no one to care for her, no one to fix her problems.

He looked at the tanker with the huge warning sign: NO SMOKING.

Since he returned from Texas, he had ignored the warning signs. Natalie didn't rely on others to solve her problems. She did it herself. Natalie wasn't ten anymore, she was a grown woman. He might not want to believe it, but all the evidence indicated that Natalie was a killer.

He turned away from the Mississippi and headed back to the office. He hoped Jane Fontenot would give him the clue he needed, because he had no idea where Natalie was.

And he was certain she wasn't done killing.

CHAPTER 24

When Frank walked into the Rue de la Course at four o'clock, students hunched over laptops occupied most of the tables. He figured the woman seated at a corner table in the back was Jane Fontenot.

He bought an iced coffee and approached her. "Jane?" he said.

Her brown eyes crinkled in a smile. "Good detective work. Have a seat, Frank."

She might be in her sixties but she was still a good-looking woman, short attractively-styled chestnut-brown hair, a firm jaw, no deep lines on her tanned skin. Unlike Corrine Peterson, who was twenty years younger, Jane appeared trim and fit, exuding an unmistakable air of femininity. No wedding band. He wondered if she'd gone on the African safari alone. Somehow, he doubted it.

"What are you doing in New Orleans, Frank? Boston's a great town."

"Except for the ice and the snow and freezing your butt off on stakeouts." His usual response. The real reasons were more complicated.

"You're interested in the Brixton murder."

"Yes. Morgan Vobitch said you're a great detective, so I figured you'd have a handle on it."

She didn't respond to the compliment, just sipped her latte. Finally, she said, "Sad case. Her kid was only ten, and I had to deliver the bad news."

"How'd she take it?"

"Okay. On the surface at least. No tears, no hysterics. She seemed unusually mature for a ten-year-old. The mother left her alone while she was working. Hooking, from what I could gather. We found her in a room at the Royal Arms, a scuzzy hotel on Royal Street. Not pretty. The killer roughed her up, slugged her with something and strangled her."

"I saw the photos in the case file. Nothing from forensics?"

"No semen, no prints that did us any good. You know how it is with hotel rooms, a zillion people have been there. They got a partial off her neck, but not enough for a match. The coroner thought the killer hit her with a flatiron, the kind they keep in hotel rooms, you know? But we didn't find one. We got fibers off the body, but that got us nowhere too. Jeannette Brixton paid for the room. For what it's worth, her toxicology report was negative for drugs and alcohol."

"Any suspects?" He tried the iced coffee. It was okay, but not as good as Dunkin Donut's coffee.

"We compiled a list of men known to frequent that particular hotel with women they paid for sex. I had a gut feeling about one guy, but his wife swore he was with her the whole night."

"Did you believe her?"

"Not really. When I talked to her the day after the murder, she had a bruise on her cheek. When I asked about it, she gave me the usual bullshit, said she fell and hit it on something."

"Who was he?"

"Frank, I may be retired, but I don't need trouble."

"Powerful guy?"

"Very. With powerful friends."

"Maybe that explains it. I assume you wrote up your notes and put them in the case file. But when I checked out the file, they weren't there."

"My notes are missing? Jesus! I put them in the file." She sipped her latte. "What's your interest in the case?"

"I'm mostly interested in the daughter. Natalie Brixton."

"You know, ten years ago I got a phone call from a woman asking about the case."

"Do you remember what she said?"

"Frank, I remember *everything* about this case. I wanted to solve this one in the worst way and I struck out. You work homicides. You know how it is. Some cases grab you by the throat and won't let go."

He sure did. A few of them still haunted his dreams. "What did she say?"

"She asked if we were still working the case and did we have any leads."

"Did she give you her name?"

"Mary Brown, Mary Smith, some bullshit name. She said she was calling on behalf of Natalie Brixton. She said Natalie couldn't call because she was in Australia and it would cost too much."

"You think Natalie was in Australia?"

"I think it was Natalie on the phone. Why are you so interested in her?"

"Keep this under your hat. It may be related to the Peterson murder."

Her eyes went wide. "You think Natalie killed Arnold Peterson?"

"Maybe. We linked the Peterson murder to the murder of Tex Conroy. You've been out of the country so you might not know about that one. They found Conroy in City Park, one gunshot to the head in both cases, ballistics report said the .38 caliber slugs came from the same gun. Conroy's from Texas, so I went there to talk to his mother. Tex went to school with Natalie."

"I knew she went there to live with her uncle, but what's Tex Conroy got to do with Peterson?"

"I wish I knew. His mother put me onto Natalie. Tex and Natalie's cousin Randy were co-captains of the high school football team. Randy fell off a cliff and died. Natalie was the only person with him. Mrs. Conroy said Tex and his friends figured Natalie pushed him."

"Why? What possible motive would she have?"

"Good question. I'm coming to that. At the time Natalie was eighteen, had just graduated from high school. When the police questioned her, she said Randy was drunk. His mother and sister confirmed this. Natalie said he got too close to the edge, slipped and fell. So they let her go."

"So? What's your point? That doesn't mean she pushed him."

"No, but when I talked to Randy's sister Ellen, she seemed indifferent about her brother's death. Same reaction when I told her about Tex Conroy. She said, and I'm quoting, *Good riddance to both of them*. Then I talked to Natalie's friend, a guy by the name of Gabriel Rojas. Rojas told me Randy had been forcing his sister to give him blowjobs."

"Yuk. How did Rojas know about it?"

"Ellen told Natalie and Natalie told him." He pulled the yearbook out of his briefcase and showed Natalie's photo to Jane. "Check out the motto. Freedom and justice for all."

Jane studied the picture. "She turned out to be a beautiful girl."

"Yes she did. I think she also turned out to be a killer."

Jane sipped her latte, her expression thoughtful. A screech shattered the silence, emanating from a machine a clerk was using to make a specialty drink for a woman at the counter. After the racket stopped, he said, "Natalie got a Social Security number when she started working as a teenager, but the last tax return filed with that number was in nineteen-ninety-five. After that, nothing."

"So you don't know where she went."

"Or where she is now. I think Rojas stayed in touch with her, but he's not talking. Now we got a murder in Boston that might be related to the cases down here." He filled her in about the Boston case.

When he finished she said, "And the Boston vic was CIA?"

"Used to be, according to the CIA-spook I met in Boston. I think Natalie picked up several fake IDs after she left Pecos. We got June Carter staying in New Orleans at the Sunshine Inn when Peterson and Conroy were murdered. Now we got Robin Adair, who most likely killed former CIA-spook Oliver James. Boston PD got her prints off a car in the parking garage and matched them to the ones they got from her apartment in Nashua, New Hampshire."

"And?"

"Boston PD ran them through IAFIS and got zip." A computerized database, the Integrated Automated Fingerprint Identification System contained fingerprints and criminal histories associated with them. Law enforcement agencies could call up mug shots, height, weight, hair and eye color, and aliases. It also included photos of scars and tattoos. If they got a match.

"So she's got no criminal record," Jane said. "And she never served in the military. IAFIS has prints of all U.S. military personnel and federal employees, including CIA agents. She might have killed Conroy because he recognized her, but why kill Peterson? Or Oliver James? Even if his CIA buddy found out she was using a fake ID and James called her on it, why kill him?"

"I don't know. I'm hoping you can help me out."

Jane gazed at him, expressionless. "Help you out how?"

"I think the Peterson murder is related to your murder case. Natalie's mother, Jeannette Brixton."

"That was twenty years ago. The trail is dead. Case closed."

"Not to Natalie. Not if she called you ten years ago to see if you were still working on it. And the case isn't closed. It's an unsolved murder."

"It might have been Natalie that called, but I'm not sure."

He took a deep breath. She was falling into the same trap he had, remembering the ten-year-old girl, devastated when she found out her mother was murdered. "Jane. It was Natalie. She wanted to know who murdered her mother. Did you give her a name?"

"Of course not! I wouldn't give a name to a voice on the phone."

"Okay. But you said you had a prime suspect and the guy had an alibi."

Jane said nothing, avoiding his gaze.

"Who's the guy?"

Her lips tightened. "A rich and powerful man. Not to be crossed."

Annoyance zinged his gut. He liked Jane Fontenot, but she was stonewalling him and he didn't like it. "I need a name. My favorite DA, Roger Demaris, threatened me today, gave me a week to nail a suspect. If I don't, he'll take me and Vobitch off the case."

"Figures. Demaris was always a bastard."

"Yeah. And if Vobitch gets dumped, he might be looking at early retirement. I need a name."

Jane's expression softened. "Underneath all the bluster Morgan's a sweet guy. Okay, promise you won't tell anyone where you got the information."

"I won't."

"Beau Beaubien. Better known as BoBo, the guy that started the GoGo Bars. But you won't get anything from BoBo. He's dead."

"Damn. When did he die?"

"Almost three years ago. In 2005 I think it was, after Katrina. You could talk to his widow. And his ex-wife."

"How many wives did he have?"

"Three, but the first one died. The second wife was the one that gave him the alibi. Joereen divorced him not long afterwards."

"You think it would do any good if I talked to her?"

"Maybe. She claimed BoBo was slapping her around. He denied it, of course."

"Did they have kids?"

"Two girls. BoBo had a son too, with his first wife. Beau Junior. He runs the Go-Go Bars now."

"What about the widow? Is she still around?"

"Frank, I haven't been following the saga of BoBo."

"Okay. I'll find her. Thanks for the name."

"Be careful, Frank. You're poking a stick into a hornet's nest. Bobo was a very powerful guy."

———

Frank mopped his plate with a slice of garlic bread and said to Kelly, "Great lasagna. Home-made, right?"

She looked better than she had last Friday, good color on her cheeks, her dark pixie-styled hair glossy. Her low-cut top accentuated her well-toned arms, not to mention her other endowments. Damn, it had been way too long since one of their ardent love sessions, a situation he intended to remedy tonight.

"Dad made it before he went back to Chicago. He's into cooking big time, thin-sliced garlic, fresh plum tomatoes, the whole bit. Mom died when I was ten. With five hungry kids, he had to cook."

"You don't talk much about your mom. How come?"

Her eyes turned somber. "It makes me sad. I never got to know her. I was her only daughter and she didn't get to see me grow up. Sometimes it's hard for me to remember what she looked like. Before she got sick, I mean." She tilted her head and her big-Z earrings swayed. "Maybe that's how Natalie feels. She was ten when her mother got murdered. Tell me about Boston."

He didn't mind talking about the murder case, but he hadn't decided what else to tell her. He recapped his meeting with Hank and Clint Hammer.

"Why did Morgan throw the guy out of his office?" Kelly said.

"Hammer made a comment about jungle bunnies and Morgan went ballistic. Man, I've never seen him so angry."

"I don't blame him. He and Juliana brought me a home-cooked dinner. It was fun. Morgan told me a bunch of New York cop stories, and then Juliana told me how they met. What a story. Morgan rescues her from a mugger and then they fall in love. I didn't know she was a ballet dancer. Then she started talking about music and art and ballet. She's amazing."

"Yeah. She calms Morgan down when he gets riled up."

Kelly gave him a speculative look. "What else happened in Boston?"

He didn't like the look in her eyes. Speculation and something else that he couldn't identify.

"I think Natalie killed the guy in Boston, using another fake ID. Robin Adair. They got prints from her car and apartment, but no hit on IAFIS."

"So you're back to square one."

"Nope. I got the name of the prime suspect in the Brixton murder."

Kelly's eyes widened. "Wow! Did you get it from Jane?"

He wagged a finger at her. "My lips are sealed. And so are yours."

"Yeah, yeah. So? Who is it?"

"BoBo, the Go-Go Bar guy. That's the good news. The bad news is he's dead. But I'm going to talk to his ex-wife, see if I can squeeze something out of her. She's the one that gave him the alibi."

"How's your reporter friend?"

Blind-sided by the question, he drank some wine, brushed crumbs off the place mat. But he could only stall for so long. The moment of truth.

"She's not just a friend. She's the woman I told you about, the one who got tangled up in my divorce. Gina and I had an affair for nine years."

Kelly gazed at him, expressionless. "Is that why she called you?"

"No," he said, irritated. "She called me about the murder case."

"Does she call you about all the murders that happen in Boston?"

Damn. He should have kept his mouth shut. But he didn't like lying to people he cared about, and he cared about Kelly a lot. "I haven't talked to Gina in two years. She saw an AP wire story about the Peterson case and thought the Boston case might be related. A rich guy murdered in a posh hotel, same MO, one shot to the head. And she was right."

Kelly looked at him. That something he'd seen in her eyes was anger.

"We had dinner."

"That's it? Dinner?"

"She's had some health problems. We talked about it after we talked about the Oliver James murder. Which she put me wise to, and for which I am grateful."

"What kind of health problems?"

This was starting to feel like an interrogation. He felt his face get hot, felt a rising tide of anger in his gut. He uncrossed his legs, about to leave the table. Forced himself to stay put. Told himself to cool it. "Breast cancer."

Kelly's eyes widened. "How awful. I'm sorry to hear it."

She went to the counter and poured herself a glass of wine. She wasn't supposed to drink alcohol while she was on pain meds, but he wasn't going to tell her what to do. She was a grownup. And pissed off about something. That was clear enough.

She came back and set the wineglass on the table, but didn't drink any. "You and Gina had an affair for nine years. That's how long Terry and I were married." She took a deep breath. "One time I had an affair."

Shocked, he stared at her. She'd never mentioned this before. As far as he knew, she and her husband had been happy. What else wasn't she telling him?

She twirled the wine glass, rolling the stem between her fingers. "One day I ran into a guy I met in college and we got talking. Terry and I were going through a rough patch at the time. Anyway, one thing led to another. It didn't last long. A couple of months. Long enough for me to get good at lying."

She gazed at him steadily, her sea-green eyes cool and distant.

"I'm not lying," he said.

"No? Look at it from my perspective. Last Friday we're sitting in my kitchen and you get a phone call and go into your double-speak routine. You're good at that, Frank. I've seen you do it. Then Kenyon arrives and you go off to talk to your reporter friend." She gulped some wine. "Then you go to Boston for three days and I don't get one fucking phone call from you. You weren't working around the clock, so I figure you must have had company."

A giant cat clawed his gut. But damned if he was going to account for his every moment while he was in Boston. Never complain, never explain.

"Meanwhile, I'm down here taking my fucking meds and entertaining my father and brother who are, for the most part, fun to be around, but they treated me like an invalid. So they fly back to Chicago, and Sunday night Morgan and Juliana come over and bring me dinner. Okay, fine, but I was figuring you'd call me and you didn't."

She gulped more wine and looked at him, frosty-eyed. "You know how that made me feel, Frank? It made me feel like a jerk."

"I'm sorry," he said. "I should have called you--"

"Not to mention out of the loop. Here I am stuck at home, who the hell knows when I'll get back to work, and then I start thinking about Ben, what a great guy he was and . . ."

He reached over and squeezed her hand.

Startled, she looked at him.

"I don't blame you for being pissed."

"Jesus. I sound like Nancy Kerrigan when the guy whacked her knee at the Olympics." She made a face and said in a whiny high-pitched voice, "Why me? Why me?" She shook her head. "Sorry, Frank."

"It's okay. You got a right to complain, what you went through."

Her sea-green eyes warmed up for the first time. "I believe you, Frank. I know you're not lying."

The giant cat stopped clawing his gut. He ran a finger down her forearm.

"I think we need to go in your bedroom so I can take off your clothes and see how your stitches are doing."

She grinned. "Frank. You are so baaad."

Natalie

2002

To celebrate my 24th birthday in April, I sent an email to Gabe. Then I went to NOLA.com to check up on BoBo as I did every morning. He was still married to Helena, still throwing parties at his house. For my birthday treat I went to the Orsay Museum. The Manet paintings were my favorites. Now, thanks to my art instructor at The Service, I could fully appreciate them. I gazed at the Olympia, admiring Manet's exquisite use of light and shadow and flattened perspective. I loved the way he painted his beautiful naked courtesan, confronting the viewer with her imperious gaze.

"I love Manet, don't you?" said a deep melodious voice.

Turning, I said, "Oui, j'aime beaucoup."

"You speak French beautifully," he said in thickly accented English. "Do you live in Paris?"

Mesmerized, I didn't answer immediately. He was very distinguished-looking: reddish-gold hair, a craggy face with a neatly trimmed Van Dyke beard. I loved his eyes. They were deep blue, almost violet.

"Yes," I said. "Do you?" Hoping he did.

"No, I live in Amsterdam. I am here for a film festival. I am a producer, and one of my films will be shown tonight at the festival."

"What is it about?"

He smiled faintly. "About a man who finds his true love in a museum."

I laughed. "And do they live happily ever after?"

"If boy meets girl, boy marries girl and they live happily ever after, there is no drama. A good film must have drama." He waggled his eyebrows and made his violet-blue eyes go wide. "*Sturm und drang.*"

"Like *L.A. Confidential?*"

"Yes. That was a fine film. My name is Willem DeVries, and yours?"

"Laura Lin." He wasn't a client, but I never told anyone my last name.

"It is my great pleasure to meet you, Laura Lin," he said, and kissed my hand. "Shall we go see some other paintings? The Rembrandts are excellent."

He was over six-feet tall and appeared quite fit, but as we walked through the museum I noticed he had a limp, and the sole on his right shoe was thicker than the left one. After a while, he said, "I am enjoying this very much, but I must go to the festival now. Would you like to come?"

Conscious of my outfit, a simple black dress that I wore when I wasn't working, I said, "I would love to, but I'm not dressed properly."

"You are dressed perfectly. After the film, I would like to take you out for dinner. Would that be all right?"

I said it would, and that's how our love affair began. At the festival Willem introduced me to several people and then we watched his film. Despite the sad ending, I enjoyed it very much. Afterwards he took me to an elegant French bistro. Partway through dinner he told me he was married. This was a disappointment, but I was glad he was honest about it. When he asked what I did for a living, I said I worked for a business in the 16th Arrondissment. I didn't want to tell him what I really did. After we finished eating, Willem said, "Would you care to have an after dinner drink at my hotel?"

My heart was beating hard and fast. I knew what this meant. Should I say it was too soon for us to be intimate? By then I loved everything about him, his looks, his intelligent discussions of art and films, even his honesty in telling me he was married. And his self-deprecating explanation of his limp—he'd been born with one leg shorter than the other—had charmed me.

Desire won. "I would be happy to join you for a drink."

At his hotel room one thing led to another as I expected. Except for one part. Willem refused to take his own pleasure until I had mine. I tried faking an orgasm, but Willem said, "Please, Laura Lin. My greatest pleasure comes from your pleasure." And so he taught me how to have an orgasm.

This indescribable feeling seemed to go on forever. Afterwards I felt both exhausted and exhilarated. Now I understood the satisfaction and contentment sex could bring. Willem asked me to stay the night. The next morning we made love again and it was even better than the first time. When I told Willem I had to work that night, he said he would wait until I finished. So I had to tell him what I did for a living. To make it sound less sordid, I said I was a high-class escort. I expected him to react with disgust but he didn't.

He was a man of the world, sophisticated and cosmopolitan. And he was married. I did not allow myself forget that.

He promised to return to Paris soon. True to his word, five weeks later he did. I took two nights off and we had a fabulous time. When Willem asked about my Asian heritage, I said my father was part Vietnamese but I didn't know where he was. Willem didn't press me. Another thing I loved about him. He was so tolerant of people. His favorite saying was *Judge not lest ye be judged.*

He couldn't visit me during the holidays, of course. He stayed with his family in Amsterdam. On New Years Eve I went to a club to hear some jazz and figure out how much money I would need to finance the Main Event. My new code word for avenging Mom. I figured it might take three years. This seemed like an eternity. The next day I asked Lin to book me as many clients as possible. He was happy to oblige.

Only once did I have trouble. One new client, an Albanian, was over six feet tall and his muscular hands looked powerful enough to pulverize rocks. He said he wanted to tie me up and pretend to beat me. I wasn't sure about the pretend part. Then I remembered what Mr. Takagi said: *What will you do if a man asks you to do something you don't want to do?* So I did my spinning TKD move and kicked him in the head. He fell to the floor, groaning. I put on my clothes and fled. The next day I told Lin about it, and Lin said he would deal with him.

Willem could only come to Paris three or four times a year. I tried not to think about him making love to his wife. He seldom spoke of her but he always told me when his sons won athletic awards or passed an important test in school. Before I knew it two years passed. In April 2004 I celebrated my twenty-sixth birthday by sending Gabe my annual email. This time I wrote: *So happy in P. Met W who is wonderful. Miss you. XOXO, IRS*

My love for Willem kept growing, and I began to fantasize about a life with him. After the Main Event, of course. But one day I went to NOLA.com and got a terrible shock. BoBo had been diagnosed with pancreatic cancer, and the prognosis was poor. I was heartsick. Here I was working overtime to save money to avenge Mom and the man who'd murdered her was going to die.

A vision of the gargoyles above Notre Dame flashed in my mind. Were the angry ancestor spirits tired of waiting for me to avenge Mom's murder? Did they decide to punish BoBo by giving him cancer? If so, this brought me no comfort. BoBo was a ruthless monster and I hated him.

I wanted to kill him myself. But my plan was not yet in place.

———

By April 2005 Willem and I had been together for three years. Well, not together exactly, but when he came to Paris, we went to movies and museums and ate superb dinners and made passionate love afterwards. For my 27th birthday, our anniversary date, Willem gave me something special. He adored the musicality of Edgar Allen Poe. His favorite poem was The Raven. As we lay in bed after making love, he would say in his deep musical voice, "Once upon a midnight dreary, as I pondered weak and weary." And recite the whole poem word for word. Or sometimes he would smile at me and say: "Quoth the Raven, 'Nevermore.'" Like it was our private joke.

For my birthday he took me to a tattoo parlor to get matching tattoos. As a symbol of our love, he said. I was thrilled. This was a far better present than jewelry or a fancy dress. A tattoo was permanent. When Willem wasn't with me in Paris I could look at my tattoo and imagine that he was in Amsterdam looking at his. And thinking about me.

Willem brought along a copy of a lithograph Manet had done in 1975 to illustrate a French translation of The Raven, and we each got tiny black ravens tattooed on our ankles. On the inside where people wouldn't notice it, Willem said. Then we ate dinner at a swanky restaurant, went back to Willem's hotel and made mad passionate love.

The day after he left I poured myself a glass of wine and took stock of my situation. By Christmas I would have enough money in my Laura Lin Hawthorn bank account to avenge Mom. Then I would be free to live life as I wished. And my greatest wish was to have a life with Willem.

I was certain he loved me. Didn't we have a permanent symbol of our love tattooed on our ankles? I began to fantasize about living with him. I wanted to feel him beside me in bed when I woke up each morning.

In November Willem called to say he was coming for a visit. "Our last tryst this year," he said. "But I'll be back in January." His promise did not fill me with joy, it depressed me.

I knew he liked spending the holidays with his boys. I don't know about his wife. I wondered if she suspected that he had a lover. I really didn't care. All I knew was that I spent the Christmas and New Year holidays alone. I had no clients. Like Willem, they were home celebrating with their families.

I made a decision. This time I would talk to Willem about our future.

The second night we went to a four-star restaurant. Over dinner we had our usual lively discussion of world events. Willem looked especially handsome in his chocolate-brown Armani suit. "What do you think of the way President Bush handled the disaster in New Orleans after Katrina?" he asked.

This startled me. Willem didn't know I was monitoring the events in New Orleans every single day on NOLA.com. And rejoicing each time I saw no obituary for BoBo.

"I feel bad for the residents," I said. To be honest I was mainly worried that if the city didn't recover, I might never be able to avenge Mom.

After dinner we went to Willem's hotel, but I didn't take my clothes off as I usually did. "Willem, I think we need to talk about something."

His violet-blue eyes, invariably full of happiness when we were together, clouded with concern. "What is it you want to talk about Laura?"

My palms dampened with sweat and my heart was beating my chest like a sledgehammer. "About you and me and where our relationship is going."

"Laura," he said softly, "you know I am married."

"You told me this on our first date and I respected you for it. But we've been together three years." I smiled. "Well, not together. You visit me, but we're not together all the time."

Willem said nothing, but I could tell he was nervous, plucking at his neatly trimmed Van Dyke beard with his fingers.

"We got ravens tattooed on our ankle. To symbolize our love, you said."

He nodded gravely. "Yes. I love you very much Laura Lin."

"If you love me, why don't you come and live with me in Paris?"

His eyes, already desolate, filmed with tears. "Laura, I love you deeply, but I cannot leave my wife. She has been my partner all these years. She is a wonderful mother. And I could never leave my boys."

Burning pain scorched my stomach. I looked at the tiny raven tattoo on my ankle, the symbol of our love. But only because we were apart. Now, every day I would look at it and see a symbol of our separation not our love. This hurt me terribly, a dagger in my heart. But seeing tears in Willem's eyes also brought me great pain. I loved him deeply, and I didn't want to hurt him.

All these thoughts whirled in my mind like debris from a terrible storm. "What about me? You won't be back until January. Over the holidays you will be with your family. I will be alone."

He took both my hands and kissed them. "Forgive me, Laura. I know this is not a good situation for you, but there is nothing I can do."

"Yes there is. You could live with me and visit your boys once a month."

But even as I said this, I knew he wouldn't.

"I want you to be happy, Laura. You are a beautiful intelligent woman. Perhaps you should think about finding someone who isn't married."

Anger boiled up inside me. "What should I do?" I said, "keep having sex with strangers for money and hope one asks me to marry him some day?" Bitter laughter spewed from my mouth. "These men are not looking for wives. You know that."

No answer from Willem. Just a closed face and sad eyes. I wanted to lash out and hurt him, as he had hurt me. But I cared for him too deeply. I gathered my purse and stood. "Willem, I can't continue our affair under these circumstances. If you change your mind, call me."

His eyes grew moist. "I love you, Laura Lin. Always remember that."

I left Willem's hotel and went home and vomited in the toilet.

———

After that everything went to hell. A week before Christmas, BoBo died.

This I learned on NOLA.com. BoBo had died in Tijuana, Mexico while undergoing cancer treatments. The article touted his rise from poverty-stricken origins to become a powerful business magnate with his chain of Go-Go Bars, scores of them all across the United States. It even quoted one of his business associates, a man named Arnold Peterson.

"BoBo had fantastic business instinct," Peterson said. "The kind of intuition and smarts you don't get in business school."

This made me want to puke.

Did Arnold Peterson know that BoBo was a murderer?

Three days later I read about his funeral, a Catholic Mass attended by hundreds of people. His son Chip said BoBo was a humble man who spent his final days "trying to get right with God."

That made me so angry I had to do some TKD moves to work off my fury. Get right with God? Did he expect God to forgive him for beating Mom's face to a bloody pulp and strangling her? I didn't want God to punish BoBo. I wanted to punish him myself. But I couldn't. BoBo was dead.

This filled me with rage.

I went out and did a five-mile run along the Seine. When I returned, hot and sweaty, I was still angry. But most of all I felt great shame. Mom had waited seventeen years for vengeance and I had failed to give it to her. I was destined to go through life haunted by the vindictive ancestor gods.

I drank a glass of water and finished reading the article about the funeral. One of his important business associates gave the eulogy, Arnold Peterson, the man who'd praised BoBo's business instincts.

Arnold Peterson seemed to be BoBo's biggest cheerleader.

Then came a list of BoBo's survivors: Helena, his third wife, and his three children, the two girls he cared nothing about and his beloved son, Chip. And two grandchildren. The list was a painful reminder of my failure.

BoBo's death had thwarted my most cherished goal: revenge.

I thought about my favorite revenge movies; *The Professional,* by Luc Bresson, and *Sympathy for Lady Vengeance,* by Park Chan-Wook. Most people took revenge by punishing the person who wronged them. They wanted the wrongdoer to suffer the same or greater pain than was originally inflicted.

What could be worse than killing someone? Once they were dead, they were dead. And now BoBo was dead.

But in some Asian cultures retribution can be far worse than the crime. Japanese warriors called Samurai uphold the family honor with revenge killings called *katakiuchi.* Such killings may involve the wrongdoer's relatives.

And what could be worse than killing BoBo?

Killing his beloved son, Chip.

I decided that this would be my new goal.

Over the holidays I had no clients, which left plenty of time to visit NOLA.com. One day there was a feature article about Chip. After graduating from Loyola, he had taken over as manager of the GoGo Bar in New Orleans. Now he was CEO of the BoBo's GoGo Bars LLC. He planned to expand his father's business empire. When asked if his two daughters might someday run the business, Chip said, "Your guess is as good as mine."

Not if I could help it.

If Chip died, BoBo's business would die too.

And clearly my romance with Willem was also dead.

Although I didn't sit by the phone waiting for it to ring, I expected a call at least. But not a word from Willem. No call, no letter. Nothing.

It was time to leave Paris. Time to forget Willem and start a new life.

After the holidays, I told Lin I planned to leave The Service in February.

He seemed genuinely disappointed. "You have been an excellent worker, Laura Lin, and we will miss you. I wish you the best of luck in whatever you do. If you ever need anything, anything at all, call me."

CHAPTER 25

Friday, 15 August 11:00 A.M.

Deep in the bowels of a federal office building in Washington, D.C., Clint Hammer punched a key on his laptop and the printer beside his desk whirred to life. His office was two floors below street level, a windowless eight-by-ten cubicle with baby-shit-green walls. The color amused him.

Plenty of shit went down inside these walls and it had nothing to do with babies. No photographs or official citations graced the walls or his desk. No file cabinets—no paper trails for someone to steal—just a gun-metal-gray desk with a padded swivel chair, and a wireless printer.

The desk faced the door. Clint Hammer never sat with his back to a door or a window. That was worse than stupid. It was asking for trouble, no telling when some sneaky sonofabitch might try to catch him unawares and overpower him. He grabbed the printout and checked his wristwatch.

Jason, his computer geek, was due any minute. Right on cue, a familiar rap sounded on the door: three knocks, a silence, another knock.

"Come in, Jason. It's unlocked."

Jason entered and approached the desk. Jason was a crackerjack researcher, a computer hacker able to access most any file no matter how well-encrypted. A wiry man in his midthirties, Jason was short, five-two at most. That was another reason Hammer liked him. Jason looked at him expectantly, his brown eyes liquid behind his thick glasses.

"I've got a new assignment for you." He showed him the computer printout. One page contained data, the other a photo and a sketch. "Find this woman. On August fourth, she escaped a police dragnet in Boston. She was renting an apartment in Nashua, New Hampshire, under the name Robin Adair, but she also goes by the name June Carson, and she might have other aliases. I want you to use the new face-recognition software to check outgoing flights at every airport within a two-hundred mile radius of Boston. Use the artist's sketch and the photo on the Robin Adair license."

Jason gnawed his lip, frowning now. "I don't know, Clint. I don't want to get in trouble. We're only s'posed to use the face-recognition program to look for terrorists."

A needle of irritation pricked his gut. "Jason, this woman killed a former CIA agent. Murdered him in cold blood and left him lying on the floor in a Boston hotel room, naked."

"How'd she manage to kill a former CIA agent?"

The needle of irritation in his gut became a shard of glass. "Never mind how! She did, and I'm going to find the bitch and make her wish she didn't."

Jason's pockmarked face assumed a hangdog look. "Whatever you say, Clint. But it'll take a while. There's a lot of airports within two hundred miles of Boston. How many dates should I check? August fourth until when?"

Pierced by stabbing pains, his gut screamed in agony. "Until you find her! I don't give a shit how long it takes. Get on your fucking computer and find the bitch that killed my friend."

"Okay, boss." Jason took the printout and backed away from the desk.

He slammed his fists on the desktop. "Soon."

After Jason left, he picked a cuticle on his thumb, recalling his escapades with Oliver during the two years they'd worked together. Oliver was a first-rate agent. He also had a way with women, which had often benefited The Hammer. While they were in Barbados, they might spot a couple of hot chicks in a bar. Oliver would pick one and leave him the other.

And now Oliver was dead. Killed by that gook pussy. The Boston cops had no clue how to find her, nor did those idiot cops in New Orleans.

He hadn't forgotten the ugly scene with the Jew-bastard Lieutenant and his greasy-Wop homicide dick. He'd fix those bastards. Down in the boonies of Louisiana, they didn't have face-recognition software. As soon as Jason located that gook-bitch, he'd make her wish she'd never been born. And those NOPD pricks would never be the wiser.

———

At two minutes past noon, she turned off St. Charles Avenue onto a street lined with magnificent Victorians and towering oak trees. Set back from the street behind a tall wrought-iron fence, Parades-A-Plenty was in the middle of the block, but every parking space on the street was taken. She circled the block, found an empty space and backed her Ford Focus into it. Towing her suitcase with one hand, gripping her laptop in the other, she trudged through the sweltering heat to Parades-A-Plenty.

Surrounded by live oak trees and dappled with sunlight, the three story Victorian had a wrap-around porch on the ground floor and a multitude of windows. The exterior was painted emerald green, accented with golden ochre trim on the shutters that bracketed the tall windows.

The house looked lovely, but she wasn't looking forward to dealing with Mrs. Reilly and her banshee squawk. She swung open the wrought iron gate, went up the walk and mounted the steps. The lower half of the door was wood, the upper portion beveled glass. The door was ajar so she walked in.

A woman seated behind a reception desk looked up. "Welcome to Parades-A-Plenty."

The banshee shriek. But Mrs. Reilly looked nothing like the woman she had envisioned while talking to her on the phone. Banshee was no scrawny turkey. Pasty-white jowls sagged from her chin. She had to weigh at least two hundred pounds. A paper plate on the reception desk held a half-eaten slice of pepperoni pizza, oozing grease.

"Hello. I'm April West. I reserved one of your rooms for a week."

Mrs. Reilly surveyed her from head to toe. Cut in an unflattering bob, her grayish hair looked like someone had put a bowl on her head and trimmed around it. Her eyes, bright blue and crafty, signaled trouble.

"Figured it was you. Everybody else who booked rooms for today called and canceled. They're worried about the hurricane." Mrs. Reilly squinted at her silently for several seconds.

The silence was a relief. If she had to listen to that voice very long, she'd get a headache.

"You look familiar," Banshee said. "Have you been here before?"

"No, never." The question unnerved her. She didn't want to look familiar, she wanted to look ordinary and anonymous. That's why she'd worn her light-auburn wig and the Vera Wang eyeglasses with pale-tan tinted glass that hid her eye color.

Banshee smiled, exposing shiny-white dentures. "Your hair is such a pretty color."

"Thank you," she said quickly. Anything to shut her up.

"You should wear green to accent it. That black suit is much too plain. Not flattering at all."

"Is my room ready?"

"Ready!" Banshee squawked. "Of course it's ready! I've been running this place for thirty years, ten of 'em by myself after my husband died, Lord rest him. He was a fine man, my Tom was, but the Lord took him and there's nothing I can do about it."

She stifled a yawn. The trip from Ithaca to New Orleans had taken two long days. Only once had she stopped to sleep.

Sensing her weariness perhaps, Mrs. Reilly said, "You're tired, aren't you dear. Well, you're going to love Parades-A-Plenty. This house was built in 1893 by a famous New Orleans architect. His name was Tom, too, just like my husband. Thomas Sully built this house in the Queen Ann style. Did you see the double Ionic columns out front? That's the tip off. Tom Sully hired the best carpenters in town to work on the house. When you go upstairs, be sure and notice the wood balustrades and the wood medallions in your room."

She gritted her teeth. "Which room is it?"

"The Blue Room on the third floor. All my rooms have hardwood floors and period furnishings, but the Blue Room is always the first room that gets rented during Mardi Gras. Walk down to St. Charles Avenue and you can see all twenty-six of the Mardi Gras parades."

"But not in August," she said, and smiled. *Shut up and give me the key to my room.* The Blue Room on the third floor. She hoped it was air-conditioned.

"Well. No, not in August. But maybe you'll come back next year."

"Could be." And maybe pigs would fly.

"Well. Let's get you registered. Can I see your driver's license?"

"Of course." She took it out of her tote bag and handed it over.

Mrs. Reilly studied her face. "You know, it's the strangest thing, but I feel like I've seen you before."

A chill rippled down her spine. "I doubt it," she said firmly. "I've never been to New Orleans."

"Hmph. Well, let's get you on my computer."

As the woman put April West's license information into the computer—click, click, click on the keyboard—she studied her surroundings.

The wallpaper was beautiful, embossed with fleur-de-lis. To her right, an archway opened onto a dining room. Below a crystal chandelier, four antique chairs surrounded a table with a polished wood top. Beyond the table, a door led to a staircase with an ornate wooden banister.

Given the period décor and antique furnishings, the flat-screen TV on the wall next to check-in desk seemed out of place. It was tuned to the Weather Channel, with the sound muted.

"There, that's done." Mrs. Reilly handed back her license. "You're going to love the Blue Room. It's got a private bath, a telephone and cable TV. And a beautiful four-poster bed."

Four-poster bed. She had an instant flashback to Arnold Peterson, trussed to another four-poster with a bullet hole in his forehead.

Banshee's grating voice jolted her back to the present.

"You get a Continental breakfast every day." Baring her dentures in a smile. "That's why we call this a bed and breakfast. You can eat in the dining room or sit out on the veranda." Her bright blue eyes widened and a look of horror swept her face. "Oh my God! Look!"

Startled, she followed the woman's gaze to the TV set. A huge swirling orange mass filled the screen.

The Weather Channel was updating the latest tropical storm headed toward the Gulf. Banshee used a remote to turn on the sound. The storm had been upgraded to a hurricane. Hurricane Josephine was west of the Windward Islands now and churning toward Haiti.

Would her bad luck never end? Why was a storm threatening the Gulf now? Her plan was in place, but she still had to seduce her target, and she didn't know how long that might take. According to an article on NOLA.com last week, Chip would return to New Orleans today to prepare for the grand opening of his newest Go-Go Bar next Friday.

"You might not be able to stay the whole week," Banshee said. "If that storm gets into the Gulf, I'm going to close up."

"Goodness, I don't think you need to worry about that yet."

The woman's doughy face hardened. "Listen here, young lady. Maybe you've never been to New Orleans, but I've lived here all my life. Tom and I stayed right here in this house for Betsy in 'sixty-five. Lord-a-mercy, I thought the roof would blow off. The walls were shaking something fierce. That taught me a lesson. I boarded the place up and left for Katrina. Good thing . . ."

The banshee voice continued, an ugly rasp. She wanted to strangle the woman. "Excuse me, Mrs. Reilly, but I'd like to go up to my room. Could you give me the key?"

The banshee-rasp stopped. Mrs. Reilly gazed at her, frosty-eyed.

"Well. I thought you might like to hear about the history of the house. But suit yourself." She opened a drawer and held out a brass key. "But mark my words, young lady, I'm keeping an eye on that hurricane. If it looks like it's going to hit us, I'm going to close the place and get out of town."

"I understand, Mrs. Reilly. You have a nice day."

She towed her suitcase through the dining room to the staircase. No elevator of course. Not in a house built in 1893. She would have to lug her suitcase up to the third floor. That might be an advantage.

Up on the third floor she wouldn't be able to hear that banshee screech.

CHAPTER 26

A loud thump jolted her awake, mercifully ending a nightmare. The four-poster bed was comfortable, and the sheets smelled fresh and clean, but the Blue Room was hot and stuffy. Not only was the air-conditioner in the window unable to cool a third-floor room with steep-slanted eaves, it was noisy, clanking a syncopated rhythm to accompany her racing heart.

The luminous dial of her wristwatch stood at 1:35.

She rolled over and tried to get back to sleep, but when she shut her eyes, Randy's face appeared, the instant before he fell over the cliff, eyes bugged out in terror. To calm herself she pictured her Japanese watercolor. In her frantic haste to escape, she had left it in Nashua. She focused on the birds circling the snow-capped mountain, willing the birds and mountains to protect her.

She finally fell asleep, but at four A.M. the air-conditioner began rattling like a hailstorm. Faint moonlight filtered through the tree outside the window, casting shadows on the steep-slanted walls. Sinister shadows like the ones that scared her when she was a kid in New Orleans, home alone in her bedroom.

She closed her eyes. This time Oliver's face tortured her, eyes accusing. Then, inexplicably, blood spouted from a hole in his forehead. Moaning, she sat up, shaking with tremors. Would she ever have any peace? Unwilling to confront more ghosts, she turned on the bedside lamp and got out of bed. Yesterday when she came up to her room, her first task was opening her laptop to access the Wifi connection. She padded barefoot to the small table in the corner and turned on her laptop.

The Weather Channel had an update. After pounding Haiti as a Category-4 storm, Hurricane Josephine had weakened, but forecasters expected it to hit Jamaica sometime today. In Haiti the storm had killed eighty people. Due to erratic wind currents in the upper atmosphere, forecasters couldn't predict where the storm might go, but they expected it to hit the U.S. coast within the next five or six days. New Orleans was within the cone of possible land strikes.

She massaged her throbbing temples. After the Katrina debacle, New Orleans officials had instituted a new policy. Mandatory evacuation orders 48 hours before a possible hurricane strike. That meant she had three days, four at the most, to complete her mission. She shut down the laptop, went back to bed and fell into an exhausted sleep.

She woke at nine-thirty, took a shower and chose an outfit suitable for a woman ostensibly here to interview for a teaching job at Loyola: a high-necked green blouse, an ankle-length paisley-print skirt and leather sandals. Unwilling to leave certain items in the room, she put the important ones in her tote: her diary, her Laura Lin Hawthorn passport and the gun. With her floppy beach hat in hand, she went downstairs and entered the foyer.

"You're too late for breakfast," Banshee shrieked, eyeing her accusingly. "I shut off the coffeemaker at nine-thirty and put away the pastries."

"No problem, Mrs. Reilly. I'm going for a walk."

The woman looked her up and down. "That green shirt looks good on you. It flatters your hair."

"Thank you."

"I didn't hear you go out last night."

"No. I was tired. Your bed is very comfortable. Do you live here?"

"Where else would I live?" said the screech-voice. Banshee gestured at a door beside the reception desk. "I have a beautiful apartment right here on the first floor."

"Really? I'd love to see it sometime."

"Why?"

"To see the fixtures you were telling me about last night."

"Well. I can't show you now. I've got to stay here to answer the phone. I just got two more cancellations. That's a bad storm brewing out there."

"Another time then." She turned and headed for the door. "I'm going for my walk." Not just any walk, to plan an escape route.

"When's your interview?" Banshee called after her. "If there's an evacuation I might close."

"We'll just have to wait and see." She went out the door and shut it behind her. When she turned and looked, Banshee was watching her. The woman was insufferable. Should she find another place to stay? That might be difficult with a hurricane coming.

She opened the wrought-iron gate, turned right and walked along the fence to the corner. A black SUV drove toward her slowly, seeking a parking space perhaps. She put on the beach hat and averted her face as it passed. Her palms dampened with sweat, and not from the brutal heat and humidity. She needed an escape route that didn't include the front door. If she had to leave in a hurry, jumping out a third floor window wouldn't be an option.

Beyond the wrought-iron fence that enclosed Parades-A-Plenty was a modest two-story house. No fence. It appeared to be a private residence, children's toys scattered over the lawn. She strolled into the yard. Flowerbeds with pink azaleas and orange day-lilies lined this side of the Parades-A-Plenty fence. She paused at the azaleas to inhale the luscious aroma. To anyone watching, she might have been studying the flowers. She wasn't.

Through the fence, she studied the back side of Parades-A-Plenty. The door centered in the porch probably led to Mrs. Reilly's apartment. She eyed the wrought-iron fence. It was only five-feet high. In a pinch, she could get over it. She continued along the fence to next house, a three-story Victorian like Parades-A-Plenty, enclosed by a wrought-iron fence. But this one was taller, well over six feet. No escape that way.

Her best escape route was through the yard with the azaleas. She turned and strolled back the way she'd come. An older white-haired man stood on the porch with his arms folded, staring at her with suspicious eyes. Her heart thumped her ribs. She gave him a pleasant smile and kept going.

When she reached the sidewalk she turned left and didn't look back.

―――――

10:15 A.M.

Frank eyed the thunderclouds hovering over the road ahead. Dark and sullen like his black mood. He hated working on Saturday. Leaving Kelly's enticing bed this morning had royally pissed him off. He could think of far more pleasant activities than driving twenty-three miles over the causeway that split Lake Pontchartrain down the middle.

Ten minutes ago he'd called Evelyn, got shunted into voicemail. Again. She was still avoiding him, but why would she change now? Avoiding him had been the story of their marriage, in bed anyway. *Not now, Frank, maybe tomorrow.* Or next week. Or next year. Or when the Pope got married ...

But the primary cause of his foul mood was Roger Demaris and his fucking deadline. The clock was ticking. Collar the person that killed Arnold Peterson by Wednesday, or Demaris would pull them off the case.

Four days, and right now he had nothing.

When he'd called Joereen Beaubien on Thursday, she said she was busy until Saturday. Seventeen years ago when she divorced BoBo, she'd collected a megabucks settlement, and her daughters, fathered by BoBo, were married. What the hell did she have to do that was so important, buy fancy clothes at the ritzy stores in the Mandeville mall? No. She just didn't want to talk to him.

Many former New Orleans residents now lived north of the lake, having abandoned their flood-ravaged homes after Katrina. Following the map, he located her house, a big Georgian colonial with an attached two-car garage. He parked in the driveway. Joereen was waiting for him at the door, tall and slender in a sleeveless lavender dress and a bouffant blond hairdo. "Mrs. Beaubien? I'm Frank Renzi."

With a wooden expression, she said, "Hello Detective Renzi. Come in."

He followed her into a living room with a cathedral ceiling and whirling ceiling fans. After the heat outside, the room felt chilly, but the décor was attractive, art reproductions tastefully grouped along pale-green walls. He sank onto a four-cushion emerald-green sofa with white throw-pillows. Joereen took the matching wingchair opposite him.

"Thanks for making time for me," he said, offering an ice-breaker smile.

"You said you had questions about BoBo." No smile.

Her eyes were cornflower-blue and her face was gorgeous, no wrinkles, no mascara, a touch of lip gloss. When she'd married BoBo in what was by all accounts an extravagant ceremony in City Park, BoBo was twenty-seven. Joereen was twenty. Now she was forty-four, and still a striking woman.

But if you were filthy-rich, you could hire a personal trainer, get your hair done twice a week . . . He stifled the thought and focused on his mission. Find out if BoBo killed Jeanette Brixton in 1988. And if he did, find out if Arnold Peterson had anything to do with it.

"I've heard some amazing stories about BoBo, how he started his business from scratch and turned it into an empire. What was he like?"

"Your guess is as good as mine. We were married seven years and I never did figure the man out." Other than her lips, not a muscle moved in her face.

"Did he ever discuss the business with you?"

"No."

"Maybe mention he was having trouble with an employee or a supplier?"

Her cornflower blue eyes regarded him steadily. "BoBo never discussed business with me. His or anyone else's."

"In nineteen-eighty-eight a woman was murdered in a French Quarter hotel. BoBo was a suspect."

Joereen blinked. "That was a long time ago."

"Yes it was. Twenty years. I spoke with the lead detective on the case. Jane Fontenot. She interviewed you after the murder, right?"

"Yes," she said, her face a smooth mask. Maybe she was having Botox treatments.

"Where were you living then?"

"In a beautiful Victorian in English Turn, near the country club."

Interesting. The Peterson house was near the country club. "You told Detective Fontenot that BoBo was home the night of the murder. He was with you all night, you said. Is that right?"

Two more blinks. "Yes."

"Seems like BoBo had a lot of friends."

For an instant he thought she was actually going to smile. She didn't.

"Yes, he did."

"Was there anyone he was especially close to?"

Her expression didn't change but her hands tightened on the arm of the wingchair. "BoBo had a lot of friends. Rich and powerful friends. Let sleeping dogs lie."

"What does that mean?"

A tiny shrug. "It means let sleeping dogs lie."

His irritation escalated to exasperation, then fury. In three days it would be high noon. Collar a suspect or you're off the case.

He gave her a hard stare. "It might also mean that you lied to Detective Fontenot. If we find out BoBo murdered that woman, you could be charged as an accessory to murder."

Her cornflower-blue eyes widened. Still she said nothing.

"Did BoBo slap you around?"

Her eyes shifted, avoiding his gaze. "BoBo had a temper, that's for sure."

"I read the transcripts of the divorce proceedings. You accused BoBo of domestic abuse. Is that true?"

A level stare from those cornflower-blue eyes. "Yes."

"Who were his closest friends?"

"Let sleeping dogs lie, Detective."

"Was Arnold Peterson one of them?"

Anger flared in her big baby blues. "Detective Renzi, I have a lot to do today. Unless you have a subpoena or some legal order to ask me these questions, I'm going to ask you to leave."

His gut burned, a slow fizz of acid, but he forced himself to maintain a cool exterior. He rose from the sofa and held out his card.

"Think about what I said, Joereen. Accessory to murder is a serious charge. If you change your mind and want to talk, give me a call."

No blinks. No smile. "Keep the card. I won't be changing my mind."

Natalie

July 23, 2008

At the agreed-upon time I went to Arnold Peterson's room on the sixth floor of the Hotel Bienvenue. As I strode down the hall I felt exhilarated, but also a bit nervous, the way an actress might feel before going onstage to face a first-night audience and the critics. Would I get what I needed? The smoking gun required to complete The Main Event.

I got there a bit late, not late enough to make him worry that his hot babe wasn't going to show up, just late enough to whet his appetite. When I tapped on the door, he opened it right away and gave me a big smile.

"You're even prettier than your pictures, Lucinda."

I ran my tongue over my lower lip. "You won't be disappointed, Arnold."

I put my fancy gold purse on the bedside table where I could easily reach it. Then I locked eyes with him and took off my clothes. First I shimmied out of my dress. Then I took off my bra and my panties. All the while his dark greedy eyes devoured my body.

Smiling playfully, I said, "You have too many clothes on, Arnold."

He unbuttoned his white dress shirt, unzipped his trousers, dropped the shirt and trousers in a heap beside the bed and stood there in his T-shirt and jockey shorts. I could see his erection pressing against his shorts.

"Let me help you," I said, accidentally-on-purpose brushing his erection with my fingers.

He pulled me closer. I felt his hot breath on my cheek, felt his erection, hard against my pubic bone. Arnold was hot to trot.

I lifted his T-shirt and stroked his bare skin. He whipped off the T-shirt and dropped it on the rest of his clothes. His torso was white and flabby. Maybe the only exercise Arnold got was when he found sexy-looking babes on the Internet and invited them to his room. Patches of dark gray-streaked hair covered his chest and his nipples were small and hard and brown.

"I can't wait to see what you've got for me," I said, easing his shorts down from his waist.

He shoved them down to his ankles, stepped out of them and pulled me close. I turned slightly to position him with his back to the four-poster bed. It was already turned down, exposing silky white sheets.

Arnold was ready to rock and roll with his sexy babe. I caressed his neck with my fingers. He ground his erection against my pubic bone. I feathered my fingers over the skin on his neck, working my right hand closer and closer to the Dokko point, the hollow spot behind the ear lobe.

Arnold didn't notice my dancing fingers. His breath was raspy and hot on my neck.

Many sensitive nerves lie beneath the Dokko point. Mr. Larson, my TKD teacher, had stressed that the Dokko point should not be your primary target during combat. It's difficult to hit if your opponent is attacking. But in other situations, applying pressure to the Dokko point can be a powerful submission technique. Your opponent will feel unbearable pain, Mr. Larson said. But he had also warned me that too much pressure can cause unconsciousness, even death.

And I wanted Arnold Peterson fully conscious for my surprise.

His arms tightened around my waist.

Before he could get a firm grip, I made a knuckle fist with two fingers, pressed on the Dokko point and twisted to shock the nerves.

He flopped backwards onto the bed, moaning and clutching his jaw with both hands. He pulled his knees to his chest and rolled side to side, clearly in great pain. His eyes were glazed and he was breathing hard, his lips pulled back in a grimace. But I had no time to enjoy my triumph.

From my bag I removed the necessary implements for my next surprise: the handcuffs and the .38 Special. When Arnold saw the gun, he stopped thrashing. I aimed it at his forehead.

"Don't even think about calling for help. One shot and your brain will be mush. This gun is loaded with hollow-point bullets."

It wasn't, but he didn't know this. In my many dealings with men I had observed that they came in two types: brainy and brawny. I figured Peterson for the brainy type. Any hint that something might destroy his precious brain would get his total attention. He stared at me. I saw terror in his eyes.

"I don't know what you're trying to pull, but if you're looking for money, forget it. I'm broke."

"I'm not interested in money." I aimed the revolver at his forehead and made a clicking sound with my tongue. He flinched.

I held out two pairs of plastic handcuffs. "Put one around each wrist."

He did as I said. Careful to keep the gun on him, I locked the other half of the handcuff that held his left wrist around the ornate wooden bedpost. His eyes followed me as I circled the bed and did the same with his right wrist. His chest rose and fell rapidly. I was certain his heart was beating very fast.

His dick was limp now, lying flaccid against his thigh.

Mr. Important was frightened out of his mind.

And the best was yet to come.

"I'm going to handcuff your ankles to the bed now." Playfully, I poked his testicles with my finger. He rolled away and clamped his knees together. "Don't worry, Arnold. I'm not going to hurt your jewels. But don't forget those hollow-point bullets. Be a good boy while I do your ankles."

Holding the gun on him with one hand, I used the other to cuff his ankles to the bedposts at the foot of the bed. Arnold didn't resist.

When I finished, I smiled at him. He didn't smile back.

Arnold was used to being in control. Now he wasn't, and he didn't like it.

With his limbs trussed to the bed, I felt safe enough to get dressed. My nakedness had served its purpose. Lull Mr. Important into a false sense of security, disable him and control him with the gun.

After I put on my clothes, I took my mini-tape recorder out of my purse.

Only then did I allow myself a tiny bit of satisfaction. But the next step was crucial. I set the tape recorder on the bed near his mouth.

"Story time," I said, and hit Record. "Tell me about BoBo."

His eyes grew baleful. But when I waved the gun, fear replaced the anger in his eyes. "Tell me about BoBo," I said. "Now, or I'll shoot you."

"I don't know what you want me to tell you."

"Tell me when you met him. And how."

He relaxed a bit, though his chest was still pumping up and down like a puffer fish out of water. "I met him in New Orleans, in October of 1988."

The words I had been waiting for. I could barely contain my excitement. Finally, after all these years, I would find out what happened to Mom.

"Where did you meet him, Arnold? Let's have the details."

"I met him at his Go-Go Bar in Central City." Peterson's eyes took on a furtive look as though he might be thinking about where this would lead.

"Go on, Arnold. What happened?"

"I was down in the dumps. My wife was giving me a hard time. I wanted her to quit working and have a baby, but she didn't want—"

"Arnold, I'm not interested in the history of your marital problems. Tell me about BoBo."

Mr. Important licked his lips. "We started talking and he cheered me up."

"How sweet. Tell me how he cheered you up."

"I told him I worked for Gillette. When I said a guy that worked in my department was giving me grief, BoBo told me . . ." Peterson's eyes flitted to the painting on the wall next to the bed. A watercolor of the Seine with pretty little boats bobbing along beneath a blue sky. How ironic.

I hadn't noticed it before. I'd been too focused on my plan.

"What did BoBo tell you?"

"He said if anyone gave him grief he hired strong-arm guys to fix them."

"And then what?"

"Nothing. I went back to my hotel."

Disappointment swallowed me like a shroud. After all the terrible deeds I had done to earn money, after all these years of planning, would Arnold Peterson thwart me? My hands gripped the gun and began to tremble.

His eyes got that panicky look again. "What do you want from me?"

I wanted him to tell me that BoBo had killed my mother, but I couldn't come right out and say this. The tape recorder was running.

I forced myself to be calm. "I thought you and BoBo were friends."

"We were. The next night I went back to the bar and BoBo was there and we got talking again." His eyes shifted to the pretty painting of the Seine.

I knew he was holding something back. "Talking about what?"

"BoBo asked me if I ever played around. I said no, I'd only been married six months."

I made an impatient gesture with the gun. Made another click-sound with my tongue.

"BoBo asked me if I'd ever tried a call girl. Not a hooker, he said, call girls are different. They do whatever you want. We could have a threesome."

Poor Mom. The cold hard iceberg invaded my gut, sent violent tremors through my very core.

"He tried to persuade me, but I refused. I didn't want to alienate him. I figured he might be helpful to my career, but I just . . . I didn't want . . . I was afraid somebody might see us or find out or something."

His admission that BoBo used call girls was something. But that wasn't what I'd come here for, not even close. "When you told BoBo you didn't want to play, what did he do?"

"He called some woman and told her to meet him at a hotel."

A frenzy of excitement sent my heart racing. "What hotel?"

"The Royal Arms on Royal Street near Esplanade."

"How do you know where the hotel was?"

He clamped his lips together and glowered at me. I placed the muzzle of the gun close to his testicles.

"Think about what hollow point bullets will do to your jewels, Arnold."

Through clenched teeth, he said, "I drove him there."

"Very good, Arnold. Tell me what happened then. I love details."

And so did my tape recorder, which Arnold seemed to have forgotten.

"It was late and he'd had a few drinks. He asked me to drive him there so I did. I wish I hadn't. Christ, I wish I'd never come to New Orleans that day. Nobody knew I was here, not even my wife. She thought I was on a business trip. I was, but things went great in Atlanta so I decided to treat myself to a few days in New Orleans. I'd never been here and everybody talked about how great it was."

Now that he was talking I was reluctant to interrupt him, but I needed him to tell me about BoBo, not business trips.

"What happened at the hotel, Arnold?"

"Christ if I know. I went back to my hotel and watched a movie."

Rage hotter than volcanic lava ate holes in my stomach. I was ready to shoot this imbecile. He must have seen this on my face.

His chest rose and fell rapidly. "An hour later BoBo called me in a panic." His voice was shaking now, and pitched higher. "He said something happened to the woman and he needed a ride home right away."

The words I had been waiting for. I could hardly breathe.

"So I picked him up two blocks from the hotel." He closed his eyes and scrunched up his face.

"Keep talking, Arnold. What happened then?"

"I drove him home. Christ, he babbled like an idiot the whole way. He wouldn't shut up." Peterson gave me a pleading look. A guilty look.

I flicked the gun. Clicked my tongue.

"He said the woman gave him a hard time and he punched her and then he hit her with a flatiron and she started to scream and . . . he strangled her." Peterson closed his eyes.

I wondered if he was trying to picture this. I was.

My throat closed up. I tried to imagine what Mom was thinking. A twenty-eight-year-old single mother trying to earn money to pay the rent. And then some important man asked her to do something she didn't want to do so he beat her to a pulp and strangled her.

BoBo the monster. Thirty-three years old.

A rich and powerful man, using women for his pleasure.

A red haze fuzzed my vision. I closed my eyes. Tried to focus. My breath came in short gasps. I felt like I'd just run a marathon. When I opened my eyes, Arnold was staring at me, a look of horror on his face.

I had to grip the gun very hard to keep my hands from shaking.

"I didn't know he killed her! Honest. Not till after I picked him up. When we got to his house, BoBo warned me not to tell anyone. He said, 'I owe you one, Arnold. If you ever need something, call me.'"

"Did you?"

"Did I tell anyone? No."

"Did you ever need something and call BoBo?"

A guilty hangdog look crossed his face. "Yes. The summer of ninety-four everything went in the toilet at Gillette. I called BoBo and he hired me to manage his GoGo bar in New Orleans. He said I'd have one of the top jobs someday. Too bad he didn't put it in writing. After BoBo died, Chip fired me."

Mr. Important was still thinking about what might have been. I wasn't.

"And you never told anyone that BoBo murdered that woman?"

"No."

"She was my mother, Arnold. BoBo murdered my mother. And you're just as guilty as BoBo. You helped him get away with it and so did his wife. She gave him an alibi and the cops let him go."

Fear blossomed in his eyes. When I shut off the tape recorder and raised the gun, the fear turned to terror.

"Please," he said, "Don't shoot me. I couldn't help it."

I had known this moment might come, but I hadn't allowed myself to think about it. Now the moment had arrived. The murderous moment.

Arnold was at my mercy, naked, trussed to a bed.

Could I shoot him and walk away with a clear conscience?

I thought about Randy, teetering on the edge of the bluff, begging me not to shoot him. But that was different. Randy killed defenseless animals like Muffy and made his sister give him blowjobs. Randy deserved to die.

Arnold wasn't the man who murdered my mother, BoBo was. But Arnold had helped him get away with it, had driven BoBo home and listened to his confession. Worst of all, rather than call the police and tell them he knew who murdered the woman in the Royal Arms Hotel, Arnold had told no one.

Because Arnold wanted to become rich and powerful like BoBo.

I aimed the gun at his forehead and pulled the trigger.

CHAPTER 27

Sunday, 17 August

Frank mopped sweat off his forehead and glanced at Miller, pounding away on the CYBEX treadmill beside him, his Saints T-shirt dark with sweat. They'd been at it for forty minutes. He hated running on machines, but it was raining like hell outside. He increased his speed, still frustrated after his fruitless conversation with Joereen Beaubien yesterday.

Wednesday's deadline loomed like a 24-second clock running out at the end of a tie basketball game. Make the shot or lose. Find Peterson's killer or you're off the case. Three days and he had nothing.

Where's Natalie? No clue. Who's her next target? No clue there either.

Miller took a towel off his treadmill, wiped his sweaty face and looked over, breathing hard. "You training for a marathon or something?"

"No, I'm pissed. Hank called last night. Not a peep from the nationwide BOLO Boston PD put out on Robin Adair." His cell rang and he snatched it out of the cup holder. "Renzi."

"Hi Franco, how you doing?"

"Hey, whaddaya know?" A familiar yearning seized him. Damn, he was glad to hear from her.

"Got a few tidbits for you. Am I interrupting anything?"

"Yeah, I'm in bed with Angelina Jolie, can't you hear me puffing?" He saw Miller's head swivel, his mouth open in a silent laugh.

"That's my Franco, always wowing the women. Where's Brad?"

"I sent him out to mow the grass." He winked at Miller. "Actually I'm on a treadmill beside my partner, Kenyon Miller." He glanced at Miller's CYBEX dashboard. "I'm three miles ahead of him."

"Total bullshit!" Miller shouted. "Don't believe it."

Along the line of treadmills, heads turned, men with grinning faces.

"Sounds like your partner knows you're a smartass," Gina said.

"True. So what's up?"

"My Boston PD source tells me the ballistics analysis on the bullet that killed Oliver James didn't match the slugs in your murder cases down there."

"Hold on." He hit Stop and stepped off the treadmill. Mopping his face with a towel, he walked to a vacant machine in the corner. "Okay, now I can talk. Hank called me yesterday about the ballistics report. He also said they've got nothing on Robin Adair. But enough shoptalk, tell how *you're* doing."

"I got thinking about what you said. Last Friday I cooked him a great dinner. No smartass remarks, Franco, I still make damn good lasagna. When Greg got home, I opened a bottle of Chianti and told him I ran into an old friend. He knew what I meant, not that I said your name or anything. Then I laid it on the line. I said maybe he wasn't interested in sex anymore, but I was." Gina chuckled, the same evil chuckle he fondly remembered. "He didn't even wait for dessert, took me to bed and fucked my brains out."

"Hey, good for you. I'm glad things worked out." But was he really glad or was he just saying that?

"So there you have it. All the news that's fit to print, and some that isn't."

"Greg needed a dope-slap and I'm glad you gave him one."

"Yeah. But you know what? I still miss you. We had some great times."

His throat tightened. "Yes, we did. So stay in touch and let me know how you're doing."

"You got it, Franco. Talk to you later."

He closed his cell. He was glad that she'd put things right with Greg. Gina was a terrific woman and she deserved to be happy. He dearly hoped the Big C didn't come back to bite her. He saw Miller heading his way, big smile on his face. "Was that your new girlfriend?" Miller said

"No," he said, truthfully, "an old one. But she's happily married. Let's hit the showers."

———

BoBo's Go-Go Bar in Central City had no lurid neon lights, no flashing outlines of big bosomed babes with sexy legs. The exterior looked almost prim, the lower half tan-brick, above it white-painted clapboards. A discreet sign above entrance said: BoBo's Go-Go Bar.

To avoid leaving a record of her destination, she'd given the cabdriver an address two blocks away and walked to the bar. The early evening air was pleasant, cool and not too humid, but her palms were sweaty.

If she played her cards right, she would soon be face-to-face with Chip Beaubien.

She entered the foyer, a wood-paneled area lined with photographs, BoBo with various VIPs, beaming his toothy smile. Beyond a wide archway, she saw well-dressed men seated on high-backed stools at the bar. No women of course, not in a club that featured sexy babes dancing in scanty outfits. Soft jazz was playing on a sound system. Not her taste, but she assumed the music would change when the show began an hour from now at eight o'clock.

When she entered the main room, a man intercepted her. He was big and brawny, over six feet tall, and broad shoulders filled his tuxedo. Dressed like a maitre d, acting like a bouncer, his frosty eyes boring into hers.

"Help you with something?"

"I'm here to speak to Mr. Beaubien."

"You got an appointment?"

She flashed a confident smile. "No, but I'm writing a magazine article about him, a flattering article. I'm sure Mr. Beaubien will be thrilled with it."

He studied her outfit, her sleek auburn wig, her elegant beige linen jacket, her matching knee-length skirt, and her gold Caparros sandals. He gave her a hard stare. "Okay. Sit at the bar, the stool around the corner at the far end so nobody'll bother you."

Conscious of men's eyes on her, she walked to end of the thirty-foot bar. Around the corner were two vacant stools. She took the one next to the wall. To her right, maroon-velvet sofas grouped around low tables filled a spacious dark-carpeted area in front of a stage. No TV sets anywhere or pictures of sexy women. Of course not. Men came here to see live women strut their stuff.

A beefy red-haired man in a white shirt and a maroon cummerbund set a cocktail napkin on the polished mahogany bar in front of her. Above a stylized line drawing of a martini glass, *BoBo's Go-Go Bar* was emblazoned on the napkin in mauve letters. "Evening, ma'am. Would you like a cocktail? Our Southern Comfort Kamikaze is the Sunday special."

"Sounds dangerous. What's in it?"

"Southern Comfort, triple sec and lime juice, over shaved ice."

"I'll try one. Could I have a glass of ice water as well?"

He smiled, his ruddy face weathered below his mop of curly red hair. "You must be really thirsty."

She returned his smile. Always make friends with the bartender. "I am."

After he left, she took a pen and steno pad out of her tote and set her tinted Vera Wang glasses against the bridge of her nose. Props for her fateful meeting. Earlier, using her well-honed makeup techniques, she had fashioned her sleek Grace Kelly look, cool and sexy but not blatantly so. She put on the sleeveless teal top she'd splurged on in Paris, clingy but not skin-tight. A boat neck exposed the skin above her breasts, but no cleavage. After donning her beige suit, she had crept downstairs, hoping to avoid Banshee. No such luck.

"Going out on the town, are you?" squawked that horrible voice.

"Have a good evening, Mrs. Reilly," she'd said, and left.

She looked at the doodles on her steno pad, two lines filled with letter B's. B for BoBo? Or Banshee? The woman was beyond annoying. She was like a cat waiting to pounce. No, cats were quick and agile. Mrs. Reilly was like a wild pig, a fat crafty creature, lying in wait for her prey.

The bartender delivered her Kamikaze with a flourish and glanced at her notepad. "What y'all writing? A novel?"

"Could be. Maybe I'll put you in it."

"Far out!" He scooped ice into a glass, filled it with water, set it on the bar and went off to serve another customer.

She pretended to sip of her Kamikaze through the straw. No alcohol to muddle her thoughts. She had to stay alert. Should she take off her jacket? No. The room was chilly. She unbuttoned the top four buttons to expose her teal blouse. The color went well with her auburn wig.

To ease the crick in her neck, she tilted her head back and saw a video camera mounted on the wall above her. She glanced around the room and spotted two more. If there were three, there might be more. Maybe Chip used the tapes to blackmail prominent businessmen as they watched the dancers.

"How y'all doing, dawlin?" said a reedy voice.

Startled, she turned. A man slipped onto the adjacent stool, gazing at her.

She'd know those eyes anywhere. Chip-off-the-old-block eyes. But she couldn't act like she recognized him. Although her heart was beating wildly, she dredged up a smile. Not a big smile, a hesitant one, as though she wasn't sure what to say. "I'm doing fine," she said in a soft voice. "How about you?"

His eyes grew frosty, Prussian-blue eyes, poised to attach like a ruthless Prussian soldier. "That depends. You a working girl?"

She knew what he meant. He thought she was a hooker. She had to play this perfectly. Dipping into her acting bag of tricks, she said with a faint smile, "Yes. But not the kind you're thinking."

His face, a carbon copy of his father's, bore a stony expression. His thick blonde hair was impeccably styled, tendrils flipped forward over his forehead, but it wasn't his looks that reminded her of BoBo, it was his attitude. A man used to getting his way in business, and with women. Supremely confident, verging on arrogant, sending a clear message: *Don't fuck with me.*

"I'm hoping to meet Chip Beaubien. I'm writing an article about him."

The frosty eyes thawed slightly. "What kind of article?"

"A feature article for the *New Yorker.*"

A glimmer of interest entered his eyes. "You write for the *New Yorker?*"

"A few articles, yes." *Careful. This is the Internet Age. He can check.*

Feigning modesty, she said, "Actually, they were restaurant reviews. I'm writing this one on spec. I sure do hope Mr. Beaubien will help me."

"What's your name?"

"April West."

He squeezed her hand. "Nice to meet you, April. I'm Chip Beaubien."

She made her eyes go wide. "Oh my God, I can't believe it. I mean, I can, but this is just so . . . strange. Meeting you like this."

He smiled, revealing well-tended white teeth. "No need to gush. I'm an average guy like everybody else."

No you're not. Your father was a killer. You're just as arrogant as he was. And you're going to pay for it.

Chip waved at the bartender who stood at the other end of the bar. The redhead practically sprinted to them. "What can I get for you, boss?"

"Make the lady a fresh cocktail. I'll have the usual. We'll be at Table 69." He got off his stool and took her arm. "Let's talk, April."

He led her to an alcove set into the back wall. One step up from the floor was a table for two set with sterling silver and white linen napkins. Chip was having his usual cocktail. Was this his usual table? It was enclosed on three sides by wood-paneled walls. To shield it from video cameras? Everyone knew what 69 meant. Did Chip bring women to Table 69 while the show was on and make them give him blowjobs?

She slid onto the semi-circular padded-leather bench. Chip slid in from the other side, snuggled close to her and smiled. A supremely confident smile.

"Tell me about April West."

She had prepared her back-story carefully. "I've been freelancing, in Boston and New York mostly. But I'd like to move up to a steady job."

"At the *New Yorker*?"

"Why not reach for the stars? Your father did."

A tuxedoed waiter delivered their drinks, another Kamikaze for her, a Manhattan with a cherry for Chip, and disappeared. She had a momentary flashback: Oliver James sipping his Manhattan.

Chip sucked the cherry into his mouth and gave her a satisfied smile. "Pops was great. Shoot for the moon, son. That's what Pops always told me."

"What was he like?" she asked, eyes wide with innocence.

Chip waved a hand. "Tell me about you. Where'd you go to school?"

"I majored in journalism at Boston University."

"Good school. Tell me about your article," He sipped his Manhattan and studied her, his rapacious eyes roaming her body.

"I thought I'd start with a summary of your father . . ." Seeing his sudden annoyance, she quickly added, "But you'd be the main focus. You know, how you took over the business when he died and made it even more successful."

"Uh-huh," he said, gazing at her, stroking his chiseled chin.

"I thought I could take some pictures so people would know what—"

"No pictures. We don't allow photographers in here."

"Or working girls," she said mischievously.

No smile. "Or working girls. This is a respectable bar, not a dump."

But not much different from the Platinum-Plus Gentlemen's Club where she'd danced topless in front of rich important men. She wondered if it had private rooms where men could get lap dances. Rooms with hidden video cameras. "Of course it is," she said. "I was kidding."

"When it comes to business I don't kid around. Would you like an appetizer? On Sunday we feature a mini-log of Vermont cheddar cheese rolled in chopped pecans." Without waiting for an answer, he snapped his fingers and their waiter instantly appeared. "Bring us the featured appetizer."

"Yes sir, Mister B," said the waiter, and scurried away.

Chip leaned back and gave her a heavy-lidded look. "April West, huh? Where you from, dawlin?"

"I love how guys talk down here. Is everyone 'dawlin'?" Easing into seduction mode.

"Waaahl, I don't know about other guys. If I like a person that happens to be female, I call her dawlin. Nothing wrong with that, is there?"

"Nothing wrong with that." *Be who they want you to be. Smile. Flatter them.*

"Boston University's an expensive school. Your folks must have money."

She wanted to squeeze his balls into little wrinkled prunes. *Money? No, my mother didn't have money. That's why she had to sell herself to your father.*

"Not really. I went there on a scholarship."

"Good for you." A broad confident smile, displaying his pearly-whites. "I got a partial scholarship to Loyola. Pops paid the rest. He never went to college. He was too busy working."

The waiter appeared with their appetizer, a four-inch roll of cheese studded with chopped pecans on a white porcelain plate rimmed with a thin maroon stripe. Two sterling silver cheese knives sat on small matching plates beside a basket of bread slices.

"Dig in, dawlin," Chip said. "You're gonna love it."

She sliced off a bit of cheese, spread it on a slice of warm bread and took a bite. "Incredible," she said. "Tangy and sweet at the same time."

"Knew you'd like it, dawlin." His bushy blonde eyebrows knit in a frown. He reached into his suit, took out a cell phone and answered. "What's up?"

If only she hadn't left her glass of ice water on the bar. She was dying of thirst, partly from nerves, partly from talking, mostly from worrying how to seduce Chip into seeing her again. In private.

Whoever called was doing most of the talking. Chip listened, frowning. After a minute, he shut the phone. "Damn Josephine."

"What's wrong?"

"You ever see that movie *Nikita?*"

Her heart almost stopped. The French film featured a female assassin named Nikita. And her code name was Josephine. "I don't think so," she said.

"Waaaahl we got a goddamned killer storm named Josephine headed our way. Forecasters say it might be worse than Katrina, mayor's about ready to order an evacuation." His fleshy lips thinned to a line. "And I got a grand opening set for Friday. Already spent a bundle on it and now I gotta cancel."

Acid boiled into her stomach. Cancel? No! Not when she was so close to completing her mission. She forced herself to be calm, dredged up a smile.

"Why? You can't be sure the storm will hit New Orleans."

"Can't be sure it won't, either. And if people evacuate, who'll come to the opening?" He patted his mouth with a linen napkin and slid out of the padded-leather bench. "Sorry, dawlin, but I've got work to do. You set right there and enjoy your drink and your appetizer and the show."

A lightning bolt of panic hit her. "But wait! You said . . ." He looked at her, his Prussian blue eyes frosty. "I know you've got problems to deal with, but can we talk again? About the article?"

"Sure can, dawlin, but not till the damn storm blows over. Enjoyed your company, April, I truly did." Chip Beaubien turned and walked away.

A black pit of despair swallowed her. She wanted to run after him, plead with him. But that would be stupid. That would destroy the confident persona she had crafted. How could this happen when she was so close to her goal?

A vision of the gargoyles atop Notre Dame Cathedral swam before her eyes, eyes that shimmered with tears. The gargoyles mocked her, accusing her, like the angry Vietnamese ancestor spirits.

For twenty years her life had been tainted by her mother's violent death. Ever since high school she had focused on one goal: Avenging her mother, who'd been brutally murdered by a monster. The devastated ten-year-old was a distant memory now.

That little girl had turned into a monster. A killer. And for what?

She took the well-thumbed snapshot of her mother out her wallet. Mom smiling into the camera on her wedding day. Mom waiting for her murder to be avenged. She felt so ashamed. "Sorry, Mom," she whispered.

The soft jazz on the sound system cut out abruptly, replaced by loud music with a disco beat. The lights dimmed and three spotlights--red, mauve and pink--darted around the stage. The brassy music grew louder, with loud cymbal crashes. Two long-legged women pranced onstage, aiming sexy smiles at the men who ogled them, their skimpy sequin-studded costumes minimized to show off their endowments.

She felt like she was back at Platinum-Plus Gentlemen's Club, felt like her life had come full circle. And she had nothing to show for it.

She took the straws out of her Kamikaze, raised the glass to her mouth, drained the liquid and left.

CHAPTER 28

Monday, 18 August

"How're you doing, Evelyn?" After six days of getting her voicemail, Frank wanted to ask his ex-wife why she'd been avoiding him, but why stir up trouble? He was glad she'd finally answered, but he wasn't looking forward to this conversation.

"Okay, I guess. It's raining up here."

As if bad weather determined your life. Miller was out of the office, but another detective could walk in any minute so he cut to the chase.

"We need to talk about your finances."

"What about them?"

"Why didn't you pay the real estate taxes on the house?"

"What do you mean?"

"What I said. Why didn't you pay the taxes? I send you money for that every month."

"How do you know I didn't pay them?"

"Never mind how I know. If you don't pay the real estate taxes, they'll put a lien on the property. You could lose the house."

"What gives you the right to check up on me?"

"I paid the mortgage on that house for twenty years, that's what."

"And I kept *that house* neat and clean for you for twenty years. Did you forget that? And took care of Maureen, too, while you were working."

Already the conversation had descended into bitterness. "I don't want to get into the same old arguments. During the divorce proceedings we signed a legally binding financial agreement. I send you money twice a month, and part of that money is so you can pay the real estate taxes on the house."

"I have other expenses."

"Like sending money to some Catholic charity every month?"

"So what if I do? The Church is a great comfort to me."

Acid flamed his gut. "You need to pay the bills before you send three hundred dollars to your favorite religious cult every month."

Uh-oh. Silence on the other end. Big mistake, calling it a religious cult.

"The Catholic Church is not a religious cult and you know it, Frank. How did you find out I sent them money? Wait, I know. You're a big important police detective. You can find out anything you want."

"Evelyn, listen carefully, because I'm only going to say this once. I paid your delinquent tax bill, but I'm not going to do it again. You want to lose the house and wind up living on the street?" And instantly regretted the question. Evelyn had enough panic attacks, calling him in the middle of the night, worried that some burglar that might get into the house and rape her.

"Don't say things like that. You're trying to scare me."

"No, I'm telling you to be more responsible. When you get my check, put it in the bank and pay your bills before you spend it on frills."

"Frills?" she said, her voice shaking with outrage. "You call it frills, helping the Church do good work?"

Good work? All the Catholic Church did was brainwash little girls into thinking sex was bad and procreation was the only reason to have sex.

"Evelyn, I'm going to hang up now. Think about what I said."

Shaking from the effort it took not to put his fist through a wall, fearing he'd explode if he didn't do something physical, he left the station and strode through the Café Beignet patio. The air was thick with humidity and dark clouds loomed overhead, but the tables were jammed as usual, toddlers, teens and adults enjoying beignets dusted with powdered sugar.

At a table in the corner a woman with auburn hair sat with her back to the tall wrought-iron fence that lined the sidewalk, her face hidden behind a copy of today's *Times-Picayune*. She wore a New York Yankees baseball cap and a Yankees T-shirt. No beignets for the Yankee fan, just a bottle of iced tea.

Infuriated by his maddening conversation with Evelyn, he entered the café and got in line. Something plinked at his mind, a vague sense that he'd missed something, something about the Yankee fan. When he finally reached the counter five minutes later, he ordered a double-shot of Americano to go. Jingling his keys, he leaned against the wall to wait.

You're a big important police detective. You can find out anything you want."

Evelyn could be as stubborn as a mule sometimes. He didn't want to call his lawyer in Boston, but if she kept pissing his money away without paying the taxes on the house, he would.

———

She watched him stride into the café. She had always been attracted to vigorous dynamic men, men like Willem and Oliver. Renzi appeared fit and muscular, energetic and quite attractive despite his hawk-like nose. High cheek bones creased his angular face below dark piercing eyes, eyes that had momentarily flashed her way. Dangerous.

Taking risks was one thing, but this was foolhardy. Renzi was a hunter and she was his prey. But something had drawn her here, an urge she couldn't define. Did she have a secret desire to be punished for her crimes?

A sudden shiver wracked her. Maybe she was thinking about Renzi because Renzi was thinking about her.

Last night's crushing disappointment had cast her into a black pit of despair. At dawn she had retrieved the latest update on Hurricane Josephine. After a hurricane hunter-plane flew over the eye of the storm at five A.M., forecasters had upgraded it to a Category-4 hurricane. Fueled by 145 mph winds, Josephine was now headed for Cuba. She dressed and went downstairs. No sign of Banshee, thank goodness. Her head was throbbing, a hangover from the Kamikaze she'd downed last night.

She rode the St. Charles Avenue streetcar to the French Quarter. Hoping to dispel her bleak mood, she walked down to the Mississippi River. Early morning fog swirled over the mile-wide waters. Hidden by the fog, a ship honking a mournful warning.

It reminded her of the time Mom took her here to see the Fourth of July fireworks. Three months earlier, a week after her tenth birthday, Mom had quit her job at the pancake house and began leaving her alone at night. She missed going to the pancake house, missed pouring all the syrup she wanted over a big waffle. But Mom said that job didn't pay enough. When the fireworks lit up the sky, Mom got excited like everyone else. But the fireworks made her sad, especially the orange ones that burst high above the river. It seemed like the sky was weeping.

Even now she could picture the orange plumes and their slow descent, sputtering out as they fell into the water like dead cinders.

Sputtering out like her plan.

Her mission was dead in the water, thwarted by Hurricane Josephine.

Thoroughly discouraged, she had walked to the Eighth District Station on Royal Street. Renzi's station. She bought a newspaper and a bottle of ice tea at Cafe Beignet and sat in the courtyard facing the station. When Renzi came out the door, she'd thought her heart would stop. Fortunately, her survival instinct kicked in and she'd hidden her face behind the *Times-Picayune*.

Every story on the front page was about Hurricane Josephine and a possible evacuation. One New Orleans resident said he wouldn't leave. "I sat in a twenty-mile backup two weeks ago when I evacuated for Gloria, and I ain't gonna do it again. I'm staying right here."

The mayor hadn't ordered one yet. He was waiting to see what happened after Josephine hit Cuba. The forecasters offered three possibilities. After entering the Gulf, the storm might veer west and hit the Yucatan Peninsular. Or veer east and hit the Florida Keys. Or, the worst case scenario, Hurricane Josephine might barrel into New Orleans with all its terrible fury.

If the mayor ordered an evacuation, Chip would cancel the opening of his new Go-Go Bar. End of story. Mission over. She clenched her jaw. She refused to abandon her mission, not while there was still a glimmer of hope. Somehow she would find a way to seduce Chip, get him alone and kill him.

And Renzi couldn't stop her. He had his own problems. In an article on the Metro page, District Attorney Roger Demaris criticized the NOPD investigation of the Peterson murder, specifically Homicide Detective Frank Renzi. Demaris said a car registered to June Carson, a person of interest, had been found in the Atlanta airport parking garage. Nothing about Robin Adair's car. Nothing about April West. Nothing about a similar murder in Boston.

But the next quote chilled her. "Now that a federal agency is interested in the case," DA Demaris said, "I think we'll get some action."

Federal agency. What agency? The CIA? She could understand why the CIA might get involved in the murder of former CIA agent Oliver James, but there was only one reason why a CIA agent would contact District Attorney Roger Demaris. Somehow they had linked the murder of Oliver James to the murders in New Orleans.

She picked up the paper and her bottle of ice tea and left the cafe.

Better not tempt fate. Frank Renzi might reappear any minute.

———

He paid for his double-shot of Americano, left Café Beignet and walked through the patio back to the station. Several customers were still noshing sugar-covered beignets, but the Yankee fan was gone. He couldn't shake the vague feeling that he'd missed something.

Unable to dismiss the thought, he mounted the stairs to the Eighth District Station, stopped on the top step and looked down Royal Street, his view partially obscured by the wrought-iron fence along the sidewalk.

And then he spotted her. The woman in the Yankee cap, heading east, deeper into the heart of the French Quarter, walking fast.

Long legs. Long strides. Damn! He knew that walk.

The woman in the security video. He set the container of coffee on the landing and bolted down the steps, but when he reached the sidewalk, she had disappeared. He sprinted to the next intersection and stopped.

He looked left, didn't see her. Did she know he'd spotted her?

To his right, four tourists in shorts and flamboyant T-shirts wandered toward him. No one in a Yankee cap and T-shirt.

Which way had she gone?

The street to his right bordered the State Supreme Court building. Nowhere to hide in that direction, but the street to his left was lined with bars, restaurants, and boutiques that sold souvenirs. Worse, Bourbon Street was one block away with dozens of places to hide. And she had a big head start.

Cursing, he ran toward Bourbon, his feet pounding the pavement. He stopped at an antique store, looked in the window, didn't see her. He looked inside the wide-open door of the bar next door. Three men sat at the bar watching TV. He kept going, running flat out now.

Damn it, he had to catch her. Two days till the deadline. If he didn't deliver a suspect by Wednesday noon, Demaris would yank him and Vobitch and the rest of the NOPD detectives off the case and give it to the State cops.

Two tourists on the sidewalk saw him coming and ducked out of the way. At the corner of Bourbon he paused, breathing hard, eyes darting everywhere. No sign of the woman with the distinctive long-legged stride. Even at ten in the morning, Bourbon Street was busy. If she ducked into a bar or some tourist-trap souvenir joint, he'd never find her.

Damn it to hell. He was positive she was the woman in the security video. And now that he'd gotten over his stupidity and denial, he was certain the woman in the video was Natalie Brixton. Doggedly determined, he kept going, slower now, pausing to look inside every rinky-dink tourist trap.

Natalie was in New Orleans and she wasn't a tourist.

She was here to kill someone. But who?

At this point he was certain she'd killed Arnold Peterson, Tex Conroy and Oliver James. She might also have pushed her cousin Randy off a cliff. Justified homicide for a rapist? In her mind perhaps.

But not according to law. And Franklin Sullivan Renzi had taken an oath to uphold the law no matter how despicable the victim might have been.

Oblivious to the tourists swirling around him, he crossed the street to check the bars and shops along the other sidewalk. Honky-tonk music wafted out of a strip joint. He eased inside, let his eyes adjust to the gloom, surveyed the room. No women, just three men seated at the bar. No dancers on stage. They were probably waiting for more customers.

With single-minded purpose, he left and peered into a small shop that sold souvenir T-shirts. A clerk stood behind the counter. No customers.

Discouraged, he kept walking. He was positive Natalie Brixton was in New Orleans, and he believed he knew why. To avenge her mother's murder, a case that had gone unsolved for twenty years.

Jane Fontenot's prime suspect was dead, but maybe Jane was wrong.

Maybe BoBo Beaubien wasn't the man that killed Jeannette Brixton.

But if BoBo didn't kill her, who did?

Maybe Natalie knew.

If she did, she sure as hell wasn't going to tell him.

CHAPTER 29

Monday, 18 August

Clint Hammer's return flight from Houston landed at nine, but Monday morning traffic in Washington, D.C. was snarled as usual, so the taxi didn't get him to his office building until 10:10. Three minutes later he entered his basement office, locked the door and stood his suitcase in the corner.

Clenching his jaw, he set his laptop on the desk, opened it and studied his notes. The fucking NOPD cops had told him about the Conroy murder, but they had withheld important information. He ground his teeth. Every time he thought about that Jew-bastard and his wop detective pal, a red haze of rage clouded his vision. Vobitch insulting him, throwing him out of the office.

The bastard would regret it.

After searching the *Times-Picayune* website for more intel, an exercise in futility, he'd flown to Pecos. His boss had given him some shit about the travel authorization but relented when he invented a story about email traffic that indicated terrorists were infiltrating Texas by crossing the Pecos River.

His two day trip to Pecos had been grueling, but gratifying.

Thrilled that a CIA agent was investigating her son's murder, Conroy's mother dropped a bombshell. Her son had gone to school with a girl named Natalie Brixton. Brixton's mother had been murdered in New Orleans in 1988. The fucking NOPD cops hadn't told him about that. Then Mrs. Conroy told him about her son's friend, Randy Brixton, Natalie Brixton's cousin. His death in 1995 had been ruled an accident, but Mrs. Conroy said her son, the now-deceased Tex Conroy, shot once in the head just like Arnold Peterson, believed that Natalie had pushed Randy off the bluff.

He ground his teeth, molar against molar, felt a sharp pain in his jaw. The gook bitch was a serial killer!

After offing her cousin in 1995, she'd disappeared, surfaced three weeks ago in New Orleans, murdered Peterson and Conroy and escaped. Because the fucking NOPD detectives were incompetent idiots.

Then she met Oliver in Boston bar and seduced him. But Oliver was no fool. Oliver had asked him to run a background check on Robin Adair. After his search turned up her bogus ID, one she'd used to rent an apartment in Nashua, New Hampshire, the bitch had murdered Oliver.

The idea filled him with rage and stiffened his resolve. He'd get that bitch and make her pay. He flexed his hands. He might not be as big as some agents, but he had big hands. Big and strong and deadly. When he found her, he'd put them around her neck and squeeze and watch her eyes bug out of her head.

A series of knocks hit his door. Jason's signal.

He unlocked the door and opened it. Jason had a smile on his usually solemn face. "I think I got something for you."

"About time." Hammer returned to his desk. "What have you got?"

"I've been working till midnight every night. It took me hours to check all the airports near Boston—"

"Tell me what you got!" Jason loved to go into excruciating detail. He didn't give a shit about that. Results were the only thing that mattered.

"I got nothing when I ran the face-recognition software on the airline passengers, but then I used the license photo you gave me for Robin Adair."

Struggling mightily for control, he said, "Jason, I appreciate your diligence. *What did you find?*"

"I figured she might have a license under a different name." A satisfied smile appeared on Jason's face. "Bingo! I got a hit at the registry of motor vehicles in the Ithaca, New York."

A warm glow filled his chest. Now he'd get the bitch. "What kind of hit?"

"She used a Vermont driver's license." Jason peered at him through his thick glasses. "No photograph because they weren't mandatory on Vermont licenses in 2004. But after 9/11 most of the New York state RMVs installed video cameras. So I used the face recognition software and the Robin Adair license photo. That's how I got the hit. A woman named April West used a Vermont DL to register a 2002 Ford Focus on August sixth."

"Excellent work, Jason. Excellent."

Jason beamed. "You want her address?"

"Hell yes! You got it?" He could hardly believe his luck.

"She had the registry mail her plates to an Ithaca boarding house." Jason held out a slip of paper. " The phone number's below the address."

A phone number. Perfect. "Thanks for all your hard work, Jason. Rest assured, I won't forget it." He never forgot anything, good or bad.

"Thanks," Jason said, clearly pleased. "I better get back to my office."

As soon as Jason cleared the door, he called the number in Ithaca, reciting the name in his mind. *April West, April West. I'll get you, April West.*

"Hello," said a female voice.

Employing the bullying tone he used to intimidate people, he said, "This is CIA agent Clint Hammer calling from Washington. Who am I speaking to?"

A shocked silence. Then, "Emily Jordan. Is something wrong?"

Yes something's wrong, you silly twit. "I understand you operate a boarding house at . . ." He read the address aloud off the slip of paper. "Is that correct?"

"Yes. What's this about?" the woman asked.

"Did a woman by the name of April West rent a room there?"

"Yes, as a matter of fact. Why do you ask?"

"It's my job to ask questions," he said. "Is she still there?"

"No. She left a few days ago."

"What day did she leave?"

"Just a moment, I'll have to check."

Anxiously grinding his teeth, he waited. Excruciating pain ran along the side of his jaw. His dentist said if he didn't stop grinding his teeth he'd need a root canal on the back molar.

"She rented a room on August sixth and left on August eleventh."

"Did she get any mail while she was there?"

"Hmm, let me think. She left on a Monday. I think she got a package from the Registry before she left. The plate for her car, I guess."

"Did she say where was she going?"

"No. She's a student at Ithaca College. She was looking for an apartment for the Fall semester. Maybe she found one, but I don't know."

"Thank you, Ms. Jordan." He closed his cell and pumped his fist.

April West wasn't looking for an apartment, she was hiding from the cops. And this time she wouldn't escape. Those NOPD cops were idiots, but he wasn't. Now he had her new alias, and the make, model and plate number of her car. And he was certain she was headed for New Orleans.

Not that he planned to tell those NOPD assholes.

When she got back to Parades-A-Plenty at two o'clock, the disgusting odor of pizza filled the foyer, aggravating the sick-ache in her stomach.

Behind the reception desk, Banshee had the mother of all frowns on her face. "Where've you been?" Her voice rose to a horrible shriek. "You have to pack up and leave. The mayor's going to order an evacuation."

Stunned, she said nothing. She never should have stayed here. Mrs. Reilly was trouble. At last, she said, "I haven't heard anything about an evacuation."

"Well. Have you seen the size of that storm? I'm not waiting till the last minute and get stuck in all that traffic."

"I can't leave today!" Not until she made one last ditch effort to avenge her mother. "I had my interview at Loyola this morning and they want me to come back for a second interview tomorrow."

Banshee stared at her. "You went to an interview in that Yankee T-shirt?"

"Of course not. After the interview I went to the French Quarter to celebrate. I bought some souvenirs. It was hot so I put on my new T-shirt."

Mrs. Reilly's face remained stony. "I doubt you'll have an interview tomorrow, but if you do, you'll have to stay someplace else. I already called my son in Houston. He's leaving right after work tonight to come get me."

No way could she allow that to happen. She forced a smile. "There's no need for your son to come here and then drive you all the way back to Houston. My best friend lives there. I'd be happy to drive you."

"You've got a car?"

"Yes. My interview is at nine tomorrow. Then I'll come back and help you load your luggage into my car and we can leave right away."

"I didn't know you had a car. What kind of car is it?"

She wanted to slam the woman's doughy face down on that disgusting half-eaten pizza. "I borrowed my daddy's car. It's a Cadillac with a big trunk and air-conditioning. The seats are very comfortable."

"Well. I suppose I could call him . . ."

"Call him now. Tell him you've already got a ride to Houston."

The idea of driving to Houston with that yammering screech-voice set her teeth on edge. She wouldn't of course. If her final attempt at completing her mission didn't work out tonight, she'd be long gone by tomorrow morning. Mrs. Reilly would be stranded in New Orleans, but she couldn't think of anyone who deserved it more.

———

"Kelly," Frank said as he loaded the dishwasher, "can you tune in the six o'clock news. I want to see if the Mayor's going to order an evacuation."

"Man, I hope not. I won't be on patrol duty this time, but you might."

Kelly left the table and went in the living room. Thanks to her physical therapy she was getting stronger, not her old athletic self but close, and now that she was off the pain meds her appetite had returned. Tonight he'd brought two takeout dinners from Zea's: pecan-crusted trout with sides of candied sweet potatoes and green beans. Kelly's favorite.

He finished loading the dishwasher, opened a fresh Heineken, got to the living room as the news jingle sounded. He sat beside Kelly on the sofa and focused on the screen. The news anchor, a somber-faced man in wire-rimmed glasses, cut to the meteorologist. A weather map showed a gigantic orange-red swirl entering the Gulf. After decimating Cuba with 155 mph winds, Hurricane Josephine had churned north. "That it will hit the Gulf Coast is no longer in doubt," said the meteorologist. "The only mystery is where."

"Where's Natalie? That's the only mystery I'm interested in solving."

"I can't believe you saw her," Kelly said. "You're positive it was her?"

"Positive. If I hadn't been so preoccupied, I might have caught her." During dinner he'd told Kelly about his exasperating talk with Evelyn, and his equally frustrating close encounter with Natalie. "I searched Bourbon Street for an hour, didn't find her." He glanced at the TV.

Now Josephine was an orange swirl in a small box in the lower right corner of the screen. Below it, numbers listed the current coordinates, wind-speed and barometric pressure, which was falling. When the program went to commercial, he said, "I talked to BoBo's widow today."

"Where is she?" Kelly drank some Heineken, gazing at him.

"Santa Monica. Unlike BoBo's ex-wife, when I asked her for the names of his friends, she reeled off a dozen. Peterson wasn't one of them, but when I asked if they were friends, she said they were. For a while anyway. BoBo hired him to manage one of his Go-Go Bars in 1995. But after BoBo's son Chip graduated from Loyola, he went to work for BoBo full time. A year or so later—she couldn't remember the exact date—Peterson left and went to work for The Babylon."

"So Peterson *did* know BoBo," Kelly said. "They were friends."

"Yes, but BoBo hired Peterson seven years after Natalie's mother was murdered. The timing is wrong. And if I don't deliver a suspect to Demaris by Wednesday noon, everything goes in the toilet. We're off the case."

He upped the volume as a clip from the mayor's afternoon news conference ran. The grim-faced New Orleans Mayor said: "Josephine is a dangerous storm. The presidents of the Gulf parishes have already mandated evacuations. At midnight I'll announce my decision about an Orleans Parish evacuation. But I strongly urge all New Orleans residents to leave now."

Frank hit the mute button. "When I told Vobitch about my close encounter with Natalie, he said he'd call the stations and ask them to run the Natalie sketch again. But even if they run it, nobody's paying attention."

A commercial came on and Kelly rose from the couch. "I gotta hit the john. Call me if the sketch runs."

He watched the muted commercial. They were better without sound, short silent comedy skits, people looking angry, happy or stupid. In the fourth one two cats were chowing down disgusting chunks of cat food. He checked the time: 6:27. Three minutes and the news would be over.

Kelly came back just as the cat food commercial ended. Frank upped the sound as the Natalie sketch flashed on the screen.

"New Orleans Police again ask for your help," said the anchorman. "If you've seen this woman or know her whereabouts, call the number on your screen." The sketch disappeared. "That's it for this newscast. Be sure to watch the crawl line on your screen for storm updates."

"Damn!" Frank exclaimed. "If anyone blinked they missed it. How long was it on, twenty seconds?"

Kelly turned to him, somber-eyed. "More like ten."

———

Seated at her kitchen table in Parades-A-Plenty, Mrs. Reilly mopped up the last bit of gravy from her Willow Tree turkey pot pie with a piece of bread. Some turkey farm up in New England made the frozen pies, and they were delicious, big chunks of turkey meat, carrots and potatoes in a thick creamy sauce tucked inside a flaky crust. The label said it was supposed to serve two. Two little people, maybe.

She eyed the small TV set on her kitchen counter. The mayor was urging everyone to leave town right away. She wished she hadn't called her son and told him not to come for her. April West said she'd drive her to Houston tomorrow, but how did she know if the girl was reliable?

That girl was strange. Saying she had an interview at Loyola to teach some course about weird religions. Saying she didn't use credit cards. Wearing a Yankee T-shirt. That's what she was. A damn Yankee.

When a commercial came on, Mrs. Reilly opened a square box that sat on the counter and took out the cake she'd bought at the bakery on St. Charles Avenue. Her mouth watered. German chocolate cake with chocolate butter frosting. Her favorite. With a long sharp knife, she sliced off a thick piece, set it on a plate and glanced at the TV. Another commercial.

The national news would be on at six-thirty and she didn't want to miss it. Britney Spears and her husband were fighting again. It served her right. The skimpy costumes that girl wore made her look like a harlot.

Mrs. Reilly set the plate on the table and lumbered down the hall to the bathroom. While she was on the toilet, the sketch of Natalie Brixton appeared on the screen.

The national news was on when she returned to the table, her bladder comfortably relieved. But her mind wasn't. There was something odd about that girl. April West didn't look old enough to be a college professor.

She had a good mind to call Loyola first thing tomorrow and check up on her. But if the mayor ordered a mandatory evacuation, all the offices at Loyola would be closed.

Mrs. Reilly picked up a fork and dug into her German chocolate cake.

CHAPTER 30

New Orleans

Clenching his teeth, Clint Hammer peered through the tiny window of the wide-body Boeing 747. Rain pelted the glass. Barely visible in the darkness, the flashing red lights of a baggage cart approached the plane. About fucking time! Now maybe the flight crew would open the doors.

When they arrived at the gate, the pilot had apologized for being twelve minutes late and said their flight was the last to land Louis Armstrong Airport due to the hurricane. As if he didn't know. He'd had a helluva time booking a seat. Unwilling to strand their equipment, none of the other airlines were flying into New Orleans. Continental Flight 2043 was full.

When the cabin door opened, only two people got up to leave. He followed them and hustled up a slanted walkway to the gate area. A gate agent was checking in three passengers. After they boarded, Flight 2043 would fly to Houston with a planeload of passengers eager to escape the hurricane threat.

Towing his carry-on suitcase with one hand, he slung his laptop over his shoulder, walked through the deserted gate area and stopped at seats reserved for handicapped passengers. He set his laptop on the flat gray platform between two seats, dug out his cell and punched in Jason's number.

Jason picked up right away. "Hey, boss, how's it going?"

"I just landed in New Orleans. What have you got for me?"

"There must be five hundred hotels in New Orleans and half the desk clerks won't even talk to me. They just say they're not taking any reservations because of the storm and hang up."

"Keep trying," Hammer snarled. "I don't give a fuck if it takes all night. Find April West and call me. I don't give a shit what time it is."

He shut his cell and rode an escalator down to baggage claim. An Avis shuttle bus would ferry him to the rental car lot. Earlier he'd managed to book the last available car. New Orleans residents hell-bent on leaving town before the storm hit had rented the rest.

233

He ground his teeth, heard molar scrape against molar. If they didn't have his car, heads would roll. At this hour he'd never get a cab. His pal at the local Homeland Security Office had booked him a hotel room, but only for one night. After that all bets were off, thanks to fucking Hurricane Josephine which had now entered the Gulf, a category four, the last he'd heard.

Where was April West?

Was she riding out the storm in some hotel room?

What if she had evacuated? Christ on a crutch, then he'd never find her!

But then he thought: April West didn't evacuate. April West was a killer, and killers didn't abandon their evil plans. April West had come to New Orleans to kill someone. He didn't know who, but he really didn't give a shit. The bitch had murdered his friend in cold blood and he was going to get her.

He yawned and set out for the Avis shuttle bus. It had been a long day.

He was ready for a stiff drink and some shuteye.

————

At ten-thirty she slipped onto the stool she'd sat on last night at the end of the bar. The music, a punishing disco beat, sent stabbing pains through her head. The place was packed, men hooting and whistling at two scantily-clad women dancing seductively onstage. The redheaded barman was mixing drinks for an anxious-looking waiter at the service area. A minute later he came over and said, his voice barely audible over the music, "What can I get for you?"

"A glass of your house red and an ice water chaser."

He grabbed a wine bottle from the shelf behind the bar, splashed wine into a glass, set it before her and went to get her ice water.

When he came back with it, she said, "Is Chip here?"

"I think he's in the office." He turned to leave, but she touched his arm.

"Could you buzz him and tell him I'm here?"

He gave her a dead-eyed stare. "I've got thirsty customers waiting." He returned to the service area where another waiter waited with a tray.

Disappointed, she sipped her ice water. Clouds of cigarette smoke hung over the room. Her head throbbed in time with the music. Chip was in his office, but he didn't know she was here and she had no way to tell him. Unlike last night, the red-haired bartender seemed cool and distant. All she could do was wait and hope that Chip would come out of his office.

Mercifully, the disco music stopped when show ended at eleven. Amidst whoops and applause, the dancers took their bows. The barkeeper was slammed, filling drink orders for thirsty patrons, who seemed unconcerned about the hurricane. Maybe they figured work would be cancelled tomorrow.

There were no TV sets in the bar, so she had no idea what was happening with Josephine. If she had her laptop she could take it in the restroom and check, but she'd left it in her room with her suitcase. She didn't dare lock them in the trunk of her car. One news program she'd seen had warned that thieves often stole cars parked on the street during evacuations. She'd locked her diary and clothes in her suitcase, but left her Yankee T-shirt and a pair of jeans hanging in the closet in case Mrs. Reilly checked her room while she was out.

At eleven-thirty the lights dimmed and the abrasive disco beat began. Two dancers came onstage, smiling their seductive smiles, prancing around in six-inch stiletto heels. Seeing them took her back to her dancing-in-the-dark days at Platinum-Plus Gentlemen's Club. A disco beat, smoke-filled air and dirty-minded men with greedy eyes who wanted her to give them a lap dance, feigning pleasure as she ground herself against their crotch until they came.

She didn't want to think about that depressing chapter of her life, or the other chapters for that matter. Being paid to have sex with men in Paris had been just as ugly, though the money was better. On the verge of exhaustion, she massaged her aching temples. She couldn't go on like this. The angry ancestor spirits were punishing her, putting Tex Conroy in her path, then Oliver James, sending hurricanes to thwart her. And Detective Renzi was still after her, the hunter that wouldn't give up.

She tried to imagine what life would have been like if she'd had a normal family with normal parents. Imagined them taking her to Disneyland, praising her when she got all A's in high school and got inducted in the National Honor Society. What if she'd gone to college, got a job as an art teacher and met some smart handsome guy? What if she gotten married and had two kids?

But those kinds of fantasies happened to other girls, not her.

Nursing her ice water, she endured the hour-long show. No sign of Chip.

By the time the show ended she felt nauseous. Her ears hurt and her head felt like someone had beaten it with a sledgehammer. Tears stung her eyes. She had sold her body to earn the money to pay a PI to get her mother's murder file, had spent months researching BoBo, only to have him die. Even then, she didn't give up. She'd focused on a new target, BoBo's son Chip, had worked even harder to earn enough money to execute her mission.

She sucked up some ice water. Her discovery that Arnold Peterson was BoBo's friend had been a major triumph. But Peterson was only a stepping-stone. Now, just when her goal was within reach, a hurricane was going to thwart her. How could it end this way?

Another show would begin at one A.M. but she couldn't endure another minute in this place. She signaled the bartender for the check. She would take a cab back to Parades-A-Plenty. At this hour, Banshee would be asleep. It would be easy to sneak up to her room, grab her laptop and suitcase, get in her car and leave New Orleans.

"Hello, dawlin. What are you doing here?"

Chip's voice. She thought her heart would jump out of her chest.

Ignoring the headache pounding her temples, she gave him a seductive smile. This was no time to act like an ingénue, this was crunch time.

"Waiting for you."

He slid onto the barstool beside hers. "I sure didn't expect to see you here tonight, dawlin."

"The bartender said you were in your office, but when I asked him to tell you I was here, he wouldn't."

His steely-blue eyes turned frosty. "Damn right. Curly knows who butters *his* bread."

A musky scent emanated from him, some cologne she couldn't identify. His shirt was rolled up to the elbows, exposing tanned, well-muscled forearms. On his left hand he wore a gold wedding band, on his right a college ring with a large sapphire. He gave her a broad smile, showing his shiny pearly-whites.

"I saw you come in at ten-thirty, dawlin. Did you enjoy the show?"

The security cameras. The bastard had known she was here all along. Alarm bells clanged in her mind. BoBo was a killer and this was his chip-off-the-old-block son. An aura of power emanated from him. Seated beside him, she felt small. Insignificant. Could she overpower him? He was bigger and stronger.

But she was smarter and motivated. Her will was stronger than his. Years of disappointments and trials had made it so.

"Your dancers are fantastic," she said. *Tell them what they want to hear.*

"Not many gals come here to watch the show. Well, a few do, but they're the type that, you know, swing the other way." He gave her a speculative look. "You're not one of those, are you?"

She removed her Vera Wang glasses and gave him a seductive smile.

"No, I'm not."

"I didn't think so. So tell me what you're doing here."

She ran her tongue over her bottom lip "You look like you've been working too hard, Chip."

"Dawlin, you have no idea. Had to cancel the grand opening of my new bar. Damn shame, all the money I spent on it, but what can I do?"

She touched his forearm, a light touch to show she was interested.

"That's too bad, but there'll be another opening won't there?"

Not if she could help it.

"Once Josephine does her thing there will." He gave her another speculative look.

She knew that look, had seen it often from many men. Knew that it meant her chances to complete her mission were improving.

"I put Marla and the kids on a flight to Chicago. Had a helluva time getting them seats. Everybody's in a panic to leave town. First thing tomorrow morning I'll hop on my corporate jet at Lakefront Airport and join them."

She could hardly believe her luck. His wife was in Chicago. Chip would stay in New Orleans tonight, but he was leaving tomorrow morning. If she had any hope of achieving her goal, it had to be tonight.

She traced a finger down the inside of his forearm. "You look like you're ready for some fun. What with your wife being gone and all."

He studied her, expressionless. His eyes, blank reflecting pools, revealed nothing. For an instant she feared she'd come on too strong. But then a subtle change came over him, a slight relaxation of his face muscles and a thrust of his chest as he straightened on his barstool.

Had she been inexperienced with men, she might have missed it. But she knew the signs and she knew what they meant: partly pride of sexual conquest and partly desire, but most of all, pride in his power over her.

His eyes locked on hers. "What did you have in mind, April?"

She shrugged her shoulders, a sensual move that never failed to excite men. Made her eyes go wide with promise.

"I thought maybe we could go somewhere and . . . relax."

He put his arm around her, leaned close and whispered in her ear, "I like your style, April. We're gonna have fun. I gotta take care of some details, might take a half hour or so. My car's parked out back. I'll pick you up outside the front door in forty-five minutes. How's that sound?"

She flashed another seductive smile. "That sounds perfect."

CHAPTER 31

1:52 A.M. Tuesday, 19 August

Awakened by his cell phone, Clint Hammer jolted upright in bed. He grabbed the cell off the bedside table and barked, "Hammer."

"Clint!" Jason's voice, high-pitched with excitement. "I found her! She's staying at a bed-and-breakfast on a side street off St. Charles Avenue. I just talked to the owner. Man, was she pissed. She screamed at me in this God-awful voice for waking her up in the middle of the night."

He pumped his fist. At this very moment the gook-bitch was fast asleep. An adrenaline rush flamed his body, hotter than napalm hitting the huts in a Vietnamese village. He wrote down the information as Jason read it to him.

"Good work, Jason. I'll handle things from here on out."

He located Parades-A-Plenty on his street map. Excellent, just three miles from his hotel. It was almost 2 A.M., the perfect time to execute a black ops sortie. Catch the enemy while they were deep in slumber. He'd done that a few times, not with a female target, but women had to sleep, too.

He flexed his fingers, imagining the damage they would inflict on her throat. Then he remembered what Jason said about the owner. If he went there now, he'd have to wake her up again. If she raised a ruckus, it might alert his target. That wouldn't do. He wanted to catch the bitch unawares.

The way she'd caught Oliver unawares, pulling a gun and murdering him in cold blood. He ground his teeth and felt a sharp pain in his jaw.

Maybe he'd call those NOPD idiots, tell them he knew where their killer was and get them over to Parades-A-Plenty. Then he'd have backup in case the gook-bitch tried to escape out a window. But the thought of asking those dimwits for help disgusted him.

No, he'd go there at sunrise when the owner was awake and sweet talk her. Tell her she'd rented a room to a dangerous killer but he'd take care of it.

A cold fury settled in his gut, a silent rage, spurring him on.

Oh yes, he'd take care of that gook-bitch all right.

———

Her head throbbed as loud disco music bled through the rest room door. Two empty stalls stood on one wall, their doors ajar. Opposite them, two sinks were set into a pink marble vanity. Above them a rectangular mirror outlined with light bulbs illuminated the room. She used the toilet and went to the sink. Her hands felt cold and clammy, the way they'd felt twenty years ago when the NOPD detective told her Mom was dead.

She ran the hot water over them and gazed at herself in the mirror. The harsh lights made her skin look sallow.

An image of the ugly gargoyles above Notre Dame entered her mind, reminders of her ancestral ghosts. Reminders of her mission. If everything went according to plan, she would avenge her mother's murder tonight.

But she had no illusions that it would be easy.

She checked her watch, the minutes crawling by like a line of cars in a traffic jam. Five more minutes to wait. She took a blister-pack of No-Doze out of her new tote, a charcoal-gray pouch with a leather shoulder strap. It was bigger than her old one, roomy enough to hold everything she needed. Her body was so charged with adrenaline she might not need any No-Doze.

No, better to be careful. Chip was a dangerous adversary. She had to stay alert. She gulped down two No-Doze and left the rest room. Loud music hit her, a visceral wall of sound to accompany the frenzied dancers on the stage.

She went to the foyer, nodded to the bouncer and left the club.

A sleek black BMW pulled to the curb in front of her. Like BoBo, Chip traveled in style, corporate jets, fancy cars. She opened the door and got in.

"Relax and get comfortable, dawlin," said Chip, smiling at her as he put the car in gear. "We're gonna have us a good time tonight."

She had hoped he would take her to a nearby hotel, but he drove to the nearest highway entrance and got on the I-10. That made her nervous. Where was he taking her? Even at this hour traffic was heavy, people leaving town to escape Hurricane Josephine, she assumed.

Chip didn't say much, just glanced at her now and then, his expression inscrutable as she prattled about how much she loved New Orleans.

When he took the Airline Drive exit off the I-10, she knew where they were going. This end of Airline Drive was lined with cheap, no-tell motels where hookers took their johns. Her moment of truth was fast approaching.

An almost-sexual feeling of exhilaration coursed through her body.

At long last she would execute her hard-earned and meticulously planned mission. Then she'd be free to live life on her terms, be anyone she wanted.

But another vision of the Notre Dame gargoyles killed her excitement. Would the angry ancestor spirits put yet another obstacle in her way? Another trial to overcome? The execution of her plan had to be perfect. She breathed deep and used her TKD focus to calm her racing heart.

Chip pulled into the Dixie Motel, a long one-story cement-block structure. No lamps outside the rooms. A red-neon sign at the midpoint of the building flashed: **OFFICE**. Chip stopped the BMW fifteen yards short of the office, took out his wallet and extracted a wad of bills.

"Go rent us a room, dawlin," he said, peeling off twenty-dollar bills. "Here's two hundred. I hate traffic noise. Tell the clerk you want a room out back. Tell him we'll be out by six. I've got a plane to catch."

She stared at him, incensed. He really was a chip of the old block. Twenty years ago BoBo had made her mother rent the room at the Royal Arms Hotel.

"You want *me* to rent the room?" she said, outraged.

His face hardened to granite. "A man in my position can't register at some cheap motel. Don't want people seeing my car either." His mouth smiled, but his eyes didn't. "Go rent the room, April. Times a'wasting."

She slung her tote over her shoulder and opened the car door.

"Hold it. Leave the bag in the car. I gave you the cash."

Leave her tote in the car? Impossible. He might look inside. "I might need it to register," she said and jumped out of the car.

Slinging the strap of the tote over her shoulder, she walked to the office. Above her head bugs sizzled against the red-neon flashing light. The gray-steel door was ajar, but a screen door protected the office from bug invasions.

She stepped inside. The walls were painted bilious green, like the slime that builds up on shower curtains. Facing the door, a microwave sat on a shelf behind the reception desk. The odor of stale food sickened her.

An older man with pale unhealthy skin stood behind the desk. His pink scalp showed through wisps of white hair. Gazing at her with undisguised distaste, he said, "Okay, missy, what'll it be?"

Feeling like a cheap whore, she set the wad of bills on the counter. "I'd like to rent a room in the back. I'll be out by six tomorrow morning."

"Show me a license. I let some underage girl rent one of my rooms, I'll get in trouble."

No way was she showing him her license. "I don't have it. My boyfriend drove me here."

The clerk's eyes hardened. "Your *boyfriend*, huh? He got a license?"

Exasperated, she said, "You want to come out to the car so he can show it to you? Or do you want to rent us a room and take the cash?"

His hand scooped up the twenty-dollar bills and shoved them into a drawer below the counter. "Gotta have a name to put on the register," he said, staring at her breasts.

"Nancy Drew," she said, knowing the idiot wouldn't get it. Would Renzi?

When the cops found a dead man with a gunshot wound in his head at the Dixie Motel and ID'd him as Chip Beaubien, she was positive Homicide Detective Frank Renzi would arrive in record time.

240

In neat block letters, the clerk printed *Nancy Drew* in the register, then plucked a key off a wallboard lined with hooks. "Room 44, out back. Leave the key in the room when you leave."

She went back and got in the BMW. Chip held out his hand for the key, put the car in gear and pulled forward.

"Which room, dawlin? I can hardly wait."

"Room 44, around back."

He looped around the one-story structure and parked in front of a room with metal numbers nailed to the door. No cars parked outside the rooms on either side of Room 44. That was a plus. Twenty yards farther along the building, a pickup truck and a red Mustang stood several yards apart outside other rooms. Other couples into their sexual games.

Far enough away not to hear a gunshot she hoped.

Chip unlocked the door, flipped a switch and waved her inside. The room stank of cigarette smoke. Directly ahead of her was a bathroom. Planning her moves, she rapidly assessed the room. It was small, no more than twelve feet square. To the left of the door, heavy maroon drapes covered a wide window. Parallel to the window, a sagging double bed with a frayed maroon bedspread took up most of the space, its headboard set against the wall of the next room.

Between the window and the left side of the bed, a narrow path led to a plastic nightstand beside the headboard. On the nightstand, a brass lamp with a red shade cast a dim red glow over the room. No luggage holder, no bureau, no TV set. Of course not. People didn't come here to sleep or watch CNN.

"What's the matter, dawlin? You don't like the room?"

Forcing herself to play the part, she beamed him a smile, part seductive, part hesitant. "It's fine, Chip. I'm just a little nervous, that's all."

Nervous didn't begin to describe her feelings. Revulsion, anger, hatred and a mountain of rage. Her secret weapon. She wanted to kill this insufferable man and get out of this disgusting room as soon as possible.

He stood by the window, a half-smile playing over his lips. "You gonna put down that tote bag, dawlin? Seems like you're holdin onto it for dear life."

"Of course." But she needed to keep it handy. The best place would be on the nightstand. Her cheeks felt stiff, but she maintained her smile.

She sauntered toward him, swinging her hips seductively.

He held out his hand. "Lemme see that thing."

No, no, no, she wanted to scream. Her heart spasmed in fear. She conjured her acting skills and forced an ingenuous smile. "Whatever for? Girls keep all sorts of stuff in their bags that they don't want guys to see."

His eyes hardened. "That's what I'm afraid of. Hand it over."

Panic turned her brain to mush. If he saw what was inside . . .

Without warning, he yanked the bag off her shoulder.

"Chip," she gasped. "That's not very nice—"

"This thing is heavy. What the hell you got in here?"

A kaleidoscope of terror flooded her mind, visions of Chip's malevolent blue eyes, spurting blood and her lifeless body on the floor of this hideous room. If he searched her tote, it was all over. "You've got a nerve. What gives you the right to search my belongings?"

Fixing her with his implacable gaze, he said, "I'm bigger than you."

He pawed through her tote and held up her tape recorder. "What the hell's this? You planning on taping our fuck-session and blackmailing me?"

Bile spewed into her throat. She feared she would vomit, forced herself to swallow. Took a deep breath and dredged up a smile.

"How could you think such a thing, Chip? I figured after we had some fun I could interview you for my article."

He pulled out the handcuffs.

Her heart sank like a stone.

Waving them in the air, he leered at her. "You into bondage? S-and-M?"

Paralyzed with fear, she stood there, unable to speak.

He hefted the tote. "Still feels heavy. What else you got in here?"

She backed up a step. Could she could do a TKD spin move and disable him? Maybe. The spike heels of her shoes were capped with metal . . .

"Well, well, well, look at what we got here."

Holding the .38 Special in his hand, he aimed it at her chest, his eyes cold and hard. "You fixin to hold me up and steal my credit cards, April?"

"Chip," she said, unable to stop the tremor in her voice, "it's not what you think. I live in New York and that can be dangerous. So I bought a gun. Whenever I go to a bar at night, I always take it with me."

His eyes glinted with anger, his face hard as granite.

His hand, steady as a rock, aimed the snub-nosed .38 Special at her heart. "Take off your clothes," he said.

————

Muttering under her breath, Mrs. Reilly put on her bathrobe and shuffled down the hall of her apartment to the reception desk in the foyer. That girl was trouble, just like she thought. She had no idea why a CIA agent was calling her in the middle of the night, but she knew one thing for sure.

April West wasn't the Little Miss Innocent she pretended to be.

She unlocked a drawer and took out the big round metal ring that held keys to all the rooms. Faint moonlight shone through the upper half of the front door, lighting her way through the dining room to the staircase. Clinging to the banister, she labored up to the second floor, grunting with each step. The second-floor hall was pitch dark. An anxious shiver wracked her.

She was alone in this huge house with that sneaky girl who'd lied to her. What if she was a killer? Another thought set her heart racing. What if the she was a terrorist? Maybe that's why the feds were after her.

Her heart fluttered, a series of rapid irregular beats. Lord-a-mercy! Was she having a heart attack? Her doctor said her blood pressure was sky-high. He wanted her to lose weight, a hundred pounds, he'd said, wagging his finger.

She leaned against the wall and pressed her hands to her chest.

She was going to die here all alone.

Moonlight filtered through the stained-glass window on the second-floor landing, casting scary shadows on the wall. She looked up the dark staircase. Again her heart fluttered. But she couldn't give in to fear. She had to find out what that sneaky girl was up to. Pausing after each step, she crept to the third floor landing. The Blue Room was the first door on the right.

Not a speck of light showed under the door.

Little Miss Innocent must be fast asleep in the four-poster bed.

Summoning her courage, she rapped on the door. Nothing. The girl must be a sound sleeper. She rapped again, harder.

A new thought almost made her wet herself. Maybe April West was gone.

What if that sneak tiptoed downstairs last night while she was watching TV in her apartment? What if that awful girl just scooted out the door, got in her car and left, leaving her poor old landlady at the mercy of the terrible storm that was about to hit them? The thought enraged her.

April West was worse than sneaky, she was a coldhearted bitch.

The girl had no respect for her elders. Abandoning her at a time like this!

She found the key to the Blue Room on the brass ring, slid it into the lock and opened the door.

Moonlight shone through the filmy white curtain above the air-conditioner in the window, enough light to tell her the four-poster bed was empty. The canvas bag that held the girl's laptop lay atop the blue comforter on the bed. A sturdy gray suitcase stood in the corner.

Maybe the girl wasn't going to abandon her after all. She wouldn't leave without her belongings, would she?

Mrs. Reilly turned on the overhead light and opened the closet door. Inside on wire hangers were a pair of blue jeans and that Yankee T-shirt. April West was a Yankee fan. It figured. How could anyone root for a team with a name like that? Damn Yankees, that's what her husband used to call them. Tom's great-granddaddy had fought for the Confederacy during the Civil War, got shot in the leg and had to have it amputated.

She checked her wristwatch. Lord-a-mercy, two-thirty in the morning.

Where was that girl? At this hour she had to be up to no good.

Mrs. Reilly left the Blue Room and descended the stairs, gripping the wooden banister, her mind whirling with questions, questions that made her head throb. The girl's belongings were still here, but what if she came back in the dead of night, took her belongings, got in her car and left town while her helpless old landlady was fast asleep?

By the time she reached the first floor, she had made her decision.

She marched through the dining room and straight through the foyer to the front door. She peered through the glass in the top half of the door. It was dark outside, but the streetlights were on. Gusts of wind were blowing the two big fir trees across the street, making them sway back and forth.

That hurricane was going to hit them for sure.

She set both dead bolts, the top one first, then the one at the bottom, and nodded with satisfaction.

If that girl tried to sneak into Parades-A-Plenty and grab her belongings and run off without waking Mrs. Reilly, that girl was in for a big surprise.

CHAPTER 32

Fear coiled in her gut like a deadly cobra.

Frozen her in her tracks, she stared at the snub-nosed .38 Special. She'd chosen the one with a matte-black finish, thinking it looked more frightening than silver. It was. Even more frightening were the implacable eyes of the man who aimed it at her.

Never in her life had she been so terrified, not when the cops questioned her after Randy fell off the bluff, not when Tex recognized her in the store, not even when the cops chased her after she killed Oliver.

She felt utterly defenseless.

Was this how Mom felt when BoBo strangled her?

This was supposed to be the stunning triumph at the end of her journey, the culmination of her quest for vengeance. Lying in bed last night, unable to sleep, she had imagined this moment in vivid detail, the fear in Chip's eyes when he saw the gun. The thrilling moment when she took control of this insufferable man, stripped him of his power and heard him beg for mercy.

But now Chip had the gun.

To avoid looking at him, she focused on the wall behind him and noticed the print. A Mardi Gras poster, a bosomy blonde with her nipples peeking out of her bra. It seemed familiar. Where had she seen it? Then she remembered the photo in her mother's case file. A poster hung on the wall above the bed where her mother lay. Naked. Dead. Another Mardi Gras poster with a busty blonde. The realization crushed her.

She was going to die in a sleazy hotel room like her mother.

"Take your clothes off, bitch."

Her insides were shaking uncontrollably, as if she'd been standing outside in a blizzard for hours. A feeling of lassitude swept over her, bone-deep weariness that made her want to capitulate. Why not get it over with? Chip just was as ruthless as his father. No matter what she did, he would kill her.

She conjured a vision of her mother, recalling the bright sunny day they had strolled along the Mississippi River, warmed by the midday sun, licking their ice cream cones—strawberry for her, chocolate for Mom. An ordinary day, peaceful and carefree, a fun time with Mom.

Do your homework and go to bed, Natalie, and I'll see you in the morning.

The last words Mom had spoken to her.

Somewhere deep within her anger stirred and became a steely resolve. Chip's father had murdered her mother and had never been punished for it. She would not capitulate. Mom deserved better. Mom deserved justice.

A jolt of adrenaline energized her. Moving seductively, she took off her clingy top and gave Chip a sexy smile. Aware of his eyes roving her body, she shimmied out of her slim black skirt.

"That's better, dawlin. I like your underwear. Black turns me on like you wouldn't believe."

She believed it all right. But what turned him on most was holding the gun on her. Having power over her. Power, the ultimate aphrodisiac. The power that enormous wealth could buy.

Shimmying her hips, she stepped closer, unhooked her lacy black bra and let it fall to the floor.

"I like your tits, April. Ditch the panties." He lowered the gun.

She took another step closer. Shoved her panties down to her ankles. Felt his greedy eyes devour her body. She stepped out of her shoes and kicked her underpants aside. Forced herself not to look at the gun. "Aren't you going to undress, Chip? I thought we were going to have some fun."

"You got that right." He tossed the gun on the bed and began to unbutton his shirt.

Waves of relief washed over her. She wasn't home free yet. Chip was over six feet tall and weighed at least two hundred pounds. But now the gun was on the bed. If she was very careful and totally focused, she might be able to save herself and complete her mission.

Eyes fixed on her breasts, he took off his white shirt, pulled off his undershirt and dropped it on the floor. Thick blonde hair matted his chest and curled from his armpits. The muscles in his arms rippled as he unbuckled his belt. He unzipped his fly and looked at her.

She ran her tongue over her bottom lip. *Take your pants off, you pig.*

He shoved his trousers down to his knees, sat on the bed, toed off his shoes and pushed off his trousers. Then he rose from the bed and took off his jockey shorts. His erection was enormous, deep red, pulsing and throbbing.

"Okay, dawlin, let's get it on."

Fixing her lips in a smile, she mustered her strength and her courage. This would be the most important move of her life. Get it right, or she was dead.

She took a breath and released it, seeking the centered calm she worked so hard to achieve during her TKD workouts. Felt the energy reach the focal point below her breastbone. Every muscle in her body tensed.

Rearing back, she spun her body and kicked him with all her might, slamming her foot against his head above the ear.

His face sagged, an instant of shocked disbelief. Like a wounded animal, he emitted a low guttural sound. Then his knees buckled and he collapsed on the floor with a thump. She pounced on him. Her strike had been a solid hit, but Chip was a powerful man, strong and muscular. His eyes were shut, but his chest rose and fell rapidly. She had to disable him before he came to his senses. Sickened by the smell of him, a gamy odor triggered by his anticipation of fucking her, she located the Dokko point below his ear. Made a knuckle fist with two fingers. Set them against the Dokko point and twisted.

Shock the nerves, but not too much.

She didn't want to kill him. Not yet.

His body shuddered and lay still. But for how long?

His head lay near the wall, his feet close to the bed.

The leg is the most powerful weapon. Mr. Larson's oft-repeated warning.

And Chip's muscular legs looked powerful enough to hurt her badly. She grabbed a pair of plastic handcuffs, knelt down and cuffed his ankles together. Checked to make sure his eyes were closed. They were. Reassured, she grasped his thick hairy ankles and dragged him closer to the foot of the bed.

Inch by inch, she heaved him closer to the bed, his body deadweight. Panting, she let go of his ankles, raised the bedspread and studied the metal bed frame. The cylindrical legs were an inch thick, sturdy enough to support any acrobatic lovers. She grasped his ankles and heaved his body closer to the leg. When his ankles were close enough, she took another set of cuffs, looped one half around the cuffs that secured his ankles and fastened the other half around the leg of the bed.

Chip's muscular legs looked powerful, but she believed the double bed and the heavy frame were too heavy for him to move. Kneeling on the carpet, she studied his face for any sign of awareness. His eyes remained closed, his lips parted, his raspy breathing clearly audible in the stillness of the room.

She rose to her feet and took the .38 Special off the bed.

It felt heavy in her hand. Heavy and reassuring.

Was Chip truly unconscious? Or was he pretending? She placed the .38 Special on the carpet beyond his reach but where she could quickly grab it. Cautiously, she grasped his wrist and raised his hand above his belly. His skin felt clammy and wiry hairs prickled her fingers. A diamond-studded Rolex with a gold expansion band encircled his wrist. Rich men loved expensive toys.

She lowered his hand, bound his wrists together with another set of cuffs and assessed his ability to resist.

His ankles were secured to the leg of the bed. Cuffed together, his hands lay on his abdomen. His erection was long gone, his penis limp and flaccid against his thigh. She'd feel safer if she could secure his wrists to something, but the flimsy nightstand wasn't an option. Chip could easily tip it over.

If she dragged his torso closer to the head of the bed, she could secure his wrists to the leg below the headboard. But she didn't dare.

If he came to before she finished, he might grab her.

Again, she assessed his ability to resist. His legs were immobilized, his wrists cuffed together. He could move his arms, but only within a certain arc. She had to stay clear of his hands.

His eyes remained closed, his raspy breathing audible as air escaped from his nostrils. He appeared to be unconscious, but for how long?

Keeping her eyes on him, she put on her clothes: First her bra, then her top, then her panties and her slim black skirt. That made her feel better. Now he was naked and she wasn't. That was part of the power game. Chip had made her undress first, but now the power equation was reversed.

Her tape recorder, slightly larger than a pack of cigarettes, lay on the floor beside her tote. She made sure the tape was inside and pushed Start. When she heard her own voice, she hit Rewind, then Stop.

Excellent. The stage was set and the actors were in place: Chip Beaubien, Arnold Peterson, and Natalie Brixton with her gun.

A soft moan startled her. She grabbed the .38 Special and aimed it at Chip. He didn't move, his eyes closed, his mouth slack, his breathing steady. She checked the time, amazed that it was 3:15. But she wasn't sleepy. On the contrary, she felt energized and excited. Now that she had Chip under control she wanted him to wake up and face the music.

A car door slammed, a loud thud, then another. Her breath caught in her throat. It sounded like the car was right outside the room. Were the cops here to raid the motel? It probably wouldn't be the first time.

She crept to the window, parted the drapes an inch and looked outside. A huge pickup truck with oversized tires was parked in front of the room two doors down. She heard a woman laugh, a rollicking laugh, the laugh of a woman about to have sex with a man.

Relieved, she turned away from the window. But the interruption reminded her that precious minutes were passing, minutes she couldn't afford to waste. Holding the gun in her right hand, she grasped the plastic cuffs fastened around Chip's wrists with her left hand. Bracing her legs for leverage, she raised his arms toward his head.

He didn't stir. She let them fall onto his belly. Still nothing.

She slapped his face. "Wake up, you slimy piece of shit."

His eyelids flickered, but his eyes remained closed. She hit him again, a sharp smack on each cheek. He grunted. Moving away so he couldn't grab her, she waited with the gun aimed at his face.

His eyes flicked open and settled on the gun. He raised his hands, saw the cuffs that bound them together. His face hardened in a frown.

"You cunt. What do you want?"

She smiled, her first genuine smile of the day. "I want to have fun, Chip."

He tried to move his legs, but couldn't. Realized his ankles were secured to the bed frame. His thigh muscles bulged as he tried to free himself. The cuffs held, but the bed moved two inches. Scowling at her, he jerked his legs.

"You tied me up, you fucking cunt."

"Now I've got the gun. One pull of the trigger blows your brains out."

His eyes, malevolent with fury, fixed on her face. "Bitch."

"'The sins of the father are visited upon the son.'"

"What the fuck are you talking about? Get these fuckin cuffs off me and we'll get out of here."

"No. I want you to listen to something that proves what a slimy shit your father was."

His cheeks reddened. "What is this some kind of revenge movie? You got some bone to pick with Pops? Hell, you never even met him."

"Your father murdered my mother."

His eyes widened. Then he laughed. "My father did no such thing."

"Yes he did. Twenty years ago BoBo murdered my mother."

"That's bullshit, those old rumors—"

"Shut up, Chip. The rumors were true and I've got the proof."

"You're full of—"

"Shut up!" She hit Play on the tape recorder.

Tell me how you met BoBo, Arnold. Her voice, loud and clear, on the tape.

Chip's eyes widened. When Peterson's voice came over the speaker, Chip said, "Jesus. Arnold Peterson?"

"That's right, Chip. Your father's pal. The man that helped him get away with murder."

"You got no—"

"Shut up and listen!" She stepped closer, aimed the gun at his face. "If you don't, I'll shoot you."

Chip clamped his lips together and listened to Peterson explain how he met BoBo in 1988. But as Peterson droned on, Chip's expression grew angry.

"That lying sonofabitch."

"Shut up. You haven't heard the best part."

Peterson described what happened when he picked BoBo up near the hotel on Royal Street and drove him home. Under her prodding, Peterson admitted that on the way, BoBo told him he'd murdered a woman in the hotel and asked him never to tell anyone.

She shut off the tape recorder. "Still think Pops was a great guy?"

"I don't believe it. You can't prove he killed that woman. Peterson got murdered in a hotel room last month. It was you, right? You held a gun on him, just like you're doing to me. Arnold lied. He told you what you wanted to hear so you wouldn't shoot him."

"He wasn't lying. He was part of it. You heard him. He picked your father up at the hotel after he murdered my mother and drove him home."

"Bullshit! Arnold would say anything to save his own skin. When he was broke, Pops gave him a job. And now, after all Pops did for him, he fingered Pops for a murder he didn't do."

Unable to believe her ears, she shouted: "Your father was a murderer, Chip. He made his wife swear he was home that night. Joereen lied for him."

"Joereen was a pain in the ass."

"Your father slapped her around."

"If he did, she deserved it."

A red haze of rage swamp before her eyes. "No, Chip. She didn't deserve it. And neither did my mother. Your father beat my mother's face to a pulp."

"She was a cheap whore like you, didn't have the brains of a flea. Fucking men was the only way she could earn money."

Rage boiled into her throat, choking her. She thought her head would explode. Deep inside her the familiar iceberg formed, a huge iceberg this time, bigger than the Titanic. An ice-mountain of hate.

"You worthless piece of shit. You're just like your father. BoBo thought women were playthings to use however he wanted. My mother meant nothing to him. He expected her to kowtow to him because he was rich and powerful. And you're as bad as he was." Shaking with fury, she gripped the gun hard to hold it steady. "Your father expected you to run the business after he died. And you did for a while, but that's over."

A crafty look appeared in his eyes. "What do you want? Money? How much do you want?"

The irony took her breath away. Just like her father, and all the other rich powerful men who thought they could buy anything with money, even forgiveness.

"I don't want money. I want revenge. I don't believe in Heaven, but I bet you do. You're a good Catholic boy. You think BoBo's up in Heaven waiting for you? He's not. BoBo's in Hell."

"Why kill me? I never did anything to hurt you."

"Your father was a murderer, Chip. Admit it!"

He stared at her, his eyes baleful. "Fuck you, bitch."

Her ice-mountain of rage exploded into a hatred more profound than her loathing of BoBo. Chip didn't deserve to live.

She aimed the gun at his forehead.

Looked into his evil blue eyes and pulled the trigger.

CHAPTER 33

5:00 A.M. Tuesday, 19 August

When her alarm clock rang at five, Mrs. Reilly struggled out of bed, put on her robe and wearily walked down the hall to the kitchen. She felt groggy from lack of sleep, but not groggy enough to forget the man that called about April West. The sneak who'd gone out last night when she wasn't looking.

She turned on the TV set to catch the Early Bird News, put on a pot of coffee and took out the cinnamon-raisin coffee cake she'd made last night after dinner. It smelled delicious, frosted with vanilla icing and chopped walnuts sprinkled on top. She took a sharp knife out of a drawer, sliced off a hunk and set it on a plate as the reporter announced the headlines.

"The mayor of New Orleans has ordered a mandatory evacuation. We'll have reports on Hurricane Josephine and local traffic conditions. And New Orleans police urgently ask your help in finding this woman."

She turned to see what woman he was talking about, but a commercial was on. Lord-a-mercy, a mandatory evacuation! And that sneaky girl had abandoned her. She set the plate with the coffee cake on her kitchen table. Her mouth watered. Should she have a bite now? No, it would taste better with coffee. By the time she washed up and got dressed, the coffee would be ready.

Fifteen minutes later she returned to the kitchen. An artist's sketch of a woman's face filled the TV screen.

The face seemed familiar. She could swear she'd seen it before.

"Police say the woman uses several aliases," the reporter said.

That got her attention. Except for the long dark hair, it looked a lot like April West. And the police were after her. The man that called last night hadn't said why he was looking for her, but she didn't think he was calling in the middle of the night because April West was someone's long-lost heir.

"If you've seen this woman recently or know her whereabouts," said the announcer, "call the tip-line number at the bottom of your screen."

Mrs. Reilly grabbed a pen and wrote the number on a yellow sticky.

Hoping no one had seen her leave Room 44, she jumped into Chip's BMW and slammed the door. In the distance, a rosy sliver of light peeped over the horizon, but dark storm clouds hung low in the dusky sky above her.

Soon it would be light. She started the car.

The digital clock on the dashboard said 5:05 A.M. Chip had been dead for ten minutes, but she couldn't think about that now.

Fearing someone might have heard the gunshot, she had removed the cuffs from his wrists and ankles and stuffed them into her tote with the tape recorder and the .38 Special. Chip's bladder and bowels had let go. Ignoring the stench, she wiped anything she might have touched with baby wipes. In the pocket of his pants she found his keys, wallet and cell phone. She had taken the keys but left the wallet and phone.

Leaving no doubt about the identity of the dead man in Room 44. After six o'clock the desk clerk would go to the room to collect the key, find the body and call the police. But so what? By then she would have left the city.

She looped around the building, drove to the exit and stopped, unable to believe her eyes. The exit was completely blocked.

Westbound traffic on Airline Drive was at a standstill, two lanes of vehicles, some towing small trailers, packed with people intent on leaving town. She glanced over her shoulder. The motel office was thirty yards away. The clerk probably couldn't see the BMW from the office, but people leaving their rooms could. She had to get out of here.

The cars blocking the entrance inched forward. She hit the blinker, signaling she wanted to turn left. Now the dashboard clock said 5:10. A sick feeling gnawed her gut. She had to get to Parades-A-Plenty, collect her belongings and leave town before they found Chip's body.

She nosed the BMW into the traffic. Mercifully, two cars stopped, allowing her to creep through the two lanes of traffic, turn left and head for New Orleans. The eastbound traffic was lighter, but the traffic signals slowed her down. She stopped at a red light opposite a big furniture store. No cars in the parking lot, not even a delivery truck, and plywood covered the large plate glass windows along the storefront.

Two cars drove up behind her. One stopped behind Chip's BMW, the other beside her. Using her left hand, she hid her face and accelerated when the light turned green. Fifty yards later she stopped at another red light and massaged her throbbing forehead.

Chip was dead, but killing him had brought no satisfaction. She felt empty inside, a yawning chasm of nothingness. After she played the Peterson tape, she had expected Chip to admit his father's guilt.

But he hadn't. Far from it. Chip had defended the bastard.

My father did no such thing. That's bullshit. You can't prove he killed that woman.

That woman. Her mother. *She was a whore. Just like you.*

As if prostitutes deserved to be beaten and strangled.

Tears stung her eyes. She should have defended her mother, but all she'd done was call him names: *You're a slimy piece of shit like your father.*

She clenched the steering wheel and screamed, "Murderer!"

And realized the woman in the car beside her was staring at her, eyes wide, mouth agape.

When the light changed, she floored the accelerator. The next light was red, but no cars were crossing into her lane. She blew through the light, desperate to get back to Parades-A-Plenty.

But when she exited at Tulane Avenue, traffic was gridlocked. Four lanes of stalled cars. Now it was 5:20. She drummed her fingers on the wheel, an anxious knot festering in her stomach. The New Orleans mayor must have ordered a mandatory evacuation. That would make it harder for her to get out of town, but not impossible. She had already done the impossible.

She visualized Chip's face. Even in death it looked powerful. Angry. Disgusting. She focused on the traffic, inching forward a few yards at a time. She made it through the next traffic signal by tailgating the car in front of her through a red light, but more stalled cars loomed ahead of her. At this rate it would take forever to get to Parades-A-Plenty, and she didn't have forever.

Soon the motel clerk would go to Room 44 and find Chip dead on the floor. She maneuvered the BMW into the right lane.

Unlike most days, vacant parking spaces lined Carrolton Avenue. She pulled to the curb, shut off the engine, wiped the steering wheel and signal wands with a baby wipe and used the wipe to open the door.

She left the keys in the ignition. With any kind of luck, someone looking to get out of town would steal the car.

———

At 5:22 Frank's cell phone jolted him awake. Foggy with sleep, he groped for the phone on his beside table and answered. "Renzi."

"Frank, it's Ernie Wilcox. I just got a call on the tip line from a Mrs. Reilly. She saw the sketch on the Early Bird News and she says the woman is staying at her bed and breakfast."

Instantly alert, he got out of bed and put on his jockey shorts. "Where?"

"In the Garden District on a side street off St. Charles Avenue. She's still on the line. Want me to patch you through?"

"Yes." He grabbed his sweatpants off the bureau.

"Hello?" screeched a voice.

"Hi, Mrs. Reilly? I understand you recognized the woman in the sketch."

"Yes. I knew that girl was trouble the minute I laid eyes on her."

"What's her name?" he said, pulling on his sweatpants with his free hand.

"April West."

"Is she there now?"

"Well. She promised to drive me to Houston, but last night she went out and didn't come back. Why are you looking for her? What did she do? "

Man, the woman's voice like a buzz saw. "I'm coming there now. What's the address?"

Mrs. Reilly told him. Then she said, "Someone already called here looking for her, woke me up in the middle of the night."

"Who was it?"

"I don't know, I was half asleep. It was the middle of the night. I don't remember his name. He was calling from Washington."

Hammer, he thought. Hammer's after her, too.

"Her suitcase is still in her room," screeched the voice. "After that man called, I went upstairs and looked. She wasn't there, so I bolted the front door to make sure she couldn't sneak in. I was afraid she'd leave without me. But then I saw that sketch this morning--"

"Thanks, Mrs. Reilly. This is a big help. I'll be there as soon as I can."

He strapped the holster with his SIG to his belt, pulled on a T-shirt and hit his speed-dial. Two rings and Kenyon Miller answered.

"Kenyon, we got a tip from the sketch. Her name is April West and she's staying at Parades-A-Plenty, a B&B near St. Charles Avenue. I'm on my way. Meet me there as soon as you can."

"Okay," Miller said, "but traffic's gonna be a bear."

He ran downstairs and got in his car, but traffic was indeed a bear, every intersection gridlocked. He dug the magnetized light out of his glove box, set it to flash and jammed it on the roof. It didn't help much, every intersection gridlocked. Cursing the traffic, he drummed his fingers on the wheel.

Natalie, aka April West, wasn't at Parades-A-Plenty now, but Mrs. Reilly seemed to think she'd be back for her suitcase. When she showed up to get it, he intended to be there. Adrenaline jazzed his heartbeat.

At last he was finally going to meet Natalie Brixton face-to-face.

Slowed by her spike-heels, she cursed herself for not bringing her Nikes. The air was thick with humidity and she was sweating when she reached the intersection on Carrolton where the trolley line began. A trolley had just arrived with a full load of passengers. The doors opened and people swarmed out of the trolley. When the car was empty, the trolley would reverse direction, go down Carrolton toward the river and turn east onto St. Charles Avenue.

She ran across the street, fished a dollar bill and a quarter out of her wallet and got in line. But it took forever for people to leave the trolley, more than forever for the driver to ready the car for its return trip down Carrolton.

When the driver allowed passengers to board, she claimed a seat by the door facing forward. Only then she allow herself to think about Chip. Despite her panic when he found the gun and held her hostage, she had outsmarted him. BoBo had died before she could punish him for killing Mom, but now his favorite son was dead. At long last, she had fulfilled her mission. But instead of feeling joyful and triumphant, she felt numb.

How could she have been so naïve? Why would Chip denounce his father? Chip was just like him, a wealthy man who treated women badly. Like his father, Chip had the same callous disregard for women. Because her mother failed to satisfy him, BoBo had murdered her in cold blood. Even after hearing Peterson tell her that BoBo had confessed to killing a woman at the hotel on Royal Street, Chip wouldn't admit that his father was a murderer.

Arnold told you what you wanted to hear so you wouldn't shoot him.

Sick with disappointment, she glanced out the window as the trolley trundled past Loyola University and stopped at a traffic light. When the light changed, a westbound trolley passed them, full of passengers, some standing in the aisle. Beyond it, the two-lane westbound street was also jammed, cars and trucks and SUVs inching along, bumper-to-bumper.

As the trolley continued past Tulane her thoughts returned to Chip. And BoBo. And Mom. Like a Samurai soldier, she had exacted her revenge. She had killed BoBo's only son. BoBo's Go-Go Bars would never again be run by anyone whose name was Beaubien. Unlike BoBo, Chip had fathered two daughters who had no interest in the business. Her victory was complete.

So why did she feel so empty inside?

Realizing she had to get off at the next intersection, she pulled the electronic cord to signal the driver. She couldn't think about Chip now. She had to focus on ditching Mrs. Reilly and getting out of town. No easy task now that a mandatory evacuation was in effect.

She checked her watch and gasped. 5:50. Ten minutes from now the clerk at the Dixie Motel would find Chip's body. Slowed by her spike heels, she set out for Parades-A-Plenty. Sullen gray clouds filled the sky, rain spattered the sidewalk, and gusty wind blew hot humid air in her face.

She pushed through the wrought-iron gate outside Parades-A-Plenty and went to the door. But when she tried to open it with her key, she couldn't. Panic hit her in waves. Had Mrs. Reilly locked up and left? Her diary was in her suitcase and her laptop was on the bed. She couldn't leave without them.

She peered through the window in the door. Banshee wasn't behind the reception desk, but the door beside it was ajar. She rapped on the glass. No movement inside. She rapped again, harder this time. After a moment, Mrs. Reilly waddled into the foyer, saw her and frowned.

Her galloping heart slowed, but she wasn't home free yet. She had to go up to her room, grab her suitcase and laptop and leave New Orleans. Without Banshee. Judging by the woman's irate expression as she opened the door, that might be difficult.

"Where have you been?" she shrieked. "You were gone all night!"

"I'm sorry. I met some friends. Are you ready to go to Houston?" She pushed her way into the foyer and stopped in front of the reception desk.

"I thought you had an interview."

"It was cancelled. I just need to grab my suitcase and we can go."

"I'm not going to Houston with you. I saw your picture on TV."

Her breath caught in her throat and icy prickles danced down her spine.

Were the police on their way? Panic-stricken, she said, "Mrs. Reilly, we made a deal. I'm driving you to Houston, like I promised."

Planting her hands on her ample hips, Mrs. Reilly glared at her. "No, you're not. I called the police. They're looking for you." Shifting her gaze, Banshee squawked, "Here they are now!"

She whirled and her heart almost stopped. Renzi was coming through the front gate. Mrs. Reilly regarded her with a triumphant smile. She wanted to kill the woman. It would be easy enough. The gun was in her tote.

But she'd killed too many people already. She made a knuckle fist with two fingers and rammed it into the pressure point between her bottom lip and chin. Mrs. Reilly's mouth gaped open, her eyes rolled up and she collapsed on the floor with a heavy thud.

Her mind was racing. What to do? Her laptop was in her room and so was her diary, locked in her suitcase. But her room was on the third floor. She looked through the window in the door. Renzi was almost to the stairs!

She plunged through the door into Banshee's kitchen, hyper alert, eyes darting everywhere. A TV set on the counter. A half-eaten piece of cake on the table. She ran down a hall past a bathroom and lunged into a bedroom. A bed with rumpled sheets. A maple bureau. Beside the bureau, a wooden door with a window in the top half opened onto a porch.

She ripped off her spike heels, put them in her tote and flung open the door. Pushed through a screen door onto the porch and ran faster than she'd ever run in her life. Behind her, she heard the screen door slam shut.

Damn! What if Renzi heard it?

Thankful that she had planned an escape route, she slung her tote over her shoulder and loped through soggy grass to the wrought-iron fence. The rain-slicked metal was slippery, but she managed to haul herself over the top. She dropped to the grass on the other side and raced through the yard toward the street that paralleled St. Charles Avenue.

Her car was in the next block. If she could get to it, she could escape.

If Renzi didn't catch her first.

Her bare feet slammed the pavement, her mind whirling. Banshee had told Renzi where she was. He must have a police radio. For all she knew, dozens of cops might be swarming the neighborhood.

Renzi could drive her into a dragnet and catch her.

She reached in her tote and pulled out the .38 Special.

CHAPTER 34

Frank peered through the window in the door. On his way up the walk to Parades-A-Plenty, he thought he'd seen someone inside, but no one was visible now. He took out his SIG and stepped inside. "Mrs. Reilly?"

Somewhere in the house, he heard a door slam.

"Mrs. Reilly! Frank Renzi, New Orleans Police. Where are you?"

Then he saw the hand. It belonged to a hefty gray-haired woman sprawled on the floor behind the reception desk. Mrs. Reilly, he presumed. He pressed a finger to the crook of her jaw and felt a strong pulse. The woman had no obvious injuries, no gunshot wound, no sign of blood, no bruises. Was it a heart attack? A fainting spell?

Or had Natalie come back and knocked Mrs. Reilly out?

Recalling the slamming door, he burst through a door into an empty kitchen. To his right was a hallway. With his SIG at the ready he advanced down the hall to a bathroom. One glance told him it was empty. He continued down the hall to a bedroom. Beside a tall chest of drawers, a wooden door was open. His neck prickled.

He pushed through the screen door onto a porch and saw a long-legged figure loping down the sidewalk beyond a wrought iron fence. Natalie! He made a quick decision. Mrs. Reilly needed medical attention, but he wasn't equipped to help her, and Miller would be here soon.

He holstered the SIG, ran across the rain-soaked yard, climbed the fence and dropped to the other side. Driven by wind gusts, rain pelted his face. He took out the SIG and ran after Natalie. She didn't have much of a head start.

Goddamn it, this time he was going to catch her.

He ran faster, his feet slamming the pavement. At the corner, he saw a flash of motion off to his right and ran that way. And there she was, thirty yards away, standing by the driver's door of a metallic-brown Ford Focus.

She met his gaze, her eyes fearful. Then she whirled and ran.

He ran after her, saw her duck left into an alley. But when he reached the alley, she had disappeared. He held his breath and listened.

No feet pounding the pavement. No sign of Natalie. Gripping his SIG, he advanced down the alley to the side entrance of a Tex-Mex restaurant. The door was shut, the window boarded up with sheets of plywood. Same thing with the store on the other side of the alley.

He dug out his cell, called Dispatch and told them to send an ambulance to Parades-A-Plenty to help an injured woman. He reeled off the address and said, "The woman that hurt her escaped, but she's on foot and I'm in pursuit. Get some squads over here to cordon off the streets."

"Frank," said the dispatcher, "be serious. Every squad I got is pulling traffic duty. We got gridlocked intersections all over town."

———

In a recessed doorway near the far end of the alley, she pressed her back against the door, hyper alert, her sweaty hands gripping the .38 Special. She heard footsteps approach. Renzi. If he found her, she would have to shoot. Bile rose in her throat. She didn't want to shoot him. She had hurt too many people already. She held her breath, alert for any telltale sound.

Mercifully, she heard nothing. Had Renzi given up?

Then she heard soft footsteps. Of course. Renzi wouldn't quit. He was a hunter and she was his prey. Her eyes filled with tears. How could it end this way? She had completed her mission. Chip was dead. Why were the ancestor spirits putting more obstacles in her path?

Resolve stiffened her backbone. She would not be captured, would not sit in some horrible jail cell to be put on trial for killing the man whose father had murdered her mother. Her hands tightened around the gun.

More footsteps. She bit her lip to keep from screaming the words in her mind: *Please don't come any closer. I don't want to shoot you . . .*

"Natalie! Throw the gun on the ground and come out with your hands behind your head!"

The air left her lungs in a whoosh. How did he know it was her?

Her heart was a machine gun inside her chest, rat-a-tat-tat-tat . . .

She sprang into the alley. Saw Renzi, twenty yards away, his hands clamped around a gun. His head jerked up when he saw her. She gritted her teeth, aimed for his legs and pulled the trigger, three quick shots.

He clutched his leg and fell to the ground. His weapon skittered away.

In the distance she heard car horns honking, but no sirens. Yet.

She looked at Renzi. He wasn't moving, one arm flung out.

Her throat tightened and her eyes misted with tears. She turned and ran.

At the end of the alley, she ripped off her auburn wig, dropped it in a dumpster and shoved the gun into her tote. She burst out of the alley and ran toward St. Charles Avenue. Her lungs burned, her legs felt like lead, and the soles of her feet hurt from pounding the gritty rain-slicked pavement.

When she reached St. Charles, a westbound trolley was coming down the tracks two blocks away. She ripped the hairpins from her French twist, let her long dark hair fall to her shoulders and jogged across the street to the neutral ground. Two lanes of cars on the westbound side were inching forward, bumper-to-bumper. Dodging between them, she reached the opposite sidewalk, panting and out of breath. Only then did she dare turn and look.

No sign of Renzi. Was he badly hurt? She had deliberately aimed for his legs. Not a kill shot. He'd dropped his gun, but he probably had a cell phone or a police radio. He was probably calling for help right now.

She took her shoes out of the tote, swiped the grit off her bare feet and shoved them into the shoes. Now the trolley was only a half block away. She waved her arms, signaling the driver to stop.

Jammed with passengers, the trolley didn't slow down.

Desperate, she stepped onto the tracks. The trolley bell changed a warning. *Ding, ding, ding.*

She waved her arms and shouted, "Please, stop."

Through the open windows, she heard passengers chanting, "Let her on. Let her on."

The trolley rumbled to a stop and the door opened. "The car's full," the driver said, scowling at her. "I can't take no more passengers."

"Let-'er-on, let-'er on," chanted the passengers.

She sprang up the steps and fumbled for her change purse.

"Forget the fare, lady. Get back of the white line so's I can get moving."

She pushed into the car and squeezed between two older black women.

As the trolley lurched forward, one of them smiled at her. "You lucky, hon. That driver wasn't gonna stop for you, no way no how, but we made him."

"Thank you," she said. "You saved my life." A true statement if ever there was one. If Renzi had called more cops to help look for her, they weren't likely to spot her in this crowded trolley car.

"You look like you all tuckered out," said the woman. "You headed out of town?"

"Yes. I'm meeting my boyfriend so we can drive to Houston."

"That's where I'm headed. Gonna take forever with this traffic."

She turned away to avoid further conversation. Her legs were shaking and the soles of her feet burned. But Renzi hadn't caught her. That was the important thing.

Other than stopping for traffic lights along St. Charles, the trolley made no more stops, trundling along beside two lanes of stalled cars headed west. By the time they rounded the curve at the end of St. Charles and continued up Carrolton Avenue, her heartbeat had almost returned to normal.

But her mind was churning. Her original plan had been to escape New Orleans in the Ford Focus, but that was no longer an option. Not only that,

Renzi knew she was here, had seen her flee Parades-A-Plenty. She checked her watch: 6:16. By now the clerk would have found Chip in Room 44 and she'd just shot an NOPD detective.

She had to get out of town fast. She also had to ditch the gun.

If they caught her with the gun, it was all over.

———

Cursing the traffic jams that had delayed him, Clint Hammer pulled his rental car to the curb and checked his Movado Swiss chronograph: 6:43. Christ, it had taken him an hour to drive the three miles from his hotel to Parades-A-Plenty, honking his horn all the way. Was everyone in New Orleans an idiot? It sure as hell seemed like it, drivers grid locking every intersection.

If he was running NOPD, he'd order every cop to issue traffic citations to those fucking idiots.

He squinted at the three story Victorian. Was this Parades-A-Plenty? There was no sign, and the rain was so heavy he couldn't see the numbers. He got out of his car, and a thousand needles of wind-driven rain slashed his face. He approached the wrought-iron gate and stopped, unable to believe his eyes.

Crime-scene tape was strung across the gate. What the fuck was this?

Sheets of rain drenched him, soaking his business suit. He hadn't thought to bring his rain gear. He'd been too intent on catching the bitch that killed Oliver. The wind was blowing harder now, gusting enough to make the limbs on two huge live oak trees in the yard whip back and forth.

The three-story Victorian was as dark as the leaden sky, not a single light showing inside. Just like the creepy Bates Motel in *Psycho*. He'd seen the movie with his wife years ago when it first came out. The shower scene had scared the bat piss out of his wife. He thought it was funny and laughed like hell.

But this no laughing matter. According to Jason, the gook-bitch that shot Oliver was staying here at Parades-A-Plenty. Hell, Jason had talked to the owner a few hours ago, and the woman had confirmed this.

And now she was gone. Sonofabitch! He should have followed his instincts, should have pounced on the bitch when Jason called. This was the mother of all fuckups. What the hell was the crime-scene tape for?

NOPD crime-scene tape. A hot poker of rage stabbed his gut.

Maybe that fucking NOPD detective found out April West was here and captured her. The thought made his blood boil.

He wanted that bitch all to himself.

He'd better go see Vobitch and find out where she was.

260

CHAPTER 35

When the trolley stopped at the end of the line, she was the first one off, relieved that no cops had stopped them. Without breaking stride, she zigzagged between two lanes of cars halted by a traffic light and stood on the neutral ground, eyeing the gas station on the corner across the street. A dozen people stood at the pumps, gassing up cars, mini-vans and SUVs, shielded from the rain by a bright orange canopy. Beyond the pumps was a large convenience store. A sixteen wheeler was parked alongside the building.

Rain pelted her, soaking her to the skin, but that was the least of her problems. She had to leave town fast, and she had no car. The cops would be looking for her at the bus and train stations. She doubted any planes were flying out of the airport. The last flights had probably departed hours ago.

The whoop of approaching sirens startled her. An NOPD squad car with flashing lights pulled into the gas station and slewed to a stop. Two officers in uniform got out. Tension invaded her gut. Were they looking for her?

Maybe not. The intersection was gridlocked, drivers honking their horns and screaming at other drivers. The cops positioned themselves on opposite corners of the intersection and began directing traffic. To avoid them, she walked twenty yards to her left and dodged between traffic-snarled cars to cross the street. The best way to get out of town might be to hitch a ride.

The sixteen wheeler was one possibility. The truck driver would probably be alone. And possibly lonely. If she played her cards right, maybe she could keep him company. But she had to do it fast. Any minute now those cops might get in the cruiser and hear an urgent bulletin about a woman wanted for shooting a cop.

When Renzi chased her, she'd been wearing her auburn wig. Now long dark hair hung below her shoulders, but she was still wearing her clingy teal top, slim black skirt and spike-heeled shoes. She took off the shoes and stuffed them in her tote. Skirting the bright orange canopy above the gas pumps, she hurried to the convenience store.

As she reached the door a young clerk came out with a hand-lettered sign that said NO GAS and trotted to the cars in line for the gas pumps.

"No more gas," he yelled, waving the sign. "The tanks are empty."

Several drivers yelled curses at him. One cop heard the commotion and looked over. She plunged into the store and joined several customers grabbing whatever was left on the nearly-bare shelves. She went to the cooler in back and took out the last cold drink: a container of raspberry-flavored ice tea. Not what she wanted, but she was dying of thirst, her mouth dry as cotton.

She studied the other customers. Which one was driving the truck?

Not the teenager in the Saints T-shirt. Not the two women. Not the tall man in the pressed chinos and spiffy brown loafers. That left the man with the reddish-brown ponytail and the full beard, the one in faded blue jeans and a Rolling Stones T-shirt, holding a box of Ritz crackers. She watched him take the last liter of Coca-Cola off a shelf and head for the checkout counter.

She followed, but as she got in line behind him, one of the NOPD cops entered the store and glanced around as if he were looking for someone.

Her heart fluttered, beating her chest like a bald eagle in a trap.

The .38 Special was still her tote. If the cop questioned her, she was dead.

She turned away to hide her face, pretended to look at the packages of chewing gum below the counter while the man in the Rolling Stones T-shirt paid for his purchases. As he turned to leave she contrived to bump into him and said, "Oops, sorry. Didn't mean to slow you down."

He turned, stone-faced, then did a fast double take, eying her clingy teal blouse. "Nothin slows me down, sweetheart," he said with a grin.

"Me neither," she said, keenly aware of the cop who was now approaching the checkout line. She set two bills and her bottle of raspberry ice tea on the counter. Saw the cop get in line behind the kid in the Saints T-shirt.

She could feel the cop's eyes on her, evaluating her, a barefoot woman in a teal blouse and a short black skirt. Her stomach revolted, spewing acid bile into her throat. She swallowed hard, felt sweat form on her forehead.

When the clerk gave her the change, she hurried to the door.

The truck driver held it open for her. "Where y'all headed, sweetheart?"

Through sheer effort of will, she managed a smile and stepped out the door. "Headed north across the lake."

"Me too." As they walked along the storefront he looked at her bare feet. "What happened? You lose your shoes?"

"One heel broke off." With a rueful shrug, she said, "Just what I needed."

Seemingly oblivious to the rain, he grinned. "Ain't that always the way? One damn thing after another. Where's your car?"

She gestured vaguely toward the street, then brushed rain off her face. "Over there, but my tank's empty and this place is out of gas."

"How far north you going? I'm headed that way." He gestured at the eighteen-wheeler.

"You got enough gas to get to Memphis?"

"You bet, sweetheart. Want to ride with me?"

"That would be fantastic! I'd be happy to pay you for your trouble."

"Won't be no trouble, sweetheart. I'll be glad for the company."

The look in his hazel eyes told her he'd like more than the company, but she'd cross that bridge when she came to it. He took her arm, guided her around a huge puddle and they hurried to his rig. He opened the passenger door and beamed her a big smile, exposing yellow nicotine-stained teeth.

"Welcome to my home away from home. I'm Paul Foster."

"Thanks, Paul. Nice to meet you. I'm Carla Jones." Easing into seduction mode. If she played her cards right, maybe she could get him to drive her to St. Louis. The St. Louis airport serviced international flights.

Perfect. Get out of town and then get out of the country.

———

While the harried Eighth District desk officer, his face a study in misery, talked to Vobitch, Hammer tried to contain his fury. The station was bedlam, the phones ringing off the hook. He eyed the clock on the wall behind the desk. Now it was 7:23. The drive from Parades-A-Plenty, another exercise in frustration because of the snarled traffic, had taken him forty-five minutes.

"He'll see you in his office," said the desk officer. "Through that door--"

"I know where it is. I had a meeting with Lieutenant Vobitch a couple of weeks ago."

An extremely unpleasant meeting, but he saw no reason to mention this to some lowly cop. He opened a door with frosted glass on the upper half and marched down a dreary hall that stank of burnt coffee. A sign on one door said: HOMICIDE. Was Renzi in there? He'd love to go in and bust his balls, but screw that. If you want information, start at the top.

When he got to Vobitch's office, he paused, gathering his outrage. Then, without knocking, he opened the door and went in. Seated at his desk, Vobitch gazed at him, his eyes venomous. The prick didn't invite him to sit down, just said in a surly tone, "What are you doing in New Orleans, Hammer?"

"Did you get her?"

A muscle jumped in Vobitch's jaw. "Get who?"

An ice pick of rage pierced his gut. He wanted to slam his fist into the Jew-bastard's face. With a supreme effort, he maintained control. "You've got a traffic control problem, Lieutenant. It took me forty-five minutes to drive two miles. Why is there crime scene tape on the gate to Parades-A-Plenty?"

Vobitch stared at him for a moment, deadpan, then smiled. "Because a crime was committed there."

Rage exploded inside him like a cluster bomb, destroying any shred of control. "Stop dicking me around, Lieutenant. Tell me what happened. Did you get her?"

"Why don't you tell me who you're talking about? Then maybe we could have a civilized conversation."

"April West, also known as Robin Adair, the bitch who murdered Oliver James. *That's* who. I know she stayed at Parades-A-Plenty last night, but when I went there just now, there was NOPD crime scene tape across the gate and the place was locked up. Did you get her?"

"No." Vobitch gazed at him, expressionless.

"You said it's a crime scene. What happened?"

"The woman we believe to be the prime suspect in two recent murders, April West if you want to call her that, disabled the owner and escaped. We put out an APB, but . . ." Vobitch gave him an evil smile. "In case you haven't noticed, we got a major fucking hurricane headed our way and as you so kindly pointed out a moment ago, we got major traffic tie-ups, which means every cop on the force is directing traffic so people can get out of town."

"So you lost her," Hammer sneered. "Where's hot-shot Detective Renzi?"

Vobitch didn't answer, his face impassive, but something flickered in his eyes. What was it? Anger? Fear? Grief? But why waste time on that? The bitch that killed Oliver was on the loose and he had to find her. "Did you post some officers at the bus and train stations?"

"How did you know she was staying at Parades-A-Plenty?"

"My assistant used some special software we've developed to find . . . certain people." He'd almost said *terrorists* but he didn't want Vobitch to call the Agency and tell anyone he'd used face-recognition software to find a common criminal. "Our software has algorithms that can compare a photograph to several million faces in mere seconds. We used the photograph on Robin Adair's New Hampshire DL."

"How'd you know she was using the April West ID?"

"I'm not at liberty to talk about that. Certain aspects of our research must, of necessity, remain confidential. Did you get her car?"

Vobitch nodded slowly. "Yup."

"What else did you get? Anything?"

The bastard smiled, his eyes wide with innocence. "I'm not at liberty to talk about that. This is an active criminal investigation."

"Fuck you! You can't withhold important information! This woman is a cold-blooded killer. We need to share our intel and find her!"

"Well, at the moment I don't have any *intel* to give you." Another evil smile. "Anything else I can do for you? We got a nice break room down the hall, might be some coffee left in the pot."

Hammer ground his teeth, molar against molar, felt excruciating pain in his jaw. A warning voice in his mind said: *Get out of here before you do something you might regret.* Ignoring the terrible pain in his jaw, he forced himself to say in a calm voice, "I'll be in touch, Lieutenant."

He ran down the hall, pulling out his cell as he went. In the lobby the phones were still ringing and the desk officer looked even more harried. He went outside and stood under the portico above the steps. Torrents of rain

264

sluiced off the portico roof, spilling down the steps. Beyond the sidewalk rainwater flowed like a river in the gutter. He speed-dialed Jason's number.

These NOPD idiots had no clue how to catch criminals, but he did. When he found the bitch that killed Oliver, she was going to die and he'd take his time doing it. Her death would be long and slow and painful.

―――――

"Thank God you're okay, Frank. I was frantic when Kenyon called and said you'd been shot. But the doctor says you're going to be fine."

Even though she had a worried look on her face, he was happy to see Kelly standing beside his bed. He tried to smile but couldn't. He felt woozy and nauseous. Any minute now he was going to throw up.

"Don't try to talk," she said. "You just got out of surgery and I know what that's like. Kenyon's here, too."

"Man, I thought you were a goner," Miller said, joining her by the bed.

"What happened?" He remembered chasing Natalie into an alley. After that everything was fuzzy. He remembered hearing shots. Did he shoot her?

"You called me on your cell," Miller said. "When I got there, you were bleeding like crazy, about to go into shock."

He flexed his left leg. That one worked okay, but his right leg felt weird. "Jesus, what'd they do? I can't feel my right leg."

"Gunshot wound through and through," Miller said. "That's why they did the surgery, hadda clean out the crap so it wouldn't get infected. You won't be running a marathon anytime soon, but you're a tough sonofabitch, Frank. Couple weeks and you'll be fine."

"What about Natalie? Did you get her?" Every time he tried to talk waves of nausea hit him.

"Stop worrying," Kelly said. "We'll get her."

"Doc said the slug didn't hit the bone," Miller said. "That's the good news. But the shock waves fucked up one of the nerves in your leg."

"The peroneal nerve," Kelly said. "That's why you can't feel your leg. The doctor said that will go away in a few days. Could have been worse. Good thing Kenyon got there when he did. You lost a lot of blood."

"Took one look," Miller said, "got you an ambulance."

He tried to speak, couldn't, cleared his throat and whispered, "Thanks."

Miller waved a hand. "Nothing to it. Relax and I'll tell you the rest, okay?"

He nodded. That made him feel worse, nausea rising in his gut.

"When you called me you were mumbling about Natalie, so I figure she shot you, right?"

He tried to remember. Drew a blank. "I guess."

"Mrs. Reilly's here too. They're keeping her overnight to make sure her heart doesn't act up." Seeing his puzzled expression, Miller said, "The woman that runs Parades-A-Plenty?"

Again he nodded. More nausea. Man, he wanted to go to sleep. But not until he found out what happened with Natalie, who had shot him apparently, though he didn't remember it.

"I found a Ford Focus with a New York plate registered to April West," Miller said, "had it towed to the police garage. Nothing important inside, but we dusted it for prints, should be able to match 'em to the ones in Boston. But here's the best part. Mrs. Reilly gave me the keys to April West's room." Miller grinned. "Man, that woman's got the most god-awful voice I've ever heard."

That he remembered. He'd only talked to her on the phone, but who could forget a voice like that?

"Found a suitcase and a laptop in the room," Miller said, "Also found a New York Yankees T-shirt and a pair of jeans hanging in her closet. Strange."

The outfit she had on at Cafe Beignet. Why was she there, he wondered. She had to be watching the news, had to know he was primary on the Peterson and Conroy murders. Was she flirting with fate? Did she want to be caught? But his head was too fuzzy to figure it out.

"Crime lab techs gonna be pissed at me for messing with a crime scene." Miller gave him a droll smile. "But my Renegade Renzi partner says sometimes you gotta break rules to catch the criminals."

And stop Natalie before she kills someone else, Frank thought.

"After they put Mrs. Reilly into an ambulance," Miller said, "I locked up Parades-A-Plenty, put crime scene tape across gate and took the suitcase and the laptop to Vobitch."

A nurse poked her head in the room and said, "Time's up folks. The patient needs to rest."

He grabbed Miller's arm, "She killed Peterson and Conroy. She came back for a reason. I think she's got another target. We need to figure out who."

Miller glanced at Kelly, "Yeah, well, unfortunately we already know who. Desk clerk at one of the no-tell motels on Airline Drive found a dead man in one of his rooms this morning. One shot to the head."

He closed his eyes. Dammit to hell. Score another one for Natalie.

"You got a name?"

"Yeah. Chip Beaubien, the bigshot that runs the GoGo Bars. You believe it? Another VIP murder and we're in the middle of a hurricane evacuation."

It hit him like a hand grenade. Chip Beaubien, the son of BoBo Beaubien, Jane Fontenot's prime suspect in the Jeanette Brixton murder in 1988.

Then the room started whirling like it did after you drank too much booze, the whirlybirds before you puked.

He pulled Miller closer and whispered, "Natalie killed him. We've got to catch her before she gets out of town."

CHAPTER 36

Wednesday, 20 August   Memphis, Tennessee

She woke with a start, momentarily unsure where she was. Then, feeling the body heat beside her, she remembered. She was in a motel room with Paul. Oddly, the warmth of his body made her feel safe. A nightmare had woken her: Chip's hate-filled eyes, the hole in his forehead leaking bright red blood, hideous images that left her sickened and sweaty.

On the drive from New Orleans to Memphis yesterday she'd had no time to think. But last night, lying in the darkness, hearing Paul's even breathing, she had sunk into a dark pit of despair. She had achieved her goal, but in the process she had become a monster. She'd killed Tex Conroy and Oliver James, men whose only mistake was being in the wrong place at the wrong time. She felt no remorse for killing Peterson or Chip. Chip's father had murdered her mother, and Peterson had helped him escape.

But killing them didn't bring Mom back.

She pictured Renzi outside Parades-A-Plenty, his eyes fixed on hers as she stood by her car. Panic-stricken, gripping her weapon, she almost shot him. But something stopped her. And later, hiding in the alley, knowing she would rather die than be captured, she had been sick with fear.

If she hadn't shot him, would he have shot her? Unwilling to kill him, she had purposely aimed for his leg. But one thing was certain.

If Renzi was alive, he was still hunting for her.

She felt Paul stir beside her. To her surprise, he'd been an enjoyable companion during their traffic-snarled, eight-hour drive to Memphis. He loved listening to music when he was driving cross-country. He had five Rolling Stones CDs, three by The Who, one by Bon Jovi. When she said she loved Joan Jett, he'd laughed and reached over to stroke her hair.

"Sit back and relax, Carla, this is gonna be a fun ride."

By the time he pulled the eighteen-wheeler into a truck stop with a motel outside Memphis, she had made her decision. Paul had helped her escape from New Orleans. She owed him her life. Having sex with strange men was nothing new. Paul might be a truck driver, but he had more class than Arnold and BoBo and Chip, rich men with a sense of entitlement who used women as playthings and discarded them. Or killed them. Last night when they had sex Paul tried his best to please her. But her mind filled with revolting memories, worse than a horror movie: her abject terror when Chip aimed the gun at her, the disgust she'd felt when his eyes devoured her naked body. After a while, to Paul's delight, she had faked an orgasm.

Now she heard him yawn. Felt his hand touch her thigh. When she traced a finger down his hairy chest, he grabbed her hand and kissed it.

"Your boyfriend in St. Louis gonna be mad?"

"Who says he has to know?"

Gazing at her with sad eyes, Paul said, "You real close to him?"

She could see where this was heading. No place good. Paul was having the time of his life. She was running for her life and she wasn't safe yet.

She gave him a quick kiss. "We better get going. I promised to meet him in St. Louis today. I get the shower first, okay?"

"Okay." His sad eyes brightened. "Want company in the shower?"

Resigned to it, she said, "Why not?"

Once Paul got what he wanted, she would hurry him along so they could get on the road to St. Louis.

Any kind of luck she'd be on a plane by sundown.

————

12: 20 P.M.

Frank watched Kelly pop the caps on three beer bottles, one for herself, the others for Miller and Vobitch, seated at her kitchen table, noshing on chips and salsa. No beer for him. He was taking antibiotics and fucking pain meds that made his head woozy.

Worse, he was confined to a wheelchair, the crucial word being *confined*. Three hours out of the hospital and he was ready to explode. The doctor wanted to keep him another day, but he'd refused and signed himself out. Kelly didn't want him to stay at his second floor condo in a wheelchair, so she'd taken a personal day and drove him to her house. Vobitch and Miller were waiting for them, had plunked him in the chair and carried him inside.

Normally he loved being with Kelly, but he needed space, alone-time to think. Having Kelly wait on him was irritating too, but that wasn't the cause of his funk. Natalie had escaped. And he was in a fucking wheelchair.

Kelly distributed the beer bottles around the table. "You want something to drink, Frank? Ice tea? Ice coffee?"

"Yeah. I'll take a big glass of Glenfiddich over ice."

"The patient's getting feisty," Miller said. "Must be feeling better."

"Feisty?" he said. "Fuck feisty. I'm pissed."

"No more than me." Vobitch drank from his beer bottle and gestured at the slider to Kelly's deck. "Fucking Josephine."

Driven sideways by the howling wind, rain pelted the glass. For the second time in two months a hurricane was pummeling New Orleans. And for the second time in two months, Natalie Brixton had killed a man and escaped. He still didn't know why she'd killed Arnold Peterson, but he knew why she'd killed Chip Beaubien. Her twisted version of revenge. Chips' father was BoBo Beaubien, Jane Fontenot's prime suspect for the murder of Natalie's mother.

Kelly set a tall glass of ice water in front of him, no Glenfiddich, and took the chair beside Kenyon Miller.

"Did Gus Walker get anything from the laptop?" Frank said to Miller. Walker was their computer forensics tech.

"Not yet," Miller said. "He had a helluva time breaking the password to open it. He found some emails from Gabe Rojas. He's still working on the hard drive, and he wants to check her Internet browsing history, too."

"What about Rojas?" Vobitch said. "You think she might contact him?"

He drank some ice water. "He's in Pecos. If she's driving, that's a helluva hike from New Orleans. But let's contact the Pecos police and have them put a watch on Rojas."

"Good idea." Vobitch picked up the leather briefcase beside his chair and pulled out two journals, the kind you could buy most anywhere, marbled black-and-white fiberboard covers with lined paper inside. "Brought you a present, Frank. We found these in her suitcase."

He picked up the top one, opened it and read the first line, written in small neat handwriting: *One night Mom didn't come home.* The date on the entry made the hairs on his neck curl. *October 20, 1988.*

The date of Jeanette Brixton's murder.

This was Natalie's diary. An adrenaline rush jazzed his heartbeat.

Kelly opened the other journal. "Neat handwriting. Looks like a diary."

"Badabing." Vobitch looked at him. "I didn't have time to read much, but now that you're on the disabled roster, you can. Might get us some answers."

"Why don't you guys hit the road so I can get started." He wanted to read every word of Natalie's diary right now. But the diary wasn't going to tell him where she was now. Or where she was going.

A cell phone rang and everybody checked their handsets. It was Vobitch's cell, but when he answered, his face sagged in disgust. After a moment he said, "When I hear something, you'll be the first to know." Then he theatrically clapped a hand to his forehead. "Check the airports?"

For Natalie, Frank assumed. New Orleans had been spared a direct hit from Hurricane Josephine. The storm had veered east but was still dumping torrential rains on the city. So far there'd been no major flooding, the pumps working like crazy, the levees holding. The mayor had announced that no one would be allowed back into the city until noon on Saturday.

"Nothing's flying out of Birmingham or Nashville," Vobitch said to whoever was on the phone. "Houston's open. So is St. Louis and Chicago."

Abruptly, he ended the call and snarled, "Our favorite District Attorney, Roger Kiss-My-Ass Demaris."

Earlier Miller had taken him aside and told him Demaris had canceled his threat to take them off the case. After Chip Beaubien's body was found, Miller said, Vobitch had gotten into a screaming match with Demaris, had threatened to call a news conference and tell the reporters that Demaris was disrespecting the NOPD, taking Detective Frank Renzi off the Peterson case as he lay in a hospital after heroically chasing the killer.

"Christ," Vobitch said, slamming his palms on the table, "Demaris thinks we're miracle workers like the cops on TV. Wave a magic wand and find out if she flew out of any nearby airports. Like the TSA is gonna help us. Anybody got any brilliant ideas about where she's headed?"

"How do we know she got out of town?" Kelly said.

Miller turned to Kelly, amazed. "You think she's still here?"

"If she is," Vobitch snapped, "we'll get her. Every law enforcement agency in Louisiana is looking for her."

No we won't, Frank thought. She's gone. He pictured the dress he'd seen in her Nashua apartment, the fancy one with the Yves St. Laurent-Paris label, recalling what Gina had said: *They don't sell clothes over here with labels that say Paris.*

"How about Paris?" he said.

"Why Paris?" Kelly said.

Irritated, he snapped, "You got a better idea about where she's going?"

One look at the sea-green eyes he found so alluring told him she was pissed. He should have kept his mouth shut. But his calf was throbbing and he didn't want to take his pain meds and he didn't want to sit in a fucking wheelchair for a week, graduate to crutches and do his fucking PT and maybe start running again in six weeks. Not to mention the real kicker. Before he left the hospital, the doctor had given him a stern warning: "No strenuous activity for two weeks. That includes sexual activity."

Screw that. He'd let Kelly hop on top. He loved watching her face when they made love in that position. Or any position, for that matter. But the look on her face now foretold storm clouds ahead. If he didn't eat some crow, they might not be getting it on for a while.

Ending the uncomfortable silence, Vobitch said, "Even if we find her, I'm not convinced Demaris will charge her. We don't have shit for evidence."

"We got the security video on the Peterson hit," Miller said. "We got the ballistics report that says she killed Peterson and Conroy with the same gun."

"But we don't have the gun," Vobitch said. He took a yellow pencil out of his shirt pocket. "Boston PD ballistics report says the slug that killed Oliver James--" He swung his leonine head, eyeballing each of them in turn. "Presuming our friend Natalie killed him. Report says the slug didn't come from the gun she used down here."

"So she got another gun somewhere," Frank said. "She was living in New Hampshire. Gun laws there are pretty loose. We could check the gun shops."

"Christ, that'll take forever." Gripping the pencil in both fists, Vobitch snapped it in half. When they burst out laughing, Vobitch glowered at them.

"I'll call Hank," Frank said. "Maybe we can get Boston PD to check the New Hampshire gun shops."

"Fine," Vobitch said, unappeased, "but we need to build a case that'll fly with a jury. Everything we got is circumstantial. No witnesses. No weapon. No prints in Peterson's hotel room."

"Got even less with the Conroy hit," Miller said. "We assume she used his car to leave City Park after she shot him, but she wiped it clean, no prints, no way to tie her to Conroy. We never found his wallet, probably dumped that too. Bet you ten cases of Bud we won't find her prints in the room where she killed Beaubien either. And we still haven't found his car."

Vobitch's cell rang. He answered. After a moment, he said, "What's up?"

Frank watched anger and disgust ripple over his boss's face.

"We got nothing on this end either," Vobitch said, and after a pause, "Thanks for calling. Let us know if you find her." He slammed his cell down on the table. "Fucking prick."

"Hammer, right?" Frank said.

"Right. Calling to say he didn't find her with his ICU software or whatever the fuck it's called. Face recognition, my ass. Peek-a-boo, I see you."

"You think he'd tell us if he did?" Frank asked.

"I'm not holding my breath." Vobitch drained his bottle of Bud.

"Where did he use this super-duper software program?"

"New Orleans bus and train stations. Not the airport. No planes flew out of Louis Armstrong Airport yesterday or today, maybe not tomorrow even."

"What if she's got another fake ID?" Kelly said.

"That's almost guaranteed." Frank touched her hand and smiled at her. "Good thinking, though."

Ignoring him, Kelly picked up her beer bottle and drank some. She was still pissed. After Vobitch and Miller left, big showdown at the OK Corral.

Vobitch slammed his fist on the table. "Dammit, she killed three people in our jurisdiction. Peterson, Conroy, now Beaubien. If Hammer finds her first, we'll never get her. You know how the fucking CIA works. Ooops, she put up a fight and my gun went off, blah, blah, blah. We gotta find her!"

"Shitload of people left town yesterday," Miller said. "Maybe she hitched a ride with somebody."

"She tried to kill Frank," Kelly said. "Maybe she's still here. Maybe she's got another target."

Frank remained silent. He didn't believe she tried to kill him. For the past twenty-four hours, he'd replayed the scene in his mind more times than he could count. When he was lying in the alley without a weapon, bleeding and defenseless, she could have shot him again and killed him. But she didn't.

"If she had a passport with a new ID," Vobitch said, jotted notes with the stub of his broken pencil, "she could fly anywhere and we'd never know. I'm gonna ask the NOPD Superintendent to call his FBI connection, get the guy to station some FBI agents in the airports."

"She'd probably avoid the airports in Atlanta or Tampa," Miller said. "To get there, she'd have to drive through areas with heavy storm damage, take a chance on the airports being open. But St. Louis is a straight shot north from here. Kansas City's close too."

"She might try to fly out tonight," Frank said. "We need to grab her before she leaves the country. Hammer's probably way ahead of us. If he finds her first, he'll make her disappear and it won't be pretty."

"If she's traveling by car," Vobitch said, "she'd go for the nearest one. I'll tell the Super to ask his FBI crony to station agents at the airports in St. Louis and Kansas City pronto." He rose from his chair and said to Miller, "Let's get back to the station. Thanks for hosting the meeting, Kelly. Let me know if our friend gets too ornery. I'll come over and give him a knuckle sandwich." Vobitch gave him a look, but Frank saw a glint of amusement in his eyes.

Miller put on his rain poncho. "Thanks for the beer, Kelly. Behave yourself, Frank. No heavy lifting." And winked at him.

Kelly went to the door with them. After a minute she came back and looked at him, expressionless. "You didn't have to bite my head off, Frank."

"Sorry. I shouldn't have opened my big mouth, especially in front of Miller and Vobitch." Judging by the angry glint in her eye, that didn't come close to appeasing her.

"Come here," he said. "I've got something for you."

"What?" Flashing him a warning look, she came closer.

He pulled her close and kissed her lips, stroking her neck with his fingers. After some token resistance, she responded with her usual passion. His groin throbbed, an achy hot bulge in his pants. His leg might not be working, but his dick was ready to go.

When they came up for air, she said, "You're just pissed about being cooped up in a wheelchair."

"Even more pissed I can't take you to bed right now and bite your ass." He caressed her face. "You're safe for tonight, but after that all bets are off."

CHAPTER 37

St. Louis 4:15 P.M.

The sun was a fiery orange ball above the Gateway Arch when Paul drove his rig into the parking lot outside a Comfort Inn near the St. Louis airport. Eager to leave, she slung her tote over her shoulder. Before she got on a plane she had an important errand to do.

Paul gazed at her with his sad eyes. "Glad to make your acquaintance, Carla. We had a good time, didn't we? For a couple days at least."

She leaned over and kissed his cheek. "Yes, we did, Paul."

Before he could say anything more, she got out and strode to the hotel entrance without looking back. She hit the revolving door and did a slow circle around the lobby past the potted plants and several people on sofas reading magazines. When she got back to the entrance, the eighteen-wheeler was gone.

She rode an elevator to the fourth floor, stepped into a deserted corridor and walked down the hall to an alcove that held an ice maker and two vending machines. A large brown rubbish bin stood in the corner. She checked the hall. Seeing no one, she took the .38 Special out of her tote, went over every inch of it with a baby-wipe and shoved the gun to the bottom of the trash bin. On the way back to the elevator she saw no one. Excellent. No witnesses. She rode the elevator to the lobby, hurried out to the cabstand, got in the first cab and told the driver she needed to get to the airport fast.

Fifteen minutes later she entered the terminal. The departures area was a madhouse, grim-faced passengers towing luggage, fighting through the crowds. At an ATM she used her Laura Lin Hawthorn bank card to withdraw a substantial amount of cash. Then she asked the woman at an information kiosk if there was a FedEx drop inside the airport. The woman said there was and directed her to it.

Dodging a stream of harried passengers, she found the FedEx kiosk, took an envelope out of the dispenser and went to the nearest rest room.

Five women stood at the sinks, washing their hands or staring into the mirror to fix their hair or freshen their makeup. She went in a handicapped stall, set her foot on the toilet rim and balanced the FedEx envelope on her

273

thigh. With a felt-tipped pen, she addressed the envelope: *To Frank Renzi, c/o the Eighth District police station.* She didn't know the exact address, but the FedEx driver would. She paused, lost in thought, then took out a scrap of paper and printed a note: *Detective Renzi. I believe this recording will solve the murder of Jeanette Brixton on October 20, 1988.*

She took the tape recorder out of her tote, ejected the Peterson tape and slid the note and the tape into the FedEx envelope. She wanted to dump the tape recorder it, but not where anyone would see her, and she could hear two women outside her stall discussing their vacation plans. Using another baby wipe, she polished the recorder and pushed it into the metal container for sanitary napkin disposal. Someone would find it when they cleaned the rest room, but she'd be long gone by then.

She went back to the FedEx kiosk. At BoBo's funeral, people had praised him, saying he was a good man. That would soon change. With a grim sense of satisfaction, she slid the FedEx envelope into the outgoing slot. Soon the New Orleans police would know who murdered her mother. Soon everyone in New Orleans would know what a monster BoBo was.

His reputation would be forever sullied.

Hurrying now, she went to the ticket counters. Long lines of passengers zigzagged through a maze of ropes in front of four counters. She wanted to buy a ticket and fly out ASAP, but that might be difficult. Thanks to Hurricane Josephine, many flights had been cancelled or delayed, forcing passengers to rebook their flights. Only six people stood in the Delta Airlines line.

Then she saw the tall dark-haired man in a black suit standing near the Delta counter, his face set in a frown. He had an aura about him, a hunter's aura, and he was staring at her, pinning her like a butterfly on a display board.

The air left her lungs in a whoosh. Was he a cop? He wasn't in uniform, but detectives didn't wear uniforms. Feeling helpless and vulnerable, she went to a nearby drinking fountain, bent down and drank some water.

How could this happen now? She was so close to making her escape, certain she was safe now that she had escaped from New Orleans. And Renzi.

Her stomach heaved and bile spewed into her throat. Fearing she would vomit, she forced herself to swallow and considered the possibilities, none of them good. Maybe the New Orleans cops had asked other police departments to post plain-clothed detectives at the airports.

But the man in the suit didn't look like a cop. Was he an FBI agent? CIA?

Was he looking for April West, a woman with long dark hair, wearing a black skirt and teal-green top?

To kill the sour taste of bile she swished water around her mouth and tried to reassure herself. She wasn't wearing a black skirt and a teal-green top now. Last night after she and Paul ate dinner at a truck stop, she'd gone to the convenience store while he refueled his truck. She bought a pastel-blue T-shirt, navy sweatpants and a pair of white canvas shoes. She put on the sneakers and threw her spike-heeled shoes in a trashcan on her way to the truck. This morning, she'd stuffed her teal-green top and black skirt into a plastic bag. That bag was also in a trash barrel.

Now she had on the navy sweatpants and the pastel-blue T-shirt, but the hunter in the suit was watching her. She had to buy a plane ticket and get out. Gathered her courage, she dug her tinted Vera Wang glasses out of her tote, put them on and recited her motto. *Be who they want you to be.*

With a confident stride, she joined the line for the Delta ticket counter. Felt the hunter's eyes on her. Needles of fear pricked her gut as he approached her. "Hello, Miss," he said. "May I see some identification?"

The fear clawed its way into her throat. "Of course. May I ask why?"

His dark eyes bored into hers, menacing eyes that said: *Don't fuck with me.*

"We're doing extra security today. Can I see your ID?"

Her hands were sweaty, but she didn't dare wipe them on her skirt. She had to act like an innocent passenger trying to get on a plane. Thankful that she'd dumped her gun at the Comfort Inn, she took her wallet out of her tote and forced herself to smile. "Has there been some sort of terrorist threat?"

His eyes were lumps of coal, dark and intimidating. "Something like that."

She gave him her Laura Lin Hawthorn passport. He paged through it, noting the exit and entry stamps. At last he flipped back to the page with her photograph. He studied it, then looked at her face.

Was he looking at her eyes? The tinted glasses masked them somewhat, but not completely.

"Where are you headed, Laura?"

"Chicago."

"Can I see your drivers license?"

Her heart jolted into a runaway gallop like a terrified horse fleeing a fire. She clenched her leg muscles to stop them from trembling. "I don't have one. Chicago's got a great public transit system. I mostly get around on buses."

He studied her passport again. "Your passport was issued in Paris."

"Yes."

"But you're an American citizen."

"Yes. Mom was too. She was born in Paris. We lived there for a while when I was little." *Be who they want you to be. Make up a story and bamboozle them.*

His face remained stony. "And you're flying to Chicago?"

"Yes."

He stared at her. "Not Paris?"

They knew she'd lived in Paris, and that's where they expected her to go.

"Nope. Chicago. It's a fun town. Have you been there?"

Annoyance flashed in his eyes. He thrust the passport at her. "Have a good flight."

He turned and resumed his position near the counter and kept watching her. Her heart jumped in her chest like an acrobat on a trampoline. Using her

TKD focus, she maintained a neutral expression, just another passenger waiting to buy a ticket. As the line to the ticket counter shuffled forward, she thought about the diary she had kept for the past twenty years.

Thanks to the diary, the cops were hot on her trail. She had intended to send it to Gabe. He was the only one who cared about her. They were soul mates, outsiders navigating the perils of Pecos High School. She'd never told him about her plan to avenge her mother's murder, but he might have guessed. Especially after Randy. Gabe had gotten her the gun, no questions asked.

But now Renzi had the diary.

If only she'd mailed it to Gabe when she had the chance. Not to his house--she didn't want to cause trouble with his wife--to his computer game business in Odessa. But for the past twenty years she had intended to do many things and quite a few of them didn't work out.

Four long minutes later she reached the ticket counter.

The hunter was still watching her.

"Hi," she said, smiling at the ticket agent. "I'd like to book a seat on the next flight to Chicago."

"Okay," said the woman, tapping her computer keyboard. "I'll see what's available. Round-trip?"

"No, one-way. Actually, I'm hoping to fly to Paris from Chicago. Is that possible?"

"I'll do my best. Do you have your passport?"

"Yes," she said, and handed it over.

"Thanks. One-way to Chicago connecting to Paris. Is that one-way, also?"

"Yes," she said. Her neck prickled. The predator was still watching her.

Could he read lips?

Five minutes later she left the Delta ticket counter with a one-way ticket to Paris via Midway Airport in Chicago. It cost more than $1,200 dollars and the clerk had said it would be a tight connection, but she didn't care about the expense and she'd worry about the tight connection when she got to Midway.

Her most important objective now was to get away from the predator.

Forcing herself not to look at him, she headed for her departure gate. Her flight left in forty minutes. But there was a long line at the security checkpoint. Another delay. As the line of passengers inched forward with their luggage she put the hunter out of her mind. Too bad she couldn't use her April West passport. April in Paris. A great song.

But after she killed Chip, her escape plan had fallen apart.

And someone had set up a dragnet.

Judging by the hunter's questions, it was clear that he believed she would try to leave the country and fly to Paris. Thanks to her diary.

By now, Renzi had probably read every entry twice.

As the line shuffled forward, she looked behind her, fearing the predator might appear. What if he checked the name on her passport?

Ten endless minutes later, using her Laura Lin Hawthorn passport, she passed through security and hurried toward her gate. Only after she boarded her flight and the plane was rocketing down the runway would she feel safe.

She dodged around two slow-moving passengers and spotted her gate. She was almost certain the predator at the ticket counter wasn't a cop. Maybe Renzi had clout with the FBI. Maybe he'd convinced them to look for her at the airports that were closest to New Orleans. Like St. Louis.

Another thought set her teeth on edge. In the newspaper article she'd read that day outside the Eighth District Station, the District Attorney had said a federal agent was interested in the Peterson case. Oliver's CIA friend?

Like a fool, she'd told Oliver she had once lived in Paris. If Oliver told his CIA friend, this could be a huge problem. Even if she escaped from Renzi, the CIA had operatives all over the world.

But she couldn't afford to worry about that now. Passengers were already boarding her flight. She strode to a corner of the deserted gate beside her own, took out her cell phone and punched in a familiar number.

A number she'd thought she would never use again.

But what choice did she have? No one else would help her.

A familiar voice answered.

Relieved, she said, "Hello, Lin. It's Laura. How've you been?"

"Laura! How nice to hear from you. How are you? Where are you?"

"About to board a plane to Chicago and continue on to Paris. Could you pick me up at Charles De Gaulle?"

"I would be delighted to pick you up, Laura. Tell me the time of your arrival."

———

Frank snuggled against Kelly, enjoying the feel of her bare skin against his. No sexual activity for two weeks? That doctor was out of his mind.

After he and Kelly made love, he usually felt fantastic, relaxed and sated, his mood flying high as a kite. Not tonight.

Tonight his mind was churning like a blender. Where was Natalie?

An hour ago Vobitch had called. The NOPD Superintendent had asked his FBI connection if he could station some agents stationed at the St. Louis and Kansas City airports, an urgent BOLO for April West who might try to fly out of the country. The FBI bigwig said he could, but he had to set it up with the Special Agents in Charge of the FBI offices in Kansas City and St. Louis.

Bottom line? FBI agents wouldn't be posted at those airports until noon tomorrow. Useless. By then Natalie would be gone.

As if she'd read his mind, Kelly said, "I can't believe she wrote all that stuff down in a diary."

"She probably didn't think anyone would ever find it."

"A woman of confidence."

"She's got balls, I'll give her that."

"Not surprising. Look at the life she led. Strip-dancing in New York, working in Paris as a high-priced escort. The meeting with her father must have blown her away."

"He's lucky she didn't kill him. Maybe he's next on her hit list."

Kelly's eyes widened. "You think she'd kill her own father?"

"I have no idea, but I plan to track down Mr. Thu Phan and talk to him. You heard what happened when I called BoBo's ex-wife. Joereen thinks she's snug as a bug in a rug in her gated community, but I wouldn't bet on it."

"Every cop in Louisiana is looking for her," Kelly said. "And thanks to your favorite CIA agent we know she didn't hop on a bus or a train."

He said nothing. Hammer was another problem, and they had too many problems already. Boston PD had Natalie's prints, but she'd murdered three people in New Orleans--Peterson, Conroy and Beaubien--and they didn't have a shred of evidence to prove she killed any of them. They had to find her.

Find her, question her and make her confess.

He pictured her standing beside the Ford Focus. For an instant, her eyes had met his. The eyes of a hunted animal, who'd do anything to escape.

If anyone threatened her, she'd kill them. That's what happened with Tex Conroy and Oliver James.

So, why didn't she kill Frank Renzi in the alley when she had the chance?

The question nagged him like a sore tooth.

"Want desert?" Kelly said. "I've got pecan pie in the refrigerator."

Grateful for the distraction, he said, "Already had my desert. You."

She smiled and her eyes crinkled, ripe with invitation.

Any other night he'd have gone for round two, but his leg was aching.

Still, thanks to Natalie there was always tomorrow. Thanks to Natalie, he would live another day to hunt down criminals and put them in jail.

Natalie might have a hit list, but so did he.

And Natalie was at the top of it.

He gingerly swung his injured leg over the side of the bed. It was sore, but not that sore. "Pecan pie first. We'll see what happens after."

CHAPTER 38

Saturday, 23 August New Orleans

"And you never told anyone BoBo murdered that woman?"
"No."
"She was my mother, Arnold. BoBo murdered my mother. You're just as guilty as BoBo. You helped him get away with it and so did his wife. She gave him an alibi and the cops let him go."

Frank shut off the tape recorder and looked at the people seated around Kelly's table. Vobitch, Miller and Kelly sat there in stunned silence. So did Jane Fontenot. He had invited her to the meeting.

Vobitch was the first to recover. Waving the FedEx envelope, he said, "This arrived at the station this morning, addressed to Frank. The sender's name is Nancy Drew."

"Nancy Drew?" Miller said, frowning. "I don't get it. That's the name she used to register at the Dixie Motel. Is that her latest fake ID?"

"She's probably got enough fake IDs to last a lifetime," Vobitch said.

Jane chuckled, a low melodious sound. "Geez, guys. Don't you know Nancy Drew? I bet Kelly does."

"Nancy Drew, intrepid girl detective," Kelly said. "It's a children's book series. When I was a kid, I loved reading them. Nancy was fearless."

Jane winked at her. "I guess Nancy didn't appeal to boys,"

"She's fucking with us," Vobitch said, glowering at Jane.

"I don't think so," Frank said. "She sent us the tape."

"And solved my case," Jane said. "BoBo murdered Jeanette Brixton, just like I thought."

"If you believe what's on the tape," Vobitch said. "Hell, she was holding a gun on the guy, could have made him say anything."

"You think Peterson would make up a story like that?" Frank said. "It dovetails with what BoBo told Jane when she interviewed him, right Jane?"

"It does indeed. BoBo claimed he was home with his wife all night and she confirmed it. I didn't believe it at the time, but Joereen stuck to her story."

"Seems like it solves the Peterson case," Miller said. "We got the diary. We got video of her in the hotel. Now we got Peterson on tape. Demaris will be thrilled."

"Don't count on it," Vobitch said. "She shut off the tape recorder before she shot him. If she got a good defense lawyer, he'd plead hearsay."

"Maybe not," Jane said. "Sounds like a deathbed confession to me."

Frank said nothing. None of that would matter if they didn't catch her.

"The FedEx came overnight express from the St. Louis airport," Vobitch said, "went out last night at six. If we'd had FBI agents there, they might have caught her." His lip curled in a sneer. "But when I told the Agent in Charge to look for an Asian woman, he gave me some song and dance about racial profiling or some fuckin thing."

Frank massaged his forehead. Still no beer for him. Just as well. His head was throbbing due to lack of sleep and the relentless questions bombarding his mind. Where was Natalie? And where was she going? "Check the passenger manifests for flights out of St. Louis yesterday."

"Yeah, but what name do we look for?" Miller asked. "Nancy Drew? April West?"

"Forget names. Check for single women in their thirties, traveling alone."

"You can fly most anywhere from St. Louis," Jane said. "Where do you think she's going?"

"Paris," Vobitch said. "We know she lived there for a while."

"You got connections with Interpol?" Miller asked. "They might help."

"I could call my buddy Clint Hammer." Vobitch barked a curt laugh, his steel-gray eyes icy. "When hell freezes over. I got some connections. Frank's got connections. We'll find her."

Frank wasn't so sure. After bamboozling the police in Pecos, Natalie had dropped out of sight, only to surface thirteen years later in New Orleans where she'd killed Peterson and Conroy. A woman on a mission. *You're as guilty as BoBo, Arnold. You helped him get away with it and so did his wife.*

It seemed clear that she'd murdered Chip Beaubien, but proving it would be difficult. No witnesses. No gun. He doubted that they'd find her prints in the motel room, and even if the desk clerk could identify her, it wouldn't prove anything. All they had was circumstantial evidence.

"Maybe she didn't fly out of St. Louis," he said. "Maybe she's hiding somewhere, waiting for the hurricane to pass and the heat to die down."

Jane locked eyes with him. "Are you thinking what I'm thinking?"

"If you're thinking we better warn Joereen Beaubien, I already did."

Jane stared into space, lost in thought. After a moment, she said, "Natalie had a tough life."

"Tough life, my ass!" Vobitch said. "She murdered three people: Arnold Peterson, Tex Conroy, and Chip Beaubien. Four if you count her cousin. And don't forget Hammer's CIA buddy in Boston."

Weary of the bickering, Frank rose from the wheelchair. Favoring his injured leg, using the crutches Kelly had gotten him, he hobbled to the slider door. The others were still talking about Natalie's tape. Kelly looked up when he opened the slider, but he waved her off and hopped outside onto her deck.

Leaves and twigs clung to the outside of the glass, remnants of Hurricane Josephine, but the air felt fresh and clean. He didn't want to hear any more speculation about Natalie. He had too many theories fucking up his head already. He was certain she had left the country and it royally pissed him off.

He set his butt against the wooden rail that enclosed the deck, recalling the night four weeks ago when he first saw Peterson's corpse at the Hotel Bienvenue. One shot to the head. Cold-blooded murder. That night he would never have guessed that a woman shot him. Even after he saw the woman on the hotel security video, he had resisted the idea.

A big mistake, one he didn't intend to make again.

Now he had to deal with the consequences.

For the past three days he had analyzed every word of her diary, reading each entry three or four times, marveling at the detail. It was like a blueprint of her life. Killing Randy, who had sexually assaulted his sister. Dancing at strip joints in New York City. Working as a high-priced escort in Paris.

And all those years she had plotted her revenge.

After reading her diary he felt like he'd come to know her. He admired her tenacity and smarts, hiring a PI to get a copy of her mother's murder file, figuring out from Jane's notes that BoBo had killed her mother, monitoring his activities until he died. And then, amazingly, focusing on a new target. Chip Beaubien. But her diary ended with the Peterson murder.

His head throbbed, a dull ache that began when he first listened to the Peterson tape and continued to plague him. With malice aforethought, Natalie had killed Arnold Peterson and Chip Beaubien. Her diary offered an explanation of sorts, justification if he accepted her desire to avenge her mother's murder. But desire for vengeance didn't justify going outside the legal system and killing people. Damned if he'd let her get away with it.

He had gone into law enforcement to seek justice for victims, no matter how repugnant their actions. Arnold Peterson and Chip Beaubien might not have led exemplary lives, but they didn't deserve to be murdered.

And Natalie had murdered them with malice aforethought.

Shooting Tex Conroy had been a matter of expediency, one that had allowed her to escape and kill again. The same with Oliver James. He didn't know exactly why but he intended to find out. Most of all, he wanted to know why she didn't kill him when she had the chance.

His memory of the incident in the alley was clearer now. He remembered hearing the shot that took him down, remembered dropping his SIG, remembered watching it skitter away. Natalie could have shot him then, but she didn't. And then she sent the Arnold Peterson tape to him. Why?

When he caught her--and he would capture her if it was the last thing he ever did--he would ask her.

I'll get you someday, Natalie. Wherever you are.

———

Charles de Gaulle Airport, Paris

When she reached the line of limousines outside Arrivals, Lin was leaning against a shiny black Cadillac. As usual, Raybans masked his eyes, but there was no mistaking his welcoming smile.

"Welcome home, Laura Lin. I'm happy to see you."

"Happy to be here," she said, putting a cheerful spin on the words as she climbed into the limo. But she didn't feel happy. She felt numb and empty, like a rotted husk of corn. She sank into the padded leather seat as Lin negotiated the airport traffic, relieved that she didn't have to fend for herself.

She couldn't do this anymore. Fake emotions she didn't feel. Fight down panic and fear. Make decisions she didn't want to make.

Life-and-death decisions.

When they got on the highway to go into the city, Lin said, "Where shall I take you? Will you be working for The Service again?" He said this in a neutral voice without looking at her.

"If you'll have me." What else could she do? Her bank account was almost empty and she would need money to hide. For years she had stalked her prey, first BoBo, then Chip. Now she was prey.

The stone-killer eyes of the predator at the airport flashed in her mind. Who was he? FBI? CIA? Oliver's friend was a CIA agent, and the CIA operated all over the world. Renzi was a hunter, too. At this very moment he was probably trying to track her down. Recalling the way his eyes imprisoned her as she stood by her car near Parades-A-Plenty, she felt a sudden chill.

Should she have killed him when she had the chance? Probably. But she couldn't bring herself to do it. And she was glad.

"I would be delighted to have you," Lin said, glancing at her, smiling. "That night when I saw you in New York I knew you were special."

But you didn't know I was a killer.

"Sit back and relax," he said. "You must be tired after your long flight."

Tired? She was utterly exhausted. Plagued by nightmares, she hadn't had a decent night's sleep in weeks. She leaned against the headrest, shut her eyes and dozed off. When she woke a few minutes later they were driving west along the Seine. Off in the distance, outlined against the pale blue sky, was the Eiffel Tower, the most famous landmark in the world.

She almost felt like she had come home. Until they passed Isle de la Cite, the Gothic towers of Notre Dame and the thin spire that towered above it. She couldn't see the gargoyles, but her mind's eye supplied them, ugly horned creatures with large wings, sharp talons and gaping mouths. Reminders of her ancestor spirits who required appeasement. A shiver wracked her.

She looked out the opposite window, saw people sitting outside a café, enjoying coffee and croissants and the brilliant sunshine. A clothing boutique where she used to shop flashed by, followed by stylishly-dressed women striding along the sidewalk. This did nothing to dispel her dark mood.

The desperate fear she'd felt at the airport were gone, replaced by despair, an endless landscape bleaker than the Alaskan tundra.

"I might need a new name," she said. "And a new ID."

"No problem, Laura Lin." He didn't look at her, but she knew he was thinking. After a moment, he said, "Perhaps you would feel more comfortable working in different city."

Comfortable? Not really, but she'd feel safer. Renzi knew she had lived in Paris. After reading her diary, Renzi would know a lot about her. By now, he had probably listened to the tape she'd sent him: Peterson's admission that he had helped BoBo escape and his account of BoBo's confession. That brought a certain amount of satisfaction. She had taken vengeance on BoBo in the most painful way possible, believing it would free her to live her life as she pleased. But that seemed impossible now. She might have banished the angry ancestor gods, but now she was on the run. Police in Boston and New Orleans were after her. And so was Oliver's CIA friend.

"Yes, Lin. A different city would be better."

"London? Berlin? Or Amsterdam, perhaps."

A sick-ache of despair engulfed her. Amsterdam?

She didn't want to run into Willem, the only man she had ever loved. She didn't want to see one of his films on a marquee, a painful reminder of that part of her life. No, not Amsterdam. No more heartache, no more married men, no more misfortune. And no more killing.

She loved speaking French, but staying in France was too dangerous. Berlin? Her knowledge of German was rudimentary at best.

"How about London? I've never been there."

"London it is. You can stay at the new-girl apartment tonight. It might take a few days to set up the new ID. Is that all right?"

"That sounds perfect. Thank you, Lin."

Bone-weary, she sank back in the plush leather seat. She wanted to sleep for a week. When she awoke, she would be someone new. Twenty years after her mother's murder, two days after avenging that murder, Natalie Brixton would disappear for good.

But who would she be then?

Her throat thickened and tears stung her eyes.

And then she thought: *Nobody special. Just another working girl. Like Mom.*

ACKNOWLEGMENTS

Creating a work of fiction is an exciting and rewarding journey, but it can also be a daunting one. Happily, many people helped me along the way.

My thanks to Carolyn Wilkins and Jaimie Bergeron for helpful comments on early drafts, and to Haley Verrin, whose suggestions about the final draft were extremely valuable. I am grateful to members of the crime-scene writers and especially to Robert P. Morris, who helped me understand the treatment of gunshot wounds. Thanks also to former police officer Robin Burcell, author of *The Bone Chamber*, for advice on police procedures. However, this is a work of fiction, and any errors or inaccuracies are mine alone.

In my research on call girls, I consulted several books, including *Call Girl: Confessions of an Ivy League Lady of Pleasure* (2004), by Jeannette Angell. I also saw *The Girlfriend Experience*, a 2009 movie directed by Steven Soderberg about a high-priced Manhattan escort, played by porn star Sasha Grey.

The main story events take place in 2008. Several hurricanes threatened New Orleans that year, but the names and details of the hurricanes in this novel are fictitious. Similarly, the hotels and the casino located in the French Quarter are fictitious.

And finally, my heartfelt thanks to you, my readers. If you have comments or questions about *Natalie's Revenge*, please visit my website: www.susanfleet.com and send me a message. I'd love to hear from you, and I'd be thrilled if you posted a review of *Natalie's Revenge*!

ABOUT THE AUTHOR

In her travels, Susan Fleet has worn many hats: trumpeter, college professor, music historian, radio host and award-winning author, to name a few. The Premier Book Awards named her first novel, *Absolution*, the Best Mystery-Suspense-Thriller of 2009. She now divides her time between Boston and New Orleans, the settings for her crime thrillers.
Visit her at www.susanfleet.com

Keep reading for a sample of Susan Fleet's next exciting Frank Renzi thriller, *Jackpot*.

CHAPTER 1

April 2000 Chatham, MA

Florence stood in her living room, peering out the picture window. No sun today, just depressing gray clouds. And no cable repair truck.

Ten minutes ago a man from the cable company had called and said they were having problems in her area but he'd be there soon to fix it. She turned and looked at her new flat-screen TV. The screen was full of snow.

Hoping to see repair truck, she stared out the window. Patches of dirty snow dotted Ginny's driveway across the street. Ginny was her only neighbor. Like many Cape Cod residents, she went south for the winter. She wouldn't be back until Memorial Day. This had been a long lonely winter, the snow piling up in huge drifts. She had to hire someone to plow her driveway so she could go out to buy groceries and visit her son.

Her heart skipped a beat. Halleluiah! There was the cable van. A man got out and hurried toward the house, lugging a big toolbox, a short chunky man wearing a blue uniform shirt. Goodness, why didn't he wear a jacket? It was chilly today, even for April.

She went and opened the front door. "Thank goodness you're here. Regis and Kathie Lee are on at ten and I'd hate to miss them."

Beads of perspiration dotted the man's forehead. Strange.

He glanced at an order form on his clipboard. "Don't you worry, Florence. I'll have it fixed in a jiffy. You don't mind if I call you Florence, do you? My boss says it's friendlier. We like to keep our customers happy."

What a nice young man, big blue eyes and chubby round cheeks. "And your name is John. It says so on your pocket. Come in. It's cold out there."

He stepped into her living room, walked past her new recliner and set his toolbox down on the rug in front of the television set.

"What's wrong with the cable connection?" she asked.

"Just a little glitch, but I'll fix it." He knelt beside his toolbox and looked up at her. "Could I have a drink of water? My boss sent me out early this morning. I've already done three customers and I'm behind schedule."

Florence hesitated. She wanted to keep an eye on him, but she didn't want to be rude. "Goodness. Here I am thinking you've got such nice rosy cheeks and you've been hard at work all morning. I'll get you a glass of water."

She went in the kitchen and stood at the sink. Having a stranger in the house made her uneasy. The ADT man had been here two days ago, but he couldn't install the security system until next week. Her son had warned her that people might try to take advantage of her. Maybe she should call him. But what good would that do? Her son was miles away and even if he wasn't, he couldn't help her. Her darling boy had come home from the Gulf War with both legs amputated below the knee. And then he got hooked on drugs.

She turned on the cold water and let it run. She was probably worrying over nothing. But her hand trembled as she filled the glass with water.

––––––

Now that she was gone he felt better. The old biddy had been watching every move he made. He hated that. His mother watched him too, whenever she could. Florence had money, but she had rotten taste. Her pink polyester pantsuit was hideous. But she'd used her winnings to buy a sleek leather recliner and a big-screen TV. He assumed the beat-up green sofa was headed for the dump.

As soon as he heard water running in the kitchen, he opened his toolbox. Inside were the tools he needed to fix the cable connection. And the other items he brought for his lucky winners. He took out a yellow plastic bag, spread open the drawstring cord and hid it on the floor behind the TV.

She came back with a glass of water and gave him a fake smile. But when she saw the surgical gloves on his hands, her smile disappeared.

He made his blue eyes go wide with innocence. "I've got eczema." He gulped some water and smiled at her. "My hands bleed sometimes. I wouldn't want to mess up your carpet."

"Oh. Well, that's thoughtful of you. The carpet's brand-new and so is the TV. I wish my husband were here to enjoy it with me. He passed on three years ago."

"Pretty exciting hitting the jackpot, huh? Lucky you."

She bit her lip, looking uneasy now.

He set the empty water glass on a table beside the recliner. "I'm about done, but I need you to unplug the TV and plug it in again when I tell you."

"Well, I don't know. It's hard for me to bend over. I've got arthritis."

He gazed at her silently. Coldly. *Do as I say you old biddy.*

With a heavy sigh, she went to the outlet on the wall, sank to her knees and pulled out the plug. Intent on her task, she didn't see him creep up behind her. Wisps of yellow-white hair curled over her collar, and he could smell her perfume, an ugly lilac scent. He plunged the plastic bag over her head, shoved her face down on the floor and yanked the cord tight around her neck.

The bag muffled her scream. Her fingers clawed at the plastic bag, but he pinned her arms behind her back and sat on her. She made grunting sounds and thrashed her legs. He pulled the cord tighter.

A minute passed. Her struggles grew weaker. Finally, she lay still.

He rose to his feet and unzipped his fly. His breathing grew ragged, faster and faster as the power swelled. The power and the glory. He shuddered as the spasm coursed through him. But there was no time to enjoy the moment.

He rolled Florence onto her back. Her mouth had sucked a deep hollow in the bag. From his toolbox he took out the nip bottle of J&B with the red letters and the red cap. His autograph. He shoved the bottle into the hollow her mouth had made in the bag. Reset the cable connection. Checked the TV. The picture was fine. He looked at Florence, lying on the floor with the yellow plastic bag over her head. Like all the others.

He folded her arms over her chest and noticed the scarab bracelet on her wrist, tiny oval stones in a gold setting. Beautiful. He removed the bracelet and put it in his pocket. He was sure she'd want him to have it.

His eyes swept the room. The water glass!

He put it in his toolbox and grabbed his clipboard. Everything was perfect, no mistakes like the other times. He blew Florence a kiss and left.

———

Later that day, a hundred miles away, Frank Renzi sat at his desk with a phone clamped to his ear. A low hum purred from a ceiling vent, sending recycled air through his office inside Boston Police Headquarters. The door opposite his desk was closed. On one wall, awards from several Boston social agencies cited Homicide Detective Franklin Sullivan Renzi for his work with underprivileged children.

Two thick murder files sat on one corner of his desk. A third lay open in front of him. Five minutes ago he'd called the victim's son. He checked his watch. Almost six. It had been a long day, but he was in no hurry to go home. And deal with more problems there.

"When did you last see her?" he said. A muscle worked in his jaw as the man poured out a torrent of anguish and rage.

"No reason to kill her. My kids are devastated. They keep asking for

Grammy. Why can't you catch the bastard?"

"George, I'm very sorry about your mother--"

The litany of sorrows continued. ". . . cameo necklace is missing."

"You're sure?" He waited. "A picture? Great! Can you send it to me?"

George said he'd Fed-Ex the photo. Frank promised to call if he had any news, replaced the receiver and rubbed his eyes. A week ago, three new cases had landed in his lap, homicides in New York, Vermont and, most recently, a Boston suburb. Three Caucasian females, the youngest fifty-nine, the oldest sixty-seven. Two were widows, one had never married, all lived alone. All three had hit the jackpot, collecting lottery prizes ranging from one million to six million dollars. In each case, cash and credit cards were readily accessible but not stolen. So far, he'd found no other links between the victims.

George's mother was the second victim. A widow, Lillian Bernard, age 63, had lived in Vermont. George, her only son, lived in California.

He opened a desk drawer and took out a pack of Merit Lights. He was trying to quit, but George's anguish had gotten to him, his voice shaking with grief and outrage. He could understand that. He was dealing with his own grief. His mother had died in three months ago.

He left the office, went out the back door and lit up. The first drag gave him a head rush. In the distance he heard the usual sounds of rush hour traffic leaving Boston, horns honking, a siren.

His cell phone rang and he grabbed it. "Renzi."

"Frank, it's Jack. I just got a call from the State Police Barracks on the Cape. We got another dead lottery winner." Jack Warner was his partner, an experienced Homicide Detective nearing retirement.

"Damn! I just got off the phone with the third victim's son. Where was this one?"

"Chatham. Mail carrier rang her bell at noon, got no response, saw her car in the driveway and called police."

"Thanks, Jack. I'm on it."

He went back to his office. As if pulled by a magnet his eyes went to the crime scene photos. Lillian Bernard lay on the floor, smothered by the yellow plastic bag that enclosed her head. The Jackpot Killer was a coward.

He couldn't look his victims in the face.

Six weeks ago he had killed Lillian. Today he'd taken another victim.

Soon there would be another. And another. Until they caught him.